THE CONSULTANT

* * * * *

LIAM MUIR

This is an ORB Press book
ORB Press *is a wholly owned subsidiary of Oceans Beyond Learning Inc.*
www.oceansbeyondlearning.com
No part of this book may be reprinted, reproduced, transmitted or utilized in any form by any electronic, mechanical, or other means now known or hereafter invented, including photocopying, microfilming, and recording, or in any information storage or retrieval system without written permission from the publishers.
Visit the ORB Press website at http://www.ORBPressBooks.com
Like ORB Press Books on Facebook:
Follow ORB Press Books on Twitter: @ORBPress
Contact the author on the web - liam@liammuirauthor.com
Like Liam Muir on Facebook: https://www.facebook.com/LiamMuirAuthor
Follow Liam Muir on Twitter: @liammuirauthor
Copyright © Lloyd Tosoff & Oceans Beyond Learning Inc.
All rights reserved.
First Published in 2013
ISBN-13: 9781484967515
ISBN-10: 1484967518

I would like to acknowledge Genevieve Appleton whose encouragement and advice on the screenplay for *The Consultant* made this novel a much better read. As well, my wife Karen spent countless hours editing and polishing the manuscript into a honed work that any author would be proud of.

Chapter 1

July, 1998 Glasgow, Scotland

Holding a duffel bag to his chest, twenty-one year old Ian MacLeod crashed into the side of a waiting cab falling clumsily onto the woman who had flagged the cab just seconds before. As she attempted to free herself from his 180 pound athletic frame, MacLeod, oblivious to her futile struggle, reached behind and slammed the cab door shut before turning his head toward the shocked cabbie.

"Drive!" MacLeod shouted.

A blood curdling scream brought MacLeod to his senses and he twisted around to face the frightened young woman.

"Get off me!" she shrieked emphatically.

MacLeod gripped the head rest in front of him and pulled himself up.

Scanning the intruder for a weapon, the driver was relieved that the out of breath young man was not armed. Not wanting the situation to escalate, he turned around and put the cab in gear.

"Where to?" the cabbie asked in a thick European accent.

"Wherever she's goin' ... and move it!" Ian shot back.

"She's going to Holiday Inn, few minutes up road," the cabbie blurted in broken English as the cab accelerated before turning north on West Nile.

Just moments before, the young woman, dressed in a plaid skirt, white blouse and short heels, was getting into the jet-black Peugeot Taxicab pulled over on St Vincent Street, across from the blinking neon sign over the entrance to O'Leary's Pub. She had been out on the town celebrating her last night in Glasgow, before her planned return to Brighton the next morning.

The woman drew away into the corner of the rear seat noticing that the young man's brow was soaked in sweat. As he tried to catch his breath MacLeod looked intently at the wide-eyed and cringing young woman.

"I won't hurt y' lass," he said gasping for air.

Ian turned and looked through the rear window of the cab just in time to see a black, high performance, older model BMW gaining on them at high speed. Ducking down MacLeod slammed his body onto the seat as the sound of the accelerating BMW grew louder. The young woman clasped her hands into a prayer like gesture, drawing her body upwards as she recoiled away from MacLeod.

"Dear God," she screamed looking down at Ian in terror.

"Just stay calm," Ian urged from his prone position.

The sound of the tightly wound engine and tuned exhaust approached from behind like a fighter jet. The BMW passed the cab at high speed narrowly missing a double decker bus making a left onto West George Street before darting back into the left lane.

"What the hell? Bloody idiot!" the cab driver yelled out as he stabbed the brakes.

Ian stayed down for a few more seconds until the sound of the speeding car was well in the distance. Sitting up he looked out the front window and saw that the car was now well ahead of them. He glanced over at the woman whose eyes were still wide in fear.

"He's a friend … of sorts," Ian stated.

The sound of horns honking and brake lights flashing could be seen up ahead as the BMW recklessly weaved in and out of traffic.

"Uh, huh," the woman said unconvincingly.

"It's OK, we're safe now … I think," Ian said looking around again.

The cabbie pulled up in front of the Holiday Inn. The driver turned, placed his arm across the back of the seat and looked at MacLeod with his eyebrows raised. Ian pulled out a wad from his pocket and handed over more than enough cash to pay the fare.

"That should cover it," Ian blurted.

Grabbing his bag and exiting the cab, Ian extended his hand to help the frightened woman to her feet. She raised her hands indicating that she did not want his help and got out on her own. Thoroughly shaken, she stood perplexed turning her head and looking around as if to regain her bearings. There were several people on the street as the cab pulled away.

"I really do apologize," MacLeod said sincerely.

"Who are you?" the woman asked, drawing her clasped hands tightly against her chest as the two of them stood a few feet apart.

"Allow me to introduce myself. I'm Ian MacLeod."

Crossing her arms with her head bowed as she peeked up at him from the corner of her eye, she trembled uncontrollably.

"Ah, you're shakin' lass."

The young woman seemed to relax slightly at MacLeod's show of sensitivity.

"Here, allow me," Ian said as he unzipped his bag and pulled out a windbreaker, wrapping it around her shoulders.

"I don't know what to say ... I'm speechless. You and that ... lunatic scared me half to death I'll have you know," the tall lanky English woman remarked as she tried to regain her composure.

"Do y' have a name?" Ian asked.

"It's Judith."

MacLeod put his hands in his pockets and cocked his head.

"Judith, I'm so sorry but I'm askin' y' to believe me now. I'm in a wee bit o' trouble and without gettin' into the details, I need to get myself out o' Glasge."

"Why should I help you?" Judith asked.

"Do I look like a bad guy Judith? I just graduated with honours from the University of Glasgow, soon to be a Chartered Accountant for God's sake. I'm harmless and I need yer help. Here look," MacLeod said as he pulled out his student ID card and flashed it at Judith.

Judith looked at the photo on the card and then back at MacLeod. With her arms still crossed, Judith cocked her head back and squinted, studying him intently. She remained silent for a few moments as Ian gave her a pleading look. Judith looked away towards the street and after a few more moments she turned toward the hotel portico and waved at the valet.

"Excuse me," Judith said summoning the valet.

The valet dashed over.

"Yes ma'am?"

MacLeod stood watching hopefully as Judith handed the valet her parking claim voucher.

"I'll be checking out of room 521 immediately. Would you mind bringing my car up? Hold my keys while my friend here waits in the car," Judith instructed.

"Right away," the young man responded.

The valet dashed off as Judith turned to MacLeod.

"Let me pack and check out."

"Certainly. I can't tell y' how much I appreciate this Judith," Ian replied.

Still apprehensive, but at the same time excited, Judith found Ian MacLeod irresistibly attractive. Not used to being in the presence of such a handsome and charming man, Judith seemed to be confused, unable to explain her willingness to help someone who was a perfect stranger, one she had every reason to be afraid of.

"I'll be back as soon as I can," Judith stated as she turned and walked towards the main entrance.

MacLeod stood under the portico with his bag over his shoulder, looking around nervously as Judith disappeared inside the hotel lobby.

"Thank God," MacLeod whispered under his breath before walking over to the main entrance to wait for the valet.

Chapter 2

Eleven Years Later

Ian MacLeod sat across from Datatime Industries CEO, Lance Mills, a short, balding man with thin pasty lips and a ruddy complexion. Mills wore a dark Armani suit as he sat at a glass and stainless steel desk in his opulent executive suite overlooking the English Channel. His eyes were lifeless as he stood up and handed MacLeod an envelope.

MacLeod was nervous as he opened it and took out the letter. He stared down, eyes wide, mouth agape as he read the words on the subject line—'Termination of Employment'.

MacLeod looked at Mills.

"But I've done nothing wrong. Ten years and this is what I get for my trouble?" MacLeod protested weakly.

"MacLeod, you're a bungler. I've no time for bunglers. Security is waiting for you, so be a man about this will you and go clean out your desk. Your days at Datatime are over," Mills said coldly.

"But—," MacLeod tried to interject.

Mills pointed towards the door.

"What part of 'you're fired' don't you get?" Mills said, interrupting MacLeod.

MacLeod got up from his chair and caught a glimpse of a porn site on Mills' computer. With his head bowed shamefully, he walked to the door and opened it, stopping and turning towards Mills.

"You'll regret this Lance, you really will," MacLeod replied.

Without so much as raising his head, Mills waved his right hand dismissively at MacLeod before sitting down.

"Get out MacLeod. We're done."

Mills' secretary, Lucy, an older woman who always wore frumpy button to the collar wool dresses and a bun in her graying hair, overheard the exchange. She looked up at MacLeod with a dismayed expression as he passed by her desk and walked down the hallway. Lucy stopped typing as she watched him disappear into his office where a security officer stood guard at the door.

An hour later MacLeod walked up the stairs towards the entrance to his flat at Brougham Manor when a court's Sheriff shoved a document in Ian's face. Ian accepted it and looked up at the officer.

"You've been served sir," the Sheriff stated heavy-handedly before turning and walking away.

MacLeod tore open the envelope as he continued down the walkway pulling out the official looking document. He stopped and stared down at it for a moment. It read, 'Court Order for Increased Spousal Maintenance'.

"Ah, fer crissake Judith!" MacLeod exclaimed angrily.

Throwing up his hands, he flung the document into the air, not watching as it landed on the sidewalk a few feet away.

A neighbor of MacLeod's who was coming up the walk, picked it up and took a look, before handing it to MacLeod with a laugh as he walked by.

"In shit with the ex, again MacLeod?" he said sarcastically.

MacLeod gave him the finger as he walked by.

"Go fuck yourself Darren," MacLeod said under his breath.

MacLeod approached the door, unlocking it and then walked upstairs to his flat where he spent the evening fretting over the day's events. Feeling overwrought, Ian decided to go for a run on the sea walk, something he did regularly as an avid jogger. He made his way down to Kings Road and began running west towards the sunset.

As the sun's warm rays cut through the chill coming off the English Channel, Ian looked toward the sails of a sloop making its way back to the harbor a mile or so behind him.

He stopped for a few minutes and watched as the sun slowly sank below the horizon until all that was left was a cobalt sky and the backlit silhouettes of a few broken clouds. The smell of the sea air revitalized Ian as he stood and took in the sound of the crashing surf. Ian was now worried about the financial pressures of the alimony he faced given the crushing debt Judith and he had accumulated during almost a decade of marriage. As he turned and looked across the water towards France, Ian wondered how much longer he could survive serving his money hungry ex-wife. He lightened up somewhat as he thought about the fact that he would no longer have to tolerate the abuse of Lance Mills.

Scanning the horizon Ian fantasized about jumping a freighter bound for southern climes. A blast of wind on his face brought him back to reality and he started the trek back to Brighton. As dusk settled over the cold, choppy waters of the Atlantic, Ian wished he had worn more than the thin Spandex pullover and jogging shorts he threw on before leaving his flat. He crossed his arms in an attempt to protect himself against the chilly breeze, noting that the only people out on the walk this late were probably tourists on their way to gamble or dine at Palace Pier. Ian MacLeod was a lone silhouette against the fading light as night fell over Brighton.

It was past ten before Ian returned to his flat, deciding to go to bed in spite of still feeling agitated. He lay on his back looking up at the ceiling and listening to the sea breeze rustling the leaves of the giant elm outside the window of his flat. Exhausted from the day's events Ian finally drifted off to sleep.

Chapter 3

As dawn broke across East Sussex Ian awoke to the sound of the birds singing outside the window. Staring up at the white plaster ceiling he remembered the night he met Judith Reid in Glasgow eleven years earlier.

He thought about how she helped him out of the mess he had gotten himself into and how just before midnight they loaded up her Austin Mini and drove through the night, arriving at Judith's home in Brighton the next morning.

Although Ian was not particularly attracted to Judith, an intimate relationship ensued and they were married within the year. Ian settled into an accountancy position with Brighton high-tech startup Datatime Industries while pursuing his certification as a Chartered Accountant. Things went downhill fast as Judith became disillusioned with the man she had thought was so exciting and charming at the quirky meeting that quite literally threw them together. As well, Ian could no longer maintain the charade of pretending to care about a woman he neither loved nor was attracted to. For another eight years they went through the motions of their loveless relationship until Judith had an affair with Barry Mason, a well-known art dealer in southern England. Judith asked Ian to leave their home in north Brighton and they were divorced a few months later, after which her new beau moved in.

Ian ended up renting a studio flat on Stanford Avenue and struggled to make ends meet while paying a good deal of the income he earned to Judith in alimony. With his marriage behind him, life for Ian consisted of going to work and jogging to stay in shape.

Rolling over Ian looked at the clock by his bed. It was 6 AM and in his waking stupor he thought he had to get ready for work until he remembered that he had been fired the day before. Ian's naivety made him a target for the brutality of people such as Mills but he had never considered moving on in his career. Now he had no choice.

He threw his feet over the edge of the bed and stood yawning and stretching before walking over and opening the door to his flat. Leaning down he picked up the morning paper catching a whiff of the hallway carpet that smelled old and musty. After a moment of disgust at how he could have ended up living in a decaying tenement in the prime of his life, Ian closed the door and looked around at the 300 square foot box he reluctantly called home.

The feeling of despair that was a regular visitor to Ian since he was unceremoniously kicked to the curb by Judith suddenly overwhelmed him. Carrying the paper in his right hand, Ian returned to his bed and sat down. A calendar featuring the skylines of the UK's largest cities was pinned up on the wall across from him. As MacLeod stared at the Gothic monoliths of Glasgow on the calendar, he drifted back in time, his attention captured by the memory of his mother, Mary Smith.

* * * * *

Sitting at the kitchen table, seven year old Ian watched as his stepfather, Thomas Smith, an overweight man in his late forties, wearing blue coveralls and carrying a lunch pail, left through the kitchen door. Ian's mother closed the door behind him and stood as if she were bracing the door at her back. A pretty, petite redhead, Mary Smith was dressed in a flower print dress and in bare feet as she stared blankly off into space. Her face was contorted in pain and her left eye blackened in spite of an attempt to hide it with makeup. She sighed mournfully. Ian looked up at his mother, his big brown eyes on the verge of tears.

"Mammy, why is he so mean?"

Mary composed herself and glanced down at young Ian.

"That's not for you t' worry about, my wee one," Mary said tenderly.

The boy placed both arms on the table as he caught his mother's eye.

"He's not my real dad, is he?"

Mary Smith looked up toward the ceiling before dropping her chin to her chest. A tiny tear glistened as it rolled down her cheek. She stepped over to her young son and leaned down to look him in the eye as she took his small hand in hers.

"He's not. Your father's name was Fraser MacLeod. He was a brave man and he loved you very much. There was a terrible accident on the North Sea and sadly, he perished, before you were born."

The wee lad sat in silence, stunned at what he had just heard.

MacLeod returned from his reverie for a moment. He thought about Thomas Smith who he had heard was now senile, wasting away in a nursing home in Aberfeldy. He remembered the day that the police came to the door of the house at 99 McIver Street, a year or so after his mother disappeared in 1984.

He recalled standing behind the partially closed front door and listening to the man who was speaking to his stepfather. Thomas Smith was wearing a sleeveless undershirt, baggy trousers and mismatched socks as the man who identified himself as Inspector Hume addressed him. It was almost as if he could hear the conversation in his head.

"Mind if I come in and ask a few questions, Mr. Smith?" Hume asked.

"Hume, you know y' got nothin' on me fer the wife's disappearance. I've nothin' more to say on the matter," Ian's stepfather replied curtly.

"I'd like t' ask the wee lad a few questions, if y' don't mind," Hume continued.

"Well the boy's not here, he's still at the daycare. You can go over and ask 'im all the questions y' want Inspector."

He remembered backing away, his eyes glued on his stepfather's clenched fist hidden behind the door.

Returning to his senses, Ian sat up straight on the bed and realized that his heart was beating wildly in his chest. He couldn't stop the stream of images from bombarding him.

A loner during his teenage years Ian had but a few friends. A school mate nicknamed 'Scarface' acted like his big brother, protecting him from trouble. It's not that Ian trusted him. In fact, he was afraid of the boy because of his reputation as a delinquent and local thug.

Ian remembered walking to school one morning when he was 12 years old. Scarface, who had dark shoulder length hair that partly hid the jagged scar across his left cheek, noticed that MacLeod had a black eye and asked him what had happened.

"I lipped him off, so 'e beat the shit out o' me," young Ian said, referring to his violent stepfather.

"That fearty drunk stepfather o' yers needs a comeuppance. I'll kill 'im for y', if y' like," Scarface said offhandedly.

Young MacLeod braced and looked at his friend.

"You're kiddin', right?"

"I'd slit 'is fuckin' throat in a minute," his friend said coldly.

MacLeod looked over at his pal's expressionless face and laughed nervously. Although they remained friends throughout their teenage years, Ian's academic interests soon became his priority. Besides, from what Ian had heard, Scarface was getting deep into the Glasgow gang culture.

* * * * *

Ian glanced down at the headline on the newspaper he had placed on the bed. 'Well Known Developer Jack Singleton Murdered in Manchester'.

Tossing the paper aside, Ian stood for a moment and looked up at the picture of Glasgow again before walking over and opening the door to his closet. He took his black pin-striped suit off its hanger and folded it neatly on the bed. Returning to the closet, he then took out the suitcase Judith had packed for him the day she sent him on his way. Placing the suitcase on the bed, Ian walked to the small chest and opened the top drawer. He took out two pairs of jeans, half a dozen tee shirts as well as the same number of underwear and pairs of socks. Ian closed the chest of drawers, which like all of the furniture in his flat, was rented. In a few minutes he was packed and ready to leave.

Ian took all of his credit cards out of his wallet and laid them on the kitchen counter. Only his Barclays bank card remained along with his ID. Walking over to his desk he took out an envelope and a sheet of postage stamps, tearing off more than enough to send a letter. Walking back to the kitchen he wrote out Judith's address but did not put on a return. After sticking on the stamps he picked up the cards and placed them into the plain white envelope, sealing it.

He picked up the envelope and stuffed it into his jacket pocket. Ian took one last look around before he picked up the suitcase and walked out the door of his tiny flat at Brougham Manor.

Chapter 4

Ian stepped on board the early bird express just before it left the station at 7:15. There was a sense of excitement and relief as Brighton disappeared behind him and he settled into his seat watching the endless English suburbs pass by on the short transit to London's Victoria Station.

It was 8:26 when Ian disembarked onto Platform 15 where he walked directly over to The District Line platform and took the six minute tube trip to St James Station. Finding the nearby branch of Barclays he closed out his account and withdrew all of the meager savings he had squirrelled away since his marriage to Judith dissolved.

After walking back to St James Station, Ian boarded the tube to Euston Station, where he purchased a train ticket to Glasgow. Walking to the waiting area at Platform 11 he noticed an attractive woman whose fine features and ochre curls made her unmistakably Celtic. Sitting alone on a bench, her head was buried in papers that sat atop a brown leather briefcase. She was wearing a tasteful but revealing burgundy silk dress and black patent leather heels that set off her petite but shapely figure.

After taking a seat on a bench directly across from her, Ian looked at the woman as he ran his hand through his unwashed and mussed hair. He rubbed his thumb and forefingers over his razor stubble, quickly taking his hand away and grimacing at how he must look.

She crossed her legs and his eye was drawn up the length of her exposed thigh. MacLeod was reminded of his pretty, strawberry blond ex-girlfriend, Heather Gordon. He remembered how he had discovered that she had cheated on him the week he graduated from university more than a decade earlier.

Ever since he had found out about the affair, feelings of betrayal and anger often accompanied the image of his roommate mounting his girlfriend.

Ian began to tap his foot on the tiled floor of the platform as the sound of her crying out in pleasure filled his head. There they were, on the blue duvet cover, naked and oscillating like two rutting animals. Ian envisioned her underwear thrown carelessly, next to his unframed degree on the small oak desk beside his bed.

He could only imagine what Heather might have uttered in the heat of passion, perhaps five minutes before he walked into his bedroom to find them looking disheveled as they sat side by side on his bed.

'*Hurry, Ian could be home any minute*,' her lilting brogue reverberated in his head as her seducer grunted away on top of her.

MacLeod flinched as he sensed the attractive woman glancing down at his tapping foot before looking directly at him as if she could read the thoughts that were going through his mind. He immediately averted his gaze.

She returned to her work and a few moments later a sheet of paper fell to the floor, landing at MacLeod's feet. He leaned down and picked it up staring at the paper for a moment and then at the woman intently. The letterhead bore the unmistakable crown, royal insignia and blue flag of the MPS, the acronym for Metropolitan Police Service.

Like most people in the UK, Ian knew that Scotland Yard was a metonym for the MPS. Ian held the paper in his hand as he stood and cleared his throat to get her attention.

"Excuse me."

The young woman looked up, seemingly surprised.

"Yes?"

"I believe y' dropped this," Ian said as he got up and handed her the paper.

"Oh, thank you so much," she replied as she took the document and smiled at MacLeod before returning to her work.

MacLeod stood there for a moment looking around before addressing her.

"I don't mean to be forward, but is that a hint of a Glaswegian brogue I'm hearin'?"

The woman raised her head.

"Maybe," she responded as her translucent blue eyes looked straight through MacLeod and then back down at her work.

MacLeod stood a few feet away with his hands in his pockets, tapping his foot.

"I'm originally from Glasge."

She glanced at Ian's tapping foot, her eyebrows raised in an annoyed gesture.

"Oh, how nice," she replied sarcastically, returning to her papers.

MacLeod's body stiffened and he looked around anxiously before clearing his throat again.

She glanced up momentarily, but ignored him.

"I'm guessin' that yer job's in London but y' live in Glasge," Ian said in a last ditch attempt to get her attention.

She looked up at MacLeod.

"And what makes y' think that?"

"Just a hunch," Ian replied looking out of the corner of his eye.

MacLeod tilted his head, glancing almost imperceptibly toward the letterhead still sitting on top of her briefcase. The young woman's eyes followed the direction of his gaze until they were both staring at the MPS insignia. Finally Ian's persistence paid off and she smiled a full toothy grin.

"Aren't you the clever one? I'm from Arran," she said picking up her briefcase and sitting it beside her.

MacLeod dreamily looked up toward the ceiling, "Ah, the beautiful Isle of Arran."

She stopped and sized MacLeod up for a moment.

"So what's your name?"

"MacLeod," Ian answered.

The young woman laughed.

"Do y' have a first name?" she asked raising her eyebrows.

MacLeod's face turned red and he responded, "Ach. Aye, it's Ian."

"Well Mr. Ian MacLeod, I'm Kyla Fraser. It's nice t' make your acquaintance," she said extending her hand.

Ian took her hand in a polite gesture. The sound of the approaching train grew louder as it pulled up to the platform. The doors opened as MacLeod looked over with a slight grimace.

"Train's here."

Kyla glanced over at the train and then up at MacLeod.

"Aye."

Ian raised his eyebrows and exhaled. He pursed his lips and looked down at Kyla.

"Well, nice talkin' to y'."

"And you as well," Kyla replied with a broad smile.

Grabbing his bag Ian sauntered toward the waiting train. Then he stopped, turned and looked back at Kyla as she was placing her papers into her briefcase.

"Kyla?"

"Yes?" Kyla replied as she looked up at MacLeod.

"Do y' ... fancy sitting together?" Ian asked half-expecting rejection.

Kyla hesitated for a moment and then smiled. "I do."

MacLeod beamed. "Great! Then let me get your bag."

"No, that's alright, I'll take it thanks."

Ian nodded in respect of her wishes and walked alongside Kyla as they made their way towards the waiting train and got on board.

Chapter 5

Ian and Kyla boarded the coach and settled into a seat for the northbound journey. They were quiet as the train pulled out of the station and got up to speed. Ian was nervous, having not dated a woman since splitting up with Judith.

As the English countryside flashed by they engaged in conversation.

"So what's in Glasge?" Kyla asked.

Hesitating for a moment, Ian wondered how he should respond.

"I was recently let go from my job as an accountant, so I decided to head back home to Glasge," Ian replied.

Kyla turned toward MacLeod her eyes studying him.

"So tell me about yourself Ian."

"Nothing much t' tell. I'm an accountant. What more d' ya need t' know?" Ian replied.

His upturned hands and silly expression made Kyla laugh.

"Any family?"

"No," Ian replied.

"So, I take it you're single?" Kyla asked.

"I am."

"Well that makes two of us then," Kyla said with a smile.

Ian was compelled to ask about the insignia on the letter that she had dropped.

"Since you know what I do for a livin', I'm curious about your line of work."

Kyla gathered her thoughts for a moment.

"Well, I'm a criminal analyst. I do profiling work for Scotland Yard," Kyla responded.

"Really? I would have expected you to say news anchor or ... fashion model," Ian said unable to contain himself.

Kyla threw back her head and laughed.

"A mild mannered accountant are y'? I'd say you're more like a wolf in sheep's clothing."

"I can assure y' lass, I'm no wolf, that's for certain. More like prey," Ian stated.

"Oh, and why is that?"

"Ach, I'm just spoutin' nonsense."

MacLeod glanced back towards the toilets and spotted someone he knew.

"Kyla, you'll have to excuse me. I need to say hello to an old acquaintance I just recognized. I'll be back in a wee jiffy."

"Certainly," Kyla replied.

Ian walked back about half a dozen rows towards a short pudgy man who was staring at the screen of his laptop. It was Jordie Dunsmuir, a school mate from his university days.

"Jordie?" Ian said as he stood beside him in the aisle.

Jordie looked up and immediately recognized Ian.

"Ian MacLeod. For the luv o' God lad, how have you been?" Jordie Dunsmuir asked excitedly.

"I'm fine Jordie, and you?" Ian responded self-consciously noticing that several passengers looked up at Jordie's boisterous acknowledgment.

"Still in Glasgow. Got a wife and two wee ones now. On my way back from London."

"Oh, you're still with RIA, the firm you articled with?" Ian asked.

"Yes I am ... as a matter of fact I'm now number two," Jordie said beaming with pride.

"You've done well."

"I suppose so. It seems like I get all the dirty work but it goes with the territory," Jordie responded.

"What's in London?" Ian asked.

"Actually I came down from Manchester yesterday where we had some trouble with an auditor," Jordie replied in his characteristically loud voice.

Ian was reminded of Jordie's habit of puffing himself up with self-importance, an attribute he became known for during their university days. The backroom talk in the accounting fraternity was that Jordie made up for his mediocre skill and intellect with the big talk of an overcompensating personality.

"I take it he didn't like the assignment?" Ian inquired, interested in the rest of the story.

"Who knows, but he's definitely terminated. How about you Ian? What 'r you doing with yourself?" Jordie asked obviously not interested in elaborating further.

Not one to draw attention to himself Ian placed his hand on the back of the aisle seat and leaned toward Jordie in an attempt to create some privacy. He looked up to make sure Kyla was not listening.

"Got married, worked for a high-tech startup called Datatime. I got divorced awhile back. It's been rough, but I've decided to start over, so now I'm headed back home," Ian said as inconspicuously as he could.

"Well I'm sorry to hear about your bad luck, but I'm glad you're gonna be back with us in Glasgow. Did y' say *Datatime?*"

"Yeah, that's right. I worked for a guy named Lance Mills," Ian added.

Jordie was clearly surprised and he adjusted his posture turning in his seat toward Ian.

"I take it you were with them for some time then?" Jordie asked.

"Yeah, I have my CA now and felt it was time to move on," Ian said reflecting on the epiphany he had just three hours earlier.

"So, what'll y' be doing for work in Glasgow, Ian?" Jordie asked.

"Not sure. I want something different and stimulating. I'm thinking about becoming a private consultant," Ian responded.

"Look, you should come and see me once you're back. I think there might be a place for you at the firm," Jordie said emphatically.

Ian was surprised at Jordie's interest.

"You're a clever lad and we could use your talents Ian. We've got clients in every major city in the UK and since you're free and single, you'd fit the bill perfectly," Jordie said trying to elicit Ian's interest.

"Thanks for the offer Jordie. I'll think about it," Ian said glancing back at Kyla.

Jordie reached into his jacket pocket and pulled out a card case.

"Here's my card. Call when you land on your feet ... really, I'm serious Ian," Jordie said thrusting his business card at MacLeod.

"Alright, Jordie, I will. I'll call you," Ian replied taking the card and placing it in his wallet.

"It's great seeing y' … G'bye Ian," Jordie said reaching out his hand.

"You as well," Ian responded shaking Jordie's hand.

Ian continued down the aisle to the toilet and as he opened the door he noticed that Jordie was twisted around watching him. Dunsmuir averted his gaze and pulled a mobile phone from his pocket and keyed in a number.

A few minutes later, Ian walked back towards Kyla, waving to Dunsmuir who was on the phone as he passed by.

As Ian took his seat beside Kyla, she smiled, feeling a surge of sexual attraction for the tall red headed stranger she had just met.

"Sorry about that. I just had to say hi to an old school mate, Jordie Dunsmuir," Ian stated.

The pair engaged in a lively conversation during the rest of the journey. Kyla was completely charmed by Ian's clever wit and captivated by the innocent sparkle in his deep set brown eyes.

As they approached the outskirts of Glasgow, Ian wondered how their serendipitous meeting would end. Ian was very attracted to Kyla and knew he wanted to see her again, but he felt uncomfortable about his uncertain situation. Arriving at Glasgow's Central Station just before sunset they both disembarked.

"I so enjoyed talking with y'. Give me a call when y' get settled. That is of course if y' want to Mr. MacLeod … who I barely even know," Kyla said with a smile.

"That'd be grand Kyla, but I don't have a phone right now. If y' give me your number I'll be in touch," Ian replied.

Kyla took a pen and a slip of paper out of her purse and wrote down her phone number. She handed it to MacLeod and after watching him put it in his wallet, waited for him to say goodbye.

"Well, I better go now," Ian said feeling like a self-conscious teenager saying goodnight on his first date.

"Aye, me too. Call me," Kyla responded.

"I promise," Ian said as he backed up a few steps.

Finally Ian turned and disappeared through the station exit onto Gordon Street.

Chapter 6

It was an early summer evening almost two weeks after Ian had arrived back in Glasgow. He had found a small flat at 666 Dundas Street and had scoured the second hand stores to furnish it in a Spartan assortment of table, chairs, couch and a twin bed. Not wanting the expense of a phone until he landed a job, Ian used a phone booth just around the corner to make calls about job possibilities he found in the classifieds. His efforts to find work were fruitless and Ian began to feel desperate with his meager savings dwindling fast.

He was reluctant to call Jordie Dunsmuir about his offer as he felt inexplicably odd about the meeting on the train. The fact that Ian didn't really like Jordie just made the offer seem unattractive.

Scouring the want-ads without success Ian folded the paper and set it down. He noticed an article on the front page headlined, 'RIA Client Completes Deal'. Picking up the paper, Ian read the article about how RIA had just completed the acquisition of an Edinburgh construction firm on behalf of an undisclosed buyer.

As he sat brooding about his lack of work, Ian pulled out the slip of paper that Kyla had given to him and stared at it for a few moments. He was torn about calling her as promised. As he scanned his austere surroundings Ian felt ashamed at how a man with a professional standing was living like someone who had just gotten off the street. There was no way he could ever have a successful and classy woman like Kyla see the way he was living. As he walked toward the kitchen, he caught a glance of himself in the hallway mirror before dropping his head and turning away. Placing the slip of paper on the fridge with a tiny happy face magnet, MacLeod switched off the light and went to bed.

A few days later, Ian decided to treat himself to a night on the town. He grabbed his jacket and walked down the stairs onto the sidewalk on Dundas Street. He remembered hearing about a spot on the river that served great burgers, where he could have a pint. Unsure as to what it was called he headed towards the river and walked around until he spotted the floating restaurant with a sign that read: 'The Clyde Eatery.'

He walked in and was escorted to an upper floor table with a great view looking west down the river. The late afternoon sun was approaching the horizon as Ian took a seat. As he sat back in his chair and took in the last warm rays of sunlight on his face his thoughts drifted to Kyla Fraser again. He looked around at the couples sitting together wishing that he had invited Kyla out for dinner.

A tall scraggly haired waitress approached and stopped to take his order.

"Can I get you somethin' to wet your whistle?" the plain freckle faced woman asked.

"I'll have—," Ian started before she interrupted him.

"I know you. I can't remember your name, but I never forget a face." she said as she held her thumb and forefinger to her mouth in a gesture of puzzlement.

Ian froze, sorting through his memory banks to find a match for her face. Even though her name tag said Mary, his search came back blank.

"No, I don't think so," Ian said abruptly.

"Well you look just like 'im. Spittin' image," she continued, doing her best to jog her memory.

"Must be someone else," Ian offered, trying to deflect her interest in his identity.

Unconvinced, she squinted as if a soft focus might prod her recall. After a brief moment Ian was relieved when she finally pulled out her order pad and pen from her frock.

"Well, what'll it be?" she asked as she threw back her tousled red mane.

"Bring me a pint of heavy or special ... please."

"OK, be back in a jiffy," she said looking Ian over inquisitively.

Ian thought about who she might be as he stared out the window at the River Clyde flowing lazily towards its opening at Newark Castle. Out of the blue it came to him.

'Omigod, she's Heather's friend Mary MacDonald,' Ian thought along with a rush of anxiety.

Ian remembered Mary as a hotheaded troublemaker who was unable to hold her tongue, always finding an excuse to be angry at something. He had an urge to run but decided it would be much too embarrassing. His apprehension notched up as he saw her returning to his table. Setting down the pint of ale, she stood over him with her hands on her hips.

"Now I know who y' are. Yer definitely Ian MacLeod. Y' went out with my best friend Heather Gordon back about 10, maybe 11 years ago," she said as if she had just solved a vexing problem.

Ian looked around at the other patrons who were doing their best to ignore the waitress's obvious imposition on Ian's privacy. Annoyed, he composed himself and looked up at Mary who had crossed her arms in an argumentative gesture.

"OK, so I am," Ian admitted.

"So what are y' doing back in Glasge? I heard you left without sayin' a word to anyone. Heather was heart broke you know," Mary declared, her voice taking on an accusatory tone.

"*Really?*" Ian blurted, his question sounding more like a statement of disbelief.

"For sure ... she couldn't believe you didn't even say goodbye or nothin'," Mary continued.

"Well let's just say I got secret information about her," Ian responded defensively.

"Oh yeah, like what?" Mary inquired, her tone now becoming confrontational.

"Well I don't think it's anyone's business is it ... although, I'm sure you have a clue, now don't y'?" Ian retorted, challenging Mary's unwelcome inquisition.

Ian stared at her crossly hoping that she would stop asking questions and leave him alone.

"OK, I'm gettin' the eye from my manager. What'll y' have for supper?" Mary asked tersely.

"Bring me the cheeseburger, thanks," Ian said his voice returning to a civil tone.

"Right away. Look, I'm off now so Monica will take over this section," Mary said her voice still carrying an indignant tone

"Great," Ian responded sarcastically, relieved that Mary's onslaught was about to end.

"Y' know she's with 'im now don't y'?" Mary said delivering one last volley of spite.

Ian's silence was deafening as his heart jumped into his throat. Mary detected his alarm.

"I'll tell them yer back. See y'," Mary said provocatively as she turned on her heel and strutted away, the swing of her hips telling everyone Ian had been put in his place.

* * * * *

Walking home to the flat he had rented at 666 Dundas Street Ian wished he had never come back to Glasgow. His encounter with Mary MacDonald had brought back a flood of memories so he didn't wait for his order, asking for the bill and leaving the restaurant as discreetly as possible.

By the time he went to bed the fallout from his encounter with Mary had become so intrusive he had trouble falling asleep. Finally after tossing and turning for several hours he drifted off.

The following morning Ian awoke as the first rays of sunlight spilled through the blinds that covered the tiny window of his flat. He lay back on his pillow face up with his hands behind his head contemplating the encounter with Mary MacDonald and how she confronted him with his ex-girlfriend Heather. Then an image of Scarface crossed Ian's mind.

'I hope we never cross paths,' Ian thought to himself as he stretched out the tension of a restless night.

Ian got up and after having a shower sat down with a cup of coffee to spend the morning looking for work. Fortunately his flat was above an internet café which meant he could log onto the web any time he wanted. After unsuccessfully surfing a few more employment sites on line and in spite of his misgivings, he decided to call Jordie Dunsmuir. He walked to the payphone, which was occupied, and after waiting a few minutes he said good morning to the elderly man as he exited the booth.

MacLeod stepped inside and closed the door before taking out the business card given to him by Jordie Dunsmuir, placing it on the stainless steel corner ledge. He picked up the handset and dialed the number. As MacLeod looked out on the street, Dunsmuir answered.

"Dunsmuir speaking."

"Jordie, Ian here."

"Ian, great to hear from you."

"I'm callin' t' find out more about your offer, if it's still open," MacLeod said as he watched an attractive young woman walk by the phone booth.

"I was beginning to wonder if I'd hear from you," Dunsmuir replied.

"Yeah, I know. It took a while to get settled," MacLeod replied.

"Well, we represent a client who is a huge national player. He was brought to us by our Managing Director, Alistair Ascot. I can't disclose anything about him because of confidentiality, but he needs a go between; someone who is arm's length. That's where you come in," Jordie explained.

MacLeod's face grimaced and he drew back.

"Jordie, I am not following you. Why a go between?"

"He believes that at least one of his business partners is not reporting profits properly. He wants to catch him red handed, from the inside."

"So, are you saying I would audit his associate without him knowing it?" Ian asked feeling somewhat confused.

"Yes, exactly. We act as an advisor and auditor on his behalf and we report any out of the ordinary findings. He's very big ... in the billions Ian," Jordie said in his predictable overstatement of everything.

"And if the payments are shorted to this client of yours, then what?"

"You simply report your findings to us here at RIA. No direct contact with the client," Jordie advised.

A burly man stood outside the phone booth giving MacLeod the eye. MacLeod motioned to the man with his finger indicating that he wouldn't be long.

"So what exactly would I be doing?" Ian asked pointblank.

"You would carry out an audit with the intention of locating the monies we believe are missing," Jordie clarified.

"How is your client connected to his partners?" Ian inquired.

"Ian, our client's partners are some of the most high profile and accomplished business people in the UK and he does many different types of deals with them," Jordie said returning to his 'big talker' communication style.

"But how do I stay under the radar?" Ian asked, concerned with the air of secrecy.

"Simple. You do all of your work after hours. We provide you with whatever you need. You will have access to safes, computers, on line information, remote and on site. The client believes he is being misled through falsified records and cooked financial statements."

"After hours? Will I have permission to be on the premises?" Ian asked dubiously.

"Of course," Jordie stated in a matter of fact tone.

"Hmm. Can you give me some idea of who I'd be auditing?" Ian prodded.

"One step at a time Ian," Jordie cautioned.

"Jordie, I'm not sure I like the idea of going into someone's place of business without their knowledge. I'd be an agent of RIA, right?" Ian asked wanting to ensure that this was not an assignment that would compromise his professional integrity.

"Absolutely Ian. I've personally already done a full audit and found nothing out of the ordinary. We know there's another bank involved other than Bentleys. He claims to have nothing to hide. Even volunteered the combination to his safe, passwords, keys to the office, the works. We're stumped."

"Interesting," Ian replied.

"He may be confident, but we still suspect he is diverting monies to his own account. We need someone who is able to look beyond the obvious. And yes, you would be working on behalf of RIA but independently like you said you wanted … you know, to be a private consultant," Jordie said referring to their conversation on the train a few weeks back.

"Well yes, but this isn't exactly what I had in mind," Ian replied unconvinced.

"Are y' at least interested in hearing about the fees?" Jordie led, hoping he could stir Ian's interest based on financial terms.

"Well, what are we talking about here?" Ian asked.

"Ten thousand pounds for no more than one or maybe two day's work," Jordie said hoping that the compensation would be a clincher for Ian.

"Jordie, no one makes such easy money."

"Ian, the client wants someone who can get to the bottom of this, and he's willing to pay for it," Jordie responded.

Ian thought about how little he actually knew about Jordie Dunsmuir. Several moments passed.

"Ian, are y' interested?" Jordie asked.

"Well, I'm willing to meet with you and your people," Ian said, the hesitation in his voice apparent.

"Great ... why don't you come into the office ... today if y' like," Jordie said coaxingly.

The man who had been waiting since Ian's conversation with Jordie began, tapped on the glass and pointed to his watch. Ian held up his index finger acknowledging the man's patience.

"OK, I'm flexible, so whatever works for you," Ian said.

"Let's make it right after lunch. The client is here for some other matters and we can meet right afterwards."

"Alright, it's a date," Ian said.

"Good, see you then Ian," Jordie replied before he hung up the phone.

Chapter 7

As Ian approached the four story stone monolith that housed the RIA offices, a feeling in his gut gave him second thoughts about Jordie Dunsmuir's offer. He stopped and tried to make sense of it but after a few moments of uncertainty, he took a deep breath and walked towards the turnstile and into the main lobby. Looking at the directory, Ian noted that RIA reception was on the fourth floor. He walked over to the elevator and pressed the call button. Standing beside him was a dignified looking older gentleman.

"Good day," the man said in a proper English accent.

"Hello," Ian replied looking the man up and down.

Ian was nervous.

'I'll just hear them out,' he thought trying to convince himself that it was a good way to break into the accounting market in Glasgow.

Ian got into the elevator with the English gentleman and watched him press floor number four.

"Ah, same," Ian said.

They got off and Ian was surprised that both he and the Englishman headed for the entrance to the RIA offices. The older man held open the glass door and allowed Ian to go in first. The butterflies in his stomach made Ian feel a bit queasy at he walked through the door and glanced sideways at the man.

"Thank you," Ian said as he entered the reception foyer.

"You're welcome," the man replied eyeing Ian before he walked down the hallway disappearing through a secured door.

"Good afternoon. My name is Ian MacLeod. I have an appointment with Jordie Dunsmuir," Ian said as he stood at the reception counter.

"Please have a seat and I'll tell him you're here."

"Thank you," Ian said as he sat down on one of the posh leather chairs that adorned the entry foyer.

A few minutes later he saw Jordie come through the secured door at the end of the short hallway.

"Ian, come on in," Jordie motioned.

"Right," Ian answered as he got up and walked towards him.

Jordie pointed his FOB at the reader releasing the heavy looking oak door and motioned for Ian to walk through.

"We'll meet in the main boardroom just over there," Jordie said pointing to a set of double doors.

As they entered, Ian recognized the man from the elevator sitting at the head of a large oak boardroom table surrounded by at least 20 black leather chairs.

At the other end of the table sat an imposing looking man who did not take his eyes off Ian. His deep set dark eyes and thick mustache made him appear very menacing.

A humongous man with a crew cut stood across the hall watching the proceedings in the boardroom. When Ian made eye contact he moved out of Ian's line of sight.

"Have a seat Ian," Jordie said pointing to a chair at mid-table.

Jordie took a seat across from Ian and began introductions.

"This is the man I told you about, Mr. Ian MacLeod."

"Hello," Ian said the unnerved feeling still simmering in his gut.

"Ian, this is Alistair Ascot, our Managing Director," Jordie said motioning to the man from the elevator.

"Yes, we've had the good fortune to have already met," Ascot said dryly putting on a charming smile.

Conspicuously, the man at the other end of the table was not introduced.

"Ian, we'd like to thank you for coming in this morning to talk about how we might work together on a very important project," Alistair Ascot said.

"Yes, Jordie has briefed me. It sounds interesting," Ian said doing his best to appear upbeat in spite of his misgivings.

"It's an extremely important engagement for RIA," Ascot stated.

"I've never done anything quite like this. Accountants don't usually get involved in what sounds to me like corporate intelligence work," Ian said nervously.

"You'd be surprised Ian. Look at the whole Arthur Andersen fiasco at the turn of the millennium. If you don't think there was some maneuvering and deceit there you'd have to be naïve," Jordie Dunsmuir spoke up vociferously.

Ascot raised his hand in a gesture that indicated he did not want commentary from Jordie. Dunsmuir shrunk into his seat dropping his head to his chest like a shamed pup.

"What Dunsmuir is saying is true Ian. RIA has been involved on several occasions as a watchdog on behalf of various governmental organizations. We have been engaged to secretly audit other accounting firms who have been suspected of engaging in questionable business activities—like taking inducements from clients involved in manipulating the markets. The criminal nature of our investigations required that our involvement remain surreptitious. Our methods were kept secret through an RIA technique we refer to internally as 'night audits'," Ascot explained.

Ian felt somewhat relieved to have the assignment Jordie had described clarified.

"So would I be doing these night audits under the auspices of RIA then?"

"Precisely Ian, but let's start with this being a single night audit for the time being. Once we know your capabilities there may be more," Ascot replied.

"So why are you so interested in me? There must be lots of people better suited," Ian asked.

"Jordie speaks very highly of you," Ascot said glancing at Dunsmuir.

Ian also looked over at Jordie.

"However Ian, it will be an arm's length relationship. Dunsmuir informed me that you are comfortable being an outside contractor. Is that correct?" Ascot asked.

"Yes," Ian replied with an affirmative nod.

"What we are doing on behalf of our client is by any definition beyond the normal professional services of a consulting firm. You need to approach this assignment with a clean slate. Normal audit techniques do not apply. There will be no formal flagging, boxing of sample files and the like. Of course we will expect an unofficial report that discloses your findings but other than that the assignment will be done under a cloak of secrecy," Ascot said.

"Can you tell me who you were acting for on the jobs you described earlier?" Ian asked having never heard of such activities within the accounting world.

"I'm afraid not Ian—top secret as you will no doubt understand," Ascot said definitively.

Ian wondered if what he was hearing was plausible.

"It takes a special individual to do this kind of work. We are very careful when it comes to selecting our people Ian," Ascot continued.

"How so?" Ian asked.

"As I said, Jordie has spoken very highly of you and I understand you went to school together. The meeting on the train may have been somewhat opportune but when we looked at your background, we were convinced that you were exactly the right man for this special assignment. Let's just say you have the right attributes," Ascot responded.

"OK, how will I communicate with you?" Ian asked.

"Once this meeting is over, should you accept the assignment, Jordie will schedule the field work and you will be contacted by text on the details. You will receive a written agenda and once you have read it, you need to commit the plan to memory because as I said previously there will be no written records to document the assignment. We will provide you with access to offices, safes, employee work stations, hard copy records, everything. We want you to photograph the materials of interest and extract data onto a modified cellular transmitter that will stream data back to us," Ascot advised.

"Why text?" Ian asked curiously.

"Because text messages are not stored on our server. Our client likes to stay under the radar," Ascot informed.

"What type of business is your client engaged in?" Ian questioned further.

"We have a very wide ranging roster of clients Ian. RIA acts as an independent agent on behalf of all of them. The nature of the client's business is of no material consequence. Our job is to provide sound financial and accounting advice and in this case to help him recover the funds due to him under the deal. I can assure you that RIA acts with the utmost of integrity and honesty in all of our firm's dealings," Ascot said.

"I must say Mr. Ascot, RIA's name is well known across the UK, so although this is not what I expected it does sound intriguing," Ian admitted.

"Well, it's important that you feel comfortable with the terms of the assignment," Ascot said.

"Gosh, I don't know. I'm not sure I'm suited for this kind of work. I'm just a simple accountant," Ian said looking around the room.

All eyes were on Ian.

"Are you at least interested in the fees?" Ascot asked.

"Jordie told me about them."

"He was referring to the base fee. There's a bonus as well, provided the audit is completed properly," Ascot said looking over at Jordie.

"A bonus?" Ian queried his interest aroused but remaining reserved.

"Double the original fee provided we are successful in recovering the missing money," Ascot said in a businesslike tone.

"How will the payments be made?"

"Your fee will be paid in US dollars into a Swiss bank account," Ascot said.

"Why a Swiss account for a relatively small amount?" Ian asked.

"The client likes to be discreet and therefore only does business using Swiss accounts and often in cash," Ascot said his voice growing impatient.

In his preoccupied state, Ascot's comment about cash payment went right over Ian's head. He looked around the faces at the meeting uncertain as to whether the offer felt right to him. The money was more than he had ever dreamed of earning and he *was* almost broke having already spent most of his savings over the past several weeks. After a few moments Ian responded.

"When do I start?"

"So you're our man?" Ascot queried.

"Yes, I accept," Ian said boldly.

"Good, we'll contact you when the first assignment is ready. Be prepared as it could be on a moment's notice," Ascot said as he looked over at Dunsmuir.

Jordie reached over the table and handed Ian a mobile phone.

"This belongs to the client's offshore holding company. All phone activity appears as if it originates outside of the UK through a proxy server. You are not to use the phone for calls, only for receiving text messages. It's capable of some very sophisticated functions, like tracking a GPS location within a few meters," Dunsmuir said in a serious tone.

"You will be provided with a data transmitter that is programmed to send to an undisclosed email recipient and a digital camera when the time comes. The laptop you will be provided is brand new, never used except to load the programs you will need. Once you have completed the job, the data transmitter, camera and laptop are to be returned to me. There are no records kept on any of the night audit work for this client," Dunsmuir further explained.

Ian was taken aback. It was clear that RIA wanted to distance themselves from the audits and he was about to ask for a clarification when Ascot finalized the meeting.

"That will be all for now. Thanks Ian, and all the best," Ascot said closing out the meeting.

"Mr. Ascot, I'm really not sure—," Ian started before Ascot interrupted.

"Not sure? About what?" Ascot asked.

"Well—," Ian started before Ascot cut him off again.

"The twenty thousand pounds you stand to earn for what could well be just a few hours of work? You'll be fine Ian. I must run to another meeting, so good luck," Ascot said convincingly as he extended his hand. Ian reached out and shook it before Ascot walked out of the room.

The prospect of earning such a large sum of money so quickly was certainly appealing. As Ian got up from the table he looked around and noticed that the man whose identity remained unknown had already left the room. Jordie escorted Ian out of the boardroom and down the hall to the elevator where they waited in silence until the elevator came. Both of them got on and as Ian watched Jordie push the ground floor button, everything seemed to go into slow motion. There was a surreal sense to the entire experience; the strange circumstances under which Ian had come upon the job, the man at the end of the table who reminded Ian of a bird of prey and the surreptitious conditions of the proposed audit. Jordie's voice brought Ian back to reality.

"Ian, you'll do a great job on this," Jordie said reassuringly as the elevator doors opened at the lobby level.

"Jordie, I have to tell you, I'm more than a little uncomfortable, so I'm really not sure if this is right for me," Ian said as they stepped out onto the polished granite floor of the ornate lobby.

"Ian, you're just the guy for this role," Jordie said reassuringly.

"Yeah, you keep saying that," Ian responded dubiously.

"Well, good luck my friend," Jordie said shaking Ian's hand.

Ian stood outside on St John's Street feeling bewildered as he watched Jordie disappear into a crowd of people on the sidewalk.

Chapter 8

After returning to his flat and changing into his street clothes MacLeod went for a walk to clear his head. Turning and walking west down Dundas Street, Ian tried to make sense of the assignment he had just accepted. His total lack of experience in what was by all appearances an undercover project was disconcerting to Ian and in spite of having taken the offer he was still ambivalent. On one hand he was apprehensive about the unfamiliar and highly irregular role he had accepted and on the other, he was encouraged by the amount of money he could earn very quickly.

After the better part of an hour he arrived at the University of Glasgow. He needed to walk the grounds around the Adam Smith Building, his alma mater, to remind himself that he was a trained Chartered Accountant—a professional.

Looking around at the neo-gothic architecture, and smelling the trees and grass, took Ian back to a time in his life when he had been free of all the worries that had come with adult responsibilities. As one of the few students to have graduated with honors from his faculty, Ian had enjoyed the status of being recognized and revered by his professors and peers, something he had not enjoyed since. Ian sat for a few minutes enjoying the warm sensation of the afternoon sun on his face before starting the return trip back to the city center.

As he walked in the direction of his flat, he saw the Artisan Roast, a small café that was a hangout for the university crowd. Ian was oblivious to the fact that down the street getting into her car was Kyla Fraser. Looking up as she opened the car door she felt a rush of emotion at seeing Ian again. She was torn between her attraction to him and the hurt she felt at being passed over—especially after he had promised to call.

Kyla slammed the car door shut and then crossed the road following him into the café. As Ian was standing in line behind two other customers he felt a tap on his shoulder.

"Remember me?" he heard a familiar voice ask.

Ian turned in surprise.

"Kyla," Ian uttered noting how good she looked with her tinted sunglasses and neatly parted hair pulled back into a tight ponytail.

"I probably have no right in saying so but I thought we had somethin' goin' on. I guess I was a fool," Kyla said trying to contain her emotions.

The two other people in line, an older gentleman and a teenaged girl, both turned to take in the impending confrontation.

Ian was cornered and without words. After a few seconds of loaded silence he spoke.

"Kyla, I've been totally caught up in trying to get settled and honestly I was about to give you a call," Ian said knowing he was stretching the truth.

Kyla just stared at him.

The teenaged girl rolled her eyes in contempt.

"I'll see you around," Kyla said calmly as she turned on her heel, threw the glass door open and walked out onto the street.

Ian hesitated before looking at the older man in line who motioned for him to go get her.

MacLeod ran after her, catching up a short distance down the street. Without saying a word he shadowed her for a few seconds. Kyla ignored him purposely, increasing her gait. Finally, and completely out of character, Ian reached out with his right hand and spun her around like a pirouetting dancer. Kyla immediately recoiled resisting his advance, her indignation showing through the dark tint of her sunglasses.

"Excuse me," she snapped before turning away.

Kyla marched off, her silk dress flowing around her shapely legs. Ian stood for a moment taking in the sight of her; the long locks of her tawny hair tied back in a ponytail falling against the small of her back. Ian sighed as she hurried down Gibson Street.

Suddenly Kyla turned around and began walking determinedly back towards Ian. Taking her sunglasses off and placing them on her head, she stopped directly in front of him. With one hand on her hip she pointed at Ian and was about to say something when MacLeod spoke first.

"Has anyone ever told y' how beautiful y' look when you're angry lass?"

Kyla stood face to face with Ian, unable to resist his cocky charm.

"Very funny, Ian—," Kyla blurted.

Kyla pointed her finger at MacLeod.

"That's no way to treat a woman," she continued.

"I'm so sorry. Can y' forgive me?" Ian asked looking at her with his head bowed slightly.

Kyla looked up at him, her arms now crossed.

Reaching out, Ian pulled Kyla towards him and passionately kissed her. Stunned for a moment, Kyla threw her head back tossing her Jackie O glasses to the ground.

"Where did y' learn to kiss like *that*?"

Not knowing what to say Ian responded with a big grin, "I've not a clue lass."

Kyla laughed and bent down to retrieve her glasses. She cocked her head and squinted at MacLeod.

"You're a charmer MacLeod, I'll give y' that," Kyla said as she studied his face for a few moments.

Reaching out she took his hand and pulled him in trail like a puppy dog towards her car.

"Where y' takin' me Kyla?"

Kyla shot Ian a seductive glance.

"You're coming home with me to Arran ... unless you have other plans?" Kyla asked stopping for a moment and looking directly at Ian.

"I've none."

They both got into Kyla's Lotus Exige. Putting it into gear she pulled out onto the street. The throaty sound of the tuned exhaust and the whine of the supercharger sent waves of visceral pleasure throughout Ian's body as they accelerated across Great Western Road towards the M8.

"I've never been to Arran before," Ian said over the exhaust note of the Lotus.

Kyla glanced over at Ian from the corner of her brilliant blue eyes.

"Ah, the beautiful Isle of Arran," Kyla said, mocking what Ian had said at the train station in London two weeks earlier.

"OK, I'm busted," Ian said as he raised his eyebrows with a silly grin.

"It's the largest island in the Firth of Clyde," Kyla said brushing back locks of windswept hair from her face.

Ian watched Kyla as she downshifted to pass the car in front of her, his eyes drawn to a hint of cleavage embraced by the cut of her burgundy silk dress.

"So Ian, why didn't you call me … really?" Kyla asked.

"Kyla, God's honest truth … I was afraid to," Ian replied.

"What are you so afraid of?" Kyla asked.

"You're such a beautiful woman."

"It's just me, Kyla Fraser … I don't bite," Kyla said flashing her eyes at Ian.

Raising one eyebrow and tilting his head, Ian looked over at Kyla.

After driving for two hours through the Scottish countryside on the M77, they passed through Kilmarnock on the way to the Ferry terminal at Adrossan. They arrived at the ferry dock nearly missing the four o'clock crossing. They were the last car on as Kyla pulled the Lotus up behind a black Mercedes convertible.

"By the way Ian, did y' ever get anything goin' for yourself?" Kyla asked as the vessel got under way.

"Yeah, I did. I'm gonna be doing some work for RIA," Ian said unsure if he wanted to disclose the nature of the engagement he had accepted.

"That's great, what exactly are you going to do for them?" Kyla asked excitedly.

"I'm starting with the audit of a partner of their client who suspects fraudulent misrepresentation," Ian responded.

"Really? Sounds like forensic work," Kyla remarked.

"RIA refers to them as—," Ian began and then thought better of what he was about to say.

"As what?" Kyla asked.

"It's kind of undercover work. I'm supposed to investigate him without him knowing about it," Ian said hoping she wouldn't press him for any more information about the job.

Ian's description struck Kyla as odd.

"Very clandestine don't you think?" Kyla remarked glancing over at Ian.

Ian thought about Kyla's comment.

The ferry pulled up to the dock at Brodick.

A few minutes later they disembarked. There was an air of sexual tension during the drive along the winding road through Arran's countryside. Finally they arrived at a small white stucco cottage just off the main road. Turning into the driveway, Ian noticed neatly kept hedges and tropical plants in the front lawn.

"Very nice," Ian remarked as Kyla pulled her car into the small garage.

"I adore it. This is my sanctuary," Kyla said affectionately.

Ian grabbed Kyla's bag from the trunk and caught up to her as she was unlocking the front door.

"I've not a thing with me Kyla," Ian remarked while closing the door behind them.

Kyla turned towards Ian after dropping her things on the kitchen counter.

"Don't worry, I've got everything you need," she said as she stepped towards him and placed both hands around the back of his head.

Ian dropped the bag as instinct took over and he pulled Kyla close, kissing her and feeling the raw pleasure of her warmth penetrating the length of his torso. He drew his head back and looked into her eyes.

"It seems like forever since I've been with a woman."

Kyla placed her index finger over his mouth as if to quiet him smiling devilishly as she took Ian by the hand. They walked up the wood stairs to a beautifully kept bedroom. Through a small window above an old oak dresser Ian could see Holy Island and the Firth of Clyde in the distance.

Kyla turned to face Ian as she removed the hair tie from her ponytail and tossed it onto the oak dresser. She shook out her thick ochre curls freeing them to fall around her slender shoulders. Then reaching behind, she unzipped her silk dress letting it drop to the floor. Soft light streamed in from the window, tracing the silhouette of her feminine form.

Ian was spellbound.

Kyla moved into his embrace. His hands followed the sculpted contours of her body until he found the nape of her neck, gently pulling upward until she offered him her lips. Time seemed to stand still as they became lost in lovemaking.

Breaking the silent afterglow as she lay with her head on Ian's chest, Kyla sighed. Ian was without words and gently pulled her head against his lips as he kissed the soft locks of her hair. Looking out the window at the faint glow of the evening sky Ian closed his eyes feeling contented seemingly for the first time in his life.

Chapter 9

As they drove back towards Glasgow, Kyla was wondering when she might see Ian again. Ian was mindlessly staring out the window when Kyla broke the silence.

"I'll be in London until Friday," Kyla stated bringing Ian back from his reverie.

Ian looked over at Kyla.

"Can I see you on the weekend then?" Ian asked hopefully.

Delighted to hear Ian's response, Kyla answered, "I'd *love* that."

Kyla had been wondering if she was being drawn towards a man that would end up breaking her heart so his response was reassuring.

Approaching the city limits Ian turned to Kyla.

"So what exactly does a profiler do?"

Knowing that murder profiling was beyond the scope of most police professionals let alone a layman she decided to keep her response simple.

"Well, it's too complicated to explain in a nutshell, but we look for connections between the victim and the killer, like Caucasians tend to kill Caucasians for example. From there we can develop a profile."

"How are y' qualified to do that kind of work?" Ian asked.

"I have a PhD in forensic psychology and I've worked with CID at Scotland Yard for the past 10 years," Kyla responded.

"Very impressive Kyla," Ian said.

A few minutes later Kyla thought about how she knew almost nothing about the man she was becoming intimate with.

"So Ian, tell me about yourself. Where you grew up, your parents, you know … what kind of a childhood you had," Kyla inquired.

Ian braced at the question and responded hesitantly.

"I never knew my real dad. He died before I was born. I had a stepdad."

"How about your Mum, your siblings?" Kyla enquired.

"No brothers or sisters, just me," Ian said hastily.

Kyla got the feeling that Ian did not want to talk about his family.

"I'll bet you were the apple of your mother's eye," Kyla said trying to lighten things up but Ian seemed to become even more withdrawn.

"My Mum disappeared when I was seven. The police came and interrogated my stepdad. I hated him. I don't want to talk about it if you don't mind," Ian said clearly upset.

As a psychologist Kyla surmised that her questions had no doubt rekindled Ian's unresolved childhood trauma so she stopped prying. They went silent as they passed by the farmlands of the rural area on the outskirts of Glasgow. She noticed that Ian seemed to be brooding, so she decided to leave him be.

MacLeod felt a rush of anxiety as his emotionally charged memory took him back in time.

* * * * *

Standing in the hallway of their south Glasgow home, tiny Ian watched as the threat of violence began to erupt between his angry stepfather and his cowering mother. As he walked in through the doorway, Thomas Smith looked around at the disarray in the kitchen. He turned aggressively towards his wife pointing his huge finger.

"Where the hell's supper?"

Mary braced, turning away, placing her hands over her face. Fearfully, she peered over at Smith. Hoping that he was not going to strike her, she dropped her hands and spoke.

"Ian's been upset. He got some sad news today about his real dad," Mary said guardedly.

Smith's eyes glared, his face turned red with rage and he bared his teeth, jutting out his massive jaw.

"I'll give y' some advice woman. Let the little bugger grow up to be a man, instead of the wee sissy yer makin' him into," Smith said belligerently.

Ian looked away so as not to make eye contact with the man that seemed to hate him so much.

Mary walked over to the stovetop, her lips pressed together and eyes averted. As she passed Smith, his eyes locked on to her, teeth gritted and jaw protruding. Doing her best not to arouse his temper, she sensed that his agitation level had decreased. Satisfied with his bullying tactic he grunted his approval.

"Aye, that's better. I'm goin' for a wee dram before supper," Smith said as he passed young Ian, giving him an angry look as he opened the door to the basement.

Smith made his way down the creaky wooden staircase.

The small lad watched him from the top of the stairs as he took two fingers of Drum out of a can and rolled a crude looking cigarette. He lit it and took in a long draw, blowing it out in two streams through his nose. Next he rubbed his thumb and fingers over his two days of razor stubble and scanned the makeshift bar. Sitting on the counter were two half empty bottles and a scotch glass with the Dewar's logo on it.

His stepfather poured a stiff glass of blended whisky and the boy got a waft of acrid smoke as it rose up from the basement. After about 20 minutes and three glasses, Smith got up from the wooden bar stool and staggered up to the top of the stairs where Ian was still sitting.

"What 're *you* lookin' at?" Smith asked angrily as he gave the innocent youngster a clout across the back of the head.

The passing urban landscape was a blur as Ian's attention returned and he became aware that he was holding his breath. He turned and glanced at Kyla, who was busily engaged in watching the road. Ian remembered what came next that very evening in April 1984.

It was the wee hours of the morning, when seven year old Ian was awakened by a loud thud. Getting out of his bed, he tiptoed over to his slightly open bedroom door. He peeked through the crack to the scene of his stepfather dragging something wrapped in the quilt from his mother's bed towards the back door.

* * * * *

Kyla's voice startled Ian. "So Mr. MacLeod, we're almost at your flat. Triple six Dundas, right?"

MacLeod sat up straight in the seat.

"Ah, yeah ... right over there," Ian said pointing towards his building, The Ayrshire.

"Are you alright Ian?" Kyla asked. "You look pale."

"I'm fine, really," Ian replied.

Kyla parked, leaving the car running. She sensed his sudden emotional shift, knowing that what she had said to him had triggered an unpleasant memory.

"So how can we stay in touch Ian?" Kyla asked.

"I don't have a mobile phone yet so we can stay in touch by email and I can meet you here at 4 PM on Friday if that works for you."

"Why no mobile?" Kyla asked.

"I haven't got around to replacing the one I left in Brighton. It belonged to my employer," Ian explained. "But I do have a new email address."

Kyla took out a notepad and handed it to Ian along with a pen. Ian wrote down his email address: 'ianmac@gmail.com'. He handed it back to her and Kyla placed it in her bag.

"Ian, I have to run or I'll miss my flight," Kyla said looking at her watch.

Ian kissed Kyla and then opened the passenger door and got out. He stood and waved as Kyla roared off towards the airport. He looked to the east as a summer storm approached on the horizon.

Ian was not in the mood to sit alone in his tiny flat so he decided to go for a walk and take in the cool morning air and the smells of the city he had grown up in. As he proceeded along Holland and crossed Sauchiehall he saw the sign over a storefront door that read 'The Crouching Tiger – Mixed Martial Arts.'

Ian walked by and noticed that there was a fight underway inside the cage. Although he was not a big fan of extreme fighting he had often watched UFC while channel surfing on nights when he was bored and alone in his Brighton flat. He stopped for a moment and peered through the storefront. One of the combatants was on the mat being beaten about the face by his opponent. Ian could see the referee trying to stop the contest, waving for the winner to back off.

As the two combatants stepped down onto the floor Ian noticed a man walking toward the fight cage that he recognized as Alex Yin. Although he didn't know him well, Ian had met Alex when they both attended university. Alex studied kinesiology but had dropped out when there were some health issues with his father and he had to go to work to support the family. Ian had not seen him for over a decade but knew he had always been into martial arts.

He noticed that Alex's opponent had already entered the cage and was standing on the canvas. He was an enormous man who looked more like a weight lifter than a fighter.

As the two men faced each other Ian thought that Alex was in for a severe beating judging by the size of his challenger.

Intrigued, Ian decided to go inside and watch. He pushed open the door and stood some distance away trying to remain as inconspicuous as he could.

He saw someone tape a sign written in felt pen on the outside of the cage. The crudely written words read 'Alex Yin vs. Fraser McAllister'. Yin was extremely toned, with well-developed biceps, a chiseled chest and a defined abdominal six-pack. Ian could see every sinew in his thickly built upper legs and he had an athletic sturdy looking neck. McAllister looked like a brute. His face was mean looking—someone you would avoid if you saw him coming your way. He was extremely muscular without an ounce of fat anywhere on his body. The referee was short, stocky and looked tough as nails. He introduced the two fighters and they began round one.

Alex assumed a defensive stance with both arms raised protectively. The big Scot kept both hands close to his face, with his head down and his massive arms protecting his body. Yin moved in with a vicious side-kick to McAllister's left hip region, but the big man didn't flinch. A lightning fast right jab to Yin's face connected hard knocking him back almost off balance. Yin planted his feet firmly and returned with a series of right and left punches that struck McAllister's forearms which he had raised up to defend both sides of his head. Yin stepped back and delivered a side kick that connected with McAllister's gut. He seemed winded for a moment but McAllister retaliated with a series of powerful body blows that knocked Alex into the cage wall. Alex was in trouble having lost the time and space he needed to stay out of the range of the big man's long arms and potent fists. Two quick head shots stunned Alex and he had no choice but to drop and roll, opening the distance between him and McAllister as he nimbly regained his feet. McAllister's timing seemed to have been interrupted by Alex's quick recovery. The huge man came at his opponent like a freight train. As he approached Yin it seemed like the fight went into slow motion as Alex waited for McAllister to enter his space. Standing his ground, Alex ducked, quickly weaving his torso to the outside of McAllister's attempted strike, twirling around some six feet away from his exposed and twisted body. Then spinning around Alex delivered a single high kick that connected hard against Fraser McAllister's head, dropping him to the mat. Yin moved in for the kill but realized he had knocked his opponent out cold and the match was over. The referee came to McAllister's aid and helped the big man up and out of the cage as Yin looked on.

Ian was exhilarated. He had often watched the Glasgow Rangers outplay their competitors and seeing Alex fight McAllister reminded him of the vicarious aggression that ran in the blood of Scottish soccer fans. Ian caught Alex's attention when he emerged from the cage.

"Hey, that was unreal … there was no contest," Ian said getting Yin's attention.

Yin, dripping with sweat, stopped and looked at Ian.

"Ian MacLeod. How the hell have you been?" Alex said as he extended his hand.

"I'm fine. I was just walking by and noticed a fight going on and there you were. You gave him some serious brain damage," Ian said still awed by Alex's fighting prowess.

"Well, let's hope not. I heard you left town in a hurry, what ten years ago?"

"What did you hear?" Ian asked.

"Well the word on the street was that you pissed off that crazy roommate of yours," Alex replied.

Ian shrugged his shoulders and raised his eyebrows.

"He's a member here you know," Alex said.

"No way," Ian responded.

"I'm serious. He could walk in right now. I hear he's in deep with the mob," Alex said, whispering as he looked around to see if anyone was within earshot.

"Thanks for the heads up," Ian responded nervously.

A man working out in the weight room nearby watched attentively as Ian and Alex conversed.

"Look, I gotta go. It was good to see you again," Ian said before turning toward the entrance door.

As Ian stepped out onto Sauchiehall he looked both ways before walking off as inconspicuously as possible. The rain from the storm he had seen approaching earlier from the east began coming down hard, so Ian ran most of the distance back to The Ayrshire.

It was 10:20 AM when he walked into his flat, soaked to the bone. He was about to make himself a cup of tea when he noticed his RIA issued mobile phone sitting on the kitchen counter. Ian walked over and plugged in the charger then snapped the phone into the jack. He pressed the silver button at the top of the device and it powered up. There was a text message notice.

Black horse & rider Gallery of Modern Art 11 AM today be prepared to travel immediately.

2009-06-01 6:26 AM

MacLeod looked down at his watch. It was already 10:30.

"Damn," he uttered as he grabbed a windbreaker and an umbrella before rushing out the door of his flat.

Chapter 10

Heavy rain fell over Glasgow as Ian walked towards the Gallery of Modern Art on Queen Street. As he approached, he could see that there was no one in sight except milling pedestrians. Even with his umbrella shedding most of the downpour, Ian's feet were already soaked and cold.

Ian arrived at the meeting place under the bronze horseman which had been blackened by age. He glanced at his watch and noted that it was 10:58. Anxiety simmered in Ian's gut as he looked around. Just then he heard a voice.

" 're ya Ian MacLeod?" the man asked in an unmistakable Cockney accent.

"Yes," Ian said as he turned to see a big heavy set man with beady eyes and coarse features.

"Well 'ere's yer orders mate," he said thrusting an envelope at Ian.

Ian took the envelope and noticed a cardboard box sitting at his feet on the ground.

"Open it and read it," the man directed.

Ian pulled out a single sheet of typewritten instructions.

Proceed immediately to the airport and board a flight to Gatwick. Then proceed via the Express to Victoria Station and get on the District Line to Hammersmith. Check into the Novatel a few minutes away. Once you are settled go to Suite #533 at Bartell Place. The night security man has been taken care of by the client and will not ask questions. We are interested mainly in bank records. We believe there may be another bank involved other than the one disclosed to our client which is Bentleys. Photos, files and whatever you think is relevant are to be downloaded to the data transmitter and then sent to us.

Ian read the document several times until he committed the key facts to memory.

'Express to Victoria, District Line, Novatel, Suite 533 Bartell Place near Hammersmith Tube.'

"Got it," Ian said as he handed the paper back to the man who folded it and placed it in his pocket.

"Then see ya la'er and don' ferget the box," the man said as he turned and walked off.

Bending down, Ian opened the flaps on the cardboard box and noticed there was a leather bag inside. Not wanting to investigate further in the pouring rain, Ian closed the flaps and stood up to find himself looking into one of several CCTV cameras around the square.

With the box under his arm Ian headed straight back to his flat.

Once inside, Ian emptied the box and laid the contents on the kitchen table.

There was a digital camera, an ordinary looking key and FOB, a USB transmitter, a laptop computer and a blank envelope. Ian opened the envelope to find a wad of bank notes which he assumed was to be used for travel and hotel expenses.

At 12:00 noon Ian set off to the airport and by 2:30 the easyJet flight was airborne. Ian settled in for the flight to Gatwick.

He deplaned just over an hour later and recited the agenda in his mind *'Express to Victoria, District Line, Novatel, suite 533 Bartell Place near Hammersmith Tube.'* After asking an airport staff member how to get to the south terminal he made his way to the Express Train Station and purchased a ticket using the cash that came with the RIA package. The trip took 35 minutes and he got off at Victoria Station where he then boarded the District Line to Hammersmith. By 5:45 he was checking into the Novatel.

He took the elevator up to Room 635 facing west overlooking Shortlands Street. The room had a small window, work station, TV and a separate bedroom. Ian stood at the window surveying the lay of the land to familiarize himself with his target, Bartell Place, a few minutes down the street. It was a typical London business district and as Ian watched people making their way home from work he realized he didn't even know the name of the company he was about to audit.

It was almost 8:00 by the time Ian finished up the dinner he had ordered from room service and placed the tray outside. Taking a look out the window, Ian noticed it was pouring and donned the black hooded Gore-Tex rain jacket he had brought in anticipation of the forecasted wet London weather. Placing the leather bag over his shoulder Ian made his way down the long hallway toward the elevator. He pressed the call button and a few moments later the doors opened and he stepped in amongst several guests and a hotel employee. When he emerged into the hotel lobby there were about a dozen people milling around. Ian was nervous as he walked towards the lobby exit that led to the hotel portico.

It took about three minutes for Ian to arrive at Bartell Place. He stood outside the main entrance in the pouring rain trying to find the courage to go inside, given it was now locked up for the night. Ian reached into his pocket for the FOB that would open the main entrance door and pulled it out holding it against the receiver. The latch released and Ian pulled the door open walking inside to a dimly lit lobby. Sitting behind a large oak desk was a night security guard who looked up at Ian as he passed by. Keeping his head down Ian walked into the elevator foyer and pressed the call button. The doors opened and Ian entered the cab, pressing the button for floor five. A few moments later the elevator stopped and Ian walked down the hall finding the door marked 533.

Ian looked around before inserting the key into the heavy mortise lock.

"Who's there?" a shrill female voice asked from inside the office.

MacLeod pulled the key out of the lock and ran towards a stairwell next to where he had exited the elevator. He opened the exit door and ducked inside listening as the office door opened and then closed a few seconds later. With his anxiety ratcheting up his ambivalence about the strange job began to shift towards wondering if he should simply abandon the audit and return to Glasgow. He heard the door open and close again, this time with footsteps and the sound of the elevator doors opening. He peeked out from the door to the stairwell and seeing no one around, he emerged and walked towards suite 533.

This time he unlocked the door and pushed it open to see a small reception area. It was stark, painted a yellowish shade of beige with nothing hanging on any of the walls. There was no reception counter and not even a chair for a waiting visitor. Obviously no one came to call except for whoever occupied the single small office.

Venturing into the short hallway Ian noticed that there was an open door to a toilet on his left and another door further down on his right. He walked to the door on his right and turned the handle pushing it open. Ian switched on the single light bulb and saw a row of shelving upon which there were a number of file boxes.

He walked back to the office where he found a cheap looking wooden desk in front of a lone window with a small safe against the wall. Next to the desk there was a corkboard with a calendar and a single sheet of paper fastened with pushpins. Ian walked into the office and looked at what was written on the paper—'CityRush 0844 888 4000.'

Worried about an unexpected visitor, Ian looked around with the intention of rehearsing an escape plan in the event that his presence was discovered. Realizing there was no other way out except through the office window, he set his leather bag down on the desk and pulled open the blind. Reflections of car headlamps and brake lights from the rain-slicked pavement of Shortlands Street, five stories below, gave Ian a moment of vertigo. Turning and looking back at the reception area Ian accepted the fact that should he be discovered there would be no choice but to storm the door and do his best to flee the premises.

He sat down and took out the RIA mobile phone from his bag and powered it up. Immediately there was a text appearing on the home screen which he selected.

Login - SXZ, Password - hellfire, Safe - 12, 22, 44, 99.

2009-06-01 4:26 PM

He got up and squatted in front of the safe as he looked at the numbers on the text message—12, 22, 44, 99. He turned the combination lock dialing in each number until the safe released. He opened the door and there standing against the inside wall of the safe were two accounting binders. He took them out and placed them on the desk. Ian flipped one of them open and noticed that it contained bank statements for 2008. He flipped open the other one and saw that the statements were from January to May 2009.

Ian wondered if the woman who had heard him place the key in the lock had been scared off by the sound of a possible intruder. If she had called someone, he could be caught red-handed in what would be a break and enter charge. Ian broke into a cold sweat before telling himself that he was letting his imagination run wild.

Gathering his thoughts, Ian noticed that on the floor of the safe there was a business checkbook as well as the bank deposit records. He reached in and picked up both of them, setting them down on the desk beside the bank statement binders. Ian opened the checkbook and saw that the checks bore the Bentleys bank insignia. There were no other records of any kind; no financial statements, no correspondence.

Unsure of what to do next, Ian got up and walked down the hall to the storage room. He looked around for a few moments before reaching up and pulling out a file box, setting it down on the floor. None of the boxes were labeled so Ian had no idea what they contained. Pulling each box off the shelf, one by one, Ian brought them into the office stacking them on the floor next to the desk.

Sitting down at the desk again, he reached into his bag and pulled out the mini-laptop he had been provided and placed it in front of himself. After disconnecting the data cable from the desktop computer Ian plugged it into the laptop and logged on to the network using the name and password from the text he received earlier. The screen came alive displaying a number of icons including one that Ian recognized as a well-known accounting software package. Ian clicked on it and it opened to a typical suite of accounting functions.

The general ledger postings displayed a simple chart of accounts; real estate holdings identified by address, revenue accounts, cost of sales accounts, management fees and general expense accounts. Ian thumbed through the bank deposits and noticed that they seemed to be exclusively made through checks. Ian flipped through a random sampling and found that there was no cash listed on any of the deposit slips. However there was a pattern to the deposits—they were weekly with transaction amounts totaling as much as

£100,000. Ian did a quick calculation in his head based on several weeks of random sampling and was shocked. The annual cash flows could be as much as £15,000,000 per year.

He was intrigued as to what kind of business could generate such huge revenues out of a nondescript postage stamp of an office. Ian looked closer at the check listings. There seemed to be a pattern to the names listed on the deposit slips—all from the same handful of numbered companies. Ian looked at the company names listed on the deposit slips: 123SXZ Limited, 456SXZ Limited and several more, all using alpha numeric combinations. The same company names appeared on the deposit record every week. Ian compared the dates from the book to the calendar on the corkboard and noticed that deposits were made every Friday without fail. There was no clue as to the nature of the business except that it received large regular payments from the same sources.

Ian then considered the possibility that the numbered companies were some sort of franchise business entities. He thought that perhaps he could answer some of his questions through review of the financial statements so he scrolled through the files on the computer desktop, but nothing obvious could be found. Ian looked down at the boxes on the floor intrigued as to the nature of SXZ's business.

He opened the Internet and typed in a Google search.

SXZ Enterprises UK

Nothing useful came back as a list of meaningless names appeared on the screen.

Ian thumbed through the folders in the first file box and found nothing. He tried another one and also came up blank. Sitting back in the chair he looked down at the three desk drawers and gave a pull on the top one. It didn't budge.

Ian typed in a new Google search.

How can I break into an old desk with locked drawers?

Ian clicked on a link named 'Dismantling a desk drawer lock with a paper clip. | Undrblog'. He read the blog and did exactly what was recommended. Pulling a paperclip from a tray that was sitting on the desk Ian straightened it and then placed it into the lock. Moving it around inside the lock he tried as instructed to contact the 6th pin that would release the tumbler assembly.

After five frustrating minutes Ian heard a click and the whole tumbler came out in his hand. Ian then picked up a letter opener and inserted it into the hollow lock and turned the mechanism which unlocked the drawers. He pulled the top drawer open and then the middle drawer where he found the 2008 Monthly Financial Statements. He set the folder on the desk and opened it up perusing the contents. After back checking the income figures against the bank deposits he had seen earlier he saw that they jibed.

Next Ian studied the expenses and noted that the biggest annual cost to the business came from a single source—payment to DM Enterprises of £6,880,000. Ian toggled over to the general ledger accounts and found DM Enterprises. There were 12 invoices ranging in amounts between five and six hundred thousand pounds billed to SXZ Enterprises for consulting services rendered.

Another line on the statement showed Management Fees payable to SXZ Enterprises in exactly the same amount, £6,880,000. Ian concluded that the equal amounts were the split in the partnership between whoever owned SXZ Enterprises and the client who must be doing business as DM Enterprises. Although interesting, the findings were of no consequence to Ian's assignment.

Ian looked around and noticed what appeared to be an access panel for a plumbing shut off valve nestled in behind the office door. It struck him as odd that there would be a shut-off valve so far away from the toilet. He got up, walked over and inspected the small square wooden panel that had been fastened over a hole cut into the plaster wall. It appeared as if it was regularly removed and refastened—the paint was worn as were the Philips head screws that fastened it shut. Ian looked around for something he could use to open it but came up empty handed. He then walked into the toilet and opened up the vanity doors. There was a Philips screwdriver sitting on the base of the cabinet. Ian picked it up, walked back to the office and proceeded to back off the screws until the panel was loose. He then pried it open with the screwdriver and there sitting in the wall space, was another bank deposit book.

Ian grabbed the book and walked over to the desk, sitting down as he flipped open the first page. It was an HMQS account, the second bank that Jordie had suspected was being used to falsify SXZ revenue. There was page after page of deposits from a single source; XYZSXZ Limited. Ian then opened up the Bentleys deposit book and flipped through until he found checks also listed as coming from XYZSXZ Limited. He scanned several weeks of the Bentleys deposits and when he compared XYZ's amounts against those from the other numbered companies it appeared that the figures were inconsistent. The XYZ deposits in both accounts followed an erratic pattern from one week to the next while checks from the other companies seemed to be of similar magnitude. A deposit made into the HMQS account on March 14, 2008 amounted to £9,900 while the next week the amount was £16,300. Ian concluded that whoever was writing the checks from XYZ was being told to write two checks; one that would be deposited into the Bentleys account for the partnership and another one to the HMQS account. SXZ was ripping off the client for what appeared to be hundreds of thousands of pounds. Ian concluded that Jordie had seen the irregular pattern but could not find evidence to show it was a fraudulent attempt at hiding profits from the client.

Ian spent a few minutes tallying the deposit slips for the entire year. They added up to £1,134,678. He wrote the amount down on a yellow post it note along with the words; 'XYZ unreported income'.

On a hunch Ian went back into the GL and found the petty cash account. It showed £55,652 in cash expenditures to office expenses and travel. Ian tried to reconcile the amount as he looked around at the meager office setup wondering whether this might have been, at least in part, payoff money to the minion at XYZ that assisted in the scam.

Ian typed in a Google search.

Companies House London WebCHeck

Ian searched for 123SXZ Limited. The search results showed that it was an active company registered to SXZ Enterprises Ltd. He then searched for XYZSXZ finding out that it too named SXZ as the parent company. It was obvious to Ian that all of the numbered companies were wholly owned subsidiaries of SXZ Enterprises set up to front the parent company. Ian presumed that the directors wanted to distance themselves from whatever liabilities might be associated with the operating companies.

Ian then took out the camera and started documenting what he had found. It was obvious to Ian that this was the incriminating evidence that RIA was looking for on behalf of their client. He snapped pictures of the post it note and the HMQS deposit book where he found the stolen XYZ monies. Ian then photographed the large checks made out to DM Enterprises and SXZ Enterprises as well.

MacLeod keyed in a text to Dunsmuir and sent it off, finishing his audit duties.

Found £1,134,678 in unreported income in HMQS account. Will send photos later.

2009-06-01 11:36 PM

Placing everything back into the safe and closing it, Ian spun the combination lock before walking over and placing the HMQS deposit book back into the wall space screwing the cover back in place. He also returned the file boxes to the storage room down the hall. Ian was about to snap the tumbler back in place after replacing the folder in the desk drawer when he noticed another folder marked 'Real Estate Holdings'. It contained papers relating to the real estate assets he had noticed earlier on the chart of accounts. He sorted through the documents and noticed one of the addresses; 1276 Hawthorn Mews, East London. Intrigued as to what might draw SXZ to East London, Ian used Google Earth to locate the address and dragged the street view icon directly in front of the address. Up flashed a daylight photograph of a three story auburn brick building with white window trim and muntins. Above the black metal clad double doors was a neon sign band that read 'Macy's Gentlemen's Club'.

"A chain of strip joints?" Ian whispered to himself in amazement at what he had found.

Ian grabbed the folder and found another address in Manchester. He typed the address into another Google Earth search: 88 George Street, Manchester, UK.

This time the street view showed a stone façade with a single door recessed into the building at street level. The sign above the entrance read 'La Femme Fatale' with a logo of a leggy female figure.

He typed in a new search on Google.

Macy's Gentlemen's Club East London

The website loaded. Pictures of big breasted women in seductive poses flashed across the home page.

Ian then noticed a tab that said 'The Backroom'. He clicked on it and was taken to an interactive site that included a chat line entitled 'For Gentlemen with Discerning Taste'. 'Click here for the best London has to offer' said one of the banners under which were fading and dissolving images of women in various stages of undress.

Ian clicked on the portal and the faces of scores of underage women appeared on the screen. He scanned the multiple images and then randomly clicked on one of the pictures—the image of an adolescent female. It transformed into a series of pictures of a pretty platinum blond in various semi-nude and nude poses. Ian estimated that she was perhaps eighteen years old. There was a bio at the top of the page.

Natasha is from Belarus. A young beauty, Natasha will satisfy your wildest desires. At 5'- 8" she is a virtual goddess. She is available immediately for any man looking for forbidden love.

07 987 664 321.

Ian had no doubt that he had come upon a porn site offering the sexual services of kidnapped and drug addicted girls—victims of the illegal sex trade. After a few moments staring at the local phone number Ian became curious. He picked up the phone on the desk and dialed the local mobile number. It rang several times until someone answered.

"Darnel speakin'. What chu want mon?" a man with a Caribbean accent asked.

"Yeah, I'd like to meet Natasha," Ian stated.

"That can be arranged. What time my friend?"

"11, tonight."

"OK mon. The Satin House in Hackney. You know it?" the man asked.

"Yes, how much?"

"She starts at one hundred pounds and then it is up to you. Your name?" the pimp inquired.

"Kenneth. See you then," Ian said.

"No mon, you'll see Natasha outside the hotel. Bye."

Ian hung up, at once shocked and disgusted at having been foisted into the midst of a highly illegal business, dealing in the exploitation of underage prostitutes. Recalling Ascot's evasive answer to his question about what type of business the client was involved with, Ian now put two and two together. His instinct to leave was overridden by his inquisitiveness as to who was behind SXZ Enterprises and why RIA's client would be partnering with them. The highly illegal nature of the business raised questions in Ian's mind as to the legitimacy of the client he was carrying out the audit on behalf of. Who were they and why would they want an obscure business relationship with SXZ in a prostitution ring?

He walked back to the storage room and one by one, thumbed through the folders in the file boxes he had placed back on the shelves. After ten minutes of searching Ian came upon a company registry document. He stood scanning the paper and there under the heading of 'Owner' was the name to which SXZ Enterprises Ltd. was registered. Ian gasped as he read the name.

Lance Mills, 1875 Decker's Lane, Brighton, UK.

"What the hell?" Ian exclaimed.

His mouth hung open and he stared wide eyed at the document. Then some of the addresses he had seen earlier in the GL jogged his memory. Ian recalled making numerous personal real estate transactions in 2006 on behalf of his former employer Lance Mills through a real estate holding company he set up for him. The business names were never disclosed but Ian remembered that there were several East End London addresses on the conveyance documents. The transactions were for commercial properties in cities across the UK.

Ian put the boxes back in place and returned to the office with the registry document in his hand. He sat down and stuffed the incriminating document into his briefcase before tapping the mouse navigating back into the chart of accounts.

He looked at the general expense ledger until he spotted the courier postings. There were regular entries for CityRush Couriers. Ian looked up at the name and phone number he had seen earlier written on the sheet of paper pinned to the tack board next to the desk.

Ian pulled out the camera and snapped a picture of the sheet of paper pinned to the board.

He added up a year's worth of courier expenses and was not surprised to find it came to over £26,880.

Ian surmised that the cash was turned into each of the club operators from a network of organized pimps. The cash collected by each operator from their street pimps must have been taken in as revenue at each club and in turn paid to SXZ by check sent on regular courier runs to whoever managed the finances at SXZ. How the club operators dealt with such large amounts of cash was obviously of no concern to either SXZ or whomever DM Enterprises represented. Ian presumed that the money continued to be laundered down a chain right through to street level. An untraceable business whose revenues consisted of laundered money with the only cost of sales being a check cut to RIA's client once a month for their interest in the business.

Ian concluded that someone must be keeping both the club operators and the pimps honest. He also wondered who supplied the drugs knowing that forcing young women into sex slavery could only be done through coercion and drug addiction.

A wave of panic overwhelmed Ian as he was beginning to sense the danger that he had gotten himself into. It was not hard to see that DM Enterprises was the client or at least somehow related, and that their participation in profits must reflect some contribution to the street level operation of the business. Not only had Ian entered the fringes of one of the most sordid and illegal businesses on the planet, he had also been inadvertently foisted back into the life of Lance Mills—a man he detested and had done his best to flee from along with the rest of his past.

Ian considered whether he should go to the police but decided otherwise. A criminal investigation would involve Ian as a witness exposing him to the obvious danger of reprisal from what was beginning to look like an organized criminal enterprise. Whoever was behind it would not take kindly to being informed on. Ian wondered how a firm like RIA, with a top reputation for professional ethics could be involved with this client.

Ian quickly returned everything in the office back to its original condition. He packed up, put on his jacket and was ready to leave before taking one last look around to ensure everything was in order.

The sound of a key in the lock of the office door startled MacLeod and he froze momentarily. He looked around in a panic before pulling up on the sliding sash to open the window. Five stories below Ian saw a downpour of wind-driven rain droplets hitting the flooded surface of Shortlands Street. Throwing his bag over his shoulder and pulling up his hoodie Ian stepped out onto the stone ledge while gripping a metal awning frame above the window opening. Holding on tightly, he used his foot to push the window closed before the driving rain made a suspicious puddle on the tiled floor.

To Ian's shock, a distorted image of Lance Mills appeared through the rain-soaked window, looking around suspiciously.

In his astonishment, MacLeod lost his footing and slipped off the stone ledge.

Hanging precariously by his arms from the metal awning, Ian looked down at the rain slicked street and passing cars 80 feet below before regaining his foothold.

Having heard something, Mills looked towards him. Adrenalin pumped through Ian's veins as Mills cautiously walked up to the window. Expecting to be seen at any moment, MacLeod remained motionless as the wind-driven rain soaked him.

It seemed like Mills was straining to see beyond his own reflection in the window against the dark rainy night. Ian's decision to bring along his dark rain jacket and black pants were a stroke of luck allowing him to blend in with the dark silhouettes of the surrounding buildings.

The sound of the torrent against the pane and the creaking of the old wooden sash could be heard along with the wind as Mills stared out through the blur of the rain soaked window. Ian could see Mills looking down at the floor, no doubt noticing that there was water. Ian desperately hoped that he would conclude that the old window was leaking due to the heavy wind and rain from the furious storm.

A few seconds later, Mills turned and walked towards the entry. Breathing a sigh of relief, Ian waited several minutes before using a free hand to push up on the sash to open the window. Soaking wet, MacLeod stepped back inside, shutting the window behind him. He threw his bag over his shoulder and walked to the entry door, carefully locking it as he left.

'Jordie, what the hell have you got me into?' Ian thought to himself as he walked down the long hallway towards the elevator. Ian got into the elevator and noticed the small pools of water forming on the floor from his rain soaked clothes. He thought about the security guard and what Mills might have said to him as he left the building. Perhaps he had alerted him to his suspicions and the guard would call Mills as soon as he saw him and his wet clothes.

The elevator doors opened and Ian hesitated for a moment noticing that he was in the opposite set of elevators across from where he had gone up. He stepped into the foyer and heard voices. He leaned around and there was Lance Mills at the security desk talking with the guard. Ian glanced over at the other end of the foyer and saw an exit sign. Without taking his eyes off of Mills, Ian walked backwards for a few seconds until he came to a long hallway that led to an exit door. Ian walked as fast as he could, the telltale sound of his sloshing shoes echoing in the cavernous lobby.

"Who's there?" Ian heard Mills ask.

Breaking into a run, Ian crashed into the panic bar of the rear exit door and fled out into the darkness of an alley and the driving rain. He glanced back just before turning the corner and saw two figures poking their heads outside trying to get a look at whoever was fleeing the building. One of them was the unmistakable bald head of Lance Mills.

Ian arrived at the hotel room and stripped off his wet clothing. He got into a hot shower and let the water run down over his bowed head as he braced himself against the shower wall. All of his suspicions about Jordie Dunsmuir and the RIA assignment were coming true.

Chapter 11

It was 10:00 AM the next morning when Lance Mills stepped out of the shower. He was about to dry himself when he heard the sound of his mobile phone ringing in the bedroom of his London hotel suite. He wrapped a towel around his waist and walked into the bedroom to find it. Mills expected a call from his wife Brigitte, who was at home in Brighton. He was anxious to check in with her after leaving a message that he had decided to stay over at his regular hotel, the Hammersmith Novatel because his flight to Paris had been cancelled. However, the real reason for his layover was lying in the king sized bed of the hotel suite—Annika—a young prostitute who had just arrived from Russia. His mobile phone was sitting on the night table in the midst of the hypodermic needle, foil packet, spoon, lighter and rubber band Mills' underage prostitute had used to shoot the Mexican heroin into one of the partially collapsed veins in her arms. Mills picked up the phone.

"Good morning sweetheart," Mills answered thinking it was his wife.

Annika rolled over and moaned as Mills attempted to cover the phone with both hands.

"Mr. Mills, I'm callin' on behalf o' yer partner," a brusque voice spoke in a Glaswegian brogue.

Surprised, Mills walked into the bathroom.

"Who is this?"

"You don't need to know my name," the voice said.

"What is this about?" Mills asked, annoyed at the mysterious caller.

"Your business arrangement Mr. Mills."

Mills knew right away what he was referring to.

"I don't know what you're talking about," Mills responded.

"Don't play cute Mr. Mills. Y' know damn well why I'm callin'."

"Look I haven't a clue who you are and I'm not about to continue talking with a perfect stranger," Mills said playing up his ploy of ignorance.

"I'm here to deliver a message," the unidentified voice warned.

"Well I'm all ears," Mills said reconsidering his avoidance tactic.

Mills did not end up on top by being timid. He was known in business circles across Great Britain as an aggressive and ruthless CEO who had taken many people down in his mercurial rise to riches and glory. Respected by few but feared by many, he was a business superstar who wielded his power without apology. He was convinced he could outmaneuver anyone including his partners in the largest criminal organization in the UK.

"You need to receive it in person Mr. Mills. Those are my orders."

Mills knew he was in trouble.

"Where do you have in mind?" Mills asked.

"You name the place."

Mills considered the request for a few moments and decided to play along.

"Fine; 11:15 outside of Callahan's in Notting Hill. How will I know you?" Mills asked.

"You won't. I'll recognize you sir," the man said feigning a respectful tone.

"See you then," Mills replied.

"Oh and don't be late Mr. Mills," the mysterious caller said before hanging up.

Mills had been introduced to his partner in the months following his award as one of the 'Top 10 CEO's in the UK', an annual business recognition program sponsored by the accounting firm RIA. The head of RIA, Alistair Ascot had made the introduction when Mills attended a gala event to celebrate the opening of an experimental drug addiction program in the city of Glasgow. It had been funded by many of the top corporations in Great Britain, including a major contribution from Mills' own company, Datatime Industries.

The vile character of the people he was dealing with made his calculated decision to partner with them in the lucrative human trafficking and sex trade business inherently dangerous. One of the perks of his arrangement was that he could satisfy his nasty addiction to illicit sex with young prostitutes whenever he was in London on company business. He kept his involvement in the business secret and no one in his legitimate professional circles knew that SXZ Enterprises even existed, let alone that he was the proprietor. The deal was that he fronted the business—financing and operating the strip joints as well as managing the money—while his partners in crime supplied the girls and the drugs as well as organizing and enforcing the widespread network of pimps needed at the street level. The profits were huge and the split was to be 50/50, with proceeds distributed monthly. Both SXZ and DM Enterprises were legitimate businesses far enough removed from the street to avoid being associated with the criminal source of their earnings. Mills knew damn well that he had been shorting his business partner by hundreds of thousands of pounds and that they may have caught on to his false reporting of profits, but he was a born gambler and loved the high stakes world of extreme risk.

Right after hanging up Mills rushed Annika out of his room and handed her £50 for her trouble before packing his bag and hurriedly leaving the hotel. He checked out and walked towards one of the taxis waiting in the hotel portico. Before he got into the cab, he looked around suspiciously to make sure that no one was following him.

Lance Mills glanced at his watch as he got out of the taxi after the short ride from the hotel to Euston Station. It was 11:10. He walked down the long stairwell from Eversholt Street to the platform at Euston Station where he would board a tube train to Heathrow before transferring to the Heathrow Express. From there he planned to catch a flight to Paris, where he was to meet a Datatime client.

Mills walked slowly scanning the crowd as he noticed the tunnel and platform that would soon be the disembarkation point for passengers riding the inbound tube train. Off to his right following the gentle curve of the glossy white metal panels that clad the cylindrical shape of the tunnel platform area was a poster advertising for the musical 'The Lion King'. Just to the right of the darkened train tunnel was a brick archway against which there was a ticket dispenser with a digital clock that read 11:15.

Lance Mills walked toward the press of people waiting for the next train. Pushing through the crowd, he looked around for any sign of being followed.

Mills stopped at the edge of the platform. The clock now read 11:19. The distant sound of the 11:20 grew louder drawing the attention of the waiting passengers toward the tunnel and track.

A young transient loitering halfway up the stairs to the Eversholt Street exit watched as a lone figure dressed in black and wearing a hoodie, moved through the crowd. The sound of the approaching train grew even louder. The man in the hoodie walked up behind Mills and with a visceral grunt made a sudden and hard impact on Mills' left side as he stood precariously close to the rail guideway below. At the same moment that the 11:20 came speeding through the mouth of the tunnel at over 30 miles per hour Mills lost his balance and fell headfirst onto the track directly into the path of the oncoming train. The noise of the slowing train and the whoosh of wind that accompanied its arrival hid any hint of the violent encounter as Mills was quite literally cut in half.

The man who struck Mills turned away, head down, calmly walking toward the stairwell as if nothing had happened. People gathered at the edge of the platform and horrific screams from the crowd echoed in the cavernous walls of the station. The killer made his way up the long stairwell in a measured pace that belied the urgency of his need to escape the scene of his heinous crime. The long haired transient youth was still leaning against the wall halfway up the stairs when he locked eyes with Mills' assassin who didn't miss a step as he spoke on a mobile phone.

"Yeah, I gave 'im the message. I followed 'im to Euston and had 'im kiss the front end of the Circle Line," the man said keeping his head down to avoid being ID'd by the numerous CCTV cameras that monitored activity around the station.

Turning and following the man, the skinny kid looked up towards the light beaming down from Eversholt Street to see the silhouette of the fleeing attacker. Arriving at the top of the stairs the young lad watched as the man disappeared down Euston Road.

Chapter 12

After tossing and turning all night long, Ian got up the next morning and hoped to see a text message that would alleviate his anxiety and get him out of London fast. After waiting the whole day, beside himself with apprehension, Ian looked at his watch. It was 5:45 and still no word from Dunsmuir or whoever was supposed to clear him to leave London. It had been almost 18 hours since Ian transmitted the data from his night audit to whoever would be receiving it at the undisclosed email address. Perplexed at how the audit could have involved his former boss Lance Mills, Ian considered the motives of RIA. The chance meeting of Jordie Dunsmuir on the train could not have been set up. However, the business world was a small place and RIA was a big player in the consulting services industry so it would be entirely possible for them to have a relationship with Lance Mills and Datatime Industries. Ian thought about the identity of the client that they so carefully kept under a shroud of secrecy. What was RIA really up to?

As he stared out the window in contemplation the news anchor's voice for the BBC caught his attention.

"Welcome to the BBC evening news for Tuesday, June 2, 2009. We have breaking news from Euston Station. Fifty-five year old award winning businessman Lance Mills was killed instantly when he was pushed into the path of an oncoming train just before the noon hour today. Mills was the CEO of Brighton based Datatime Industries and was thought to have been in London on business at the time of his death. Scotland Yard is investigating."

MacLeod turned and walked over to the TV. He picked up the remote so he could turn up the volume.

The story segued to the scene of the incident at Euston Station. A man in his mid-fifties was being interviewed by a BBC reporter.

"I'm speaking with police spokesman, Detective Chief Inspector Harry Cosgrove of Scotland Yard. Can you tell us what happened here today Inspector?" the reporter asked.

Presenting himself in a dignified and officious manner, his tall physique, neatly trimmed mustache and greying hair gave Cosgrove a commanding appearance.

"Well there's very little to go on right now and we have not yet been able to gather witness accounts that might corroborate what actually happened here today. However we do suspect foul play," Cosgrove stated.

Ian's blood pressure skyrocketed as a rush of adrenalin shocked his system. He switched off the television.

Just then the familiar sound of a text message beeped on the RIA phone.

You are cleared to return to Glasgow.

2009-06-02 5:36 PM

By 6:45 Ian was checked out of the hotel and on his way to the airport. By 9:45 he was on an easyJet flight climbing out of Gatwick.

* * * * *

Back in Glasgow, Ian awoke Wednesday morning panicked over the news that his ex-boss Lance Mills had been murdered. He showered and then proceeded directly to RIA headquarters at 29 St Vincent Street. Ian was angry and extremely agitated when he arrived.

"I need to see Jordie Dunsmuir right away," Ian blurted to the startled receptionist.

"I'm sorry sir but he's in a meeting at the moment," the receptionist stated.

"Please interrupt him. I have urgent business," Ian demanded.

"I'm sorry but—,"

"Listen, you don't want me making a scene do y'?" Ian said forcefully.

"No sir ... just a moment," the receptionist said nervously looking up at Ian as he leaned on the counter.

The receptionist rang Jordie who was in the boardroom.

"Jordie, I have Mr. MacLeod here and he says he has urgent business to discuss with you," the receptionist said, recognizing Ian from the initial meeting with Ascot and Dunsmuir.

"I'm in a meeting at the moment," Jordie's voice said loud enough for Ian to overhear.

Ian reached out and grabbed the phone from the receptionist's hand.

"Jordie, if you don't see me there'll be big trouble my friend," Ian said threateningly.

"Ian, settle down. I'll be right out," Jordie responded.

Ian handed the phone back to the receptionist.

"My apologies," Ian said to the flustered receptionist.

A few seconds later, Jordie came through the big oak door.

"Ian, please come in," Jordie said apprehensively.

Ian followed Jordie into his office across from the boardroom they had met in a few days earlier. Ian noticed that there was a meeting underway with Ascot and the same unidentified man he had seen at his first meeting with RIA. He was wearing a scowl as he looked up through the glass sidelight making eye contact with Ian.

"Who is that?" Ian asked.

"I don't see that is any of your business Ian," Jordie said motioning for Ian to go into his office.

MacLeod became very agitated pointing toward the boardroom.

"Jordie, your client's partner was my ex-boss, Lance Mills."

"Calm down Ian," Jordie said shrinking away from MacLeod.

"Do y' know where Mills is today?" MacLeod said as he leaned over Dunsmuir's desk.

"I've no idea," Dunsmuir replied as he cringed even further.

"On a slab at the London Morgue. He was murdered, Jordie."

"Ian, calm down," Jordie said motioning with both hands.

"Calm down. That's all you can say? You knew I was going to set Mills up for whoever killed him didn't you? Didn't you Jordie?" Ian asked accusingly.

Alistair Ascot overheard Ian's loud voice and walked in on the conversation.

"MacLeod, how are you?"

"I've been better," Ian replied as he looked at Ascot.

"I gathered that. We could hear everything you said. I suggest you try to control yourself."

"You knew who I was investigating didn't you?" Ian accused, pointing his finger at Ascot and then Jordie.

"Quite an imagination you have MacLeod. Don't be ridiculous. Why would we do such a thing?" Ascot inquired.

MacLeod stood toe to toe with Ascot.

"Enlighten me," MacLeod said provocatively.

"You think too much MacLeod," Ascot shot back.

"Oh yeah? How do you explain that Mills, my ex-boss, was the client's partner who coincidentally was murdered right after the audit? What am I supposed to think Mr. Ascot?" Ian countered.

Ascot crossed his arms and looked directly at MacLeod. He shrugged his shoulders.

"You said it, MacLeod ... coincidence," Ascot replied persuasively.

MacLeod looked over at Dunsmuir before returning his piercing gaze to Ascot.

"I told Jordie I worked for Mills."

"MacLeod, I'm sure there's nothing to it. I assure you, all of this is fortuitous," Ascot calmly replied.

MacLeod pursed his lips and nodded his head grudgingly, looking first at Dunsmuir and then at Ascot.

"Sure," Ian said dubiously.

"No one can connect you to this thing in any way provided you don't draw attention to yourself. I wouldn't worry about it," Ascot stated reassuringly.

Ian looked across the hallway and out the window of the boardroom for a moment, knowing he had left a trail of damning evidence—airline and hotel records, fingerprints and video surveillance tapes. He also had no alibi.

MacLeod turned to Ascot and Dunsmuir.

"What about the sex trade business?"

"What are you talking about?" Ascot asked.

MacLeod reached in his jacket pocket and pulled out the corporate registry document showing that Lance Mills was the owner of SXZ Enterprises. Unfolding it, he thrust it directly in front of Alistair Ascot.

"This! Perhaps you recognize the name," MacLeod replied sarcastically.

Ascot glanced at the document before taking it from MacLeod and handing it to Jordie Dunsmuir.

"How very unprofessional of you to take personal possession of original audit materials, MacLeod," Ascot admonished.

MacLeod remained in a confrontive stance, toe to toe with Alistair Ascot who remained stone faced except for the slightest movement of his right eyebrow.

"Recovering the client's money was our only interest in having you audit Mr. Mills," Ascot said in a matter of fact tone.

MacLeod stared at Ascot in contempt for a moment before responding sarcastically.

"Aye, the client ... who I know nothing about."

MacLeod threw both Ascot and Dunsmuir a piercing look before taking a seat across from Dunsmuir.

"OK gentlemen. What's next?"

Surprised, Ascot took a different tact.

"Ian, maybe you should take some time for yourself. Relax and take your mind off of things. Jordie, do we have an address for Ian so we can send over a nice bottle of single malt?" Ascot queried.

"Ah no, actually we don't," Jordie said realizing his omission.

The last thing Ian wanted was for anyone to have his address given the threatening turn of events. Ian interjected quickly.

"There's no need for that Mr. Ascot. I'm fine, really. Just a bit shocked at the news that's all. You're probably right. It was most likely an accident—a heart attack or whatever. I'm ready to get back to work on the next assignment," Ian said wanting to show that he had regained his composure.

"Well, you're jumping the gun a bit aren't you? We haven't recovered the money from the first assignment yet MacLeod," Ascot said glancing over at Dunsmuir.

"Yeah, as Alistair said in our first meeting Ian, we have to assess your skills first," Dunsmuir added.

MacLeod looked at each man, realizing they were stalling. He was now certain that he had been set up and was about to be thrown to the wolves. He needed time to figure out their game and to extract himself from the tangled web Ascot and Dunsmuir were weaving.

"What more do you want? I told you exactly where to find over a million pounds of unreported income for your precious client, didn't I? Isn't that performance?" Ian offered emphatically.

Ascot thought about it for a moment. The fact that MacLeod had uncovered the sordid details of Mills' business was commendable and proved how smart he was. He considered the possibility that MacLeod might go directly to the police and blow the lid off of something much bigger than he could even imagine. However, the scenario was unfolding as planned and MacLeod would eventually be apprehended as the suspect in the Mills murder. Keeping him on a close leash might be expedient for the time being now that he had become a potentially dangerous threat. Ascot put on his reading glasses and pulled out a paper from his suit pocket. After reading its contents for a moment he looked up over the top of his glasses.

"Alright MacLeod. We do have another job in Edinburgh. Are you ready to travel?"

"I can be."

"It is much more complex than the last audit and involves a good deal of money," Ascot advised.

"What are the details?" Ian asked.

Ascot seemed to size MacLeod up, uncertain as to his motives given his emotional display earlier.

"Let's just say we have a situation on a construction deal that has gone askew. The client has been shorted several million pounds of expected profit and would be grateful for its recovery. In any case MacLeod, I must run so you can expect the contact to be in touch," Ascot replied.

"I'll do my best to recover your money, sir," Ian stated resolutely.

"The client's money, MacLeod," Ascot clarified. "Our man will be in touch."

MacLeod looked at Ascot carefully. There was something about him that felt malevolent. His disingenuous smile and charming demeanor could not hide the fact that he had no one's best interest in mind but his own. Ian felt his skin crawl.

Ascot watched MacLeod's face carefully as he extended his hand. MacLeod made sure he appeared interested as he shook it.

Ascot walked out and left Jordie and Ian alone in the office.

Jordie tried to shift Ian's focus. "Oh, by the way, let me get the account information where your fees are being deposited. I'll be right back."

Ian looked around nervously and spotted a piece of paper on Jordie's desk. He tried to make out the name scrawled on the slip torn out from a small note pad. Reading upside down Ian was shocked. The name was Kyla Fraser.

"What the—," Ian blurted.

Just then Jordie returned.

"Ian, here's the account info. The cash is already in the bank," Jordie said thinking Ian would be happy to hear that he had been paid.

Ian took the slip of paper and looked at it: CH 23 2649853709 Balance $15,000.00 USD.

"It's an account at Zurobank, a Zurich branch actually. The client deals with them exclusively in US dollars, through us of course. We handle all of his financial dealings."

"A Scottish businessman who deals with a US bank located in Zurich? Why is that Jordie? Has he got something to hide?" Ian asked pointedly.

They stood and looked at each other for a moment.

"We made the first deposit but I suggest you contact the bank right away and get your own password. Our CFO down the hall will do it with you since she set everything up and they know her well," Jordie said choosing to ignore Ian's comment.

Ian's mind was drawn back to the slip of paper on Jordie's desk that had Kyla's name on it.

"Jordie, am I being followed?" Ian asked.

"Why do y' ask *that*?" came Jordie's retort.

Ian looked down at the slip of paper next to where Jordie's hands were clasped on the top of his desk. After realizing that Ian was staring at Kyla's name written on the slip of paper, he looked up at Ian who was waiting for an answer.

"Ian, we handle the lion's share of professional tax returns in Glasgow."

"I'm sure you do," Ian replied.

"Look, if there's someone following you, it's not to my knowledge Ian," Jordie said with a hint of annoyance in his voice.

Ian looked at Dunsmuir unconvinced.

"Let me take you down the hall to Janet McComb's office and she'll take care of the Swiss banking procedures which you will need to know about," Jordie said as he got up and motioned toward the door.

The pair walked down the hall until they came upon an office door with a sign on it that read 'Janet McComb – CFO'. Dunsmuir knocked before walking in.

As Ian entered her office, he noticed an attractive fashionably dressed woman of about 45 with a trim figure.

"Janet, this is Ian MacLeod," Jordie said gesturing to Ian.

"Nice to meet you Ian. Have a seat won't you," she said in a proper English accent.

"Janet will take care of things from here Ian. Stay in touch," Jordie said.

"Sure, see you later," Ian replied as Jordie turned around and walked back to his office.

Ian looked over at Janet McComb wondering how she fit into the scheme of things.

"So Ian, it's very simple. Your money has been temporarily deposited into one of a series of trust accounts that we administer on behalf of the client. The name and security protocols on that account can be changed very easily transferring control over to you. I will make a call to Zurobank and then you will get on the line and set up your own password and so on and then you'll be on your way."

"Alright," Ian said watching Janet as she nervously darted her eyes and fidgeted with her pen.

"They are very discreet. As long as you have the account number, the right answer to a passcode and the password, you will have access to the money. They don't ask any other questions," Janet advised.

"Alright," Ian said agreeably.

Janet dialed the number.

"I'd like to speak to Adrianna please," Janet said to the Zurobank receptionist.

Ian couldn't make out what was said to Janet but it was obvious that Adrianna was not in.

"That's fine. I'll speak to Claudia, thank you."

Ian heard a faint voice on the other side answer as Janet turned away speaking softly.

"Sienna," Janet said in a barely audible voice.

After explaining the purpose of the call, Janet handed the phone to Ian and excused herself from the room.

"Good afternoon, my name is Claudia. I understand we are transferring the ownership of this account today. Is that correct?"

"Yes it is."

"Each time you call or access your account electronically, you will be asked to select one in a series of some category such as artists, colors, musicians, writers and so on. Can you provide me with a list of eight in a series so we can start a file for you Mr. MacLeod?" the service advisor asked.

Ian thought for a moment and decided he would use authors to reflect his interest in old English literature.

"I'd like to use the following names: Poe, Shakespeare, Thomas, Burns, Joyce, Conrad, Chaucer and Nabokov," Ian said as he scrawled down the list on a post it note pad that had been sitting on Janet's desk.

The service advisor read back Ian's list and then moved on to the next step in the process.

"If you don't mind, I'd like to ensure you understand this procedure by asking you to identify the sixth name in the series you just established for your file."

"OK, that would be Conrad," Ian responded.

"Thank you. Next you will need to key in a password on Ms. McComb's computer which she advised is up on the Zurobank site. Can you do that?"

Ian sat down in front of Janet McComb's computer and was directed by Claudia to a new page on the Zurobank site.

Ian keyed in his password.

"Next we can change the name on the account," Claudia advised.

Ian was thoughtful for a moment.

"Can I change the name later?" Ian asked.

"Of course. This is a trust account currently administered by RIA so now that you are authorized with the passcode and password, only you can access it."

"Good, let's leave the name for the time being then," Ian decided.

"No problem sir," Claudia replied.

After thanking Claudia for her assistance, Ian went to the door and invited Janet back into her office apologizing for the inconvenience.

Ian was ready to leave when he hesitated and sat back down.

"A couple of questions, if you don't mind Janet?"

"Of course," Janet replied.

"Look, I don't mean to be forward, but I am intrigued with the whole Swiss banking thing ... you know, it seems so furtive or whatever," Ian said trying to sound interested.

"Oh no, it's very common for people with money to protect their wealth with offshore and Swiss bank accounts," Janet said informatively.

"Protect it from what?" Ian asked.

Janet rarely had anyone interested in her so she was quite willing to be talkative.

"Could be that the money needs to be secured from a family member or that it needs to be tax privileged from the country of origin and other reasons," Janet said enthused that Ian seemed sincerely interested.

"Like the proceeds of crime," Ian said looking for a response from Janet.

Janet looked at Ian, her expression suddenly turning from open and apparently charmed to annoyed and angry.

"Mr. MacLeod, I think we're done aren't we?" Janet said crossly.

"Yes, I suppose we are," Ian said as he got up and left her office.

Chapter 13

Ian was troubled that he had allowed himself to be conned into taking the job with RIA and now worried that he was about to be offered up as a patsy in the Mills murder. There was little doubt that he could be implicated based on the trail of circumstantial evidence he had left behind him since taking on the night audit role. He typed a search into the browser of his laptop: 'Lance Mills murder.'

The search came back with a number of hits. He clicked on one and began to read.

Suspicions Aroused in CEO Killings

Scotland Yard believes that the suspected killing of Brighton executive Lance Mills may be related to the murder of Jack Singleton. Mills and Singleton were killed within four weeks of each other.

Ian recognized Jack Singleton's name as the businessman murdered in Manchester that he had read about in the newspaper the day he left Brighton. He recalled that Jordie had said he was returning from Manchester when they first met on the train and had alluded to having concerns about one of his auditors.

Ian typed in another Google search on his laptop. 'Illegal sex trade UK.' A number of hits appeared on the screen and a link within the text caught

Liam Muir

MacLeod's eye, 'Glasgow Mob.' He opened the link. More text appeared as well as another link, 'Bud Paisley.' MacLeod clicked on it.

Bud Paisley (gangster)

From Wikipedia, the free encyclopedia

Bud Paisley, known as the "Scottish Godfather",[1] was a notorious Glasgow-born mobster who built a violent reputation on the streets of Scotland in the 1960s, and who then went on to take charge of organized crime there for over thirty years. He was born September 1940 [2] in the industrial area of The Clydebank, Glasgow.[3] He died in Glasgow on 6 April 1990—suspected to have been gunned down by associates of his successor Douglas McMurphy [1]—at the age of 50.

Ian was intrigued. He clicked on the link to Douglas McMurphy.

Douglas McMurphy (businessman)

From Wikipedia, the free encyclopedia

Douglas McMurphy [1] is said to be the kingpin of SOCKS, an acronym for *Scottish Organized Crime Kings* given to the Glasgow mob when McMurphy took control after the violent murder of his predecessor, Bud Paisley. McMurphy has made a reputation as a legitimate businessman and his company DM Enterprises is housed in a prestigious penthouse overlooking the area surrounding Glasgow. Known for his contributions to philanthropic causes throughout Great Britain McMurphy has gained the respect of political and business figures across the UK. He was born December 12, 1962 [2] in the Baillieston area of Glasgow. [3]

Ian clicked on another site.
Images for Douglas McMurphy

Dozens of pictures came back showing a man who by all accounts was a revered member of the Glasgow social elite. The face indeed was that of the man he had met with, but had not been introduced to in RIA's boardroom. Ian scanned the photographs until he came upon one that showed both Douglas McMurphy and Alistair Ascot shaking hands with the now deceased Lance Mills. The caption read 'Awards Dinner for Top CEO's'.

MacLeod had become a pawn in a cover up for the gangland murder of Lance Mills, a killing that had been planned in advance of the so called 'night audit' he had performed. The audit was simply a convenient mechanism to put Ian in the right place at the right time. The fact that Ian had found the missing money for them to recover was of much less importance than ensuring there was no mob connection to the death of Lance Mills. Mills had paid for his disloyalty with his life and his murder would fall onto Ian's shoulders simply because it would appear that he had both motive and opportunity.

A rush of panic overcame Ian as he remembered his last words to Lance Mills, *'You'll regret this Lance, you really will.'*

As he sat and stared out the window in a state of disbelief, MacLeod heard the familiar text message tone on the RIA mobile phone. He picked it up and opened the message.

Glasgow Central inside the doors next to Jessop's 12:45

2009-06-04 10:16 AM

Ian picked up his jacket and left the flat. He made his way over to the train station on Union Street and seeing the double wood and glass doors next to Jessop's he went inside to wait.

As Ian stared out onto the street, he heard footsteps behind him followed by the now familiar voice of the Cockney, " 'ere's yer instructions."

Ian turned around and took the paper from his hand.

Take the train to Edinburgh and get off at Waverly. Book into the Ibis Hotel. You are to go to the site office for Dundee Constructors at the waterfront redevelopment named Montrose Shores. The night security people have been taken care of and will not ask questions. Go late, just after 10 PM, the site clerk will be expecting you. He will provide you with access to the site office where you will find hard copy files as required. Our contact will give you a laptop loaded with software that will allow access into the contractor's information system with no restrictions. Login, password and job numbers will be provided. Once you are done stay at your hotel until you are cleared to leave.

Ian read the document and committed the key facts to memory.
'Waverly, Ibis, Dundee Constructors at the Waterfront.'
"OK," Ian said.
He handed the paper back to the Cockney.
The Cockney folded the paper and placed it in his pocket.
"Ascot told me there would be no records," Ian said.
"I' 'll go in the rubbish la'er," the man answered.
"I'm sorry, what's your name?" Ian asked.
"I's none o' yer business mate," came the man's answer.
Ian pressed the man.
"Ascot said there was to be no record of my involvement or of RIA's," Ian stated sternly.
"Don' know 'im and don' work fer 'im," the man answered.
"Well who do you work for then?" Ian asked.
"Shu' yer fockin' mauf ... 'ere's yer tools," the Cockney said handing over a laptop.
The Cockney walked away.
Ian returned to his flat, packed his bag and headed off to catch the train from Queen Street Station, a few minutes away. By 1:05 Ian was on the train to Edinburgh's Waverly Station.

Chapter 14

"Kyla, we're meeting in the situation room. Cosgrove wants you in on the briefing to answer questions," Detective Jeremy Blatherwick said as Kyla looked up from her desk at Scotland Yard Headquarters.

Kyla caught up with Blatherwick as he walked down the corridor towards one of the main meeting rooms. They entered the room and took a seat along with the rest of the Homicide Command Unit.

Both Detective Chief Superintendent Bill Pilling and Detective Chief Inspector Harry Cosgrove stood at the front of the room at the smart board. Pilling spoke first.

"Good morning everyone. We believe that our latest murder case could possibly be related to the Singleton file which we are investigating in co-operation with Manchester police. It appears, by all witness accounts, that Lance Mills was pushed into the path of the tube train. We do not believe this is a random act. We know that a call was made to Mills' mobile phone at 10AM on the morning of the murder. Mobile phone records and triangulation of mobile transmission towers in the vicinity showed that the call in question came from a location outside of the UK. However, that does not mean it did not originate from the killer given the technology available to smokescreen such calls. Unfortunately without the connection of a name to a number the call is not particularly helpful to the investigation team at this time. Our questioning of Mills' executive assistant at Datatime Industries where he was the CEO, didn't prove very fruitful as she was not aware that he was even in London. We know that he stayed the night before at a hotel in the Hammersmith district. We have assembled a task force to investigate both the Singleton and Mills murders, most of whom are with us in this briefing. That's all from me for now. Cosgrove will take it from here as I must be off to the fifth floor for a media briefing," Pilling said.

As Pilling left, Cosgrove stepped up front and center, his six foot trim frame and salt and pepper hair giving him a commanding bearing as he began to speak in a measured and self-assured manner.

"We've assigned an investigation team to this case consisting of six officers. We have also brought in Ms. Kyla Fraser who will be lending us her skills in murder profiling. What we have to work with so far is as follows," Cosgrove said as he pointed to the smart board while he continued speaking.

The words on the screen read: 'pushed onto track, room 324 Novatel, hotel video footage, Top 10 CEO award, Glasgow CCTV footage'.

"Before we cast a broad net over both of the murders, let's focus on the latest one; the Mills case. We have not ruled out a disgruntled client or associate who he may have had a relationship with. However, when you hear Kyla's profile you will see why we are not pursuing that angle at this time. He wasn't a popular guy to say the least but Datatime was, on the surface, a top flight organization. It even won several international awards. Making it into the 'Top 10 CEO's in the UK' was Mills' biggest accomplishment. Without disclosing anything or divulging details on his death, Woods made a call to his accounting firm RIA this morning to ask for a list of business associates. We'll be following up with his business contacts at Datatime, his personal banker at Lloyds, his wife, existing and former employees and any other person of interest that comes up during the investigation. I'll have Kyla expand on how this murder may tie into Singleton's in a minute," Cosgrove said.

Kyla sat up when she heard RIA's name and noted it in her iPad.

Cosgrove continued, "In spite of the fact that we have him on video capture from Euston, the alleged killer could not be ID'd as he was wearing dark clothing and a hoodie. We questioned some witnesses but no one got a very good look at the suspect. So far there's no reliable physical description but it appears that he is very athletic, given his perfect timing in sending Mills into the front end of a train as it approached the station at 30 miles per hour. There was a young lad standing in the stairwell at the station who may have seen something. The suspect walked by him on the way out talking on a mobile phone. He needs to be tracked down as he may be a key witness.

Also, there's one other piece of CCTV footage from Euston that we need to follow up on—"

Cosgrove paused for several seconds before speaking again.

"...We have a tip from an informant who said we should check out a lead. Could be a red herring, but we are cross referencing the height and build of the Mills' suspect to a figure seen in CCTV capture from Glasgow. It's available to the team for review on the case event code," Cosgrove said motioning to the junior officer in charge of running the computer and smart board.

Kyla asked, "What is the event file number?"

"@58900854," Cosgrove responded as it was put up on the smart board. Kyla noted the number in her iPad.

"What about physical evidence that might have a DNA link? Is there any at this point?" asked Detective Janine Woods.

"Given the large crowd at Euston at the time of the murder there is no reliable physical evidence at the scene," Cosgrove noted.

"Do we know who was the last person to see Mills alive?" asked Woods.

"Johnson has been assigned to interview staff at the hotel where he stayed. His wife said he left a message about the cancellation of his flight to Paris the day before his murder. She said he always stayed at the same London hotel when he was on business—The Novatel near Hammersmith. We'll review the hotel security video in due course. We are also compiling a list of every male employee who left Datatime in the last three years as a starting point for the investigation," Cosgrove said looking over at Kyla Fraser.

Kyla made a note of the cancelled flight to Paris.

"Why just male employees?" one of the junior investigators asked.

"A perfect segue for Ms. Fraser to brief us on her profiling. Kyla?"

Kyla walked to the front of the room.

"Jack Singleton and Lance Mills, both prominent businessmen, were killed within weeks of each other. According to the profiling data, the perpetrator is likely a male between 28 and 40 who has suffered a history of physical and psychological abuse at the hands of a violent father with a weak or completely absent mother. This is someone who hates male authority figures and is targeting other male power figures who represent his sense of being wronged or oppressed. Although the killer may not be a psychopath, he has a lot of thwarted anger towards his victim archetypes. He is very smart and will probably continue to kill. Now that it has hit the news he may take a rest, but I personally doubt it. The murders have occurred in different cities so we are looking to eventually establish a geographic pattern should the killings continue," Kyla stated.

"How will you do that?" asked Detective Blatherwick.

"Well, we have just linked the murders to each other, so we need to do more background work to establish commonalities between the killings which will take some time," Kyla replied.

"Anything else?" Cosgrove asked.

"No, I'm done for now sir," Kyla replied.

"Any further questions for myself or Ms. Fraser?" Cosgrove asked.

Cosgrove looked around the room. There were none.

"OK everyone, you've heard the facts, so let's get out there and do our job," Cosgrove said closing the meeting.

Kyla proceeded to her office and sat down at her desk. She thought about Cosgrove's reference to RIA during the briefing. As Kyla recalled Ian's furtive description of his RIA assignment, instinct took over and she dialed RIA's Glasgow phone number on her mobile phone.

"Good afternoon, RIA."

"Yes, I'm calling from Scotland Yard. I'd like to speak with someone about one of your clients, Mr. Lance Mills," Kyla stated.

"Is this Detective Woods again?"

"No, it's an associate," Kyla said, feeling satisfied that she had adequately identified herself by inferring that she was a police officer.

"Please hold a moment."

A few moments later Kyla heard a voice on the line.

"Jordie Dunsmuir speaking."

Although Ian had mentioned it in passing while on the train from London, Kyla did not recognize Jordie's name.

"Yes, my name is Kyla Fraser, with Scotland Yard. I'd like to ask a few questions relating to one of your clients."

"Did you say Kyla Fraser?" Jordie asked with noticeable surprise in his voice.

"Yes, that's correct."

Jordie raised his eyebrows as he looked wide-eyed at the slip of paper with Kyla's name written on it still sitting on his desk.

"How can I help you? We're already cooperating by compiling a list of Datatime vendors from our audit records," Jordie said defensively.

"RIA's name came up in a briefing this morning and no doubt you have been contacted by another investigator, but I am interested in whether your firm might have represented the other gentleman involved in my profiling work," Kyla elaborated.

"Profiling?" Jordie asked, stunned.

"Did you or your firm know of Jack Singleton?" Kyla asked.

Jordie braced.

"Ms. Fraser, our client lists are highly confidential and I am not at liberty to disclose any such information," Jordie said in an attempt to blockade Kyla by toeing the company line.

Kyla sensed that Dunsmuir was stalling.

"Shall I get a warrant?" Kyla said knowing her threat could not be enforced given her advisory role in the case.

Jordie became flustered. Kyla's name had ended up on his desk because he was told to tail Ian MacLeod and the tail had followed the pair to her home on Arran. He was informed that MacLeod may have had a relationship with a woman named Kyla Fraser. Dunsmuir never expected her to suddenly emerge in an official role in a murder investigation.

The 'night audit' project was under Jordie's control and he would be held responsible if anything went wrong. Having Scotland Yard prying into RIA's business was not an option, especially given that one of their best kept secrets was that alleged crime boss Douglas McMurphy was their biggest client.

"For what? What do you want to know exactly?" Jordie asked anxiously.

"I am looking for common threads between the demise of both Lance Mills and Jack Singleton," Kyla elaborated.

"What in the world do you mean by that?"

Kyla picked up on Jordie's anxious tone.

"Mr. Mills' death was a homicide, as was Singleton's."

"You're kidding," Jordie replied in a feeble attempt to sound surprised.

"Surely you knew about Mr. Mills. It was all over the BBC," Kyla led.

"I don't watch much news Ms. Fraser."

"Mr. Dunsmuir, why do I get the feeling that you are not being forthcoming?" Kyla asked trying to bait him.

"I'm just being careful as the firm has a very staunch position on disclosing private information about our clients," Dunsmuir replied.

"They were both clients weren't they Mr. Dunsmuir?" Kyla asked.

"Look, I could get fired if I disclose such facts," Jordie offered guardedly.

"So the answer is yes?" Kyla asked fishing for an answer.

"I can't say, Ms. Fraser."

Kyla let the line go silent for a few moments.

"Well, thank you for your cooperation Mr. Dunsmuir. If I have any further questions I will get back to you."

"Fine, I'm sorry I couldn't be of more help," Jordie said wanting to get off the line before anyone overheard the conversation.

Kyla hung up the phone. She thought about what Dunsmuir might be withholding but since she was not an official investigator on the case she would have to turn over her findings to the detective team. She knew something was amiss; she just couldn't put a finger on it. She decided not to share her conversation with Jordie Dunsmuir for the time being.

Chapter 15

Ian checked into the Ibis Hotel in Edinburgh at 5:15 Thursday afternoon. After settling into his room and ordering room service, he logged into the hotel's internet and began a Google search.

Dundee Constructors Edinburgh Scotland

As Ian expected, the search returned numerous results including a Wikipedia link. Ian clicked on the link.

The Dundee Group is the largest general contracting organization in Scotland and the eighth largest in the UK. The organization's main emphasis is on commercial, institutional and multi-family residential construction sectors. The corporate head office is in Edinburgh, Scotland with branch offices in Manchester and London. The organization is privately owned by the Dundee family and is governed by a diverse board of directors with real estate, banking, legal and accounting backgrounds.

He then clicked on the Dundee logo at the upper right of the page.

The Dundee website loaded, with pictures of big construction projects appearing and fading across the home page. He clicked on the tab that said 'Meet Our Team' and the faces and bios of a number of executives including the CEO, Clive Crawford appeared. Ian clicked on Crawford's image and found out that he was an engineer who graduated with honors from the

University of Manchester and had earned his MBA in Canada at Rotman, an internationally acclaimed business school. He looked to be in his late forties, with a commanding appearance framed by thick auburn hair, a prominent chin and deep set intelligent eyes.

Ian noticed that the Executive Vice President was a youngish looking man named Joseph McMurphy. Ian couldn't help but wonder if he was related to Douglas McMurphy or whether it was just a coincidence.

He then selected the 'Projects' tab and a lengthy list of current projects filled the screen. Ian scrolled through the projects until his eye caught the name of one in Manchester, the Singleton Building, tagged with a 'new' banner. The project description said that it was a mixed use commercial and residential project being developed by Manchester based Singleton Developments. Ian was taken aback, recognizing the last name of the developer who had been murdered in Manchester. Now hyper vigilant, Ian reflected on Jordie's comment during their conversation on the train, *'we had some trouble with an auditor.'* Ian was certain that he had walked into the midst of a gangland conspiracy.

Ian shifted his focus to the task at hand, and clicked on the project he was supposed to be auditing—Montrose Shores. It was a massive mixed use project located on reclaimed land on the Edinburgh waterfront with a completion date slated for November 2010. Ian read the project description further and found out that the development was being financed through a public-private partnership between the City of Edinburgh, the Scottish Government and a large developer—The Montrose Shores Partnership.

Ian looked at his watch and saw that it was almost 9:45, close to the time he was to meet with the site clerk. He picked up the hotel phone and heard the front desk operator answer.

"Can I help you Mr. MacLeod?"

"Yes, would you be so kind as to call me a cab right away," Ian asked politely.

Ian hung up and left the room, taking the elevator down to the main lobby.

He took a taxi to the Edinburgh waterfront and got out in front of the project sign that read Montrose Shores. The site was massive, covering the entire north shore of recently reclaimed land from waters that were once part of the Firth of Forth. Ian had noted that the project was valued at almost £500 million, one of the largest mixed used projects of its kind ever undertaken in the UK.

The site was fenced, bustling with trucks, men and equipment pouring concrete high above the ground level using high intensity floodlights. Ian stood by the entrance to the site office. A young man of about 25 dressed in jeans, a vest and hardhat approached from inside the fenced site. He opened the gate and faced Ian.

"Are you MacLeod?" the young man asked.

"Aye," MacLeod answered.

"I'm Jeremy, the site clerk. I'm to let you into the site office."

"Change in plan Jeremy," Ian stated.

The young man looked surprised.

"I'll be able to access everything I need right from my hotel room. I assume you provided the laptop?" Ian asked.

"Maybe," Jeremy answered cautiously.

"Whatever. It will get me into the file system so I'll start with electronic access. If I need hard files, how can I reach you?" Ian asked.

"One meeting was all I agreed to, so you can take it up with Mr. Dunsmuir. Too risky," Jeremy replied.

Ian wondered how much Jeremy had been paid to act as a turncoat against his own boss.

"Fine. Do you actually know Mr. Crawford?"

"Never met 'im, just seen him once or twice," Jeremy said looking around nervously.

"Is it a good company?" Ian asked.

"It was. The Project Manager says the Dundee family just got bought out. There's a new second in command ... a guy named Joseph McMurphy."

Ian now surmised that Joseph was indeed related to Douglas McMurphy, possibly his son.

"Can y' tell me more?" Ian pressed.

Another man appeared and approached from behind the site clerk. Jeremy turned around and recognizing him, addressed MacLeod.

"No, we don't accept unsolicited sales calls," Jeremy said deflecting suspicion.

Jeremy turned, closed the gate and walked away.

"Fuckin' salesmen," he quipped as his work mate passed by.

MacLeod realized he had stumbled onto a big piece of the puzzle thanks to Jeremy. It appeared that Crawford's days were numbered at Dundee which explained why he was stockpiling a nest egg for himself. How he was pulling it off right under the nose of McMurphy was gutsy to say the least, Ian thought.

Returning to the hotel Ian turned on the laptop. He realized he had little information upon which to base his audit and therefore his first order of business would be to review the cost reports to get a sense of the magnitude of the monies at stake. Ascot had told him that this audit would be much more complex and involve a great deal of money. Since the deal between McMurphy and Crawford was a mystery he would have to undertake the audit blindly in order to find the missing money.

The computer he was working on no doubt had come from Jeremy, the site clerk. He lifted it up and inspected the various tags on the underside and there next to the serial number was a Dundee Constructors logo and inventory barcode sticker. Ian placed the laptop back down on the desk and studied the screen. Ian knew that a company as big as Dundee would have a very sophisticated system with remote access as he looked at the array of icons on the desktop.

There was a small diamond shaped icon that appeared to be the access portal to Dundee's information system. Ian clicked on it.

A large icon appeared—ConNET along with Dundee's logo—followed by a login dialogue box. He typed in the login information and the screen displayed a graphic user interface that read 'Welcome to Dundee ConNET'. Ian clicked on it and it came up with another dialogue box asking for a job number. Ian typed in L2356 and all of the files for Montrose Shores appeared. He clicked on the accounting folder.

Typical accounting categories flashed onto the screen;

Assets
    AR
Liabilities
    AP
    PR
Profit
    GL
Reports

Ian clicked on Reports and a menu of date ordered cost reports appeared. He clicked on the latest one dated May 09 and scrolled down to the bottom line.

Estimated Bid Profit	Buy-Out Profit	Projected Final Profit
£12,325,000	£34,510,987	£21,724,377

The profit had almost tripled from the time the project was bid until it was underway, but then it had dwindled by millions of pounds according to the final projection.

A quick study, Ian had paid attention during an audit practicum he had been selected for by Glasgow's largest General Contractor, Highland Contracting. It enabled him to find out the basic mechanics of the construction business. During lunch with one of the Project Managers Ian was informed that profit margins included in the initial bid on fixed price, lump sum contracts were usually set very low in order to be able to compete against the other bidders. He was also told that during the early phase of compiling trades for the project, additional profits called 'buy out' were added to the bottom line through tough negotiations with vying subcontractors. As well, design modifications undertaken to reduce costs were carried out through tradeoffs called value engineering with the goal being to bolster profits by only giving back 50% of the actual savings to the owner. Overall the strategy was to gain several percentage points on the profit line before the project was out of the ground. Based on the buy-out profit shown on the cost report, that was exactly what was done on Montrose Shores.

As he studied the cost report further he wondered why the final profit projection was so much lower than expected—almost £13 million pounds shy. Either there was a big glitch that increased costs or there was something fishy. A forty percent reduction in anticipated profit deserved a flag.

Next Ian clicked on the accounts receivable icon to find out how much monies had been billed to date and paid to Dundee.

Contract Value	% Complete %	Billed	Earned Profit	Cash Position
£493,467,900	60	70	£20,567,588	£78,234,678

It was obvious that Dundee was claiming they had already taken in almost all of the projected profit and that they had been able to get the client to pay far beyond what the real progress of the work actually was.

The cash Dundee had in its hands exceeded £78 million pounds, none of which could legally be claimed by Dundee as profit until the project was complete and all payments had been made under the contract. As a Chartered Accountant Ian had to have a good working knowledge of the law as it pertained to taxation and commercial transactions. He wondered how much of these trust funds had been spent by Dundee as payoff money so far.

Next, Ian clicked on the accounts payable icon and a long list of vendors appeared on the screen. Ian scanned through all of the typical vendors such as concrete and lumber suppliers, then began doing random audits of those that didn't fit into typical construction categories. After almost two hours he came upon one in the labor category, Blackstone Ventures.

After toggling between the purchase order registry, vendor billings and check registries, a pattern of monthly purchase orders, invoices and payments began to take shape. Upon further examination he found documentation that the payments to Blackstone were for general labor costs over the duration of the project. Clicking on the payroll module Ian noted that

Dundee didn't seem to have any direct payroll costs so payments to an outside labor provider would be difficult to dispute.

He then executed a search looking for other postings for labor costs for the project. The screen filled with several vendors including one that looked legitimate, a known labor broker named CCS, an acronym for Construction Crewing Services who supplied labor across the UK. Upon further examination Ian found that all of the large billing amounts attributable to CCS had been reversed and charged to another Dundee project under a job number miscoding error. Ian suspected that the reallocation of labor costs incurred through CCS was an expedient move specifically aimed at justifying the large and falsified labor expense from Blackstone. There was no doubt in Ian's mind that the real labor *had* been provided by CCS and *not* by Blackstone. He remembered another tip he had learned from his mentor during his audit practicum.

'*If something doesn't look right, it probably isn't,*' Auditor John Maitland used to say.

Ian typed in a Google search.

Labor Providers UK

The top search result was for CCS Construction Crewing Services but there was not a single search result for Blackstone Ventures.

Next Ian executed a search on the UK Companies House website. He keyed in Blackstone Ventures and was not surprised to find out it was registered to Clive Crawford of Edinburgh, Scotland.

Ian inputted a payables search and found that the payments to Blackstone added up to £2,986,610.

Ian sat back with his hands behind his head. Crawford had faked losses through costs that attributed to a shell corporation. But how could he pull it off himself? He must have had an accomplice. Ian's knowledge of accounting processes pointed to someone who could make postings and approve invoices in the accounting system without scrutiny.

"I'll bet Crawford is cutting the Project Accountant and the Project Manager into his little scam," Ian said aloud.

There was no need to drill down any further as Ian believed he had enough on Clive Crawford to see that he had bilked almost £3 million pounds from his criminal counterpart Douglas McMurphy. MacLeod now had everything he needed to finish up except for one crucial piece of information; the bank account number that Clive Crawford was supposed to have made deposits to on behalf of his partner, Douglas McMurphy.

The digital clock on the bedside table read 2:12 AM and Ian decided he would sleep on his next move.

* * * * *

"Dundee Constructors, how may I help you?" asked the receptionist.

"May I speak with Clive Crawford?" Ian asked politely.

"Who shall I say is calling?"

"Just tell him it's about the McMurphy deal," Ian stated.

"Aye, just a moment please."

A few seconds later the receptionist came back on the line.

"Mr. Crawford is asking for your name?" the receptionist inquired.

"Tell him I represent Mr. McMurphy in his business arrangement," Ian replied.

"Hold please."

Crawford was on the line in short order.

"Who are you?" Crawford asked.

"McMurphy sent me. You must have known you'd eventually hear from him didn't you?" Ian bluffed.

"I've no idea what you're referring to," Crawford said in a weak attempt at lying.

"Yes you do," Ian said continuing his cool intimidating tone.

"How do I know you are who you say you are?" Crawford pressed.

"I have the password to your network, unrestricted access to the filing system and I'm carrying out audits on all of your fraudulent business transactions on the Montrose Shores project," Ian said trying to rattle Crawford.

"Bullshit. Only key personnel have access to unrestricted levels of our information system," Crawford challenged.

"Do you ever think that you don't pay your people enough to stay loyal? Maybe they've been bought out like everyone else in this deal," Ian retorted.

"How do I know you're not bluffing?" Crawford asked.

"I do not think you want to try me," Ian said continuing to poke at Crawford.

There was silence on the line.

"I know you're working on your retirement plan now that your days at Dundee are numbered. You seem to have a lot to hide Mr. Dundee," Ian said accusingly.

"It's Crawford."

"Of course. That's the name right here on the contract."

"Contract?"

"You heard right. You of all people know about contracts. I suggest that you meet with me today, in the next hour actually, because now that there is a price on your head you only have one choice," Ian said threateningly.

"Look, I do not want any trouble so—,"

"You're already up to your neck in shit pal and if I come back empty handed, my backup won't be so willing to negotiate," Ian said cutting off Crawford in mid-sentence.

The line was silent for a few seconds.

"OK, where do we meet?" Crawford said his tone now more conciliatory.

"How about we meet at a coffee shop downtown."

"Alright. Let's meet at the Scotsman Hotel on Market Street. In the restaurant. It's private."

"I'll meet you there in 30 minutes," Ian said as he hung up the phone.

Ian looked at his watch. It was 2:25. He then picked up the phone and dialed Jordie's direct line.

"Dunsmuir here."

"Jordie, I'm getting close to finishing up with Dundee," Ian advised.

"How the hell did you get finished so fast? I expected you would take a few days to uncover this deal," Jordie said surprised.

"Jordie, you've been out of the mainstream of audits for too long. I can access an information platform anywhere in the world if I have the passwords to get into the system. I just followed my instincts and found what I was looking for right here in the hotel suite. I just need to know what he did with the money and then I'm done."

"But how could you do all that online?" Jordie said obviously not quite convinced by Ian's story.

"All your client's partner had to do was show GL entries on the revenue side and issue false PO's on the expense side and bingo they pocketed the value of the phony cost entries. I saw it right away. After some searching I found the vehicle. There is no such vendor as Blackstone Ventures; it's a shell corporation they used to skim out money that was owing to your client. It's all in the data that I'll be sending over once I confirm where the client's money can be recovered," Ian explained.

"That's amazing Ian. You did all that in one day? Great work," Jordie said excitedly.

"Look, this guy is smart. Your suspicions were spot on, but I can't prove anything until I see where he channeled the funds. There was a Swiss bank account right?" Ian asked.

"Ah, yeah, there always is with the client's business deals. Dundee has access to a specific partner account that the client strips out once a month and aggregates it into a master account. The problem is there have been no payments beyond the finder's fee when the original deal was made. He has claimed cost overruns which we don't buy," Jordie offered.

Ian made a mental note of Jordie's disclosure and remained silent.

"In my view you've done your job Ian and the client can take it from here," Jordie said.

"Yeah, but I presume you want me to find out where the money is?" Ian asked.

"The client has his own methods of extracting such information, so we should just leave it to him Ian," Jordie advised.

"Alright, I'll finish up here and be back in Glasgow by this afternoon."

"I'll be letting the client know about your findings right away so he can deal with the situation in Edinburgh," Jordie advised.

'Not before I do,' Ian thought.

"Fine Jordie. I'll talk to you later," Ian said.

They hung up.

Ian looked at the time. It was now 2:45 and Ian had only a few minutes to make his meeting with Clive Crawford.

Arriving at the restaurant in the Scotsman Hotel, Ian quickly recognized Crawford. Walking over to where he was sitting Ian introduced himself.

"Clive Crawford I presume?"

"Yes," Crawford said nervously.

"I'm McMurphy's man," Ian said as he took a seat across from Crawford.

"So what is this all about?" Crawford asked as if their phone conversation had never happened.

"Crawford, this isn't a social call so I'll be short and to the point. You're gonna die if you don't pay up what y' owe," Ian threatened.

Crawford drew back.

"How do y' know that?" Crawford asked.

"Because Douglas McMurphy does not take kindly to people stealing from him."

"I did nothing of the sort. We had a profit sharing agreement in addition to the finder's fee already paid to him. The performance side just didn't pan out like everyone thought it would. That's the way it goes in construction. There were unforeseen circumstances … weather, schedule delays, labor increases and cost escalations. It happens all the time," Crawford said as if he was making a sales pitch.

"I'm not here to listen to your lies Mr. Crawford. I'm here to collect my boss's money."

Crawford became combative.

"Listen, he was supposed to be paid ¾ of the original amount of profit we had in our bid—that was the deal. We weren't even low bidder so one of our board members said he knew McMurphy well and approached him asking him to apply some pressure to certain officials at the city. McMurphy got a check for nine million pounds as an advance for his influence in getting us the job. He got the city's project manager to turn a blind eye and approve our revised cost estimates which supposedly included price escalations. The balance of the £12 million pounds was dependent on actual costs coming in as expected. They didn't so he wasn't paid the extra three million. That's business fair and square. Maybe I should call Dunsmuir," Crawford said trying to throw Ian off.

Ian raised both palms in the air.

"Go ahead. They keep their relationship very discreet. McMurphy may be the silent partner here but I can assure you that all hell is about to break loose on you Crawford if you refuse to pay up," Ian said in a last ditch attempt at convincing Crawford to comply.

"Look, I'm not sure what you do for McMurphy but I've told you the truth. The threshold to trigger the balance that he expected came and went. I do not owe him the money," Crawford said smugly.

Ian stared at Crawford for a moment.

"What about the falsified job costs and payments made to Blackstone Ventures for almost £3 million pounds?" Ian asked making his final move.

Both of them stared at each other for a few moments.

"Look, you're about to be whacked if you do not come clean pal … end of story," Ian warned.

Crawford finally capitulated.

"So what's the deal then?" Crawford asked.

"No deal. You give him the money you owe, full stop."

"Look, I can make this entire mess go away," Crawford said contritely.

MacLeod stared at Crawford for a moment.

"How did you get away with this Crawford, especially with McMurphy's own blood sitting right beside you?" Ian said, trying to bluff Crawford with the information that the site clerk had given him.

Crawford's anxiety turned to anger.

"That entitled little prick, wouldn't know concrete from mud. He's gonna run this company into the ground once I'm gone, so I had to make hay while the sun shines."

"So, he didn't have a clue?"

"Not a clue," Crawford added.

"How long has McMurphy's kid been at Dundee now?"

"You sound like you don't know much about the man you work for," Crawford said surprised.

"It's a big company. I just do what I'm told," MacLeod replied.

"Young Joe got parachuted in when we took over the Singleton project after Singleton's death. Poor bastard couldn't pay off the mezzanine loan that McMurphy shoved down his throat so I think it was them who put him in permanent foreclosure, if you get my drift. I'm supposed to teach McMurphy's kid the ropes but I have no time for 'im. Already walks around like he owns the place. I didn't want to step down but McMurphy gave the Dundee family an offer they couldn't refuse," Crawford stated bitterly.

"Alright, let's get this bit of business done Crawford," MacLeod stated.

"I can write you a check," Crawford offered.

"OK, make it payable in US funds to 'deposit only in trust to RIA Partners'," Ian instructed.

Crawford took out a calculator and keyed in some numbers and then wrote out the check and handed it to Ian.

Ian held it up in front of him. It read $4,300,234.00 USD. The name on the check was Blackstone Ventures Ltd.

"That's the right number I swear, perhaps plus or minus a few dollars on the exchange rate that's all," Crawford said urgently.

"It'll have to be certified and I need the bank account number and password," Ian stated.

"I can deposit it into the joint trust account for you," Crawford said.

"No, my instructions are to ensure it is done personally," Ian responded.

"I was told never to disclose their banking information. Jordie Dunsmuir was right there when we made the deal and he made that very clear," Crawford said nervously.

"Have you ever met Douglas McMurphy?" Ian asked.

"No, everything was arranged through RIA," Crawford replied.

"I figured so. Crawford, I work for McMurphy. He calls the shots pal. If you don't give me the information I'm asking for I'll make one call and some very nasty people will be here within a few minutes to extract it out of you ... or your Project Manager. Do y' understand?" Ian threatened.

"Robbie knows nothing, I swear. He just kept his mouth shut."

"I'm sure ... for a price," MacLeod quipped.

"Look Mr. whatever your name is, I'm not screwing with you ... but what's the difference if I deposit it or if you do?" Crawford asked.

"Trust. Your business relationship with us is over, Crawford. My orders are to personally make sure the funds get into the account," Ian said definitively.

"Then why don't you already have the bank information with you?" Crawford asked suspiciously.

"Like I said, McMurphy and RIA do not talk except when he wants his cash. Other than you, there's only one person at RIA that has the banking information on this deal. The money you owe him is dirty and you know it so he stays far enough away to make sure he can't be connected to this or any other deal. My job is to recover the money. Then I make one call to McMurphy, he calls RIA and the account will be stripped and closed forever. As long as the account is active and you have access, you're a risk pal. I am instructed to get it in the account, so there's no more discussion on the issue," Ian said looking Crawford square in the eye, doing his best to convey an air of finality.

Crawford was squirming in his seat. He pulled out a Zurobank business card from his leather business folder and laid it on the table in front of him. Ian could see that the banking information was written on the card.

"Alright, the passcode is one of the following."

Ian watched Crawford's hand shake as he scrawled the words.

'Yellow, red ...'

Ian grabbed the business card.

Crawford looked up in surprise.

"You won't need this anymore," Ian said as he placed the card in his shirt pocket.

Crawford was speechless.

"By the way, I heard McMurphy thought you were gonna screw him on the Singleton project. That's probably why he dropped his son in, to keep an eye on you," Ian said trying to bait Crawford for information.

"No way, I already cut the first kickback check. As long as I'm still in charge I'll make sure he gets paid every bit of what we owe fair and square. I don't want any more trouble," Crawford replied.

"What do you know about Singleton's death?"

"Just what I read in the papers and from the little interaction I had with him before we took over that job. He told me he was having trouble with McMurphy over the mezzanine financing. The word was that the mezzanine funding was laundered money," Crawford replied.

"Laundered or drug money?" Ian lured Crawford.

"I've no idea. When we did the deal, Dunsmuir told us they would be running money through the job as extras and that Dundee would offset them with trumped up credits through the backdoor," Crawford continued.

MacLeod got up from his seat.

"Enough small talk, let's go to your bank," Ian stated wanting to finish up.

Both men left the restaurant and walked several streets to a Bank of Scotland branch on Princess Street. Ian stood with Crawford as he certified the check and handed it to Ian.

"Now go back to your office after I leave. I suggest you forget you ever met me or anyone else on this deal," Ian instructed.

"So, I'm gonna be OK, right?" Crawford asked his voice now cracking with worry.

Ian nodded half-heartedly, feeling for Crawford's predicament. He gave Crawford a final glance before he turned and walked north down Bridge Street. It took six minutes for Ian to reach the Zurobank branch where he had the check deposited into the bank account number Crawford had given to him.

Chapter 16

Ian arrived back at the hotel at 3:43, a few minutes after depositing the certified check into the Zurobank account. He sat down at his computer and accessed the client's site on the web.

He opened up his own account and confirmed the balance. It was $15,321.01 USD. He then dialed the Zurobank number in Zurich.

"Good afternoon, Zurobank, how may I direct your call?"

"I want to make a transfer between accounts please," Ian said.

"Right away sir."

Moments later another female voice came on the line.

"Hello, this is Adrianna, how can I assist you?"

"I'd like to do a transfer please. The name's MacLeod, Ian MacLeod."

"Certainly. The fourth in the file passcode sequence please," Adrianna asked.

"Burns," Ian responded.

"Thank you sir and what are the details?"

"Details?" Ian asked feeling flustered.

"The account numbers you wish to transfer to and from sir."

Not wanting to raise an alarm bell he decided not to close out the account completely.

"I wish to transfer $4,000,000 from CH23 2649853755 to CH23 2649853709," Ian advised, speaking slowly and clearly.

"Just a moment. The last five digits again ... of the account we are transferring from please."

Ian looked down at the business card he had taken from Crawford.

"5-3-7-5-5," Ian replied.

There was a moment of silence on the line as Ian heard the sound of keystrokes on a keyboard.

"These are both accounts belonging to RIA in Glasgow. I don't recognize your voice sir. Usually I deal with Janet on these accounts," Adrianna said as she continued keying in the information Ian had given her.

"Ms. McComb is ill. The flu that's going around is brutal. I'm the senior accountant on the file so I'm filling in for her," Ian said trying to hide the nervousness in his voice.

Once again there was silence on the line.

"How unfortunate, give her my best," Adrianna finally replied.

"Yes, I will."

"Alright sir. Are you near a computer?" Adrianna asked.

"Yes, I'm on the Zurobank website as we speak."

"Please enter the password for the account from which funds are being transferred," Adrianna instructed.

Ian keyed in the word 'sacredlamb' into the screen for the RIA account.

"OK, I'm done."

"Thank you and now the same for the account the funds will be transferred into," Adrianna instructed.

Ian keyed in the letters 'broadsword.'

"Done," Ian said.

"The transfer is complete. Is there anything else I can do for you today?" Adrianna asked politely.

"No, that's all thank you," Ian said his tension becoming almost unbearable.

"Thank you for using Zurobank and have a good day sir," Adrianna said closing out the transaction.

"You too and thanks for your help," Ian said trying to contain himself.

Ian hung up the phone and stared at his computer screen. The balance in his account read $4,015,321.01.

Ian had a rush of anxiety as he took in what he had just done. He had no idea what had possessed him to steal the money but the shock of Mills' killing and the realization that he had been set up to take the fall for a crime he did not commit had thrown him into an adrenalin fueled battle of wits driven by instinct. For the first time in his life MacLeod had gotten out of his head and into the razor's edge world of survival. He felt alive like never before.

Ian looked at the bedside clock. It was exactly 3:57.

He did not transmit the data. Instead, he placed the mobile phone, camera and USB transmitter into his briefcase before packing up. He left the room with just 15 minutes remaining to make the 4:20 back to Glasgow from Waverly Station.

* * * * *

It was 3:59 when the custom painted gun metal grey Porsche Cayenne rounded the corner as Clive Crawford walked towards his office, briefcase in hand. Screeching to a halt the back door flew open and two huge men, both sporting crew cuts and wearing black leather jackets, jumped out and grabbed Crawford. Crawford struggled, screaming for help but it was to no avail as the two burly men forced him into the backseat.

The tires spun in response to the 500 horsepower motor and there was white smoke in the air for almost a street as the SUV sped off. A few minutes later they arrived on a deserted portion of the Edinburgh waterfront less than 300 meters across the breakwater from Dundee's massive construction site. There in front of the car was a stack of rusty pipe piles sitting out in the open surrounded by a dozen or so abandoned tractor tires. The wind was blowing hard, whipping up whitecaps across the open water of the Firth of Forth. It was a clear day so the shoreline and rise of Fife could be seen in the distance. The back door opened and Crawford was pushed out onto the dirt. He got up and stood unsteadily, looking confused and terrified as he watched the driver walk around the back of the high powered SUV where the two burly men were now holding Crawford by the arms.

"Yer gonna cough up the money y' stole y' fuckin' thief," the driver said as Crawford looked in horror at the menacing black pistol pointed directly at his head.

Crawford pleaded, "Don't do this, I paid the money … to the red headed guy who said he was your partner … I gave him a certified check … please."

"You did what?" the gunman replied incredulously.

"I paid the guy you sent to talk to me … you know, McMurphy's man," Crawford responded.

"Who?"

"He didn't give his name but he said he would take care of the money for you guys and he promised nothing would happen to me," Crawford said pleadingly.

The man with the pistol looked over at his cohorts and raised his eyebrows.

Crawford began shaking as the two big Europeans held him by the arms.

"Pal, you're a deid man."

"No … please, I have a family," Crawford implored.

"Everybody's got a family. Now on yer fuckin' knees."

Crawford looked fearfully at his executioner. Bracing his legs against the ground as the two big men tried to force him to his knees, he struggled valiantly. With their full weight on his body Crawford finally surrendered as he bowed his head and went limp. The two men got up and stood by as he slumped, his body almost fully bowed over, head nearly touching his knees. He began to shake uncontrollably as the driver placed the gun less than a foot away from the back of his head.

A single shot rang out as Crawford dropped to the ground, blood trickling from a head wound. Another three shots rang out in rapid succession—two into his back, the other into his hip. Then the driver pushed over his lifeless torso and looked at the dead man's face.

The executioner walked back to the still running vehicle followed by the two henchmen.

"Get in," the driver said.

The two men obeyed.

They pulled away as the driver dialed a number on his mobile phone.

A gruff voice answered. It was Douglas McMurphy.

"He's deid, boss."

"OK."

"But there's a problem. He didn't have yer money."

"What?"

"Crawford said he gave a red headed guy, claimin' to be on the payroll, a certified check," the driver replied.

"Don't fuck with me," the voice on the speakerphone shot back.

"I'm deid serious boss. That's what he said."

"Ah, fer crissake, Dunsmuir's harmless bean counter is turning out to be our worst fuckin' nightmare," McMurphy said.

"What d' y' want me t' do boss?"

There was a moment of silence on the line.

"Head over to the Ibis and find him. He should still be there. Jonas knows what he looks like," the voice on the other end said.

"Kill 'im?" the driver asked.

"Of course not, just bring 'im back to the warehouse. Once he loses a finger at a time he'll hand over the money. Then I'll personally slit 'is throat."

The driver ended the call and turned to his cohorts. "Y' gotta love McMurphy. He's a fuckin' animal."

The two big men remained silent.

The Cayenne headed towards the Hotel Ibis. As the Cayenne crossed the corner of North Bridge and High, the big German, Jonas cried out, "That looks like him there, on the bridge."

MacLeod was crossing the North Bridge several hundred yards away.

"Are y' sure?" the driver asked as he slammed on the brakes.

"Yah ... from a meeting with the boss," Jonas shot back.

The driver spun his head around to catch a glimpse of the distant figure.

In an instant he cranked on the wheel and applied full throttle, lighting up the rear tires and fishtailing the SUV, straightening as they headed north towards the bridge and their target.

As the sound of a high powered vehicle approached from his rear, Ian turned his head to see the gun metal SUV racing towards him down Bridge Street a few hundred yards away. Ian saw the familiar sight of the Scotsman Hotel ahead on his right where he had met with Crawford earlier. He began to cross the North Bridge when he heard the SUV closing in. The entrance to Waverly Station was over 50 feet below the bridge deck on Market Street. Ian leapt over the bridge rail onto the narrow cantilevered cornice, ducking to avoid detection. He heard the SUV go by unable to stop in the heavy traffic and then the sound of screeching tires as it came to a halt some distance beyond the face of the hotel. Ian thought quickly as he looked around for an escape route. Below him was a scupper and rainwater pipe that made its way down the face of the hotel to the top of the last bridge pier. From there it was another 18 feet to the roadway on Market Street. Ian threw his overnight bag 50 feet to the road below. He could now see a single figure running towards him on the bridge sidewalk brandishing a pistol.

"Out o' the way," the man's voice yelled at the pedestrians crossing the bridge.

They scattered, turning and running in the opposite direction away from the man as he fired a single shot that grazed Ian's scalp. Ian winced as the burning sensation stunned him momentarily. He regained his bearings and leapt onto the top of the large copper scupper attached to the face of the old hotel. Another shot rang out ricocheting off the stone face but Ian had no time to ascertain the whereabouts of his assailant as he landed on the scupper and his weight fell against the stone face. Ian could sense his would be killer directly behind him standing on the bridge sidewalk.

"Where dae y' think yer off to lad?" the man said lining up a shot and firing again in the same instant as Ian's gyrating body dropped as he tried to regain his balance.

The shot sliced through the outer flesh of MacLeod's right flank and ricocheted off the stone face in front of him. He screamed in pain almost losing his balance as he gripped the wound with his hand. He forced himself to stay conscious at the sickening sight of his own blood. The instinct to survive drove him to contort his body in spite of the pain as Ian reached his right leg down setting it onto one of the metal brackets that connected the scupper to the stone cladding. He quickly lowered himself with one hand on the scupper and the other on a metal bracket that tied it to the stone wall. Ian let his weight swing free and he now hung with both hands, each around one of the metal brackets. Ian waited for a fatal shot but there was no report—no fatal last instant of life because there were no more rounds left in the gunman's weapon. He had forgotten to reload after putting four rounds into Crawford.

"Ah for the luv 'o the fuckin' Irish," the gunman yelled out realizing he was out of ammunition.

Ian looked up in shock as he recognized the man's voice and the long scar across the left side of his face.

"Danny?" Ian uttered.

Chapter 17

Sirens approached in the distance as blood ran down Ian's pant leg almost to his knee. The pain was anesthetized both by Ian's focus on escape and the endorphins that were now flooding his bloodstream. Ian grabbed hold of the rain water leader with one hand and while applying pressure with the rubber soles of his shoes he transferred his grip from the metal bracket to the pipe that led to the ground. Quickly he shimmied down the length of the pipe to the top of the bridge pier below as the shooter ran back to the car hoping to intercept MacLeod on Market Street. Although the pipe actually continued past the overhanging cornice, it penetrated the stone, making it impossible to continue his shimmy. He sat down to catch his breath when a flood of images flashed across his mind at the shock of seeing his old nemesis, Danny McGinnis.

* * * * *

Danny and Ian met when they were in primary school and had kept in contact with each other after Danny moved across town when Ian was 12. McGinnis was as deeply troubled as Ian but because he seemed to lack any real emotion he was able to cope, thriving within the dark culture of delinquency. He acquired his nickname 'Scarface' after a street fight left him with a long, jagged cut on his left cheek.

A year older than Ian, Danny made up for his 160 pound wiry stature with big attitude and physical toughness. His long wavy hair and sparse adolescent beard framed the rough features of a menacing face. Ian once saw him almost 'curb' a fellow who Danny claimed had ripped him off for a bag of dope. Horrified, Ian watched Danny make the guy go down on his hands and knees.

"Now put yer fuckin' mouth over the curb hawfwit," Ian heard Danny say.

Slowly dropping his head, the poor soul started shaking like a leaf and begging for mercy. Ian panicked as he watched Danny place his boot behind the guy's head preparing to drive his face into the concrete.

"No Danny," Ian said.

McGinnis looked over at Ian with cold, lifeless eyes as he balanced on one foot. Having made his point, Danny released his foothold and stepped back.

"It's yer lucky day bitch," he said as he gave him a vicious kick to the ribs.

The guy moaned as he laid there clutching his side, pleading eyes looking up at Danny like a sinner who had been given absolution.

As they walked away Ian asked, "What the hell did y' do that for?"

Danny, calm as could be stared straight ahead barely flinching as he walked along.

"The dimwit owed me. Claimed I sold 'im shit. He won't do it again now will 'e?"

Ian was always nervous around Danny after that.

As young men they shared a rented duplex on Kingsbridge Crescent in south Glasgow but rarely saw each other. Ian spent most of his time at university as well as working part time while Danny slept all day and was out almost every night. In spite of having heard rumors that his roommate was an associate of SOCKS, Ian turned a blind eye not wanting to know the truth about Danny McGinnis.

Late one afternoon a few weeks after his graduation, Ian was alone in his room furnished with his entire worldly possessions consisting of a small oak desk and a bed covered in a blue duvet. Ian was admiring the unframed degree that lay on his desk when he heard Danny come home with a friend.

"Last night was a close call," the stranger's voice said.

"No worries. While you lumbered along like a stuck pig I chased 'im through the woods until 'e reached the boat dock. I shot 'im in the back and shoved 'im in the river," Ian heard Danny say.

Startled at the shocking admission, Ian gasped.

"I thought I heard somethin'. MacLeod, are y' home?" Danny called out.

"Who's MacLeod?"

"My roommate. Must 'ave been Felix."

"Yeah, the only pussy you've had lately," the stranger quipped.

Ian heard the two of them laugh.

"No way. MacLeod's lassie is a nice little piece of ass. I tagged 'er right in there, a few days ago," Danny said.

Ian bristled at his friend's admission of betrayal.

"Anyways, g' ahead."

"When I heard the shot, I was sure we were in deep shit. How do y' know he was deid?" the visitor asked.

"I watched 'im drown," Danny remarked.

Ian froze, his eyes wide in shock.

Danny and his friend continued the conversation as the pungent aroma of marijuana smoke wafted into Ian's room. The unmistakable sound of a toke drawn through pursed lips could be heard under the door.

"So where's yer roommate?"

"Ach, he's at school, an egghead. Doesn't have much of a life y' know," Danny said not knowing that his friend had graduated and that classes were over.

Ian's heart raced as he listened to the conversation. Measuring every breath, he sat silently at his desk hoping Danny would not walk into his room.

"It's suppertime and I'm hungry. Let's head over to the pub at the Ardmay," Danny said.

"No arguments from me Danno," his friend responded.

Finally after 15 minutes of sitting frozen in his chair, Ian heard them leave as the screen door creaked and then slammed against the front door jamb. Waiting a few minutes, Ian emerged from his bedroom and looked around, seeing the roach in the black ashtray and a large caliber pistol lying on the coffee table. Fearing Danny would remember the gun and return to fetch it, Ian decided he needed to get out quickly. Walking to the window he looked for any sign of McGinnis and the stranger. Sitting on the window sill was Danny's old cat Felix. Sensing that the coast was clear, Ian walked to the door. Taking a deep breath he opened it and stepped out onto the porch closing the door behind him. Just as he removed the key from the lock he nearly jumped out of his skin at the sound of Danny's voice.

"Ian, what are y' doin' home?" Danny asked.

Thinking on his feet, Ian composed himself.

"Oh hey Danny, I just finished classes for the day and was about to go in."

Uncertain as to whether Ian may have already been inside Danny replied, "Look, don't bother goin' in ... James and I were about to hit the pub. Why don't y' join us? He's waitin' 'round the corner."

Ian knew Danny was suspicious so he quickly agreed.

"Sure ... I could use a pint," Ian said trying his best to appear nonchalant.

Danny watched intently as Ian walked down the steps toward him.

"Come on, I'll introduce y'," Danny said not breaking his gaze.

Ian knew that Danny was on to him, but he didn't blink as they continued to lock eyes. Finally as Ian closed the gap, Danny was forced to break his poker stare and put his arm around Ian leading him toward his friend James.

"J-man, this is my roommate Ian ... you know ... the one I've been tellin' y' about," Danny said making the introduction.

"Aye, so you're the lucky bastard," James remarked as he shook Ian's hand.

"What do y' mean?" Ian asked.

"Oh, nothin'. Danny tells me you've got quite a way with the lassies, that's all," James said with a silly grin.

"Really?" Ian said doubtfully, looking straight at Danny.

Remembering the distinctly human sound from Ian's room earlier Danny was convinced that he and James had not been alone in the house during their conversation.

The three of them walked about halfway down the path towards Kingsacre Road before Danny stopped.

"Oh shite, I need to go back to the house for a minute. James, I'll meet you and Ian at the park, by the pub ... y' know," Danny said as he rolled his eyes towards Ian.

Ian knew the park well. It was more like a playground but had a treed area that was secluded—a perfect place for clandestine dealings. He also noticed the exchange between them but James, who seemed a bit daft, was oblivious to Danny's cues.

"Why, did y' forget somethin'?" James asked.

Danny tried to contain himself at James' stupidity and took in a quick breath that hissed between his teeth.

"Yeah, remember our conversation earlier? Well I left somethin' on the table," Danny said watching for a telltale reaction from Ian.

Ian remained expressionless. Sensing danger and now fearing what Danny's motive might be Ian tried to appear calm while formulating his next move. Ian's instincts took over as he watched Danny walk back on the path toward the house. Once out of sight, Ian executed his plan.

"Oh crap, I completely forgot I told Heather I'd go with her to the Rangers game tonight," Ian said in his best attempt to sound convincing.

James laughed remembering what Danny had told him about Ian's girlfriend, his big gut rolling with each chortle. He was obviously as dumb as he looked choosing his words for a veiled insult instead of the ruse Danny had set in motion.

"Ach, she'll find someone else to do ... oops, I meant somethin' else that is," said James grinning.

Ian looked James up and down, concluding that his fat and out of shape appearance put him at a significant disadvantage. Unlike James, Ian was tall and lithe, his muscular frame some 70 pounds lighter than the 250 pound thug that was about to become his pursuer. It was now or never.

Taking a quick breath Ian bolted down the asphalt pathway.

In a split second he heard James' voice say, "Hey, where d' ya think yer goin'?"

Almost immediately he heard James a few steps behind him, both of them running down the pavement—portly predator and nimble prey. Ian blocked out everything except his focus on escape. Every movement was intent on survival as Ian strained to draw massive amounts of air into his lungs to drive each lunge forward. The rubber soles of his jogging shoes slammed into the concrete sidewalk sending waves of exertion up into his hips and torso as he turned left down Kingsacre Road. After almost a quarter mile his legs were burning from the full tilt sprint.

Standing at the intersection of the path that led through the green area to Ardmay Crescent, he turned and saw James on the verge of collapse, bent over trying to catch his breath about a hundred meters behind.

"Bloody boat-licker," Ian said out loud.

Ian's breathing was labored and deep. He then saw that James was on his mobile phone and surmised that Danny was already in pursuit so he resumed running, deking down another path that doubled back towards the house. Once he was well out of sight Ian crossed the grassed area and ducked behind the unkempt hedges that lined the back of the yards of the row houses along Kingsacre Road. Safe in the secluded green space Ian tried to catch his breath as sweat drained out of every pore in his body soaking his tee shirt. His senses remained on high alert for what seemed like an eternity, on the lookout for Danny's black older model BMW between breaks in the row houses along Montford Avenue.

Ian glanced at his watch. It was going on 9:00 and he had been hiding for almost an hour. Ian assumed Danny was focusing his search in the neighborhoods west of the Hampdem Park Stadium. The sun was almost down and dusk began to fall as Ian emerged from the secluded green space onto the street and started walking towards the house. He desperately needed to get his wallet and personal belongings so he could flee Glasgow.

After standing watch outside the house for a few minutes, Ian cautiously walked up the front steps stopping on the landing to take a good look around before inserting the key into the door lock and turning the handle. He slowly pushed open the weather-beaten door and scanned the darkened entry and living room. Off to his left he heard a thud. In a split second Ian turned toward the place where he heard the sound come from. His eyes darted back and forth, his ears straining and heart beating wildly in his chest. Then, from behind the door came Felix calmly looking up as Ian nearly collapsed to the floor.

"Felix," Ian said as he let out a sigh of relief.

The adrenalin shock focused Ian and he packed all of his essential belongings into an old duffle bag and set it on the floor in front of the entryway. He grabbed his wallet and a wad of cash he had stashed in the drawer of his dresser. Ian then rushed over to the window to ensure that he was safe to leave only to see Danny getting out of his car.

"Oh no," Ian said to himself.

Ian ran past the door grabbing the duffle bag knowing that the only escape route was through his bedroom window. As he entered his bedroom he stopped for a moment deftly using his heel to close the door while slamming his left hand against the wall to switch off the bedroom light. Throwing the duffle bag onto the bed Ian went to the window and unlatched the old wooden sash and pulled up on it. It wouldn't budge.

"Move, dammit," he exclaimed.

He tried again without success.

"No … please … come on."

Ian took in a deep breath and using all of his strength finally got the sash to lurch up about halfway before coming to a stop. Ian grabbed the bag and threw it down onto the grass below. Just as he heard McGinnis insert his key into the lock, Ian placed his right hand and buttocks on the sill and using his left hand for leverage behind the partly open window, he swung both feet through the opening. Sitting with his legs dangling outside and his face looking through the glass, he twisted his body until he was face down. Ian froze for a moment as he heard the front door open and then close.

"Oh shit," he cursed to himself as he heard footsteps coming towards his room.

Just outside his door he heard Danny say hello to old Felix.

"How's my tiger doin'?"

Ian heard a voice in the next yard.

"Are y' alright there lad?"

Ian ignored old Mr. Nairn hoping he would disappear.

Next came James' muffled voice outside the bedroom door.

"I'm sorry Danny, I should have held 'im. He just buggered off soon as you left before I even said a word."

Again came Mr. Nairn's voice, "Ian, I can come over and help y' down if y' like."

Ian, too caught up in the situation to register the absurdity of an 86 year old man trying to assist him in an escape attempt, just hoped that the neighbor's voice was feeble enough so Danny did not hear it.

Ian strained to make out what Danny and James were saying.

"Well, I've no doubt he heard us, but he better be smart enough to keep 'is mouth shut or they'll be hunting 'im down after they kill us first. That guy I hit last night was a big wheel with the construction down at the docks. The eejit was on the take," Ian heard Danny say.

As silently as possible Ian slowly lowered himself by supporting his weight on the sill with his forearms clenched against his chest. When he let go, gravity took over and he slid about three feet breaking his fall by grabbing on to the sill with both hands. Hanging in mid-air for several seconds, Ian was loath to let go for fear of being heard when he hit the ground. After hanging on for several more seconds he began to tire and his fingers lost their grip. He had no choice but to let go. His body dropped to the ground with a muffled thud. Losing his balance in the approaching darkness Ian fell hard against the house, recovering quickly.

"Oh dear, Martha, the lad fell," Mr. Nairn exclaimed.

Ian looked over the fence hoping Mr. Nairn could see him motioning to stay silent, placing his index finger to his lips.

Back on his feet, Ian grabbed his duffle bag with his left hand and ran to the corner of the old house. During his descent he caught a sharp protrusion on the sill that cut into his right hand. He winced in pain looking down in the dim light to see the extent of his injury. Blood was oozing from a long cut down the length of his right middle finger which Ian wiped onto the canvas duffle bag.

Stealthily making his way toward the street Ian covered the distance of the width of the house in a few seconds. He heard Danny call out his name through the open window.

"Ian, I know yer out there, I heard y' fall. Where did y' get to lad?"

"He's around the corner," Mr. Nairn said oblivious to the nature of the situation.

"He's on the move," Danny exclaimed after glancing over at Mr. Nairn.

Knowing this was his chance to escape, Ian broke into a full run holding his duffle bag to his chest with both hands.

Turning quickly, Danny slammed into big James who had been standing directly behind him. They both fell. Danny found himself clumsily wrapped around his friend's big torso.

"Get out o' my way y' fat bastard," Danny shouted angrily.

Danny leapt up and ran toward the front door but it was too late. By the time he got down the front steps Ian was a street away.

"Damn, we're back to the wild goose chase again thanks to you, y' hawfwit," Danny said as James stood behind him.

Danny turned to go back into the house to get his keys, violently shoving James out of the way.

After a few streets Ian slowed down to catch his breath and walked the last 100 feet to the bus stop at Castlemilk Road. Luckily, the bus arrived just as Ian approached, so Ian waved urgently to make sure the driver noticed him. Jumping through the open doors Ian prayed he would never see Danny McGinnis again.

Ian paid the fare and took a seat near the stair to the upper deck as he tried to make sense of what had just happened to him. Looking down at his right hand he noticed that the bleeding had stopped from the cut on his middle finger. As he caught his breath, he looked around at the handful of people riding the bus. Relieved at his escape Ian dropped his shoulders and caught the smile of an attractive older woman sitting across the aisle from him. She reminded him of his mother. Smiling back Ian adjusted his duffle bag between his legs and glanced out the window as McGinnis' BMW pulled up alongside the bus.

"Shit," Ian said out loud as he looked down from the dimly lit bus.

The woman stared at Ian as if she was trying to understand his unprovoked expletive.

"Sorry," Ian blurted as he grabbed his bag and started up the staircase to the upper level.

Ian panicked knowing that McGinnis would not relent in his pursuit. For ten nerve racking minutes, he watched from the rear seat on the upper level as Danny's BMW tailed the bus. As they neared their destination in downtown Glasgow, Ian got up, walked down the stairs and stood by the front exit door.

As soon as the bus came to a halt and the door opened, Ian grabbed his bag and launched into a full tilt run down Stockwell Street. He was a few hundred feet away when he heard the screeching tires of the BMW as it accelerated towards him. Looking over his shoulder he knew his only hope of escape was to scale a wooden fence he had noticed many times before on Hutcheson Street, a street away.

Ian didn't look back as he heard Danny accelerating, darting recklessly in and out of traffic with the obvious intention of running him down. Expecting to be thrown into the air at any second by the crushing force of the BMW's sharply sculpted hood, Ian could almost feel the heat emanating from the front grille of the 'max'd' 325i as it closed in for the kill. Leaping for dear life a split second before impact Ian rolled onto the pavement with his duffle bag held to his gut. MacLeod's rugby playing days came to his aid as he curled up and let the momentum of his body break his fall as he dropped to the ground. Upside down in the midst of a shoulder roll, Ian saw the flash of Danny's car as it flew by down Stockwell Street, its tires dropping off the curb from the sidewalk screeching rubber as they made contact with the road. The BMW came to a halt and Ian saw backup lights as Danny slammed the car into reverse only to be blocked by a city bus that had come up on it from behind. McGinnis had no choice but to now go around the street in order to intercept MacLeod.

Ian's heart was beating explosively as he lunged back into flight, hanging a left down Hutcheson Street toward the fenced in lot. Ian stopped and threw his bag over the fence and then launching himself he gripped the top edge of the rail pulling his body up and throwing his legs over dropping down into the vacant treed lot. Exhausted, he fell to the ground lying on his back. Ian looked up at the surrounding buildings that framed the night sky, thanking his lucky stars that he was still alive. Slowly he got to his feet and contemplated his next move.

He heard the BMW as it slowly drove by in the opposite direction having gone around the street. All Danny could do now was circle street by street hoping to spot him so Ian waited until he no longer heard the whine of the supercharger and rumbling exhaust note of the 300 horsepower engine.

He put on a dark hoodie before pulling himself up and peering over the fence. Tossing his bag onto the sidewalk Ian propelled himself over it landing back on Hutcheson Street. Walking quickly he turned at St Fredericks looking around nervously for any sign of McGinnis. As he reached the corner of George Square and began walking west he spotted the BMW coming towards him.

Thinking quickly Ian pulled the hood over his head and ran over to the grassed area inside the square. With his back turned to the road Ian tried to appear inconspicuous by kneeling down under the cover of one in a group of five smallish elms that lined the edge of the green space. The BMW stopped and then the motor died.

"Ian? MacLeod?" Danny yelled through the open passenger window in his unmistakable Glaswegian accent.

Ian ignored Danny's call.

"Hey you!" Danny shouted in an attempt to get Ian to turn around.

Ian was still for a moment before grabbing his duffle bag and launching into a full tilt sprint across the square towards a small group of tourists out on a late night stroll. After a few moments Ian glanced back and saw Danny brandishing a pistol as he ran in hot pursuit on the other side of the tourists. Hoping that Danny would not risk a shot that would catch innocent people in the crossfire, Ian made a dash for St Vincent Street perhaps a hundred yards beyond the iconic statue in the center of the square. Roosting pigeons scattered as Ian heard Danny's yell.

"Outrun this y' fuckin' hawfwit."

A shot rang out and Ian heard the hiss of a bullet pass by his left ear and then ricochet off the stone pedestal that supported the brass statue at the corner of the square.

In his peripheral vision Ian saw the few people around the square duck for cover as Danny took another shot that again narrowly missed Ian as it careened off into the construction site across the street.

Danny had lost his senses in his effort to gun down his friend and looked around realizing the scene he had just caused. He knew that a Strathclyde police cruiser, siren blasting would be along momentarily so he turned and ran back towards his parked vehicle to make his getaway.

Ian spotted a young woman dressed in a plaid skirt and white blouse getting into the backseat of a taxi pulled over on St Vincent Street about fifty feet ahead. The neon sign of O'Leary's pub reflected off the rear window as Ian ran towards the open door of the idling cab.

Chapter 18

As he sat atop the bridge pier, immobilized by his ordeal and narrow escape from death, Ian jolted back into action from the trance-like state. It had been less than a minute since he had been shot and now standing on the concrete pier, Ian quickly removed his belt, as if by instinct. He noticed that the thick leather had been scarred by the bullet that had torn through his flesh. He looped the belt around the protruding frame that supported a floodlight and gripped it with all of his strength swinging for a couple of oscillations before hanging in mid-air. His feet dangled ten feet from the ground and Ian knew there was a good chance he could sprain an ankle when he hit the pavement which would cripple his escape and mean certain death at the hands of Danny McGinnis. Ian let go and landed hard feeling the pain of impact in waves that resounded through his torso.

Ian gathered his wits, grabbed his bag and high-tailed it down Market Street to the entrance of Waverly Station. The bloodied belt lay where it fell on the stone pavement of Market Street. An old man who had been watching stopped as Ian hustled by limping slightly as his body braced against the gash in his side.

"You should have that looked at lad," he cautioned.

"I'm alright," Ian blurted as he focused on finding the station entrance.

Ian pushed open the door and ran down the stairs threading in and out of people as he rushed towards the platform. With just seconds to spare he jumped through the doors of the train and watched as they closed. Now a fugitive from the most powerful criminal organization in Great Britain Ian came to terms with what he had just done. There was no turning back and he would have to find a way to survive knowing he would be hunted down for keeps by the mob and pursued as a wanted murderer by Scotland Yard.

As Ian stood by the door amidst a throng of passengers, he looked down at his bloodied clothes. Alarmed, he unzipped his bag and pulled out his blue windbreaker, tying it around his waist in an attempt to cover up the evidence of his wound as best he could. Ian saw a transit police officer walking towards him, so he turned and threaded his way through the crowded coach until he arrived at the rear car. He took an empty seat and breathed a sigh of relief that he had somehow survived.

As the train approached Queen Street Station in Glasgow, Ian got up and stood by the exit. Danny's Porsche was fast enough to have outpaced the train to Queen Street station by a few minutes so Ian knew he would have to be careful. It was quite possible that Danny and his two thugs would be waiting for him at the station exit on Dundas Street. The fact that Ian had absconded with four million dollars of their money could mean that the entire taskforce of SOCKS Glasgow would be on a manhunt for him by now. Fortunately for Ian, it was only 100 feet from the Dundas Street station exit to the door of The Ayrshire where he lived.

Ian disembarked and headed towards the exit. The portico was abuzz with taxis and cars picking up and dropping off passengers. There was no sign of Danny's SUV amongst the dozen or so vehicles on the street so Ian put his head out the door and looked down Dundas Street. There was McGinnis, leaning on the side of his Porsche Cayenne, waiting for Ian to walk out of the station.

'Just my luck,' Ian thought as he struggled to come up with another plan.

Ian went back into the station and found a toilet off platform number seven. He set his bag on the counter and turned on the cold water tap to splash water on his face. He undid his jeans and looked at the flesh wound above his right hip. He realized that the belt he had left on the street in Edinburgh may well have saved his life, deflecting the .357 caliber slug's trajectory enough to only result in a surface wound. It was still oozing but the bleeding had stopped. After using a paper towel to dry himself, he opened up his bag and pulled out the RIA issued mobile phone. It looked intact having survived the fall from the bridge, but Ian dared not turn it on knowing full well that it would transmit a GPS signal that would give away his location to anyone monitoring it.

He picked up his bag and walked back into the station spotting a nearby payphone. Ian picked up the receiver and dialed 999. The connection rang twice before an operator answered.

"999, what is your emergency?"

"There's a gun metal grey Porsche Cayenne on Dundas Street just east of the Queen Street station with three men armed with automatic weapons threatening to kill people. Get the police here fast," Ian said urgently.

"What is your name and location?" the operator asked.

"My name is James Ferguson and I'm at a payphone inside the Queen Street Station as we speak. Hurry before they kill someone."

"The police are on their way sir, please stay put as they will want to interview you."

"Right," Ian said before hanging up.

Making his way back to the main entrance Ian heard sirens approaching, so he stuck his head into the portico and saw McGinnis looking about trying to ascertain where the sirens were coming from. Then he saw McGinnis jump into the driver seat and slam the door closed. The sound of the Porsche's exhaust note was music to his ears. Ian's ad hoc plan had worked. The Cayenne made a U-turn and took off down Dundas Street in an attempt to evade the Strathclyde cruisers on their way to Ian's 999 call.

MacLeod made a dash for the entrance to The Ayrshire and the safe haven of his flat as no one knew where he lived except Kyla. No sooner had he closed the glass door, there were two brightly colored Strathclyde cruisers screeching to a halt on the street outside. Several police officers scanned the area in search of the reported Cayenne to no avail as Ian walked up the stairs to his flat.

Ian inserted his key and pushed open the door closing it behind him. He set down his bag and walked over to his bed where he collapsed in fatigue.

Chapter 19

"Dunsmuir, come to the boardroom," crackled the intercom in Jordie Dunsmuir's office.

Jordie braced, knowing something was wrong when Ascot used that tone of voice. He glanced across the hall and saw Ascot sitting with the client, Douglas McMurphy and CFO Janet McComb. Jordie got up from his desk and walked over to the boardroom, knocking before opening the large oak door and entering.

"Good morning," Jordie said as if it were a question.

"Have a seat Dunsmuir," Ascot said harshly.

Jordie took a seat as far away from McMurphy as he could.

"I've spent the last 20 minutes being brought up to speed on some disturbing news about your wonderful friend Mr. Ian MacLeod. You seem to have brought a traitor in amongst us Jordie," Ascot said accusingly.

Immediately Jordie knew something had gone very wrong with their plan. Janet sat with her head down like a prisoner awaiting execution.

"Yeah?" Jordie uttered hardly able to make his vocal cords work.

Douglas McMurphy was sitting to Ascot's right, silent as usual, but Jordie knew he could explode at any second.

"Jordie, did you know that MacLeod got a hold of the account number, passcode and password to the client's Swiss bank account on the Dundee deal?" Ascot queried.

"What—,"

"Answer the question. Yes or no?" Ascot demanded.

"No," Jordie replied in a state of shock.

"Well somehow he conned Crawford into giving up more information than would have been extracted through ... let's say more physical methods," Ascot said glancing at McMurphy.

Dunsmuir was speechless.

"Do you have any idea what he did with the information he got out of Crawford?" Ascot inquired sarcastically.

"He did what we asked him and confirmed that payments were being made to a dummy company instead of being deposited to the Swiss account we set up for the deal. I'm still waiting for him to send the data as we speak ... he must have got sidetracked over the weekend," Jordie replied.

McMurphy nearly launched out of his chair.

"Oh, he got sidetracked alright. He slipped right through your hands, you dumb shit!" McMurphy said angrily.

"Jordie, somehow he got the client's business partner to write him a certified check so he could deposit it into the client's account and then he transferred the money presumably into his own Swiss account which you and Janet set up for him ... four million dollars Jordie," Ascot explained further.

Jordie looked over at McMurphy.

"He duped me," Jordie admitted.

"He duped you? That's all you can say, you stupid little turd?" McMurphy blurted furiously.

"I'm sorry."

"Oh, you're gonna be sorrier than you'll ever know," McMurphy threatened.

"Jordie, listen carefully. You are going to find MacLeod and then you're going to get him to return the client's money. Do you understand?" Ascot said in a no-nonsense tone.

"How am I going to convince him to do that?" Jordie asked with fear now written all over his face.

"That's your problem Dunsmuir," Ascot said devoid of any empathy for Dunsmuir's predicament.

Ascot turned to Janet McComb.

"Janet, that will be all thank you. Clean out your desk. You're fired," Ascot said dryly.

"But, I did nothing," Janet protested.

"Precisely," Douglas McMurphy said scornfully.

"Janet, the client wants you terminated. I'm sorry," Ascot said without so much as looking at Janet McComb.

Janet, looking shocked, got up from her chair and left the room giving Jordie a final glance of disdain as she passed through the boardroom door.

Jordie slowly got up and started for the door before stopping.

"What if I can't get him to meet with us?" Jordie asked, his eyes filled with panic.

McMurphy's black expressionless eyes stared at Jordie as he raised his right hand to his chest thumb cocked, index finger pointing at Jordie. He dropped his thumb and raised his bushy eyebrows, his lips curling back in a sneer.

Jordie returned to his office shaking so badly he was hardly able to stand. After sitting down at his desk and taking some deep breaths he opened his computer and began searching for any record of contact information for Ian MacLeod.

Ian had not forwarded the requested data nor was a fix on his GPS location known since he had left Edinburgh. Jordie surmised that Ian had either discarded or turned off the equipment and now he knew why. Then he remembered Kyla Fraser. He had her and Ian tailed by one of the client's men. He found the mobile number for Rupert Bertwistle, the contact he had used for all of the client's unsavory business. Jordie dialed the number.

"Bertwistle 'ere," the voice said in a thick Cockney accent.

"Yeah, it's Dunsmuir. I've got a job for you," Jordie said.

"I'm all ears."

"I want you to get me a location on MacLeod."

"Oh, another one's gone fer a dumper 'as it?" Bertwistle said with a chuckle.

"McMurphy would be pissed if I told him about your mouth."

"Don't worry, mum's the word. So what's the nit'y grit'y?" Bertwistle asked.

"I need you to find out where Kyla Fraser lives ... you know the woman who he was with when you were assigned to keep an eye on MacLeod after we brought him in on the last project a couple weeks back. But be careful. I found out she's with Scotland Yard so don't screw this up. Since he was with her then, I have to hope that she is still in contact with him," Jordie explained.

"I know where the lit'le bird lives," Bertwistle noted.

"Good. You're gonna bring me MacLeod in one piece without Ms. Fraser's knowledge. Understood?" Jordie stated in a serious tone.

"Y' can depend on ol' Rupert, y' know that."

"Look, don't underestimate this guy. He's very clever."

"Consider it done. Oh, and if he's no' with 'er?" Bertwistle asked.

"Then I'm screwed," Jordie said with an air of finality.

"I'll do wha' I can, as always."

Jordie hung up the phone and contemplated his predicament. He looked at a file folder on his desk. The file label read: Jack Singleton, Singleton Developments – Manchester.

Chapter 20

After Ian did not show up as promised or answer his emails, Kyla began to worry and spent the weekend wondering what had happened to him. She was sure that she and Ian really had a connection and it seemed out of character for him to simply not show up or try to contact her—even if they were in the early stages of a budding love relationship.

Kyla arrived at Scotland Yard late in the day on Monday and was seen walking to her office by Cosgrove.

"I heard you called in late—not feeling well?" Cosgrove asked.

"No, I'm fine now. I caught a later flight."

"Alright. See me in my office in a half hour and I'll give you the latest on the investigation. In the meantime, read this report from Edinburgh ... there's been another CEO murder," Cosgrove said as he handed Kyla a brief.

"OK, see you then," Kyla responded as she turned down the hallway towards her office scanning the document.

Kyla sat down at her desk absorbed in thought, poring over the Edinburgh report, when Detective Woods poked her head into her office.

"Kyla?"

Kyla looked up.

"Oh, hi Janine."

"Did you hear we have a breakthrough on the Mills case?" Woods asked.

"No. What?" Kyla responded.

"We have now identified a suspect," Woods stated.

"That's great," Kyla replied.

"We found more video capture from the Novatel. We identified the suspect as an individual who just recently left his job at Datatime—Ian MacLeod. There's an APB going out on him as we speak," Woods said excitedly.

"Ian MacLeod? From where?" Kyla asked anxiously.

Kyla's heart felt like it was in her throat.

"Brighton," Janine replied.

"Really! That's … such … good news," Kyla said, doing her best to hide the look of shock on her face.

"Yeah and get this. According to Mills' assistant, MacLeod uttered a threat when Mills fired him recently. Looks like a slam dunk. We'll talk later," Woods said as she continued down the hall.

Stunned at the news, Kyla hastily logged onto her laptop. She pulled out the access code assigned to the video footage referred to in the first briefing of the Mills case. She keyed in the code, '@58900854.' There was a single media file marked Glasgow (1). Kyla clicked on it and watched the black and white footage of a young man wearing a light colored windbreaker as he came into the camera's range stopping under the horse and rider statue Kyla recognized as being the one at the Modern Art Center in Glasgow. He held an umbrella which she could see even in the grainy footage was shedding a hard downpour. She noted the digital time on the video was 10:58 AM. A minute later a heavyset male came into view and handed him something. Both men stood for a few moments until the larger figure took back a sheet of paper and folded it before walking away. The younger man bent down to pick up a cardboard box and then looked up directly into the CCTV camera.

"Omigod," Kyla gasped under her breath.

Kyla sat in astonishment trying to wrap her head around the implications of a meeting caught on tape between Ian MacLeod and whoever the other man was. Then she remembered that she needed to get to her meeting with Cosgrove. Composing herself, Kyla walked down the hall to Cosgrove's office. As she walked through the doorway she noticed a man standing in front of the window with his back to her, so Kyla stopped and waited for an introduction.

"Kyla, I know you don't usually get involved with the Yard's informants, but I'd like you to meet Rupert Bertwistle. He has some new information for us," Cosgrove said gesturing towards the heavyset man.

The man turned towards Kyla who was taken aback, recognizing Bertwistle from the video capture she had just watched. He was the man who met with Ian under the bronze statue. Kyla's head was spinning at a developing story she was not sure she wanted to hear, but she collected herself and extended her hand.

"Nice to meet you Rupert," Kyla said, noticing that Bertwistle was ogling her.

She felt an immediate dislike for the crass looking man as he impolitely thrust out his enormous hand in response to Kyla's. After a brief handshake Kyla quickly withdrew her hand and they both sat down in front of Cosgrove's desk.

Bertwistle made obvious his once over and then addressed Cosgrove.

"Now she's a bit of awright if I do say so meself chief."

Kyla ignored Bertwistle's comment.

"As I said, Rupert has some very interesting information about our suspect," said Cosgrove, handing off the conversation to Bertwistle.

"Some very important people wan'ed that Mills bloke called out. From wha' I 'eard they hired a fella by the name o' Ian MacLeod to find out about his indiscretions, you know pilferin' money 'n such," Bertwistle said darting his eyes between Kyla and Cosgrove.

Kyla noted that Bertwistle's story was consistent with the description of what Ian had told her he was going to be doing for RIA.

"How do you know that?" Kyla asked.

"Because no one's got 'is ear to the ground more than me luv. I personally 'anded MacLeod 'is orders. I'm told they needed 'is skills in coun'in' money 'n such and 'e got paid dearly for callin' out that backhander. I'm also told 'e 'ad a grudge against Mills being 'is former boss and all so 'e took things into 'is own hands. I s'pose 'e must've enjoyed pushin' Mills onto the track and seein' 'im cut in two cause he couldn' wait to do in that poor bloke in Edinburgh. Blood changes a man Missy. Anyways that's wha' I'm tellin' y'."

Kyla bristled at Bertwistle's callous accusation and was even more shocked to hear him bring up the Edinburgh case especially because it had just been shared with national law enforcement. She was suspicious about Bertwistle's motives.

"This is absurd. Sir, it's obvious who this man works for when he's not spreading lies and getting paid for them," Kyla said, her eyes flashing with anger at what she was hearing.

"Kyla, calm down," Cosgrove cautioned.

"It's ridiculous to think we'd believe a criminal. Scotland Yard isn't that naïve are we sir?" Kyla asked imploringly.

"Well I don't disagree that the story is a bit far-fetched," Cosgrove added.

"It's no cock and bull story if that's wha' yer tryin' t' say," Bertwistle replied.

"Sir, if he's saying that there are other people in on this then why aren't we investigating them instead of a nondescript accountant from Glasgow?" Kyla asked vehemently.

Cosgrove was taken aback and stared at Kyla for an instant before speaking.

"How do you know he's from Glasgow Kyla?" Cosgrove asked drawing back his face in surprise.

Kyla looked at Bertwistle and then at Cosgrove wondering how she could recover after letting the cat out of the bag.

Bertwistle smirked. The irony just seemed too good to be true as he watched, entertained, while Kyla squirmed in her seat searching for words.

"Well ... the video you quoted ... you know, at the first briefing sir, obviously brought in by Bertwistle, since he's in it, was shot in Glasgow. I'm assuming the suspect lives there," Kyla replied.

Bertwistle turned to hear Cosgrove's response his growing amusement becoming hard to contain. Kyla cringed in anticipation of Cosgrove's next question.

"What are you smiling at Bertwistle? You find this funny?" Cosgrove asked annoyed at the loss of decorum unfolding in his office.

Kyla was relieved to have the focus shifted from her onto the vile man sitting next to her.

"Yes, so why don't you tell us who the *real* killer is Mr. Bertwistle?" Kyla asked unable to contain the contempt in her voice.

"I told y' wha' I know," Bertwistle responded smugly.

Cosgrove studied Kyla's demeanor and then looked over at Bertwistle.

"Kyla the reason you're in on this meeting is to match the profile as it exists to MacLeod as the suspect," Cosgrove said looking at Kyla.

Once again Bertwistle tried to contain himself.

"Yeah, y' must 'ave qui'e a profile on 'im Miss Fraser," Bertwistle said with a Cheshire smile pasted on his crudely featured face.

"I'll do my best sir," Kyla said her brilliant blue eyes flashing angrily at the man sitting beside her.

How Bertwistle was privy to her romantic interest in Ian, Kyla had no idea. She didn't know how he could have found out but somehow he seemed to know more about Ian MacLeod than she did.

"OK, let's get back to work. Thanks Rupert, you've been very helpful. I'll make sure you're taken care of. Kyla, I'd like to talk to you after Rupert leaves," Cosgrove said escorting Bertwistle to the door.

Cosgrove took his seat.

"Kyla, what was that about? I've never seen you act like that before," Cosgrove asked staring in disbelief at the woman he had so much respect for.

"Sorry sir. Bad chemistry I guess. I found the man to be a vile and horrid excuse for a human being. He's a parasite," Kyla said hoping her explanation would allow her to sidestep her behavior.

Cosgrove considered her response for a few moments.

"Hmm. Kyla, how do you know that MacLeod is an accountant? Other than me, only Johnson is privy to that information," Cosgrove said still bothered by what he had witnessed.

Kyla sat up straight trying desperately to think of an answer.

"Well, your informant did say, 'MacLeod has skills in countin' money 'n such.' After all, I am a profiler, sir," Kyla answered.

Cosgrove was silent for a moment.

"Alright, fair enough. Let's get back to work shall we?" Cosgrove said ending the meeting.

Kyla got up from her chair and was about to leave Cosgrove's office when he addressed her.

"Kyla, I'm sending Detective Johnson down to Brighton to interview MacLeod's ex-wife. I'd like you to tag along," Cosgrove stated.

"Ex-wife?" Kyla blurted taken completely by surprise.

"You sound surprised. Kyla, is everything OK?" Cosgrove asked.

"Yes, of course. Where and when, sir?" Kyla asked as her heart skipped a beat.

'I'm interviewing his ex-wife ... that I didn't even know existed,' Kyla thought unable to comprehend how absurd the situation was becoming.

"Thursday morning in Brighton. You and Johnson are taking the early train."

Chapter 21

Kyla sat next to Detective Inspector Kenneth Johnson as they approached Brighton on an overcast summer day. Small droplets of rain streaked across the window as the train passed the outskirts slowing down as it rounded the gentle S curve that led to the Brighton train station. Kyla had been engrossed in thought, finding the developments in the murder case and now the impending meeting with Judith Mason bizarre.

'I hardly know Ian and now I'm meeting with his ex-wife to profile him as a suspect in a murder investigation. What on God's green earth have I gotten myself into?' Kyla thought as she stared out the window.

She turned to speak to her partner for the day.

"So how are we going to conduct the interview Ken?" Kyla asked.

"My goal is to find out anything she might know regarding his whereabouts and then I'll defer to you on his relationships with her and his ex-boss Lance Mills," Johnson replied.

Kyla was not a good liar. She had been intimate with Ian MacLeod and knew exactly where he lived in Glasgow. Her double life was beginning to wear on her conscience and she was well aware of the implications of shirking her professional duty as a member of the criminal investigation community.

They got up to disembark as the train stopped at the Brighton Station platform. Once they got off, they found a cab and proceeded to Judith Mason's home in North Brighton.

"There's the house over there," Johnson said as the cab came to a halt.

Johnson paid the cabbie as Kyla stood nervously sizing up Ian's ex-wife's residence. It was a relatively upscale home in a nice neighborhood. One you would expect of a doctor or a lawyer.

"Shall we?" Johnson asked.

Johnson was a senior investigator with 20 years under his belt; a proper British chap with good manners.

"Yes, by all means," Kyla answered.

They climbed the four steps to the landing and rang the doorbell. In a few moments the large oak door swung open and a woman of about 35 appeared. She was plain and had a severe look about her, with thin lips and eyes that didn't show much warmth. Her mousy brown hair was pulled back into a tight knot giving her the bearing of a schoolmarm. At 5'8" she looked down at Kyla's petite 5'2" frame.

"Hello, I'm Judith Mason. You must be from Scotland Yard. Please come in," she said not bothering to wait for an introduction as she turned and walked inside.

"This is Kyla Fraser and I'm Detective Inspector Kenneth Johnson," Johnson said noting Mrs. Mason's stand-offish demeanor.

Judith showed them into the Great Room and seated them on a white fabric sofa.

"Can I offer you anything?" Judith asked as she took a seat in a black leather chair across from her visitors.

"No, thank you, this won't take but a few minutes. We have some questions about your ex-husband Ian MacLeod."

"Yes of course. Have you found him yet?"

"No not yet. We were hoping you might help us out with a bit more information than we currently have on him," Johnson led.

"Well they didn't say much when they called and said you wanted to talk with me about Ian. Why are you so interested in him?" Judith asked concerned with the police involvement.

"He's become a suspect in a murder investigation Mrs. Mason," Johnson said anticipating that there would be an alarmed response.

"What?" Judith exclaimed incredulously.

"We believe he pushed his former employer Lance Mills into the path of an oncoming train at Euston Station. He's also being investigated for another homicide in Edinburgh," Johnson said as a matter of course.

"Impossible," Judith said refusing to accept what she was hearing.

"I understand your feelings Mrs. Mason but if you don't mind answering a few questions we'd appreciate it. Ms. Fraser here is actually one of the country's leading profilers on serial murders and that is why she is with me—to further her understanding of his psychology and behavior patterns," Johnson continued.

"These allegations of murder are ridiculous. Ian is one of the mildest mannered and meek people you'll ever meet. He wouldn't hurt a fly. He is gentle and tender and I defy you to convince me of such heinous accusations," Judith said combatively.

"You sound like you miss him dearly Mrs. Mason," Kyla said gently.

"Well ... not really. My husband Barry and I have split up over the fallout from his disappearance so things are topsy-turvy right now," Judith said, the stress in her voice belying her staid appearance.

"I'm sorry to hear that," Kyla said compassionately.

"Oh, he can be such a bonehead, Barry can. I'm sure we'll patch things up if he ever gets over his snit. It was over money. Ian walked out on his alimony obligations, so I'll have to look to Barry now. We argued and I told him to get out. We haven't talked since the middle of May," Judith said trying to make light of her admission.

"Mrs. Mason, when was the last time you saw Ian MacLeod?" Johnson asked.

"Not since late April," Judith advised.

"Did he enjoy his job? What made him want to leave Brighton?" Johnson queried.

"He detested the place ... hated Mills ... for good reason. But would he kill him? He wouldn't have the guts for one thing," Judith proclaimed.

"So you have no idea of his whereabouts?"

"Not a clue. Those silly buggers at East Sussex call themselves police. They wouldn't lift a finger to find out what happened to him," Judith said derisively.

"Do you think he might still be in the area ... around here for instance?"

"No, he's originally from Glasgow, so my bet is he ended up in that godforsaken place," Judith advised.

"That's where Ms. Fraser hails from," Johnson said with a chuckle.

Kyla was silent, watching as the last woman Ian had been with gave her insight into the man she loved.

"Kyla, do you have any questions for Mrs. Mason?" Johnson asked handing off the interview to Kyla.

"Yes, thank you. Judith, may I call you Judith?" Kyla asked respectfully.

"Of course. That's my name," Judith snapped back.

"Did Ian ever lose his temper? You know, become abusive when his stress level became high?" Kyla asked.

"No, absolutely never. The most emotion I ever saw from Ian was his anxiety and panic attacks," Judith replied.

"How did he express his anger towards his boss Mills?" Kyla queried.

"Oh, he'd curse him and be very frustrated, but he never threatened to act out if that's what you mean," Judith said defensively.

"How about his family of origin? What do you know of them?"

"All dead. His biological father died in the sinking of the North Sea oil rig Ocean Harvester. Ian said it broke up in 100 foot swells in January of 1974, a month before his birth. His mother married Ian's stepfather who he hated with a passion. She vanished into thin air when Ian was very young ... just a boy. His stepfather Thomas Smith beat him to within an inch of his life many times until Ian finally broke free when he was 17. He moved in with his friend at the time, Danny McGinnis, who is one of the nastiest people on the planet according to Ian. That's how we met—he literally fell into my cab while trying to escape from McGinnis when I was visiting Glasgow in 1998. He said McGinnis tried to kill him. He fled Glasgow with me and ended up here in Brighton. The rest is history," Judith explained.

Remembering her conversation with Ian during the drive back from Arran, Judith's description of Ian's family relationships was not surprising to Kyla and it furthered her understanding of his pysche.

"I have no further questions Mrs. Mason. Thank you for your time."

"Well, do you think he's a serial killer?" Judith asked.

Kyla sensed that Judith wanted some comfort to settle her anxiety about her ex-husband.

"It's not my place to make assertions about guilt or innocence. My job is to provide a personality and behavioral profile based on personal history and other background factors. I have no opinion at this juncture in the investigation. If I knew him like you do, perhaps I could offer one," Kyla said trying to remain objective and non-judgmental for Judith's sake.

"He's not a killer. Never in a million years Ms. Fraser. I don't care what you come up with. You're barking up the wrong tree," Judith said conclusively.

"Thank you Mrs. Mason, we'll be on our way now," Johnson said ending the conversation.

Kyla and Johnson made their way to the train station and boarded the express back to London.

As Kyla stared out the window of the London Express, she recalled Judith's words, *'He's not a killer. Never in a million years Ms. Fraser'*. Strangely, her words gave Kyla comfort. Having been intimate with Ian, she knew for certain he was not capable of killing anything.

Chapter 22

Kyla was deep in thought as she drove along the M8 from the Glasgow airport. There was new evidence in the Mills case. The flight that Lance Mills claimed had been cancelled the day before his murder was confirmed to have taken place. He was also seen with a young female companion on hotel video. Why Mills had lied and how the young woman fit into the narrative was unclear. There were also new developments in the Singleton case. Mobile phone records showed that he had received and made several calls on the evening of his murder. One incoming call was traced to Jordie Dunsmuir, the man she had spoken to on the phone after the initial briefing, so Kyla now knew he had lied to her about what he knew. Singleton had made another call traced to a man who had gone missing, an accountant from Manchester with no connection to either RIA or Singleton, baffling investigators. Detectives were following up and planned on interviewing Jordie Dunsmuir in the coming days.

Then the name of the old acquaintance Ian had encountered on the train trip to Glasgow popped into her head.

"For the luv o' God, that was Jordie Dunsmuir," Kyla said out loud.

There was something off with Dunsmuir and the entire situation; Ian's secretive behavior, Dunsmuir's nervous avoidance, the Mills connection and now another murder in Edinburgh. Kyla was bewildered.

Kyla continued along the M8 to Strathclyde police headquarters on Stewart Street and parked her car. Finding the main entrance, she walked up to the reception area.

"How can I help you ma'am?" the on duty officer Constable John Kendrick asked.

"I'm with Scotland Yard, the name is Kyla Fraser. I'd like to speak to the investigator, if he is still here, who was in charge of a disappearance that occurred about 25 years ago in Glasgow," Kyla said while flashing her Scotland Yard security card.

"Do you know the name of the investigator or the person who disappeared?" Kendrick asked.

"Not directly," Kyla replied.

"If you go through the main area you'll see a bank of offices. I will let the Chief Superintendent know you're on your way. Your name again?"

"Kyla Fraser. Thanks so much."

Kyla proceeded through a set of double swinging doors. She saw a gentleman in uniform standing by the door to his office.

"Ms. Fraser?" the pleasant looking older man asked.

"Yes," Kyla answered as she approached him.

"It's a pleasure to meet you. Come on in and have a seat," Chief Superintendent Jim Thompson said motioning to the chair sitting in front of a large oak desk.

"Thanks for seeing me," Kyla said as she sat down.

"So how can I be of service?" Thompson asked as he took his seat across from Kyla.

"I'm looking for some information on a man named Ian MacLeod. I believe his mother disappeared when he was very young. There must have been a police investigation," Kyla said.

"Alright, let me check our records and see if anything comes up."

After several minutes Thompson spoke.

"Ah, here it is. My search for Ian MacLeod brings up what was believed to be an unsolved homicide investigation," Thompson said looking up at Kyla over his glasses.

Kyla was taken aback. Thompson continued.

"The woman's name was Mary Smith, Ian MacLeod's mother. She disappeared in 1984. It was suspected that her husband Thomas Smith murdered her. The inspector was a fella named Hume. He's retired but we still hear from him now and then, so I can get in touch if you'd like," Thompson offered.

"I'd very much appreciate that Chief Superintendent," Kyla responded.

"Let me see if I can dial him up for you."

Thompson dialed Hume's number and Hume answered.

"Gordon, this is Thompson over at central headquarters. Would you have some time for a lovely lady from Scotland Yard? She'd like to ask a few questions on the Mary Smith case from back in the eighties."

Kyla couldn't hear Hume's reply but she hoped it would be positive.

"Fine, I'll give her your address and she'll be along. Ms. Fraser, when would you like to pay a visit to Inspector Hume?" Thompson asked while placing his hand over the mouthpiece.

"Right away, if he's up to it," Kyla replied.

"Can she come over say in 30 minutes or so?"

Kyla gathered by Thompson's facial expression that he had said yes.

"Alright, I'll send her on her way."

Thompson hung up and wrote down the directions to Hume's home in Langbank. After thanking Thompson, Kyla drove to Gordon Hume's home. She opened the front picketed gate and found herself in front of a small single story bungalow with a roof that looked like it was in need of repair. She knocked on the front door. After a few moments the door opened and a man of about 75 answered.

"Ms. Fraser?"

"Yes," Kyla answered.

"Gordon Hume, come in and have a seat. Can I get you some tea?" Hume asked.

"No, I'll be brief and then be on my way thanks."

"Alright," Hume said as he sat down on a recliner across from Kyla.

"Tell me a bit about the Mary Smith case."

"Well, I never found the proof I needed, but as far as I'm concerned she was murdered by her husband Thomas Smith. He was a very crass individual with a violent temper and a drinking problem. The word from the neighbors was that he drank every night and was very abusive, especially to his stepson, a wee boy not seven years old," Hume said describing the case details as if it were yesterday.

"What happened to the boy after his mother vanished?" Kyla inquired.

"Oh, Smith kept him. He eventually found another woman, Carlene as I recall and they lived together as unhappy as ever the word was. It was a sad story indeed. Why social services didn't take the boy away is a mystery, but he put up with Smith right through his teens," Hume said in a measured voice.

"What do y' mean?" Kyla asked.

"The word was that young Ian suffered terrible beatings on a regular basis," Hume continued.

"Did Ian have any friends that I might interview?" Kyla queried.

"Well, I do recall there was a lad named Danny ... the last name slips me, but give me a minute. He had a bad reputation as well ... criminal actually. He's now an enforcer with the local mob."

"Danny McGinnis?" Kyla asked, recalling the name from her interview with Judith Mason.

"Yes ... that's it," Hume replied.

"Thank you so much, you've been very helpful Mr. Hume. I won't take up any more of your time."

"My pleasure. It's nice to have some female company. My dear wife Helen passed away last year. Beautiful lass, miss her dearly," Hume said.

"I'm so sorry," Kyla responded.

"Thank you, Ms. Fraser. I'll show you out," Hume said as he got up and escorted Kyla to the front door.

* * * * *

Kyla made her way back to Strathclyde headquarters. Once again she was sitting across from the Chief Inspector in his office.

"In my conversation with Hume he brought up the name Danny McGinnis. Do y' know of him?" Kyla asked.

"Of course we know of McGinnis. He's on the top of the list of bad guys in Glasgow. He's suspected to be a shooter for Douglas McMurphy, the man behind SOCKS. Very dangerous individual," Thompson noted solemnly.

"Can he be brought in so I can talk to him?" Kyla asked.

"Hmm. I'll see what the lads over in organized crime or homicide can do. Stay here, I'll be right back," Hume said as he got up and left his office.

Kyla sat for a few minutes trying to process the new information she had gathered from her morning at Strathclyde and her visit with Gordon Hume.

She began to formulate a profile on Ian's personality in her mind. She now knew that he was a man who could have a lot of unresolved anger and might, at least unconsciously, want payback.

'But could he be homicidal?' Kyla asked herself.

Thompson returned to his office.

"We'll pick him up and have him here within the hour. Our Detective Black says he knows where to find him," Thompson advised.

"Thanks so much for this. Do you have a spot where I can set up a laptop?" Kyla asked.

"Absolutely, come with me over to homicide. That's where you'll be interviewing him. Be careful, he's a bad one you know," Thompson cautioned.

Kyla spent the next hour and a half on line researching while she waited for McGinnis to be brought in. She Googled SOCKs and found out that they controlled almost all of the major crime rings in the UK as well as exerting power over a wide range of legitimate businesses. According to sex trade watchdog, 'Take Action', SOCKS had recently made major inroads into the sex trade industry exerting control over most street level pimps in the major metropolitan centers in the UK. Douglas McMurphy was known to be a white collar crime boss who in spite of his mob connections was respected within business and social circles throughout the UK.

She then Googled RIA and found out that the managing partner was Alistair Ascot. She also found out that Ascot had been nominated for an Order of the British Empire by the Cabinet Office in recent months and was expected to be knighted within the year. His close ties with Home Secretary Gordon Kinsey and his influence over government policy makers made him a formidable power broker within business circles in the UK.

"Interesting," Kyla said softly as she jotted down Ascot's name next to McMurphy's.

Kyla was beginning to see how McGinnis was connected to McMurphy, and Dunsmuir to Ascot.

"Ms. Fraser?" the middle aged detective asked as he poked his head into the office Kyla was occupying.

"Yes."

"I'm Detective Black. We have Danny McGinnis waiting in interview room one," Black said sizing up Kyla as he motioned to her.

"Thanks," Kyla said as she followed him.

"Mind if I ask what yer looking for with McGinnis?" Black queried.

"I'm a profiler and I need some background information on people who may be suspect," Kyla replied as both of them walked towards the interview room.

"Is McGinnis a suspect?" Black pried.

"You know the answer to that Detective. Everyone's a suspect until someone's arrested and charged," Kyla responded wondering why Black was so interested in her motives for interviewing Danny McGinnis.

Kyla arrived at the interview room and Black opened the door. She walked in to find a surly looking man in his mid-thirties sitting with his right ankle resting on his left knee, arms behind his head. Kyla was surprised that McGinnis was not the repulsive monster she had expected. She found that his dark hair, green eyes, and chiseled features were not physically unattractive. Kyla noticed a long, jagged scar across the left side of his cheek as Danny sat up straight, shocked to see an attractive female interrogator walk into the room. As she placed her notebook on the table she noticed that Black had not closed the door. She walked over and saw Black leaning against the wall seemingly listening in. She pushed the door closed and turned toward McGinnis.

"Relaxed are you Mr. McGinnis?" Kyla asked.

"Ah, no, not really. This is not my idea of a good time … yet," McGinnis said looking Kyla up and down.

Ignoring the innuendo, Kyla continued, "I'd like to ask you a few questions about your relationship with Ian MacLeod."

The look of surprise on Danny's face did not go unnoticed.

"What the hell? Who are you?" Danny asked.

"My apologies. Kyla Fraser, I'm with Scotland Yard."

"Good on y'," Danny said dismissively.

"Mr. McGinnis, what do y' do for a living?" Kyla asked.

"I work for an honest day's pay. What's it to y'? And what's MacLeod got to dae with this?" McGinnis asked.

"Mr. McGinnis, I'm a serial murder profiler and I'm investigating a number of murders that have occurred over the past month or so …"

"I do not know nothin' about no murders," Danny interrupted appearing nervous.

"I didn't say you did," Kyla stated calmly.

Kyla had been watching Danny's body language as the interview proceeded.

"What do y' know about Ian MacLeod?" Kyla asked.

Danny braced ever so slightly but enough to be perceptible to Kyla.

"I know nothin'," Danny uttered.

"You and he were childhood friends, I know that," Kyla continued with her line of questioning.

"He was a fuckin' loser," Danny said crudely.

"How so?" asked Kyla.

"No guts. He let people push him around like his stepfather," Danny replied.

"Thomas Smith?" Kyla asked.

"Yeah, beat the shit out of 'im most every night. MacLeod shoulda killed 'im. I would 've," Danny said with the swagger one might expect from a thug.

'No doubt,' Kyla thought continuing to study McGinnis.

"When was the last time you were in touch with Ian?"

"I don't remember," Danny snapped back. "Look, unless you've got somethin' on me, I'm leavin', otherwise let me see my lawyer."

Kyla looked at Danny intently, deciding that it was futile to continue the interview.

"Fine, you're free to leave. Thanks for your time Mr. McGinnis," Kyla said crossing her arms defensively.

Danny got up from his chair and walked towards the door sizing up Kyla as he left.

Inspector Burns of Homicide walked in.

"How did it go with Mr. Personality?" Burns asked.

"Well, that's not what I'd call him. Can't you guys nail him on anything?" Kyla asked.

"His boss is untouchable here in Glasgow. He owns half of the UK. Nobody messes with McMurphy. Between you and me, I think he owns

Strathclyde as well, so watch out what you say here, especially to him," Burns said under his breath motioning his eyes towards Detective Black.

"You mean cops on the take?" Kyla asked.

"You didn't hear it from me. Let me show you out if you're done here," Burns said motioning to the door.

Kyla was escorted out and got back into her car. She sat for a few minutes trying to take in what she had learned about Ian MacLeod and his old friend Danny McGinnis. As the names of the various characters passed through her mind—Ascot, McMurphy, McGinnis, Dunsmuir—Kyla had a sinking feeling that Ian had gotten himself into an inescapable world of trouble.

Chapter 23

Alistair Ascot arrived at the RIA offices on the stroke of nine as usual. After saying hello to Priscilla he walked directly to Jordie Dunsmuir's office. Jordie was not there so Ascot went back to the front desk.

"I take it Dunsmuir has not arrived at work yet?" Ascot queried.

"No, it's unusual isn't it? He is always here before eight every morning," Priscilla replied.

"If you don't mind, call his home and see if we can find out where he is," Ascot said as he stood at the reception desk.

"Do you think something has happened to him?" Priscilla asked worriedly.

"No, I just need to talk to him, that's all," Ascot replied.

"I haven't checked the overnight voice mail yet. Maybe there's a message there."

"Let me know," Ascot said as he proceeded to his office.

After taking off his jacket Ascot dialed Douglas McMurphy's direct line.

"Hello," McMurphy answered.

"Ascot here. Dunsmuir hasn't shown up for work. Do you know anything?" Ascot asked.

"I know that his bad judgment cost the operation $4 million dollars. Just assume he's left town ... permanently. Look, I gotta go. I have my man McGinnis here, so let's talk later," McMurphy said abruptly.

"How unfortunate; he was a good man," Ascot said regretfully.

"Yeah sure, you'll read about it in the papers tonight. They've already found him floating face down in the Clyde. Look, the scum may be on to us. There was an untimely interview down at CID Strathclyde yesterday with a

Scotland Yard profiler who has been poking her nose into business she might be sorry for—Kyla Fraser. Do y' know who she is Ascot?" McMurphy asked cynically.

"Yes, I know—," Ascot started before McMurphy cut him off.

"Bertwistle says she's fucking Ian MacLeod for crissake. How in the hell did Dunsmuir allow an outsider, who was hooked up with a little piece of ass from Scotland Yard to get on the inside? Jeezus Alistair, your little patsy is turning the tables on us," McMurphy said angrily.

"Douglas, we'll catch him, don't worry."

"Yeah right. Well, I've already sent Bertwistle down to London to try and deflect the Yard's attention away from us and onto MacLeod. I think your plan to frame him was ill conceived," McMurphy said exasperated.

"How much does CID or the Yard know?" Ascot asked concerned.

"Enough to make me very uncomfortable," McMurphy stated.

"Douglas, stay with the plan. Let the police deal with Ian MacLeod. Kyla Fraser will look like a complete fool when her sordid little affair with a murderer blows up in her face," Ascot advised.

"Look, I gotta go," McMurphy said ending the conversation.

McMurphy hung up and turned his attention to Danny McGinnis who was sitting on a chair in front of him surrounded by his two burly henchmen, Jonas and Grigor. The view from 30 stories up was spectacular and Danny was mesmerized as he could almost see the mouth of the Clyde off in the distance.

"Danny, are you with me here?" McMurphy asked.

"Yeah, I'm listenin'," Danny said smugly.

"How in the hell did you get pulled into homicide and interviewed by the lead profiler for Scotland Yard?"

"How d' y' know that?" Danny asked, sitting up straight in his chair.

"McGinnis, I own shares in Strathclyde you dumb shit. I know everything and everybody in this town," McMurphy stated belligerently.

Danny just sat there and stared defiantly at McMurphy.

"Danny, first of all, when you get pulled into Strathclyde it draws attention to me and I don't like attention … at least not that kind. Second, I don't pay you to be a hero, I pay you to eliminate problems. What were you thinking when you tried to kill MacLeod? These two guys told me you made them drive around in your fancy fuckin' car while you took pot shots at him and watched him escape. Have you lost your mind? This guy is a valuable asset you eejit. He's worth four million dollars to me alive and that's the way he stays until I have a talk with him. After that he's all yours and not before. Understood?" McMurphy chided.

"Yes sir," Danny replied doing his best to sound repentant.

"Now you can redeem yourself by getting MacLeod and my money back. If you don't, Dumb and Dumber here will be feeding you to the fishes—soon. No offense boys," McMurphy said glancing up at his two henchmen.

The two goons smiled as if they had been given a compliment.

"I'll get 'im if it's the last thing I do," Danny promised.

"If you don't, it *will* be the last thing you do. Capicé?" McMurphy threatened.

"Crystal clear boss."

"Word on the street is that MacLeod was seen at a pharmacy near Queen Street station, so I suggest you stake out the vicinity. You have until Friday to sanitize the situation," McMurphy stated.

McMurphy looked over at his henchmen.

"Now get him out of here," he said with a single wave of his hand.

Jonas and Grigor picked Danny up by the elbows. Danny flung them off, shaking himself indignantly.

"I can walk myself out. I'm not deid yet," Danny blurted angrily.

Danny swaggered out of McMurphy's office towards the entrance to the prestigious penthouse suite from which DM Enterprises ran its empire.

"Follow him and don't let him out of your sight," McMurphy ordered his thugs.

Danny walked to his Porsche Cayenne and stopped before getting in. He lit a cigarette and let the smoke curl up as the butt hung from his mouth. Glancing back towards the residential entrance to the building on St Vincent Street, he saw Jonas push open the door. His partner, Grigor was right behind him. The two 300 pound, over-developed Europeans made quite a comical sight as they lurched out onto the sidewalk.

"They really are stupid," Danny said loud enough for the two big men to hear as he watched them look around.

"Hey meat, I'm over here if yer followin' me," Danny taunted.

The two enormous enforcers stopped dead in their tracks.

"Fuckin' hawfwits," Danny yelled out as he flicked his butt towards them in contempt.

Danny jumped into his vehicle, starting it and slamming it into gear before they knew what to do. The high powered SUV laid two long strips of rubber along St Vincent Street as Danny accelerated away. He could see the two of them in his rearview mirror lumbering like giants towards their minivan. The tires of the Porsche screeched as Danny threw it around the corner at Elmbank Street. Pedestrians turned their heads as the unmistakable whine of twin turbos and roaring exhaust warned of an approaching maniac behind the wheel of a menacing looking super-SUV. Danny put the 520 horsepower Porsche through the gears, hitting almost 130 until he slammed the ceramic brakes hard in order to negotiate a right turn at Sauchiehall. Two pedestrians narrowly missed getting struck as the hurtling SUV sped down the busy street braking again to negotiate a left at Dalhousie where it accelerated until almost losing control turning left at Great Western Road. By the time Danny found the on-ramp to the M8 the minivan was nowhere in sight.

"And McMurphy thinks he's safe with those two morons?" Danny said laughing out loud.

Danny continued along the M8 until exiting at Springburn Road. He knew McMurphy didn't make idle threats and he was not going to be the next body floating down the Clyde if he had his way.

Chapter 24

Ian walked fast as the sun set on an overcast evening in Glasgow. The gathering clouds looked ominous and the smell of the air foretold of the approach of a summer rainstorm. MacLeod had left his flat just once since returning wounded from Edinburgh on the previous Friday. The items on the pizza joint menu downstairs had sustained him for the past seven days while he recovered from the bullet wound above his right hip.

The muscles in his side ached with each step he took and the semi clotted injury still oozed lymph as the wound slowly granulated a scab beneath a gauze bandage. The street was filled with people dashing home from work and Ian was careful not to collide with anyone so as not to open up his wound.

Ian had not ventured outside during the day but since it was almost dark he felt as if he blended into the crowd as he walked down Sauchiehall Street, now lit up with street lights and neon signs. McMurphy's goons, the two Europeans were walking in the opposite direction across the street when they spotted MacLeod.

"Hey look … it's MacLeod," Jonas said excitedly.

"Yah, it's him for sure," Jonas' partner Grigor confirmed.

"We need to take him by surprise," Jonas said.

The two big enforcers had little time to put their plan in motion as Ian was less than a street away. They dashed across the street onto the busy patio of a small coffee shop where people were sitting at tables enjoying their beverages on the cool summer evening. A few of the patrons looked up as the humongous men arrived running full tilt almost crashing into a table of young locals.

"Slow down lads, they'll no' be outa lattes anytime soon," a severe looking Scottish lad in his mid-twenties said mockingly.

Those at his table and a few others sitting nearby laughed.

"Watch your beak, bitch," Jonas said dismissively, more interested in his quarry than the smartass sitting at the table.

The young man, Angus, who had made the humorous comment took offense to the big man's insult and stood up as if to defend his honor. Jonas and Grigor ignored him and stood in wait for Ian to appear around the corner where the treed walkway met the storefront of the coffee shop.

"Angus, forget about it. Those dudes look big and freakin' mean," said one of Angus' mates at the table.

As Ian walked past the corner of the coffee shop, Jonas grabbed him around his arms and torso, immobilizing him. MacLeod struggled in vain, outmuscled by the big enforcer.

"Hey y' fuckin' shitebag," young Angus MacPherson shouted.

Grigor turned towards Angus and laughed at the tall wiry scot whose stern angular face was contorted in a mounting rage.

"What's so funny, y' big fuckin' rhino," Angus yelled fearlessly.

An instant later he delivered a single vicious kick to the balls of the imprudent Ukrainian who dropped to the ground in pain. The rest of Angus' pals sitting at the table jumped into the melee and began to pummel Grigor who had assumed a fetal position both in reaction to the groin kick and to protect himself from the swarm.

Taken by surprise at the feisty group of Scots, Jonas looked on as he held Ian who was in no shape to resist. While the rest of his pals surrounded the humiliated and injured Grigor, Angus confronted the big German.

"Let 'im go, skinhead," Angus demanded.

Skinny Angus, as tough as he might have been, looked like a mouse threatening an elephant.

The big German had no choice but to release his grasp on Ian in order to grab his weapon and fend off an impending attack from the group who had taken down his partner. Ian fled down the street as Jonas pointed his weapon at Angus. MacPherson's pals and onlookers dispersed at the sight of the weapon but Angus crossed his arms and stood his ground.

"Now back off," Jonas exclaimed, threateningly.

Jonas used his free hand to get Grigor to his feet. Angus remained defiant as the two big thugs backed away.

"That'll teach y' to fuck with the Scots y' numpty-heided muppets," Angus MacPherson shrieked as Grigor and Jonas disappeared down the street.

* * * * *

MacLeod doubled back to his flat knowing he was in deep trouble having been spotted by McMurphy's henchmen. He stopped at the payphone and pulled out a business card Kyla had given to him bearing both her business and mobile phone numbers. He picked up the receiver, inserted some coins and dialed the mobile number.

"Kyla Fraser speaking," Ian heard her answer over the hands-free phone in her car.

"Kyla, it's Ian."

"Ian, where are you? Are you alright?" she asked.

"Aye, I'm in Glasgow and OK. I don't have much time. I need to tell you the truth about the job I took—," Ian started before Kyla interrupted.

"Ian, they think you killed Mills, but I know you didn't."

"Kyla, I'm in big trouble. I stole $4 million dollars from the mob."

"Ian, why?" Kyla asked as her mouth dropped open and her eyes widened.

"There's no time to explain. I was shot by a hit man named Danny McGinnis."

"Omigod, I just interviewed McGinnis at Strathclyde," Kyla replied clearly upset at Ian's disclosure.

"Look, I need your help or I'm a deid man," Ian said anxiously.

Kyla was silent for a moment.

"I know someone who might help us. Stay put and let me call you back at this number," Kyla instructed.

"Fine, but hurry. McMurphy's goons are looking for me as we speak."

Ian hung up the receiver and stood vigilant inside the phone booth. The passersby on the street all looked suspicious to MacLeod and he was becoming more paranoid with each passing second.

Kyla speed dialed a call to her friend Nigel Cambridge. The phone rang several times before there was an answer.

"Kyla, to what do I owe the pleasure?"

"Nigel, forgive me but I'll have to dispense with the niceties. I need your help. My good friend has been wrongly accused of murder and is being hunted down by the Glaswegian mob for stealing their money. He's in Glasgow and says they are in hot pursuit," Kyla said hurriedly as she drove along the M8 from the airport.

Cambridge raised his eyebrows before responding.

"Good friend? How in the world did a Scotland Yard profiler get involved with such an unsavory scoundrel? Who is he to you, Kyla?"

Kyla slammed her hands on the steering wheel.

"Nigel, please don't go there. Just trust me... he's in over his head for reasons that escape me at the moment, but you have to believe me Nigel, he's innocent. Can you help?" Kyla asked pleadingly.

Cambridge rolled his eyes and sighed.

"Alright. I'm in Crewe at the moment, leaving in the morning. Under the circumstances, I'll meet your ... friend on the platform at Crewe train station. He needs to get himself on the next—," Nigel started.

As he sat on the end of the bed of his hotel room he glanced at his Oyster Perpetual Rolex watch.

"... make that the last train out of Glasgow tonight. I can't promise anything more than riding with him as far as my home in Salisbury, but that will at least get him off the beaten path and out of the mob's dragnet. He'll have to fend for himself after that. Tell him to keep his head down."

"Alright Nigel, I'll pass that on to him. His name is Ian MacLeod. He's a tall, good looking red headed lad," Kyla replied.

"Kyla, my dear, I suggest you get him moving and tell him to make himself scarce in Crewe as I can't meet him before 6 AM. I'm sure we'll have a lot to talk about later," Nigel said, ending the conversation.

Kyla dialed MacLeod who picked up the phone on the first ring.

"Hello?" MacLeod answered peering nervously onto the now rain-soaked street.

"Ian, listen carefully. I have contacted an associate by the name of Nigel Cambridge. He's a lawyer who consults with Metro on occasion. He's a former MI5 operative and he knows his way around having worked closely with SOCA in their pursuit of mob activities. Nigel's in Crewe at the moment on a case and he can't hook up before 6:00 tomorrow morning. He's willing to help you get as far as Salisbury where he lives. We'll decide what to do next once you get there."

"What is SOCA? And why would he help me?"

"Serious Organized Crime Agency, but never mind that now. Get on board the 11:30 overnight London express and be sure to get off at Crewe," Kyla directed.

"Kyla … thanks so much," Ian said, the stress in his voice palpable.

"Remember, his name is Nigel Cambridge. He's a tall, slim gentleman with a close-cropped mustache and a distinguished bearing. You won't miss him. He said to stay off the streets; McMurphy's men will be everywhere. I'll be in touch through Nigel. Godspeed Ian."

"I better go," Ian said before hanging up the phone.

MacLeod exited the booth and broke into a full sprint towards his flat.

Chapter 25

A torrent of rain driven by strong winds swept over Gordon Street, sending rivulets of water rushing along the curb. Suddenly a blast of wind and water made people headed for Glasgow Central Station turn their backs against the onslaught. The tires of a lone taxi cut two ribbons through the flooded pavement before finding shelter from the rain under the portico. The rear door of the cab opened and a lone figure emerged.

Grigor and Jonas had been ordered by Douglas McMurphy to head over to Glasgow Central. They had no sooner arrived when Grigor pointed out the window at the figure running toward the station entrance.

"Hey, that looks like MacLeod," Grigor said excitedly.

"Yah," Jonas agreed.

Jonas picked up his mobile phone and pressed a speed dial, putting his phone to his ear.

"Yeah, what's up?" McMurphy answered.

"I think we saw him, going into station," Jonas said calmly.

"OK. No point in making a scene. There's only one last train at this hour, the London overnight express with limited stops. We'll flush 'im out at Preston. You two pay a visit to McGinnis. If he's not home he'll be at his friend James Ot's place. Give 'im my best," McMurphy stated.

Jonas ended the call and started the car before pulling away.

It was exactly 11:30 PM as MacLeod slipped through the doors of the Virgin Star. A few moments later the doors sealed and the train lurched forward. Ian felt a flood of relief as coach number four passed the south entrance of Glasgow Central Station on its way to London.

Ian was agitated and kept looking around nervously as the train passed through the suburbs south of the city center. Kyla's warning about McMurphy's dragnet put Ian on high alert.

He found a seat and did his best to relax for the next hour or so until he felt the train slowing and the lights of the stop at Preston appeared in the distance. A minute later the train came to a full stop and within a few seconds Ian noticed that there were two men who seemed to be looking around suspiciously in the coach ahead of his. Alarmed he got up and headed towards the rear of the train not stopping to look back, walking the length of all eleven coaches until he came to the toilet in first class.

MacLeod opened the door and entered the toilet.

The sound of unintelligible voices could be heard approaching the rear of the coach.

Ian looked around in a panic and noticed that there was an access panel in the ceiling. He reached up, unlatched and removed the panel, placing it up against the wall. Straining for a split second Ian tried to ascertain the whereabouts of his pursuers.

"There, the toilet. It's the only place he can be," Ian heard a barely audible voice say.

Ian had just seconds to hide in the train's air conditioning duct. Standing on the change table, he placed one foot on the handicap grip that returned into the wall and then launched himself up into the opening, shimmying his body as far as he could into the duct space hoping the background mechanical noise would mask his stirring. He began to feel claustrophobic.

"It's not locked. Knock on the door," a baritone English voice uttered.

"No answer. What d' ya think?" an Irishman asked.

"Open it and take a look see," the Englishman instructed.

With his arms outstretched Ian could see his watch. The green phosphorescence on the dial showed it was 12:47 AM.

Ian heard the automatic toilet door open and footsteps enter the tiny space. The whooshing sound of his labored breathing seemed to amplify and echo inside the metal duct. Sweat began to trickle down his brow. Ian focused on controlling his urge to panic as he heard the sound of probing hands picking up the access door that was propped up against the toilet wall. Ian braced himself for the worst. Then another voice piped in.

"Gentlemen, we're now way overtime on this stop. I have to release the train or they'll start asking questions."

Ian surmised that the voice was that of the conductor. His heart was beating furiously.

"OK. He's not here. Looks like he may have given us the slip and gotten off somehow," the Irishman advised.

Ian heard the door to the toilet close and less than a minute later the train began to move. Ian couldn't wait any longer as the soreness of his still tender flesh wound was unbearable in the cramped position he had assumed. Disoriented by the centrifugal force exerted on his body as the train rounded a corner, Ian began to back himself out of the air duct. His legs were dangling from the opening when he heard the door to the toilet open.

"Excuse me," an elderly female voice said in a surprised tone.

"So sorry, repair underway, I won't be but a moment," Ian answered back, his voice echoing from inside the duct.

"My good man, do you not know to lock the loo when you use it," the woman answered indignantly as she left the toilet and closed the door.

Ian slid down and dusted himself off as he looked in the mirror. He knew that every police site served by the UK criminal intelligence network, every airport, train station, bus depot and seaport in the UK would be onto him by now.

As Ian opened the door he was met by the same prim and proper English woman who had scolded him just moments before. She drew back as Ian emerged from the toilet.

"A slight problem with the exhaust fan. I'll finish up later," sweat soaked Ian MacLeod quipped with a wink as he deftly slid by.

Chapter 26

It was almost dark as Jonas and Grigor watched from a distance as James Ot pulled up to his house in the northern outskirts of Glasgow.

"We've got the right house," Jonas advised.

Waiting a few minutes, the two men crept silently on the other side of a row of shrubs that lined the property. They pushed their huge bodies between two large Junipers and sidled up beneath the parapet wall at the edge of the slightly elevated porch. Grigor moved to the edge of the stair that led two steps up to the porch floor. Jonas waited silently for a few moments before signaling to his partner to move in. On cue, Grigor silently ran up to the door just as the lights went out inside the single story bungalow.

"The lights just went out," Grigor whispered to Jonas who remained behind the porch wall.

"OK, they know we are here."

"We go in now?" Grigor asked.

"Yah, you take a run at the door and I back you up," Jonas advised.

Grigor stepped back a few paces and then launched his 300 pound hulk against the door easily tearing the lock out from the jamb and flinging the door open as he hurtled inside falling onto the floor with a huge thud.

A volley of shots rang out.

The slugs burst through the partially open door as well as through the air at the empty house across the street. One of them found its mark tearing into human flesh as Grigor screamed in agony from a bullet wound to his buttocks. Jonas had counted four shots and did not hear the telltale sound of reloading so he knew that Danny's .357 had just three bullets left. He pulled out his Glock 17 and armed it. His orders were clear that McGinnis was to be beaten to death so Jonas had to be careful not to kill McGinnis before they captured him.

"You'll never take me alive y' fuckin' hawfwits," Danny's voice dared.

Jonas figured that if Danny was in the room he would be able to see the outline of Grigor and he would have finished him off by now. He surmised that Danny was hiding behind a wall. He remained silent holding his gun in his right hand and the one kilogram bat in the other. He aimed his Glock at the large picture window to the left of the front door and fired two rounds sending shards of glass in all directions. Immediately he heard three more shots in rapid succession. After holstering his gun he burst into the house leaping over Grigor who was moaning in pain.

The sound of a gun magazine being ejected came from behind the wall to Jonas' left so he lifted the bat and swung as he rounded the corner. The bat made a sickening thud as it connected with James' left shoulder breaking the bone just below the head of the humerus. He screamed and dropped like a stone to his knees. McGinnis slammed in another 7 round magazine and raised the .357 Magnum toward Jonas just as the bat came down and knocked it to the floor breaking Danny's right forearm. Jonas swung again, this time low, breaking his right knee cap. He then calmly reached out and switched on a light illuminating a pathetic looking and agonized Danny McGinnis writhing on the floor. The pistol had been flung several feet away. James Ot looked terrified as he stood frozen behind Danny, who was holding his right arm desperately looking for a way out. The incapacitated Danny McGinnis grimaced as Jonas set his bat on the counter and reached down to pick up the gun from the floor. Danny pushed himself on his backside towards the door. Confident that McGinnis was no longer a threat, Jonas looked over at Grigor, his blood soaked partner, now sitting up on his unwounded butt cheek.

"You OK Grigor?" Jonas asked.

"Yah, yah, I'm OK."

"Get yourself to the minivan and wait for me," Jonas instructed as he picked up a roll of paper towel off the counter and threw it at him.

He turned and pointed the pistol directly at James' head and fired it. James' head exploded in a spray of flesh, bone, brains and blood onto the kitchen floor. Jonas tossed the gun aside and looked at Danny McGinnis who had not flinched at the gore he had just witnessed.

"Now Danny, I have my orders, which you will no doubt understand. Sorry pal," Jonas said as he picked up his bat from the counter where he had laid it down.

"Yer a halfwit German mother—"

Danny never had a chance to finish his insult as the first bat swing slammed into his left shoulder with crushing force, pulverizing the bone. Danny screamed in agony as another blow came to his left thigh, then another to the mid-calf portion of his right leg. Danny lay on the floor powerless, looking up at his assailant in shock. Jonas continued pummeling Danny as instructed, from the bottom up. Danny had stopped screaming and now stared blankly at the ceiling. Jonas walked over to the kitchen sink and poured a large pot of cold water, walking back to Danny.

"Sorry pal, but McMurphy said to keep you awake," Jonas said as he threw the water onto Danny's face. Danny moaned, coming to in a pool of diluted blood that was now flowing freely over the linoleum floor.

Jonas continued the brutal beating until McGinnis was still with his head turned to one side barely breathing. Jonas lined up one final blow to the back of Danny's skull and then threw the bat aside, stripped off the prophylactic gloves and pulled out his mobile phone. Leaning over the body Jonas snapped a single picture of Danny's death mask and immediately sent it to Douglas McMurphy.

"Goodbye my friend," Jonas said as he picked up the bat and the blood stained gloves walking towards his wounded partner who had made his way back to the minivan.

Jonas dropped the mobile phone on the concrete sidewalk. He retrieved a small sledgehammer from his vehicle, walked back, and with a single swing he crushed the phone into a thousand pieces. Calmly he walked over to the minivan and placed the sledgehammer into the cargo area and pulled out a broom and dustpan. Jonas walked back over to the sidewalk and swept up the remnants of the device onto the dustpan and carried it over to the minivan placing the contents into a plastic Ziploc bag, zipping it shut. He threw the bag, broom and dustpan back into the cargo area and closed the rear hatch.

Unbeknownst to Jonas or Grigor, Danny McGinnis' girlfriend Heather Gordon was cringing in the closet of James' spare bedroom, frozen in fear. She had heard the shot that killed James Ot and the blood curdling sounds of the lengthy beating of one of the most notorious criminals ever to have walked the streets of Glasgow. Danny McGinnis was dead.

Chapter 27

Ian's senses were heightened as he walked toward the front of the train, his bag in his hand. Walking through several coaches Ian was in the second from the lead coach when he saw a man staring straight at him. He was gaunt and harmless looking with beady eyes and a five o'clock shadow. As soon as the man saw Ian, he averted his eyes but continued to glance up several times as if trying to confirm Ian's identity. Just as he came into range Ian heard the telltale double click of a picture being taken from an iPhone. Ian looked down and saw the device held in the man's palm pointed towards the aisleway. MacLeod continued until he entered the lead coach where he spotted two seats right at the bulkhead. After making sure that they were not reserved he sat down and got himself ready to make a dash for the exit when the train stopped at Crewe, about forty-five minutes ahead.

MacLeod sat silently for the next half hour watching the lights of farmhouses that dotted the English countryside through the window of the fast moving train. The train began to slow as it approached the station stop at Crewe. As the station came into view the train lurched to a halt and almost immediately the doors opened. It was just past 3:00 AM as Ian leapt from his seat and scrambled through the open doors onto the platform, walking quickly away from the train.

MacLeod surmised that the man with the beady eyes had forwarded the pictures he had taken to McMurphy as confirmation that Ian was still on the train. No doubt there would be an army of SOCKS henchmen waiting on the platform when the train arrived at Euston Station at 6:15 AM.

* * * * *

It was 5:57 AM as Ian waited out of sight in an alcove off the main platform. Approaching was the man that Kyla had described to him the day before on the phone. As the man walked by, Ian stepped out and silently trailed him closing the distance quickly. The man suddenly spun around and stopped dead in front of Ian. He looked at MacLeod for a few moments as if he were sizing him up. Taken off guard, Ian was flustered, surprised that the man he tried to follow without being noticed had detected him.

"Mr. Cambridge?"

The man looked sternly at Ian.

"When you follow someone, always stay in the flank, otherwise you make it rather obvious; and yes, I am Nigel Cambridge," the man said as he looked around cautiously.

"Am I glad to see you," Ian stated breathlessly.

"There'll be time enough for introductions once we're on our way," Cambridge said motioning to a nearby ticket counter.

Ian followed Cambridge as he walked up to a Virgin service counter.

"How can I be of assistance sir?" the female ticket agent asked.

"Two tickets through to Salisbury please," Cambridge replied.

"No problem. You'll be on the 7:01 to Birmingham New Street, then you'll disembark and board the 8:12 Cross Country to Bristol Temple Meads, disembarking and boarding a train to your destination in Salisbury via Southwest arriving at 11:10 PM," the ticket agent advised.

"Yes, yes, that will be fine," Nigel noted as he glanced at the time on his watch.

Ian stood right behind Cambridge looking around nervously.

"Here are your tickets. Your train will depart on the adjacent platform. Thank you for choosing Virgin."

As they walked over to the platform where the 7:01 would arrive Nigel spoke, looking straight ahead.

"Once they get ahold of the video from that CCTV camera over there, they'll have a make on me. Unfortunately I have a very familiar face amongst law enforcement and the mob so they may put two and two together," Nigel remarked.

"What should we do then?" Ian asked.

Nigel stopped for a moment and turned towards Ian, pointing at a recess off to the side of the main station area.

"Follow me," Nigel instructed.

They walked over and stopped inside the alcove.

"It's important as a precautionary measure that we board the train separately," Nigel stated.

"Do you really think they'll link us together?" Ian asked.

"Only if we make it obvious. They're very resourceful and I understand there is a lot at stake."

Ian looked at Nigel blankly.

"The money," Nigel said raising his eyebrows and gesturing with open palms.

"What do you mean?" came Ian's response.

"Kyla told me that you have a sizable sum of the mob's money."

Ian looked intently at Cambridge for a moment.

"Well, stealing the money was an act of opportunity, I suppose. I was told that the mob used Swiss bank accounts and when I became aware of their intention to frame me for the Mills murder I decided to take things into my own hands. I duped a guy named Crawford into giving me the banking details on the account he and his sketchy partner were using to siphon off monies from a big construction project in Edinburgh. I got him to certify a check that should have stayed in his partner's Swiss account but I transferred the money to the account RIA set up for my fees," Ian explained.

"How very clever of you. I'm sure Douglas McMurphy was not impressed," Nigel acknowledged.

MacLeod raised his eyebrows in surprise.

"I know who runs SOCKS," Nigel continued.

"I almost got whacked by their hit man, Danny McGinnis," Ian mentioned with a sigh.

"They'll stop at nothing," Nigel said glancing over at Ian.

Nigel cocked his head and was lost in thought for a few moments before he spoke again.

"I'll ride with you as far as Salisbury."

"Then what?" Ian asked.

"I hate to say it but given the story you have told me, your prospects are not very favorable," Nigel replied.

"That's comforting," Ian replied sarcastically.

"Cheer up! You'd be dead already if it wasn't for Kyla. The train's about to arrive, so let's go," Nigel said commandingly.

* * * * *

It was 9:15 when the pair stepped off of the Cross Country at Bristol Temple Meads. Nigel and Ian were walking toward their next connection when they were spotted by the British Transport Police.

"124 to dispatch," Special Constable Arnie Smith radioed.

"Dispatch, 124 go ahead," the voice crackled over Smith's walkie-talkie.

"I've got a positive ID on the wanted felon. He's with a middle aged male."

"124, track them but do not engage. Repeat, do not engage. Suspect may be armed and dangerous," the dispatcher advised.

"Roger that," Smith responded as he walked towards the pair.

Nigel spotted the constable immediately and turned to Ian whispering a barely audible command.

"Listen closely. The police have spotted you. Go into the toilet to your right. I'll distract the constable. Count to 60 and then barrel out full tilt and run towards the ferry landing not a minute from that exit over there. Take the ferry until it stops and then flag a taxi to the Salisbury A bus station. I'll let Kyla know that's where you'll be," Nigel said before turning to the constable who was standing watch over his target.

Ian ducked into the toilet as Nigel beckoned the officer, who appeared discombobulated at being spotted.

"Is there anything I can help you with?" Nigel asked.

"Your friend, what's 'is name?" Smith asked officiously.

"Who?" Nigel responded.

"The bloke who just went into the toilet," Smith said becoming annoyed.

Nigel suddenly gripped his chest and fell to the floor.

"I think I'm having a heart attack, please help me," Nigel groaned.

Smith looked distraught as he knelt down at Nigel's side. Ian opened the door to the toilet peeking out to see Nigel lying on the floor. After standing still for a moment Ian launched into a sprint toward the exit door on the other side of the platform area, quickly disappearing outside.

Smith looked up just in time to notice MacLeod's escape. Immediately he radioed dispatch.

"124 to dispatch."

"Dispatch, 124 go ahead."

"The subject has escaped."

"Confirm subject has escaped?"

"Affirmative."

"Confirm you are giving chase?"

"Negative. Am attending medical distress in other subject older male."

"Copy that. Backup should be on site momentarily."

Ian jumped aboard the waiting foot ferry and paid his fare. His heart was beating wildly as he waited for the ferry to get underway. Finally the little watercraft disembarked along the scenic River Avon.

A swarm of British Transport Police arrived to see Constable Smith attending to a man in apparent medical distress.

"What's the problem Smith?" his superior officer Corporal Jennings asked.

"He seems to have had a heart attack. I've called the medics," Smith responded.

Nigel sat up and looked around at the crowd that had formed around him.

"I seem to be feeling much better now. A touch of indigestion I reckon," Nigel said doing his best to appear serious as he got up and dusted himself off.

"Is this the man who was with the suspect?" Jennings asked.

"Yes sir."

"Sir, may I see your identification please?" Jennings asked.

"By all means. So sorry for all the commotion," Nigel said, smiling at the crowd.

Jennings ignored Nigel's comment and studied his identification.

"What is your relationship with Ian MacLeod sir?" Jennings asked.

"Never heard of the man," Nigel answered.

"You were seen with him by Corporal Smith here," Jennings countered.

"The young corporal is mistaken. I don't know what your interest is in this MacLennan fellow but he's of no interest to me. Now if you don't mind I'd like to be on my way before I miss my train," Nigel advised.

"His name is MacLeod and he's wanted on suspicion of murder. We'd like to ask you a few questions down at headquarters if you don't mind?" Jennings asked.

"I certainly do mind. You have no reasonable suspicion that would give you the right to detain me. Your constable mistakenly thought I was with someone. Do you see anyone else here? Unless you can show me evidence that I was aiding and abetting a criminal then I suggest you get out of my way," Nigel said as he handed Jennings his business card.

Jennings studied Cambridge's business card for a few moments before turning to Smith.

"You obviously were mistaken Smith. Mr. Cambridge you are free to go. My apologies and I hope you are feeling better," Jennings said skeptically.

"Thank you and good day," Nigel said as he walked towards his waiting train.

Although Jennings had no reasonable grounds on which to hold Cambridge, he suspected he was lying.

"You two follow him while I check the CCTV footage to corroborate either Smith's or Mr. Cambridge's story," Jennings instructed two of the other constables.

Nigel glanced behind him and as expected, he was being tailed. At the other end of the train station Nigel noticed a car rental booth and he proceeded directly to it. Once he reached the booth he stood in line waiting for a service agent as the two police officers watched from a distance. After several minutes Nigel was the next customer and approached the counter.

"I would like to rent a car and I want to pick it up at Trowbridge in about an hour," Nigel stated.

"Of course sir. What would be your pleasure?" the agent asked.

"I'd like something in an SUV," Nigel advised.

"Let me see what they have available," the service agent said as he looked at his computer screen.

Nigel looked at his watch. He had only a few minutes to catch his train to Salisbury.

"Sir, we have a 2009 Range Rover available, but it's quite expensive," the service agent advised.

"I'll take it. Please ask them to have it ready when I arrive in Trowbridge. Would you be so kind as to pick me up at the train station?" Nigel asked.

"Of course. We'd be happy to accommodate you sir," the agent said agreeably.

A few minutes later Nigel walked toward the platform and noticed that his train was about to depart so he broke into a run as did the two policemen tailing him. Nigel boarded the Southwest to Salisbury a few moments before it departed at 9:10.

"116 to dispatch," one of the constables radioed.

"Dispatch, 116 go ahead."

"Subject just boarded the train to Salisbury."

"Copy that 116," said the dispatcher.

The dispatcher then posted a notice for all police authorities to be on the lookout for Nigel Cambridge's whereabouts and travel.

Ian spent 25 anxious minutes going from dock to dock until he reached The Cottage Ferry Landing. He leapt from the boat as it was mooring and spotted a waiting cab, running towards it.

"Can you take me to Salisbury?" Ian asked the cab driver as he leaned through the open passenger window.

"Sure. It'll cost y'," the driver said in an East Londoner's accent.

Ian jumped into the cab and a few minutes later as they passed by the train station he wondered how Nigel was faring.

Thirty minutes passed before the Southwest arrived at Trowbridge and Nigel disembarked. He looked around and spotted the Enterprise driver who would take him to his waiting rental car. Nigel scanned the platform and immediately noticed the telltale garb and obvious demeanor of waiting plainclothes police agents. He glanced outside and saw the insignia of the Wiltshire Police inscribed on the door of a late model Vauxhall Vectra.

After fifteen minutes Nigel pulled out of the Trowbridge Enterprise car lot onto County Way. Nigel leisurely drove the first few miles along West Ashton Road turning right onto the A350. He watched closely as the two officers in the police cruiser behind him kept their distance not wanting to blow their cover.

Nigel knew that there were many dirt access roads that crisscrossed the open fields east of Westbury a few miles up the road. He looked behind him as he passed through Westbury and noticed that the single cruiser had been joined by another one—a rally tuned Mitsubishi EVO.

As Bratton Road approached Nigel maintained his speed with the two police vehicles following well behind. At the last second, Nigel signaled and then cranked on the steering wheel nearly rolling the Range Rover in a sudden right turn. He continued down Bratton Road. At Newtown Road Nigel turned right again past the gravel pit until he reached the end of Long River Road where he came to a stop. The two police vehicles stopped at the corner and maintained surveillance.

"54 to dispatch," the officer in the EVO said into the microphone.

"Dispatch, go ahead."

"Vehicle has come to a stop."

"Tail but do not apprehend."

"10-4."

Nigel looked in the rearview mirror and could see the police vehicles trying their best to stay out of sight. He picked up the hand held Garmin GPS that he had taken out of his bag at Trowbridge which had now picked up satellite reception. He selected home via direct which showed that it was 25 kilometers as the crow flies to his home in Woodford Valley. He wetted the suction cup on the back of the Garmin and secured it to the dash directly in front of him so he would be able to monitor his progress towards Woodford.

Nigel reached down and moved the terrain response controller on the full-time all wheel Range Rover to the 'grass' mode and then adjusted the suspension height. He put it in gear and then began to move slowly off road down into a drain swale that eventually led to a dirt trail that disappeared across the field all the way to the distant horizon.

Both police cars followed reaching the end of the paved road. The Vectra's front air dam almost ripped off as it negotiated the ditch between the paved road and the dirt trail. Nigel proceeded down the wheel rutted trail for a few minutes and then turned the wheel towards the open grass plain pushing the Rover's accelerator to the floor. The big SUV began to porpoise leaping into the air and then slamming back down with each dip and roll in the open grassy field. A long trail of choking dust streamed from the back of the Range Rover blinding the drivers of both police cars. The officer in the EVO darted off to Nigel's left to avoid his dust trail so he could maintain eye contact with the Range Rover. The Vectra was nowhere in sight, either bogged down or lost inside the thick dust that churned out from the Rover's big all-terrain tires.

Groves of trees passed by on Nigel's left and he could see that the high powered and nimble EVO was gaining on him with sirens blasting and lights flashing.

He looked at the speedometer. It read 60 miles per hour and the big SUV was being outdone by the lighter EVO. The two vehicles reached Shrewton Road at Chittern and the chase returned to the public roadways. Speeds reached in excess of 70 miles per hour as they passed through Shrewton. Nigel turned onto the B3083 knowing exactly where he had to lead the EVO. This was Nigel's back yard and he knew it well. The Rover left the road headed east traversing the open countryside once again.

'In for a penny, in for a pound," Nigel thought knowing the solemn consequences of his actions should he be apprehended for aiding and abetting a wanted felon.

Nigel surmised that the EC135 Police Eurocopters had no doubt been dispatched from London and would be intercepting him at any minute so he had to act fast. He glanced at the Garmin handheld on the dash. He spotted his target approximately two miles northeast—a geographic landmark consisting of a deep depression perhaps 75 feet wide and 100 feet long that was filled with runoff water. There was a thicket of trees approximately 300 feet beyond the depression. He turned slightly to the left to line up the landmark with the course that both vehicles were tracking at high speed. As they crossed a freshly plowed field, black dust could be seen for miles so Nigel had but moments to outmaneuver the EVO before they would be spotted by the police helicopters.

"There it is," Nigel said as he slowed down and allowed the EVO to come up alongside him.

The young police officer sitting in the passenger seat was motioning to Nigel to pull over. Instead of watching what was coming at him the EVO's driver had his eyes glued on the Range Rover. Both vehicles continued along the grassy field slamming into a line of hedges sending leaves and branches flying.

"Bye, bye," Nigel said calmly as the 5,400 pound Range Rover flew into the air across the dry streambed that led to the deep depression just to his left.

Landing hard on the Rover's front suspension on the other side of the streambed, Nigel noticed that the EVO was no longer in chase. He looked behind him and saw that it had nosed almost out of sight into a deep drop off that had been excavated by a farmer as an irrigation measure.

"I do hope the two lads are OK," Nigel said as he turned right towards the A303.

Nigel almost lost control as the tail of the Land Rover slid to the left eventually righting itself turning direction towards an opening in the thick woods barely wide enough for the big SUV to get through. Nigel breathed a sigh of relief as he got the Range Rover back onto the paved road.

Within ten minutes Nigel arrived home in Woodford. After pulling into the driveway he left the Range Rover running while he got out and opened the garage door. Nigel got into his small innocuous Renault, backing it out to make room for the Range Rover which would no doubt now be the focus of a police manhunt. Nigel drove the Renault to Salisbury Bus Station A to pick up Ian who was sitting on a bench outside looking impatient.

"Care for a lift?" Nigel said as Ian turned in surprise.

Ian quickly jumped into the passenger seat and they drove off.

"What are *you* doing here?" Ian asked.

"It seems I've been unwittingly foisted into your life threatening dilemma," Nigel responded calmly, glancing over at MacLeod.

Nigel recounted his cross country car chase as Ian sat spellbound at what he was hearing.

"Well, won't they be on your doorstep as soon as we arrive?" Ian asked anxiously.

"No, my official address is in London—my apartment—so they will go there first. They'll track me down in Woodford but it will take some time. I didn't do anything wrong other than break the speed limit at Shrewton. To my knowledge there are no speed limits off road so it's my word against the dim witted cops' who negligently nose-dived their police car into a water filled ditch. However, I'm sure Scotland Yard will be paying me a visit in the next day or two once they find my country address," Nigel explained.

They eventually arrived at Nigel's country home next to the Wheatsheaf Inn on The Ave in Lower Woodford.

Safe for the moment, Ian spent the evening filling Nigel in on the events of the past several weeks.

"I don't even know what day it is," Ian remarked.

"It's Saturday."

"Things have been so crazy since I took the bullet in my side," Ian stated.

"You've been silent on the issue until now," Nigel said, surprised.

"I was too busy trying to survive, in case you hadn't noticed."

"Well, let's take a look," Nigel replied.

Ian pulled back his shirt to expose the still open wound just above his hip bone.

"Oh my, aren't you a lucky man. Another inch deeper and you would be missing a kidney and perhaps even bled to death. That will heal quite nicely. We just need to keep it bandaged for a spell."

After Nigel treated the injury, the two of them shared several stiff drinks before Ian passed out, sleeping well for the first time since his violent encounter in Edinburgh a week earlier.

Chapter 28

"A marvelous view isn't it?" Douglas McMurphy asked his guest Alistair Ascot as they looked out over the panorama of Glasgow from his opulent offices high above St Vincent Street.

"Yes, it certainly is," Ascot agreed.

The two men sat for a moment sipping the 40 year old Highland Park single malt McMurphy had poured for them.

"Wonderful scotch as well," Ascot complimented.

"They say the Highland Park whiskies are the finest in the world. Pride o' the Orkney's for sure. Even the 12 year old is a cut above the rest," McMurphy said with pride as he looked over at his collection standing on a stainless steel liquor service in the corner.

"You live a good life Douglas … protect it."

"Yes I intend to," McMurphy replied.

"So what have you done with the Mills situation?" Ascot queried.

"I've already bought off the club operators so we can take all of the action now. Since we already control the streets and the drug trade I'm setting up a new front for the prostitution ring and the club owners will have no choice but to abandon their deals with Mills. Mills' single employee, his accountant, has been made an offer and she'll be working for me now. We'll be making all of the profits and SXZ will just dry up as if it never existed," McMurphy advised.

"And if the police investigation into his murder turned up unwanted evidence?"

"I'm not concerned in the least. All of the records pertaining to SXZ's operations were cleaned out and destroyed. There is nothing left as far as we know. Besides, Mills was smart enough to distance himself from his seedy underbelly so there are no connections to us Alistair," McMurphy responded.

"Good work Douglas."

"On another more important matter, we lost MacLeod's trail," McMurphy stated.

"I was wondering when you'd broach the subject," Ascot said passively.

There was a moment of suspense as Ascot sat up in the custom made Italian leather chair and looked over at McMurphy as he slouched behind the ultra-modern glass and chrome desk that adorned his office.

"MacLeod slipped through the dragnet in spite of your connections and my task force that should have flushed him out. The only thing we do know is that he's still in the country," McMurphy stated.

"Not good. Every day that he is on the loose is a threat to your organization, not to mention putting you personally under the scrutiny of the authorities. Need I also mention that RIA's reputation is at risk as we have exceeded ethical and professional boundaries by collaborating in the so called discipline that your brutal henchman McGinnis meted out so freely? Right now the culpability for Mills' death points directly at MacLeod and we need to keep it that way while Scotland Yard builds a case against him. For the moment the spotlight has been deflected away from SOCKS. We don't want a repeat of the debacle Dunsmuir orchestrated in Manchester. We've done our part, now you need to do yours. MacLeod must be found, notwithstanding whether you ever retrieve the four million dollars Douglas," Ascot advised.

"You're preachin' to the converted Alistair. I still don't know why you and Dunsmuir thought we needed to cover up the Mills hit, especially after the Manchester fiasco. Dunsmuir's judgment was to say the least bad. My people are always clinical and leave nothing for the scum to use against us. We should have left well enough alone."

"Hindsight is always 20/20 Douglas. Dunsmuir saw an opportunity that he felt was too good to pass up given MacLeod's history with Mills and his skill set. It's too late to second guess and besides Dunsmuir got his just reward for his errors. Now down to business. As your advisor I recommend that we extend the dragnet to find MacLeod."

"OK, how do you suggest we do *that*?" asked McMurphy.

"I can pull some strings that will tighten the noose around MacLeod's neck and you can use your insider contacts at Strathclyde," Ascot replied.

Alistair Ascot had managed to keep his close relationship with his client Douglas McMurphy a secret and maintain an appearance as one of the most respected and influential men in Great Britain.

"So, what actually happened that you let MacLeod slip through your fingers?" Ascot queried.

"I hate to admit it, but based on what my lads told me it appears that MacLeod evaded detection by hiding in an AC duct in one of the train's toilets," McMurphy responded sheepishly.

"For heaven's sake man, is he that smart? Or are your people that daft? He's made us look pretty foolish by uncovering Mills' dirty laundry and second guessing our plan to frame him. Then he answers back by cleverly stealing four million dollars with the click of a mouse, evading capture and very deftly sidestepping a legion of some of the nastiest thugs on the planet. Shameful really Douglas," Ascot admonished.

"I know. We've made an example of McGinnis and the scumbag club owner who helped Mills rip us off and I will be punishing those responsible for the latest blunder as well, believe me," McMurphy admitted in exasperation.

"That won't help us if MacLeod talks. He knows too much. You must find and kill him," Ascot directed.

"We will, if I have to put all of my resources on it Alistair," McMurphy promised.

"How in the hell could they miss finding him?" asked Ascot.

"They found an access panel leaning up against the wall in the toilet but didn't bother looking further," an embarrassed McMurphy admitted.

"Douglas, I'm deeply troubled by such incompetence. MacLeod's knowledge of RIA's connection to SOCKS could prove to be both our undoing," Ascot cautioned.

McMurphy remained silent.

"I've got to be off now. Keep me posted," Ascot said as he got up and headed to the big oak door of McMurphy's private office.

He stopped and turned toward McMurphy.

"Oh, by the way, did you ever deal with Janet McComb as planned?"

"Uh, no, not yet. It appears she has disappeared. No trace anywhere," McMurphy responded.

"She's dangerous Douglas. She knows everything about me and about the real nature of our consulting agreement," Ascot counseled.

"We are working full time on locating her."

"Douglas, now that Dunsmuir is gone, it would be best if the inside details of our business stayed just between you and I," Ascot said ending the conversation.

* * * * *

After seeing Ascot to the private elevator McMurphy picked up the phone and dialed his assistant Alison.

"Ali, get ahold of the twins and have them bring Detective Black in to see me please," McMurphy requested.

"Only half of them is available sir," Allison replied referring to Grigor's injury.

"Oh yeah, well get Jonas to track him down and bring him in. You've got Black's number right?" McMurphy asked.

"Sure do."

McMurphy swiveled around and looked off in the distance towards the estuary of the Clyde thinking about the situation MacLeod had created for them.

An hour or so later, Jonas showed up at McMurphy's door with Detective Black.

"Thanks Jonas. Close the door."

Jonas closed the door and the Detective walked into McMurphy's office.

"Black, have a seat," McMurphy said motioning to the chair in front of his desk.

Detective Black, a 20 year veteran of the Strathclyde police and a lead homicide investigator, took a seat across from McMurphy.

"CID Homicide is just about to release the details of the double murder that occurred the other night off Crosshill Road," Black stated.

"Any leads?" McMurphy asked.

"Aye, McGinnis' girlfriend apparently heard the whole thing. Your thugs weren't very thorough or discreet. They didn't look around before they beat him to a pulp. It was very messy. She was extremely traumatized, so she hasn't been able to make a formal statement as of yet."

"Get me her address. Pay off whoever y' need to, just get it," McMurphy urged.

"Right. One thing Douglas. The guy with the bullet wound in 'is ass needs to stay away from legitimate medical treatment. McGinnis' gun is in ballistics as we speak, and if the medical community comes forward with a slug, I won't be able to cover it up. As well, I've heard rumblings out of Edinburgh that they have slugs from a murder there as well. I hope it wasn't McGinnis' work."

"Mind yer fuckin' business Black. You get paid well enough. Just get me the address will y'."

Black remained stone faced unfazed by McMurphy's belligerent comment.

"Look I called you over today to do me a favor," McMurphy said as he walked over and set down the two crystal scotch glasses he and Ascot had used on the liquor service.

"Yeah, what's that?" asked Black.

"I need to get my hands on some CCTV video capture," McMurphy said as he walked back to his chair and sat down.

"Not that easy to do. I'll need to have cause to get the tapes released," Black said in a serious tone.

McMurphy opened a drawer and pulled out a wad of cash held in a thick rubber band.

"Here's cause," McMurphy said as he tossed the cash into Black's hands.

Black shuffled the wad.

"Yes, I think this will do just fine. What exactly do you want?" Black asked as he looked up at McMurphy.

"Word is that someone we're very interested in got off the 11:30 Glasgow to Euston train at Crewe. It was a big surprise to us and we want to know how he could have escaped a very tight dragnet," McMurphy explained.

"I'm sure you know that kind of video is unreliable, so the information will be of limited value," Black advised.

"Just get me the video Black," McMurphy replied.

"Alright, leave it with me. I'll be back with something for you to look at," Black stated.

"How soon?" asked McMurphy.

"Dunno, probably tonight," Black responded.

"I'll be here. Let me walk down with you," McMurphy said as Black got up to leave.

McMurphy's phone rang just as the elevator doors opened onto the main floor.

"Yeah," McMurphy answered curtly, as he waved goodbye to Black.

"It's Jimmy," a voice answered.

Jimmy, one of McMurphy's watchdogs on the street, had been staking out the fight club after another SOCK's street thug had reported seeing MacLeod a few weeks earlier speaking to Alex Yin. He had reported the sighting to McMurphy after a photograph of MacLeod had been circulated when the dragnet for his capture was set up.

"The Chinese guy you want to talk to is at the club as we speak."

"Alright, stay with him until I get there."

McMurphy ended the call and dialed a number.

"Hey Charlie, I want you and your tough guy pal Amilio to meet me at the fight place over by Holland and Sauchiehall."

McMurphy ended the call and walked through the cool air of a cloudy day in Glasgow, arriving to find Charlie and his associate Amilio waiting at the door. Charlie Campbell was a curly red headed native from Fort William, tough as nails and unforgiving in a fist fight. Amilio Carini was a short, dark haired Italian, whose family moved from Silicy when he was a teenager. He was one of the many enforcers on McMurphy's payroll and had a reputation that preceded him.

"What's up boss?" Charlie asked.

"You'll see. Just stay cool and let me do the talking. No weapons," McMurphy advised.

"OK boss, whatever you say," Charlie answered obediently.

The two enforcers followed Douglas McMurphy into the gym. McMurphy stopped and looked around until Tommy Stewart, the owner spotted McMurphy's familiar face and walked over.

"Mr. McMurphy. How can I be of assistance?" Stewart asked.

"I'm looking for a Chinese guy," McMurphy replied.

"Chinese guy you say. Well, we have more than one Asian member, but you might be referring to Alex Yin," Stewart stated.

"Is he around?" McMurphy asked.

"As a matter of fact he is. He's in the showers I believe," Stewart responded agreeably not wanting any trouble.

"Thanks," McMurphy said as he walked toward the change rooms.

McMurphy pushed open the door to the sight of three men in various stages of undress.

"Get lost," McMurphy said to the men.

The big Scot, Fraser McAllister, turned his massive head, raising his eyebrows, as he stood naked at his locker.

"Who the fuck are y' talkin' to asshole," McAllister said challenging McMurphy's demand.

"Don't be a wise guy meathead. Just get out," McMurphy said in a measured tone.

McAllister puffed out his massive chest and set his jaw defensively, his muscular body glistening with water droplets and his short hair still dripping wet from the shower he had just stepped out of.

"Get stuffed," McAllister said ignoring McMurphy and rummaging through his locker.

Douglas McMurphy held out his hand to stop his two henchmen who moved toward McAllister in defense of their boss.

"Are you a tough guy?" McMurphy asked McAllister.

"Tougher than you are dad," McAllister said disrespectfully before turning and confronting McMurphy.

"Oh really?" McMurphy said as he cocked back his head and raised his bushy eyebrows. McMurphy grinned, putting McAllister off guard. Fraser McAllister was standing with his feet planted firmly on the tiled floor, his legs slightly bent and spread apart as if preparing for a fight. His brawny arms hung by his side as he welcomed McMurphy to make the first move by motioning with his fingers.

"Show me what y' got gramps," McAllister taunted.

With the dexterity and reflexes of a man twenty years younger, in a lightning fast move McMurphy kicked McAllister viciously in the balls with his expensive Italian leather pointers nearly tearing into the flesh of his scrotum. As McAllister keeled over in pain, he threw another violent kick to the middle of his face, breaking his nose and sending him reeling.

"Y' broke my fuckin' nose," McAllister yelled holding his hands to his face.

"Now get the fuck out before I kill y'," Douglas McMurphy said sneering.

The two other men quickly grabbed the naked and humiliated Fraser McAllister by the arms and threw him through the doors to the main gym. A few seconds later Tommy Stewart came crashing through the doors.

"What the *hell* are you lads up to?" Stewart asked as Amilio and Charlie moved towards him.

Amilio and Charlie grabbed Tommy by the arms and escorted him back out into the main gym area. Tommy knew better than to resist.

Alex Yin had heard McAllister's angry voice and had positioned himself to be able to see the escalating confrontation reflected in one of the dressing room mirrors. Expecting the worst, he hastily put on his street clothes in anticipation of trouble. Just as he heard Stewart being escorted through the doors, Alex grabbed his bag and attempted to walk out of the change room. He appeared from behind a row of lockers and was met face to face by Douglas McMurphy.

"Are you Alex Yin?" McMurphy asked.

"Who is asking?" responded Alex calmly.

"I am," McMurphy stated staring at Alex coldly.

"And you are?"

"Your worst fuckin' nightmare if you're not careful," McMurphy warned.

Alex recognized Douglas McMurphy.

"OK, so what if I was Alex Yin?"

"Then we have business to discuss," McMurphy stated.

"Alright, talk," Alex said staying as unruffled as the man who was confronting him.

"I was hoping that would be your job Alex," McMurphy said standing his ground.

"How so?" Alex queried.

"Do you know Ian MacLeod?" McMurphy asked point blank.

Alex noticed how edgy the two enforcers standing behind McMurphy were getting.

"I barely know him. He happened to stop by awhile back. Hadn't seen him for like 10 years," Alex replied.

"Where is he?" McMurphy asked.

Alex braced. The two men behind seemed ready to pounce and Alex knew they were packing from the bulges in their jackets.

"I have no idea," Alex said remaining unflustered.

"No? Well maybe my two guys here can convince you to remember," McMurphy threatened.

Alex looked at the exit from the change room and tried to imagine how he could get through the three thugs who were blocking the door. McMurphy motioned to Charlie and Amilio and they moved toward Alex. Alex raised his arm, palm out in a halting gesture.

"Stop!" Alex commanded.

It was as if the two enforcers had hit a brick wall. They stood wide eyed for an instant.

In a lightening move, Alex launched into a 360 leg kick torqueing Charlie's head and slamming his body into Amilio knocking both men to the ground. McMurphy was stunned at the deft move and stepped back as Alex landed and instantaneously kicked McMurphy in the midsection so hard the big man fell on his rear end grimacing in pain and gasping for air. The two thugs recovered and were coming at Alex from behind as both of Alex's elbows met their attack with vicious force breaking Amilio's nose on contact and nearly blinding Charlie. As Charlie Campbell lost his balance and fell backwards, the feared Amilio Carini yelled out in pain as blood spilled from his nose.

Alex ran for the door hurtling into the main gym area and then out onto the sidewalk where he disappeared down Holland Street.

The three men all looked at each other, dazed, as they attempted to compose themselves.

"That was pathetic you pussies. What d' y' call *that*?" McMurphy asked as he caught his breath.

"Boss, shall we go after him?" Charlie asked, his face red with shame.

"Yeah sure and if y' catch 'im tell 'im he can have both your jobs. Now get lost," McMurphy replied angrily, slamming through the change room door.

As he walked out into the gym area, there was Fraser McAllister naked as a jaybird, still doubled over in pain, his nose swollen and eyes almost shut. Tommy Stewart didn't say a word and had obviously cautioned the others to remain silent in the face of the most powerful crime figure in Great Britain.

"I want his address and telephone number, now!" McMurphy demanded.

Tommy went over to his office and looked through his rolodex until he came to Alex Yin's name. He wrote down his contact information and handed a slip of paper to McMurphy. McMurphy grabbed it and stormed out of the gym walking out into the fading daylight.

His phone rang. Hitting the talk button McMurphy answered.

"Yeah."

"Black here. I got your information."

'Fine, meet me at my office," McMurphy said abruptly ending the call.

"I need a goddam stiff drink," McMurphy said out loud grimacing.

A passerby laughed at McMurphy's comment.

"What the fuck are y' laughing at asshole," McMurphy said motioning aggressively sending the skinny man running down the street.

He arrived back at his office to find Black had already arrived.

"Here's the capture you wanted," Black said handing a disk to McMurphy.

"Thanks. Do y' fancy a wee dram?" McMurphy asked pointing to his scotch collection.

"No, I better be on my way," Black replied.

McMurphy saw Black to the private elevator. After pouring himself a single malt he sat down to watch the video capture. It didn't take long to see Cambridge's face as it jumped off the screen.

"Ah, for crissake."

McMurphy picked up the phone and dialed Ascot's mobile number.

"Ascot here."

"Guess who I just saw on the same Crewe CCTV capture as Ian MacLeod? Would y' believe Nigel Cambridge ... you know, the MI5 guy who almost broke through the veil a few years back," McMurphy stated.

"Hmm, I thought I finished him off. He's no longer MI5 ... my good friend the Home Secretary himself made sure of that. The whole investigation was dropped," Ascot replied.

"Well given how we've been outpaced and outmaneuvered it's too coincidental to not connect him somehow to our Mr. MacLeod," McMurphy said.

"Well we don't know that for certain, but if Cambridge is involved with MacLeod, that Douglas, will be a very trying problem for us. I must go as I'm late for a board meeting. We'll talk later," Ascot said before hanging up.

Douglas McMurphy looked out over the lights of the city he owned as he walked over to his prized scotch collection holding an empty crystal scotch glass in his hand. Perplexed at how he had been outmaneuvered by a nondescript minion like Ian MacLeod, he looked down at one of his most cherished bottles, one that he had never opened. He set down the glass and picked up the bottle inspecting its label—MacLeod's Glen Grant 1954 / 50 Year Old.

Then he looked more closely at the name of the bottler—Ian MacLeod Distillers. McMurphy laughed.

"Jeezus. If he's as good as this scotch, we're in big trouble," McMurphy said as he looked up and stared at his own reflection in the expanse of glass that surrounded him.

"He's a fuckin' accountant for crissake."

Chapter 29

Detective Chief Inspector Harry Cosgrove sat in his Scotland Yard office listening to informant Rupert Bertwistle.

"The skinny on the street is that MacLeod went AWOL after killin' a business associate of McMurphy's. The bes' part is tha' 'e pilfered a couple million pounds of dir'y cash. They're more than a lit'le pissed off ... enough fer a kill order," Rupert Bertwistle said.

"Are you serious? Do you have any information on his whereabouts?" asked Cosgrove.

"The word is 'e left Glasgow in a big hurry after takin' a bullet in Edinburgh and evadin' capture from McMurphy's personal shooter, who's now waitin' for the down elevator at the fockin' pearly gates," Bertwistle replied.

"Who was the shooter and how does MacLeod fit into the mob?" Cosgrove asked.

"McGinnis, tha's 'is name. 'e was beaten to death a few days la'er. Punishment comes swift in me circles," Bertwistle said raising his eyebrows.

"Did you hear my question Rupert?" Cosgrove asked.

Bertwistle laughed heartily.

"I 'eard y'. Y' know what 'e is? A bloody accoun'ant. Tall and thin ... 'e's no tough guy I'll tell y' that much," Bertwistle said barely able to contain himself at the image of Ian MacLeod outmaneuvering Douglas McMurphy's top hit man.

"Yes, we know who he is, but what about the mob connection?" Cosgrove queried wondering why Bertwistle found the conversation so humorous.

"Dunno, but 'e seems to 'ave a lo' o' friends 'arry. There was a Chinaman. Word is that 'e beat the livin' daylights outa McMurphy's lads. Barely go' a punch thrown is wha' I 'eard," Rupert Bertwistle said his voice becoming animated.

"His name?" Cosgrove asked.

"Dunno, but it happened at a figh' club in Glasgow ... Crouchin' Tiger I think it's called."

Cosgrove took a moment to write in his notes.

"How did MacLeod escape and evade capture? I mean the mob have people all over the UK don't they?" Cosgrove asked.

"'e slipped onto a train and has now vanished. They're lookin' for 'im everywhere," Bertwistle replied.

"Do you know which train he took?"

"No' a fockin' clue. Word is McMurphy's very frustra'ed," Bertwistle responded.

Again Cosgrove penned what he had heard in his notebook.

"Why would they want him dead if he has their money?" Cosgrove asked.

"Dunno. Bu' if youse wan' my lowly opinion, I think 'e knows too much 'n' they wan' his mauf closed permanen'ly."

"OK, well once again Rupert, the Yard thanks you for your cooperation and we'll make it worth your while," Cosgrove said getting up to shake Bertwistle's hand.

"Yeah, no problem ... glad t' be of 'elp as usual 'arry," Bertwistle replied as he walked to the door.

The meeting ended and Bertwistle left. Cosgrove sat for a few moments trying to make sense of the news Bertwistle had given him. He called Strathclyde and confirmed that hit man Danny McGinnis had indeed been executed a few days earlier. He picked up the phone.

"Gladys, convene the CEO task force for an update meeting," Cosgrove directed.

"No problem sir," Gladys responded.

Two hours later all members of the task force were present as Cosgrove stood at the front of the room.

"We've got some new developments in the case. It seems that the main suspect Ian MacLeod has not been acting alone as we previously suspected. It is believed that while he was in Glasgow he contacted an Asian man who is a martial arts expert. As well, the latest information shared with us from Lothian placed MacLeod at the scene of a shooting on the North Bridge in Edinburgh," Cosgrove stated.

Each new twist in the case intrigued Kyla, and it was now her opinion that the perpetrator was a mob hit man. Her suspicions were further aroused after hearing about Jordie Dunsmuir's murder which was a suspected gangland killing. Dunsmuir's murder seemed to link RIA to mob activities, otherwise why would they kill him? Given his evasiveness when she questioned him, and his connection with Ian that led to Ian's involvement with RIA and subsequent suspicion in Mills' death, Kyla was convinced that Dunsmuir played a pivotal role in what appeared to be a conspiracy. Dunsmuir's phone call to Singleton before Singleton's murder as well as a number linked to the mob less than an hour before the killing all pointed to possible criminal connections. As well, she was certain that RIA and Douglas McMurphy had close ties that seemed to point to Managing Director, Alistair Ascot. She was not yet able to find proof that would exonerate Ian for the Mills murder but she knew her instincts pointed in the right direction.

Kyla listened intently to what Cosgrove was saying.

"New information from both the British Transport Police as well as the Wiltshire Constabulary now points to a new accomplice by the name of Nigel Cambridge, an ex-MI5 operative," Cosgrove stated.

Kyla's heart sank knowing full well that it was because of her that Nigel was now implicated.

"It seems Mr. Cambridge has been helping MacLeod to evade capture using his extensive experience as a secret service agent not to mention his extraordinary driving skills. He outran a highly trained pair from Wiltshire in a 25 kilometer off road run across the Salisbury Plain just after MacLeod and Cambridge were spotted together at Crewe. We believe they are somewhere in Southern England and we are working on possible locations as we speak. We now have information that SOCKS has a special interest in Mr. MacLeod. Apparently, in addition to allegedly killing Mills, he is in possession of a couple million pounds of their money. So, it appears that he does have connections to the mob," Cosgrove elaborated.

Kyla's previous knowledge of this new development heard directly from Ian himself made her very uncomfortable and she fidgeted in her chair.

"How could he have a personal connection to Mills and be associated with the mob as well?" Detective Woods asked.

"Good question. I don't have a good answer. We are basing our allegations on both circumstantial evidence and on information provided by an informant," Cosgrove responded.

"But is he still the primary suspect?" Detective Vishnumurti asked.

"For the Mills case, it appears so. The help he has been able to muster may point to some sort of conspiracy to evade capture, especially with a guy like Cambridge who possesses highly trained operative skills. How MacLeod could have come to know Cambridge, who had ties to both the investigation of organized crime during his time at SOCA as well as being known to us as an outside consultant, is perplexing," Cosgrave said, shaking his head.

Kyla squirmed and glanced around the room.

"We also need to track down the Asian man in Glasgow who happens to be a martial arts expert. He apparently took on a couple of McMurphy's thugs and made fools of them so he is a very skilled fighter. Of possible interest is McMurphy's former personal shooter, a guy named Danny McGinnis who has since deceased," Cosgrove continued.

"What's the story on McGinnis?" a voice at the back of the room asked.

"He was the victim of a mob execution. According to our informant, he was beaten to death with a baseball bat for allowing MacLeod to escape," Cosgrove answered.

"Kyla, any thoughts?" Cosgrove asked.

Kyla composed herself and responded.

"No … sir," Kyla said as she tried to hide her obvious discomfort.

"OK, here's the action plan. Team A will go to Glasgow and track down a martial arts expert who our informant believes may have a connection to MacLeod. He fights at a club called the Crouching Tiger. Although it's not likely he is involved as a co-conspirator, we need to find out what he knows. I also want you to visit Strathclyde and find out what you can about Douglas

McMurphy and the activities of his organization. There's a possible connection to the recent killing of an RIA executive, Jordie Dunsmuir. Team B will go to Crewe and Wiltshire and interview members of the BTP and the Wiltshire Police. You will also go to Brighton and dig up more on the relationship Mills had with MacLeod. There are also possible clandestine links to RIA that may shed light on the case. Team C will visit Edinburgh and get all of the details surrounding the killing of Clive Crawford as well as a possible connection to MacLeod who may have been the victim of a shooting. We also need to bring in the young transient who may be able to ID MacLeod as Mills' killer. I want to find out how MacLeod went from being an accountant to working for the mob in very short order. Something really smells about this whole thing. It's the 15th today and we will reconvene the task force in a week. I expect results from all of you. That'll be all. Kyla, see me in my office."

Kyla walked the hallway on the way to Cosgrove's office with a sickening feeling of anxiety and guilt over her undercover activities during the past several weeks. She wondered if she should tell all which would mean being stripped of her role and the finish of her career with Scotland Yard.

"Kyla, have a seat," Cosgrove motioned.

Kyla took a seat across from Cosgrove.

"You didn't have much to add during the meeting. Are you alright?" Cosgrove asked.

"Yes, I'm fine," Kyla said trying her best to calm her nerves.

"So what do you make of all this?" Cosgrove queried.

"I don't know, I'm quite perplexed at the new developments," Kyla replied.

"So when you and Johnson interviewed MacLeod's ex, you didn't see any red flags that might point to a secret underground lifestyle or involvement with the mob?" Cosgrove asked.

"No, nothing at all. He seemed like a very ordinary guy who worked hard in his job. He's a Chartered Accountant, a professional. One thing that did come up was that he left Glasgow under duress back in 1998 in an attempt to escape the guy you talked about in the meeting—Danny McGinnis. Apparently, according to his ex-wife, they were friends and roommates before that," Kyla replied.

"Kyla, why didn't you say something before now?" Cosgrove asked seemingly annoyed.

"I assumed Johnson put it in his report to you," Kyla responded defensively.

"Alright. Well that's an important piece of information that we need to track down. Perhaps MacLeod has had an ongoing relationship with the mob both prior to and since then. Those Glaswegians are a tough bunch you know," Cosgrove stated.

"I'm at a loss sir."

"Well given the direction that this case has taken, as far-fetched as it may seem, it appears that MacLeod is somehow entangled with the mob. How Cambridge fits into this is even more curious," Cosgrove stated.

"It doesn't add up sir," Kyla said emphatically.

"How so?"

"I just don't get MacLeod as having the profile of a killer," Kyla responded.

"We'll see. Look, I have to run," Cosgrove replied.

"Thank you, sir. One thing, I'm off for a bit so would you please keep me abreast of the developments in the case?" Kyla asked.

"Of course, I will call you personally as things unfold."

Kyla returned to her office, packed her briefcase and left for her home on the Isle of Arran.

Chapter 30

"Home Secretary's office, how can I direct your call?" a mature female voice asked.

"It's Alistair Ascot calling. I wonder if I might have a word with him, Geraldine?"

"Oh, yes Mr. Ascot, I'll see if he's available. Just hold a minute please," replied the executive assistant to Home Secretary Gordon Kinsey.

Alistair Ascot had been friends with Kinsey since before they both graduated from Oxford in 1980; Ascot with an honors degree in law and Kinsey who read law and eventually went on to gain a masters in political science. They had maintained a friendship over the years and Ascot had been a big supporter of Kinsey's political career since day one.

"Alistair, it's good to hear from you. To what do I owe the pleasure?" Kinsey said opening up the conversation.

"Gordon, you know me. I never call without an agenda."

"That is what I've always liked about you Ascot; you don't beat around the bush," Kinsey remarked.

"Small talk has always bored me to tears. It's the pastime of the mediocre as far as I'm concerned," Ascot said arrogantly.

"So true, but that's how I make my living on behalf of the people I serve Alistair. How can I help?" Kinsey asked remembering how in their early days, he and Ascot would often square off with each other in a cut and thrust of intellects.

"Well, I hate to ask, but we had a young chap who turned rogue on us Gordon. He was assigned as an auditor on one of our largest accounts and ended up stealing almost three million pounds from the client. He is also being investigated for murder, including our very own Jordie Dunsmuir, who was my second until he was found floating in the Clyde," Ascot said feigning lament.

"Oh dear, how unfortunate. Can I ask who the client is?" Kinsey asked.

"I'd rather not disclose that as you'll understand the confidential nature of the situation Gordon."

"What about the whereabouts of this scoundrel?" Kinsey asked.

"Well that's why I'm calling. He's evaded capture so far; even Scotland Yard can't get their hands on him so I'm told. I was hoping that you could give me clearance to use the resources of the military and perhaps even MI5 to tighten the noose around this dangerous fugitive's neck," Ascot explained.

"By all means, I'll arrange to have the top man at MI5 coordinate the situation as your personal contact. Just a moment and I'll raise him on the other line," Kinsey said putting Ascot on hold.

Ascot waited until Kinsey came back on the line.

"The chap's name is James Stoddard. I'll send his particulars over via email once we finish up," Kinsey advised.

"Very good. Well, I know you're a busy man Mr. Home Secretary so I'll let you on with your day sir," Ascot replied pandering to Gordon Kinsey's well known sense of self-importance.

"Yes, and Alistair—," Kinsey started.

"I know, keep this between the two of us."

"Good, well cheers then," Kinsey said before hanging up the phone.

Alistair Ascot had planted the seeds he needed to cast a bigger net for the capture of Ian MacLeod.

He turned to McMurphy who was sitting with him in the boardroom listening in on the entire conversation.

"That is one of the benefits of power Douglas. What you do with a hoard of weapon toting thugs I do with political clout," Ascot said with an air of conceit.

"Yeah, well I'm not sure which is worse, Mr. Power Broker—guns or lies," McMurphy stated with a sneer.

"What is the latest on MacLeod?" Ascot enquired.

"I paid a visit to the gym where the Chinese guy works out," McMurphy replied.

"And what did you find out?"

"Nada, the guy beat the shit out of two of my toughest lads before he got away," McMurphy said in an annoyed tone.

"Douglas, this is becoming very disappointing."

"I'm disappointed as well. But in defense of my lads this fella is as good as Bruce Lee, maybe better," McMurphy replied.

"Have you been able to find him?" Ascot asked.

"We're trying. So far nothing," McMurphy admitted.

"OK, what else?"

"We've heard through our inside contacts that our Cockney friend is a turncoat and has been double shifting it with Scotland Yard as a paid informant," McMurphy said.

"Do we have any further use for him then?" Ascot asked.

"He knows the location of Ms. Fraser, who we now need as collateral," McMurphy replied.

"Agreed, get him in for a conversation and if it's going to be messy leave me out of it. I don't do well at the sight of blood," Ascot said making a grimaced face.

"Already arranged. My guys should have him secured at the warehouse by now. I'm headed over after we're done," McMurphy advised.

"Call me when you know her address and we can plan a visit."

McMurphy left 29 St Vincent Street and drove to a secluded warehouse in the west dock area of the Clyde wharves. The warehouse was secured with a heavy steel door insulated against sound leakage and was equipped with CCTV cameras to warn of any intruder who dared snoop around the perimeter. McMurphy buzzed the intercom when he arrived.

"I'm here, let me in."

The big steel door opened and there sitting in a heavy custom made steel chair, arms and legs strapped down to prevent him from moving, was Rupert Bertwistle. Standing around him were several of McMurphy's men.

"Boss, I'm so glad yer 'ere. These silly fockers have me strapped into this contraption ... talk some sense into them," Bertwistle said agitated and obviously fearing the worst.

"Is that thing running?" McMurphy asked referring to the camcorder a few feet away from Bertwistle.

During such interrogations McMurphy recorded what he referred to as 'training videos'. The record button was never actually pushed for the dreaded snuff films, but McMurphy knew the value of the myth that propagated on the streets at the mere rumor of their existence. Fear was McMurphy's only stock in trade.

"Yah boss," enforcer Jonas replied.

"Don't worry Bertwistle, we're just gonna have a wee conversation about the virtues of loyalty. Are y' a believer in allegiance and trustworthiness Rupert?" McMurphy asked staying well back and out of view of the camera lens.

"Well I sure as fock am. I'm proud to say I'm a company man," Bertwistle said in a voice that was strained and anxious.

"Which company are you referring to Rupert?" McMurphy asked.

"You know the answer ... yers of course," Bertwistle replied in a feeble attempt to deny his betrayal.

"Jonas, turn on the TV," McMurphy ordered.

A short clip came on showing Bertwistle entering and leaving Scotland Yard on multiple occasions.

"Turn it off."

"That's not me. The bloke looked like me, but no fockin' way is that me boss," Bertwistle said maintaining his innocence.

"Why 'r ya sweatin'? Y' fuckin' traitor," the Irish voice of Connor O'Sullivan taunted.

"Shut up," McMurphy said remembering that it was Connor who let MacLeod slip away in Preston.

'You're next you sawed off Irishman,' McMurphy thought as he picked up a hammer in his gloved right hand.

"You've done some good work for us over the years Rupert so I'm gonna be compassionate here. Just don't lie to me," McMurphy said looking straight at Bertwistle.

"OK boss."

"I want the address of the woman you tailed for Dunsmuir ... Kyla Fraser."

"Yeah, no problem. But yous don't need to keep me in this god-awful contraption if that's all y' wanna know," Bertwistle said, the fear in his voice now palpable.

"Her address Rupert?"

"I can't remember the exac' number or nothin', but she's over on Arran, straigh' across from the island, Holy Island I think it is. Lit'le white stucco cot'age righ' off the road. Red tile roof as well. Yous can't miss it," he said, his eyes wide with dread.

"OK, that's helpful. Now what about Scotland Yard? What have y' told them about us Rupert?" McMurphy asked as he slapped the hammer into his palm.

"God's hones' truth, I said very lit'le, yous got'a believe me boss. I got kids, trouble and strife, and bills comin' ou' o' me yin yang. I needed the extra money tha's all. I was just playin' along with them, feedin' them bollocks, nothin' more," Bertwistle said as beads of sweat formed on his brow and soaked his shirt.

"You're a liar. I don't fancy liars. Cut his fuckin' tongue out," McMurphy ordered as he stepped back.

"No, no ... please boss," Bertwistle pleaded before clenching his jaws in anticipation of the coming attempt to open his mouth.

The Irishman donned a balaclava before he walked over to the 'truth chair' as it was referred to among McMurphy's lieutenants. Jonas put on a rubber fisherman's jacket and then pulled on a pair of prophylactic gloves before picking up a surgeon's scalpel. He walked over and stood in front of Bertwistle and then nodded his head to Connor O'Sullivan who was standing directly behind Bertwistle. The Irishman slammed the Cockney's head back against the steel headrest and while Rupert struggled against being restrained O'Connor belted his head so that it could not move. Jonas picked up a piece of surgical gauze and waited for McMurphy.

"Turn the camera off for a minute," McMurphy commanded and Jonas walked back and pretended to switch off the device.

Douglas McMurphy walked over to Bertwhistle's side.

"Yer a scumbag liar y' no good fuckin' English cocksucker," McMurphy uttered in the instant before he swung the hammer smashing Rupert's left jawbone leaving him screaming in agony.

He then walked around and did the same to Rupert's right side.

"OK, that should do it. Get the rest on tape," McMurphy said while stepping back to avoid the gory mess that was to ensue.

Rupert's eyes were wide in terror, jaw muscles rendered useless as the two henchmen opened his mouth exposing his vulnerable tongue. Jonas deftly gripped the end of Bertwistle's tongue with the surgical gauze and with a single forcible slice excised it to a rush of blood that poured down the front of Rupert's jacket. He slumped, hanging by the head restraint, passing out from the excruciating pain. Jonas dropped the muscular organ along with the bloody gauze into a nearby trash can.

"Jonas, make sure you bring the camcorder back to the office for anyone who thinks moonlighting is a good idea," McMurphy instructed while making eye contact with the two other lieutenants standing off to the side in terrified astonishment at the brutality they had just witnessed.

"OK boss, what's next?" Jonas asked.

"Come here," McMurphy beckoned as he walked away with his arm around Jonas.

"Yah boss."

"How's your partner's sore ass doing?" McMurphy asked feigning concern.

"Oh much better, he be back soon," Jonas replied.

"Good, good. Now I want you to finish Rupert off and float 'im. Once you and that mouthy little mick have him in the river, get rid of the Irish troublemaker too," McMurphy whispered.

"Das is no problem boss," Jonas responded as O'Sullivan strained to hear the exchange between the two of them.

"OK boys, thanks. That was good work," McMurphy said as if he were acknowledging the exemplary efforts of a construction crew.

Waving as he turned toward the door, McMurphy walked out into the warmth of a beautiful day and closed the big steel door behind him.

"Now Ms. Fraser, you're next on the agenda," McMurphy said as he got into the passenger seat of his silver Range Rover.

"Drive."

Chapter 31

Team A, which consisted of Detectives Woods and Johnson arrived in Glasgow on June 17th. After being briefed by the Strathclyde investigators they were given videotape copies of CCTV coverage showing a passenger who fit Ian MacLeod's description leaving Glasgow Central on June 13th. They were also filled in on the recent murders of James Ot and Danny McGinnis. After thanking the investigators they set about tracking down the person of interest from the fight club.

"Our first stop is going to be 'Crouching Tiger'," Kenneth Johnson advised.

"Right," Detective Janine Woods acknowledged as they walked the short distance from their hotel room to the gym on Sauchiehall Street.

They arrived just after 10:00 AM and entered the premise as owner and trainer Tommy Stewart was refereeing a fight that was underway. The detectives watched as the two opponents sparred in the ring when Johnson spotted Fraser McAllister standing at ringside, his nose bandaged and both eyes sporting the yellow and black circles of a broken nose.

"Hey, look at that guy. These fights must get very violent," Johnson noted.

"I detest this so called sport. They'll all be brain dead by the time they reach middle age," Woods remarked.

"Let's go over and see what we can find out," Johnson said.

The two detectives walked over and stood beside McAllister, who glanced over at the pair. Johnson took advantage of being seen.

"The black guy's got a quick left jab doesn't he?" Johnson said in an attempt to engage McAllister.

"Yeah, he fights like an animal."

"Looks like you do too. What happened?" Johnson asked knowing he should have shown his badge before talking to anyone.

"Didn't happen in the ring. I was suckered," McAllister replied.

"Street fight?" Johnson asked.

"Nah, I don't do that shit," McAllister responded.

"Oh, so …?" Johnson led.

"Sonuvabitch barged into the change room and kicked me in the head when I was bending down to put on my socks," McAllister said lying to save face about what really happened.

"Did you report it to the police?" Johnson queried.

"Are you nuts? The man owns the fucking police according to Tommy," McAllister said glancing at Johnson and pointing to the referee in the ring.

Johnson's curiosity was aroused by the big man's admission, but he instinctively decided to curtail his informal questioning and wait for the referee to finish so he could introduce himself as a police officer, albeit out of jurisdiction.

When Tommy Stewart left the ring and walked over to his office, Johnson and Woods followed and introduced themselves.

"Excuse me, my name is Detective Kenneth Johnson and this is Detective Janine Woods. We're both with Scotland Yard. We're conducting an investigation that might involve someone who works out at this gym. Can we ask you a few questions?" Johnson said as both of them flashed their badges.

"Not sure if I can help but go ahead," Tommy Stewart stated.

"Are you the owner?" Johnson asked standing in the doorway with Woods behind him taking notes.

"I am. The name's Tommy Stewart."

"We're looking for a Chinese fellow who is quite a martial arts expert. Apparently he works out here," Johnson stated.

Stewart's sudden braced demeanor did not go unnoticed by Johnson.

"Why are y' looking for 'im?" Stewart asked defensively, his instincts telling him not to trust the police.

"We'd like to ask him a few questions about his association with a murder suspect," Johnson said candidly.

Knowing he had better not deny Alex's membership at the gym, but being cognizant of the risks associated with Douglas McMurphy, Tommy chose his words carefully.

"OK, he's a member here, but he's not been in for a while now. Don't know where he is," Stewart offered reticently.

"Do you have an address for him?" Johnson asked.

Tommy Stewart wrote down the address and handed a slip of paper to Johnson.

"Alex Yin, but you won't find him there. One of the guys who knows him well says he's not available," Stewart replied.

"Oh and why is that?" Johnson asked.

"I'm sure y' know the answer to that Detective. I've no more to tell y'," Stewart stated hoping to end the interview.

"What about his buddy you referred to who knows him well?" Johnson inquired.

"The black guy who just finished sparring," Stewart responded pointing over to the locker room.

"His name?" Johnson asked.

"Kenny Jones. He's in the showers."

"Thanks for your cooperation Mr. Stewart," Johnson said as he offered his hand.

Tommy Stewart reluctantly shook Johnson's hand.

"Let's have a word with Kenny Jones when he comes out," Detective Woods said as they walked back toward the cage.

"What do you think?" Johnson asked.

"I'm not sure, but these guys are scared," Janine Woods replied.

"I have a hunch that the big lad with the broken nose has more information for us," Johnson said motioning towards Fraser McAllister.

"I agree. Shall we show him our badges?" Woods asked

"That's what I'm thinking. You do the talking this time Janine," Johnson replied.

"Alright."

The two detectives noticed McAllister talking with a couple of his cohorts in the weight room, so they approached him.

"Mind if we have a few words?" Detective Janine Woods asked as both of them flashed their badges.

"Hey, y' hoodwinked me back there," McAllister said obviously annoyed at Johnson.

"We're with Scotland Yard. I'm Detective Woods and this is Detective Johnson. You are?" Woods led.

"Fraser McAllister's the name."

"Just a couple of questions Fraser. We're looking for a fellow who works out here by the name of Alex Yin. Sound familiar?" Wood asked.

"Of course," McAllister answered.

"Have you seen him lately?" asked Woods.

"Not since he disappeared out those doors on Monday night. He hasn't come back," McAllister responded motioning with his head at the gym entrance.

"Really? What happened?" Woods asked.

"Who said anything happened?"

"Fraser, when did you break your nose? And who barged into the change room to break it?" Woods asked pointedly.

Fraser McAllister knew he was cornered but he had been told to keep his mouth shut for his own good. He had already seen firsthand the viciousness of Douglas McMurphy and was not about to draw any more attention from a man that would not think twice about having him killed.

"I'll no' be saying anything more to you or to yer slippery friend," McAllister said turning away from the detectives.

"The injury looks fresh. Did it happen on Monday night by any chance?" Woods asked, looking for any sign of reaction from McAllister.

McAllister was silent ignoring any further questions.

"Well thanks for your help," Woods said and both of them turned and walked back toward the change rooms.

"These guys had a visit from the mob on Monday night. They are all frightened Kenneth. My bet is that Alex Yin was the target of their visit and it did not go as planned. Alex Yin is on their hit list because he likely knows where Ian MacLeod is," Woods said conclusively.

After several minutes Kenny Jones walked into the main gym area.

"Kenny Jones?" Detective Woods asked blocking Jones' way.

"Yeah, who are you?" Jones asked surprised at being confronted.

"Detective Woods and this is Detective Johnson. We're with Scotland Yard."

"OK," Jones said tentatively.

"We understand that you know Alex Yin quite well," Woods led.

"We're friends, not close or anything," Jones offered.

"Do you know where he is?" asked Woods.

Kenny looked around to see if anyone was listening.

"Can we go somewhere else?"

"Sure, where?" Woods inquired.

"Outside, away from here. There are too many ears. But you leave first and wait for me around the corner," Kenny Jones said nodding his head towards the entrance.

"Fine."

Jones watched as the two detectives walked out onto the street and disappeared out of sight. Tommy Stewart had been watching from his office and got up and stood in the doorway as Jones walked toward the entrance.

"I hope y' were careful in what you said to those two. The mob is watchin' every move in and out of that door Kenny. You'll lead them right t' Alex if you're not careful lad," Stewart cautioned.

"Yeah, yeah, thanks for the heads up Tommy. I'm leavin' now. See y' later."

Kenny Jones walked out into the light rainfall that had just started. The smattering of rain left dark droplets on the sidewalk filling the air with the unmistakable smell of summer as they quickly evaporated. He looked down the street at the two detectives standing on the corner of Holland and Sauchiehall. He then noticed two shady looking men across the street who, as Tommy had cautioned, were undoubtedly watching the comings and goings of anyone who visited the fight club. He turned and walked in the opposite direction of where the two plainclothes detectives were waiting.

"That's strange. He seemed so cooperative in there," Woods said looking over at her partner Detective Johnson.

Johnson surveyed the surroundings and noticed the two men across the street smoking cigarettes and trying to appear casual.

"He's smart. The two thugs over there are watching. Keep your eye on which direction Kenny goes while I flag a cab," Johnson said scanning the area for a taxi.

A few moments later a taxi pulled up and the two detectives got in.

"Just in time to get out of the rain," the driver noted.

"Turn right over there," Woods directed.

The cab proceeded to Pitt Street and turned right.

"There's Kenny up ahead. Pull over."

The car stopped and Kenny looked at Janine Woods, who had opened the door.

"Kenny, get in. We know what is going on," Woods said as she moved over to make space for Jones.

Jones jumped into the back seat.

"It's very important that we talk to Alex Yin. We believe his life may be in danger," Woods said.

"Well then, so is mine," Kenny responded.

"What do you mean?" Kenneth Johnson asked.

"He's at my flat."

"Will you take us there?" Johnson asked.

"Alright."

The cab took the three of them to a small apartment building across town where they got out.

"Let me go in first to give him a heads up," Kenny Jones said.

A few minutes later, Kenny motioned from the front door for the two to come up.

"Alex says he'll talk to you but he doesn't know anything."

They walked into Kenny's small flat where a nice looking man in his late twenties was sitting on the couch.

"Alex Yin?" Johnson asked.

"Yes."

"Woods and Johnson from Scotland Yard. Can we ask you a few questions?" Johnson asked.

"I guess so," Alex said guardedly.

"Alex, do you know an individual by the name of Ian MacLeod?" Johnson asked.

"Why do you ask?" Alex responded.

"We are investigating a series of murders, one of which is thought to have been perpetrated by Mr. MacLeod. We have information that he visited you at the fight club just prior to that murder," Johnson elaborated.

"MacLeod? That's crazy. He wouldn't hurt a fly," Alex responded.

The detectives shared a glance before Johnson turned back towards Yin.

"What was the purpose of his visit?"

"He came in to watch a fight. I hadn't seen the man in ten years," Alex responded.

"So you have no information about his activities subsequent to your meeting with him?" Johnson asked.

"No, and we actually barely knew each other. We attended the same university, that's all. Our encounter was purely coincidence," Alex replied.

"OK, care to tell us what happened on Monday night at the fight club Alex?" Detective Woods asked.

"I have no idea what you're talking about," Alex said attempting to deflect the question.

"Who broke Fraser McAllister's nose?" Woods pressed.

Alex appeared to be surprised.

"I have no idea," Alex said raising his hands in the air, seemingly annoyed at the line of questioning.

A few moments passed before Woods continued.

"So you have nothing further to say?"

"No, I'm sorry I can't be of help," Alex stated uncooperatively.

Woods crossed her arms, obviously frustrated. Johnson interjected knowing further questioning was futile.

"Well, thanks for your time. If you do remember anything call me at this number," Johnson said handing Alex his card.

The two detectives left Kenny Jones' flat and walked out onto the sidewalk.

"He's stonewalling," Woods said to her partner.

"No doubt. He is obviously afraid for his life," Johnson said as he hailed a taxi.

Chapter 32

Kyla was anxious to know what had transpired in the Edinburgh team's review of the shooting that occurred on the North Bridge over Market Street. She had heard from Cosgrove that according to the Lothian and Borders Police investigation it was believed that Ian had been shot by an assailant while attempting to escape. Kyla had to feign surprise when Cosgrove informed her of the new development.

She dialed up the lead investigator on the Edinburgh team, Detective Jimmy Whiteside.

"Whiteside here."

"Hello Jimmy, it's Kyla Fraser."

"Kyla, how are you?"

"I'm fine, thanks. I'm calling about the MacLeod investigation. What did y' find out in Edinburgh?"

"Well, where should I start? They told us that Crawford, the construction executive, was executed in signature gangland style—bullet to the back of the head. There were a series of photos leaked from security video to the police of MacLeod skulking around Crawford's construction project on the Edinburgh waterfront placing him in the vicinity of the murder," Whiteside noted.

"Whoever leaked the photos must have wanted him seen. The connection is weak, circumstantial at best," Kyla responded.

"Let me continue. Witnesses described a male matching MacLeod's description trying to escape a shooter who chased him along the North Bridge over Market Street. MacLeod must have taken a slug because according to an elderly man who was an eye witness, MacLeod left a damaged bloodstained belt below the bridge."

Kyla's mind raced.

"Are you still there, Kyla?" Whiteside asked.

"Yes, the phone reception is often bad here on Arran," Kyla responded.

"Can you describe the belt?" Kyla asked recalling that Ian wore a wide heavy leather belt with paisley embossments.

"From the photos it appeared to be brown leather with some sort of repeated designs on it. In any case, the DNA from the belt was analyzed and there were no matches to the database so it could well be MacLeod's," Jimmy commented.

"Jimmy, something doesn't add up. If you're saying that the execution in Edinburgh was a signature gangland hit, then whose signature was it? If MacLeod was the shooter why was he being pursued and shot at? It doesn't make sense," Kyla speculated.

"According to eyewitnesses and one man who actually captured the action on his mobile phone, the person that shot at MacLeod matches the description of a well-known hit man named Danny McGinnis, who was recently murdered in Glasgow. I checked with Strathclyde and they have reason to believe that a single gunshot to the back of the head is McGinnis' MO, which was the cause of death for Singleton as well. They are currently underway with ballistics on the .357 Magnum retrieved from the McGinnis murder scene, known to belong to him. If it's a match to the slugs found at the scene of the North Bridge shooting and those extracted from Crawford's body, then we know McGinnis is our man. However, if our informant is right and MacLeod is in possession of mob money, until ballistics clears him, there is reasonable suspicion that he is involved in Crawford's murder," Whiteside concluded.

There was a moment of silence before Kyla responded.

"We need to confirm that the belt is MacLeod's," Kyla urged.

"Yes, if we knew conclusively that it was his belt it would help exonerate him as the time frame between the bridge shooting and the time of the Crawford killing don't add up. However, he's still a suspect in the Mills murder," Whiteside said definitively.

"OK, thanks for the update Jimmy."

Kyla was torn. She was reticent to step up to help prove Ian's innocence given the risks to her career. Kyla thought for a few minutes before she picked up the phone and dialed her friend and co-worker Janine Woods.

"Hello," Janine answered.

"Janine, it's Kyla."

"Kyla, how are you?" Janine asked.

"Fine Janine. I'm gonna tell y' something that could end my career and I need you to keep it between us until I decide to disclose it," Kyla said hoping her friend would agree.

"What are we talking about here?"

"I just got off the phone from a conversation with Jimmy Whiteside up in Edinburgh. He has concluded his review of the Edinburgh incident and he doesn't believe that it is likely that MacLeod is guilty. At least not of murder," Kyla stated.

"OK ... that's interesting, go on," Janine said wondering where Kyla was about to go with the new information.

"I've been doing some investigation on my own based on case evidence and I think that MacLeod got caught up in a situation that arose out of a job he took with RIA in Glasgow. He's a Chartered Accountant who they hired to look into profits that were missing in deals between one of RIA's clients and his business partners. Based on the Dunsmuir killing and phone records that placed him in Manchester at the time of the Singleton murder, my theory is that Dunsmuir was a go between for Douglas McMurphy and a higher up at RIA. That individual is the Managing Director, Alistair Ascot. I believe they are in collusion. I also think MacLeod was brought in as a patsy and had nothing to do with any of the killings including Mills. It is a serial pattern Janine, perpetrated by one of the most little understood serial murder types—the mob hit man. I believe that the now deceased Danny McGinnis was the murderer."

"Interesting theory Kyla. What has this got to do with your career?" Janine asked suspiciously.

Kyla ignored the question.

"According to his bank, Singleton was in trouble and could not get financing for his riverfront project in Manchester. I believe that McMurphy stepped in and provided him with the money he needed to salvage his business. Given mob involvement, the money was obviously dirty and that's where things went sideways leading to Singleton's death. I have no proof but that's how it appears to me," Kyla continued.

"Go on …," Woods led.

"Jimmy Whiteside said that if they had MacLeod's DNA it would clear him from being anywhere near the scene of the murder in Edinburgh because the timelines just don't work. He could not have been shot by the same weapon suspected to have been used to kill Crawford just minutes after the fact given he was on foot which would place him an hour away from the murder scene. Even a taxi ride would have taken at least 20 minutes. So … what if I could get you something with MacLeod's DNA on it?" Kyla asked knowing she would be setting off alarm bells.

"Kyla, what are you saying?" Janine asked shocked at the implications of Kyla's question.

"I'm saying that I was in a relationship with MacLeod, albeit early days, before I had any knowledge or suspicion about his culpability. I'm in love with him Janine."

"Alright, I'm gonna stay calm here. You have definitely jeopardized your career at Scotland Yard once this gets out," Janine advised.

Kyla was silent, not knowing what to say.

"Kyla, I'm gonna go out on a limb for you and trust that you will be forthcoming when the time is right. What do you have?" Janine asked.

"I have a toothbrush that I can get to the DNA lab in Edinburgh. Whiteside said they have DNA on the belt so it should be easy to get a match if the belt is his," Kyla said.

"Do it, and I will authorize a requisition to have the article checked for DNA. As soon as we have results, within the week, I'll call you. Even if it is his belt, it doesn't absolve him of the Mills murder Kyla and that one is much more damning in evidence against him," Janine cautioned.

"I know, but I am beginning to think Ian has been set up all along. He's just too naïve for his own good. I know he's not guilty of anything except perhaps bad judgment. Thanks so much for understanding Janine," Kyla said relieved.

Kyla hung up the phone hoping that Janine would keep the secret to herself for the time being. She found the toothbrush and carefully placed it in a plastic Ziploc bag. She grabbed her purse and jacket and headed off to Edinburgh.

Chapter 33

Nigel and MacLeod were upstairs in a room at the Wheatsheaf Inn next to Cambridge's home waiting for supper to be sent up from the pub below. They dared not stay at Nigel's cottage because the police could be snooping around at any time, once they found his country address.

Cambridge studied Ian as they shared a pint of ale.

"So tell me about you and Kyla," Cambridge pried.

Ian averted his eyes for a moment before looking back at Cambridge.

"I met her when she was returning from her job in London," Ian replied guardedly.

"How long have you known her?" Nigel asked looking up over his beer mug as he took a long draw.

Ian felt that Nigel's questions were invasive and he hesitated for a moment before responding.

"Just a few weeks," Ian replied.

"Really? I would have thought longer. I've known her a long time and found her to be a very careful young woman. She must think very highly of you Ian," Nigel said impulsively.

Ian felt suddenly defensive toward his rescuer who had downed several pints of ale since early afternoon.

"How do *you* know her?" Ian countered emphatically.

Nigel looked up at Ian from the corner of his eye before responding.

"It was a warm August evening, perhaps five years ago. I had recently been let go from what had been a long career with SIS ... I was devastated.

Those scallywags sitting in their wainscoted offices on Whitehall Road are no more than puppets to the bloodsuckers who pull their strings. My investigation began to name some very big players who were as crooked as a tree root and as hidden from scrutiny. They arranged to have the gutless mannequins who watch over our fine country run me out and threaten to ruin me. In any case, I love French cuisine so I was sitting alone at a table at a bistro in Soho when I saw a lovely young woman walk in off the street. I can still recall her burgundy silk dress cut just so, if you know what I mean and I must admit I was spellbound—"

Ian cleared his throat and braced at Cambridge's intimate musings. Cambridge looked at Ian before continuing.

"...In any case, there were no other tables available, so like any gentleman, I stood and gestured to the empty chair across from me. She smiled and declined by motioning with her hand. I sat down and looked over at the maître de who I knew quite well. He walked over to her and must have said something favorable about me as she nodded before looking at me with a smile. Before I knew it we had shared a lovely dinner over two bottles of Grand Cru Chablis," Cambridge said eloquently.

Ian was sitting up straight listening intently, his eyes wide and brow furrowed.

"Nice," Ian said belying his true feelings before turning and looking out the window hoping he had heard the end of Nigel's spirit fueled, quixotic narrative.

Nigel got up and placed his mug on the tiny bar. He picked up a bottle of Brandy, unscrewed the cap and poured several ounces of the amber liquid into a large snifter. He took a sip then followed up with what was more like a gulp. Ian could see that Nigel had a huge tolerance for alcohol but was nevertheless getting quite inebriated.

"So what happened?" Ian asked unable to resist his growing wariness of Nigel and the curiosity that now gripped him.

Nigel studied Ian for a moment.

"Nothing really. We enjoyed each other's company, I told her a few spy stories, called a cab and we both went home," Nigel said wistfully with a glance over the top of his snifter as he intentionally goaded Ian.

Ian surmised that there was a reason beyond platonic friendship that Nigel had readily volunteered to help Kyla. He hated to admit it, but he felt jealous. He searched for a way to change the subject but couldn't find one. It was as if he was no longer in control of his emotions.

"Why are you helping me Nigel?" Ian asked doing his best to hide the suspicion in his voice.

Nigel had already emptied the glass so he walked over and poured himself another one. He turned towards Ian, his eyes rolling almost imperceptibly.

"Truthfully … I've no idea. I suppose it's my relationship with Kyla," Nigel said slurring his words slightly.

Nigel looked at MacLeod. He reflected back to when Kyla contacted him and asked for his help. He had to see first-hand, the man she was so intent on protecting. He had responded as if he were a swashbuckling knight-errant off to save a damsel in distress. Now, deeply conflicted and ambivalent about the young man who he had committed himself to helping on behalf of the woman he secretly loved, Nigel searched for a way to save face from the rising conflict.

Nigel walked up behind Ian, placing his hand on his shoulder.

"Let's change the subject. She's obviously fallen head over heels for you MacLeod and no doubt for good reason," Nigel said softly.

Ian sat in silence for a few moments feeling very uncomfortable. He had counted the number of drinks Nigel had consumed and decided to cut him some slack.

"The shooter you mentioned—McGinnis— is dead," Nigel blurted.

Ian turned and looked at Cambridge, surprised.

"How?"

"I'm not exactly sure, but I read in the papers that it was a suspected mob hit. Apparently it was very violent," Cambridge advised.

"I'm not surprised," Ian responded.

There was a knock on the door. Nigel walked over and answered it, taking the tray that the kitchen downstairs had sent up containing dinner. He placed it on the table and beckoned Ian, who was still reeling from what had felt like an onslaught.

"Come Ian, let's break bread," Nigel said in an attempt to make amends.

Nigel and Ian shared dinner and then sat in front of the old stone fireplace as Nigel continued downing several more glasses of brandy while MacLeod nursed another pint. As drunk as he was, Nigel seemed to be able to remain coherent, and engaged in a thoughtful conversation with Ian.

"Now the question is how do we vanquish McMurphy's criminal empire while Kyla proves that you are innocent?" Cambridge asked.

"What about Ascot? It seems he's more than just McMurphy's advisor," Ian countered.

"Well, based on what you have told me, it seems that RIA is engaged to set up McMurphy's action and then collect and account for the money he makes from all of his illegal dealings," Nigel responded.

"All I know is that Ascot and Dunsmuir hired me and they were there every step of the way with McMurphy, who was always in their boardroom. The brains behind RIA must have known everything that was going on, including the murders," Ian stated putting down his beer.

"Hmm. If there is indeed any criminal connection between SOCKS and RIA it will be exceedingly difficult to prove," Nigel said stroking his mustache with his thumb and forefinger.

"If we knew just how much money flowed through RIA on behalf of SOCKS it might lead us to how Ascot and his firm figure into this puzzle. We've got to catch Ascot red-handed," remarked Ian.

"Yes, but how?"

"What if we could get Ascot's personal financial records? You know—show money with no verifiable source, or maybe paid from one or more of the many corporate tentacles within McMurphy's criminal empire," Ian proposed.

"Ian, we would need to get on the inside to do that. What do you propose?" Nigel asked.

"The only way to get inside is through Janet McComb, their CFO. She handled all of RIA's—and if my hunch is right—McMurphy's financial dealings," Ian replied.

"So how do we get her to expose them?" Nigel asked.

"I'm not sure. But I do know there's a master Swiss account where all funds from SOCKS' global criminal activity are aggregated once every month. Our only hope is to convince Janet McComb to divulge the information on the aggregate account. She would be a star witness against McMurphy and Ascot," Ian said.

"We need to get to Ms. McComb. Without her the veil is impenetrable," Nigel said as he walked over to the window.

Outside, the flashing lights of police cars surrounded his home.

"Looks like Scotland Yard and Wiltshire Constabulary finally tracked me down. How unfortunate for them I'm not at home. Care for another brandy?" Nigel asked chuckling, too drunk to see that Ian was having a pint of beer.

Both Nigel and Ian watched as police officers piled out of the three police cruisers and grouped together with a handful of plainclothes Scotland Yard detectives. After conferring for less than a minute, the bullhorn from the Wiltshire police came to life.

"Nigel Cambridge. You are surrounded. Come out with your hands up. You have one minute before we use tear gas and break down the door," the voice on the bullhorn stated officiously.

"Stupid fools. Why don't they knock on the bloody door and find out if there is anyone home," Nigel said reeling slightly from the effects of his inebriated state.

Ian cracked the window to better hear what was going on outside. He could hear pub owner Fred Carlisle speaking to the police.

"Look, the man's not home. I've not seem 'im for almost a week. He said he was away on business in Scotland and he's not returned. I've a bloody key to his house if you want to get in," Carlisle's voice could be heard right below the window.

"Damn Nigel, what about the Range Rover in your garage?" Ian asked anxiously.

"I returned it to the depot in Salisbury while you caught up on your beauty sleep the day after we arrived. The good lads were kind enough to give me a lift back," Nigel said calmly.

After fifteen minutes of searching inside Cambridge's house and looking around the property, the convoy of police cars left empty handed.

"Fred's a good man. Follows instructions well," Nigel said as he watched the taillights of the cars disappear down The Ave.

Nigel finally passed out on the couch, so Ian covered him with a blanket and went to bed.

As he lay awake, reflecting on the few short weeks since leaving Brighton, Ian wondered how this would all play out. He also wondered what had really happened between Nigel and Kyla.

Chapter 34

It was early afternoon when Kyla's phone rang. The name on the call alert was Janine Woods.

"Janine, what did y' find out?" Kyla asked nervously.

"The DNA was a perfect match. MacLeod is apparently not a killer, at least not Clive Crawford's," Janine Woods said feeling relieved for Kyla.

"That's a good start and what I needed to hear luv," Kyla said hardly able to contain herself.

"Kyla, you must disclose your relationship with MacLeod," Janine stated.

"Janine, I fully intend to, but not before he is proved innocent."

"Look girl, he's in way over his head. Whatever he did to anger the people who are after him, he needs to turn himself in so we can offer him protection," Janine advised.

"I know, but honestly I've not a clue where he is Janine. I wish I did," Kyla said, knowing her words were a half truth.

"Well, your little secret is safe with me for now," Janine said trying to comfort Kyla.

"Thanks Janine and keep me posted please," Kyla said before hanging up.

Kyla dialed Nigel Cambridge's mobile number.

The sound of Nigel's mobile phone ringing could barely be heard over the deluge of rain as it fell onto the roof of the Wheatsheaf Inn. Nigel walked over, picked it up and pressed the call button, holding the device to his ear.

"Nigel speaking."

"Nigel, it's Kyla. I have good news. There is evidence now to clear Ian of the Crawford murder," Kyla stated.

"That is good news. However, things are heating up at our end. The Yard's hounds are closing in on us so MacLeod and I will have to leave Woodford soon," Nigel advised.

"Try to hang in there for a bit longer. Everyone is working very hard to get to the truth of the matter and in the end Ian will be proved innocent," Kyla replied.

"Well let's hope so. I must say, stepping into MacLeod's predicament is more than I bargained for Kyla," Nigel replied.

"I can't thank you enough," Kyla responded.

"Let's hold the applause until the final act," Nigel said as he looked over at MacLeod.

Kyla went silent for a few moments remembering the night she met Nigel. She was charmed by his clever wit and flamboyant character as well as being impressed with his SIS background. Although he was careful not to divulge state secrets, she was spellbound as he recounted the many exciting and dangerous situations he had encountered during a long and illustrious career with MI5. The fact that he had also been educated as a lawyer inspired her to recommend that he be brought in as a special consultant to 'The Metro' on cases involving organized crime. The two developed an ongoing friendship and had often met for lunch when Kyla was in London on Scotland Yard business. Although she sensed Nigel's infatuation with her, she respected him for having the good judgment to be satisfied with having her as a valued friend.

"You're a gem Nigel. Let me speak with Ian, please," Kyla said.

"Certainly," Nigel said as he handed the phone to Ian.

"Kyla, how are you?"

"I'm fine Ian, and pleased to report that there is new evidence clearing you of the Crawford murder," Kyla said happily.

"That's great news."

"Well, it's too early to celebrate yet, but soon everyone is going to see the truth about who *is* responsible for the murders—"

There was silence on the line for a moment.

"… Be careful Ian."

"Yeah, you too—," Ian said hesitantly.

Ian looked over at Nigel who was staring out the window at the falling rain.

"I ... I just wanted to tell you—," Ian said softy, looking down at the floor.

"Yes?" Kyla responded in an expectant tone.

"I'm not good at expressing myself, but I am so glad you spotted me that day outside the café," Ian replied almost in a whisper.

"Me too luv," Kyla said biting her lip.

Nigel placed his hand against the wall and turned his head towards Ian. Ian and Nigel locked eyes just as Ian hung up the phone.

* * * * *

Harry Cosgrove had just stepped into his office after a briefing with the investigation task force. Review of videotape secured from Glasgow Central prior to the departure of the 11:30 PM Virgin train showed that Ian MacLeod arrived at the station by taxi and ran into the station entrance. Further review of videotapes showed that known associates of SOCKS searched trains along the Glasgow – Euston route, ostensibly looking for MacLeod. One videotape showed MacLeod disembarking at Crewe.

Cosgrove had also been briefed by his London team that they had located and interviewed the transient youth who had witnessed the Mills murder. The youth positively identified the face he had seen as that of Danny McGinnis.

Jimmy Whiteside's report from Edinburgh all but absolved Ian MacLeod of Clive Crawford's killing on the waterfront. Having heard the preponderance of evidence now unfolding in MacLeod's favor, Detective Janine Woods decided to break her vow to Kyla and disclose the results of the DNA test on the toothbrush. She walked into Harry Cosgrove's office.

"Sir, may I have a moment?" Woods asked.

"Of course, have a seat Woods."

"I received an anonymous piece of evidence in the form of a toothbrush with Ian MacLeod's DNA on it. I had it analyzed and it matched the blood DNA from the Edinburgh belt. MacLeod got shot but he was not the shooter. The ballistics and everything else in Jimmy's report points to Danny McGinnis as the killer. The DNA cinches it sir. The transient lad's positive ID on McGinnis takes MacLeod off the hook for the Mills murder as well. It looks like MacLeod has been wrongly accused," Woods said nervously.

"And *where* might I ask did you get the toothbrush?" Cosgrove asked dubiously.

Detective Janine Woods thought for a moment before responding.

"From Kyla Fraser, sir ... Ian MacLeod is her lover," Woods admitted.

Cosgrove's mouth was agape and his eyes wide.

"Good God, how could she withhold information like that? She has an obligation of full disclosure for crissake," Cosgrove said, shocked.

Fortunately for Woods the conversation was abruptly ended.

"Sir, I have a James Stoddard from MI5 on the line," Cosgrove's assistant Gladys said.

"Fine, put him through," Cosgrove said sounding annoyed.

"Inspector Cosgrove, this is James Stoddard of MI5."

"What can I do for you Mr. Stoddard?" Cosgrove replied.

"I've had a request coming down from the highest office to stick my nose into a Scotland Yard murder investigation. I know it is highly irregular for MI5 to get involved but there is reason to believe that we have a threat to national security with what may be a rogue ex-MI5 operative by the name of Nigel Cambridge. The Home Security office has information that has led us to suspect that Cambridge may be masterminding a planned vendetta against government agencies. He and this Ian MacLeod fellow seem to be collaborating and are now thought to be together in an attempt to evade capture," Stoddard explained.

"That is the most ludicrous thing I've ever heard. It won't be necessary to have MI5 involved as we are close to solving the case," Cosgrove said expecting Stoddard to stand down.

"Too late sir, we have operatives on the move throughout the country in an attempt to flush out these two dangerous fugitives. The Home Office has mandated a cooperative effort to catch, and if necessary, kill them both," Stoddard countered.

Cosgrove knew that MI5 was capable of falsifying charges to justify their own agenda. A mandate may have in fact been sanctioned for MI5's involvement but Stoddard had the discretion and the power to decide the fate of his quarry.

"Without due course of justice? That's absurd," Cosgrove said with growing annoyance at the interference from MI5.

"Those are my orders sir," Stoddard replied.

"Well your orders are trumped up bullshit Stoddard," Cosgrove said angrily.

"I believe the sanction is clear. You continue with Scotland Yard's protocol and we with MI5's. There is no need to coordinate per se. If you find them, you simply turn them over to us. Understood?" Stoddard said dismissively.

"No, not understood. You're talking about state sanctioned murder if I'm not mistaken," Cosgrove said now enraged.

"I'm under Ministerial orders, so perhaps you should take this up with your superiors, who I believe have been apprised," Stoddard said officiously.

"Fine," Cosgrove said slamming down the receiver.

"Jeezus, this stinks," Cosgrove said exasperated.

Cosgrove was deeply disturbed at Stoddard's call and stewed for over an hour reading over the reports he had received from the debriefing. The task force investigation now pointed clearly to SOCKS as the perpetrators of the murders MacLeod was suspected of.

'This is a cover up and someone has friends in very high places,' Cosgrove thought to himself as he picked up the phone and placed a call.

"Hello," Kyla's voice answered.

"Kyla, it's Cosgrove."

"Hi there."

"Why didn't you tell me about your relationship with Ian MacLeod? You know that you have given me no other choice but to invoke Yard policy and relieve you of your duties?" Cosgrove asked.

Kyla was shocked that Janine had broken her confidence.

"I do," Kyla responded plaintively.

"Look, I understand the dilemma you are in. The good news is that MacLeod is clearly innocent. He's been set up," Cosgrove continued.

"What do you mean?" Kyla asked, surprised to be hearing this from her superior.

"I think people having influence over government officials at the highest level are behind these murders. This is the work of a professional hit man and the mob," Cosgrove concluded.

Kyla breathed a sigh of relief.

"Sir, now that the cat is out of the bag, I can confide in you that I have conducted my own investigation. I have reason to suspect that Alistair Ascot may be in collusion with Douglas McMurphy and that MacLeod was a hapless victim of his own naivety. He took on a murky role as an auditor come patsy for a mob sanctioned hit on Lance Mills. They knew he had the motive and history with his ex-boss and all they had to do was put him in the right place at the right time. What are you going to do?" Kyla asked.

"I'm not sure. I just got off the phone with the top guy at MI5. There's a sanctioned shoot to kill order against Ian MacLeod and his apparent partner Nigel Cambridge."

"That's insane. We can't let this happen sir," Kyla said, deeply disturbed.

"Well sit tight. I'll let you know what develops."

Kyla hung up the phone. Her heart was pounding. The involvement of MI5 meant almost certain death for both Ian and Nigel.

Chapter 35

Nigel stood by the window holding a corner of the curtain while peering out at a suspicious looking pair sitting in a Black Audi across the street.

"I looked into Janet McComb," Ian stated getting Nigel's attention.

"Yes?" Cambridge replied.

"She is no longer with RIA."

"Really," Cambridge replied as he let go of the curtain.

"I tracked down her home number in Glasgow and the answering machine is full. She obviously hasn't checked it."

"What do you think has happened?" Cambridge asked.

"She's probably dead," Ian said fearing the worst for her.

"Or, she's gone underground," Nigel remarked.

"Possibly," Ian replied.

"What would you do if you were fired from an organization that was tangled up with the mob?" Cambridge queried.

"I'd definitely make myself scarce," Ian agreed.

"However, I'm sure she needs to work. How does she survive?" Nigel asked.

"Maybe she rents a flat in the outskirts and runs an ad in the paper for bookkeeping services," Ian proposed.

"With value added given her prowess as a CFO … like, can do full financials or something like that," Nigel added.

"Very plausible," Ian said.

Ian was sitting at the computer when Nigel's mobile phone rang. Recognizing Kyla's number, Ian answered it.

"Hello."

"Ian, it's Kyla. I have some very disturbing news."

"What is it?"

"My boss Cosgrove knows about us, so my days at Scotland Yard are over—," Kyla stated before Ian interrupted.

"That's terrible."

"That's not the worst of it. Apparently, you are now the target of a state sanctioned kill order issued by MI5."

"You're joking. Let me put you on the speakerphone," Ian replied disbelievingly, before pushing the speaker button.

"Kyla, it's Nigel here as well."

"Hi Nigel. No, I'm not joking. I was told by Cosgrove that MI5 has been authorized to pursue you with a shoot to kill order, if necessary," Kyla responded anxiously.

"If I can get through to Janet McComb and convince her to divulge what she knows about the crooks she worked for we can turn the tables," MacLeod said earnestly.

"You don't seem to understand, Ian. There's a bullseye on the back of your head," Kyla said emphatically.

"So can they actually do that Nigel? Shoot to kill?" Ian asked incredulously.

"That is a naïve question. Does the CIA hold such powers? Of course. The Home Office would not order such barbaric actions, but SIS could and obviously did. We are no longer safe anywhere in Britain, I'm afraid," Nigel stated.

MacLeod was silent for a few moments before addressing Kyla.

"Kyla, it is imperative that we locate the former CFO of RIA, Janet McComb. She is no longer at RIA and we suspect she has gone underground. She's our only hope as we believe she knows everything about SOCKS. You need to check local papers for bookkeeper ads. It's daunting but important that we find her," Ian stated.

A knock on the door put both Ian and Nigel on high alert.

"I'll do my best—," Kyla began before Ian muted the phone.

Nigel went to the door and peeked through the peephole.

"It's Fred Carlisle," Nigel said as he opened the door.

"Sorry to bother you Nigel, but there are a couple of seedy looking chaps hanging around the pub asking questions about you. Thought you should know," the pub owner said.

"Thanks Fred," Nigel replied.

Nigel closed the door and walked over to the window.

"They've found us," Nigel said as he peeked out the curtain at the Black Audi S6 parked on the street.

"Kyla—," Ian blurted before she interjected.

"I heard all of that. I'll do what I can. Please stay safe. Call me as soon as you are able," Kyla said anxiously.

"We'll call as soon as we can. Gotta go."

Ian ended the call and looked at Nigel.

"What should we do?" Ian asked.

"Pack up and meet me behind my garage," Nigel stated.

"Alright."

Nigel walked outside onto the street and saw two thugs sitting in the Audi S6. He turned and quickly crossed the parking lot toward the house hoping they wouldn't spot him.

MacLeod was waiting at the rear of the garage and Cambridge motioned to him to join him at the front of a dilapidated building that looked like an old shed. Cambridge pulled up on the old garage door and there sitting next to his little Renault was a racing green Aston Martin Vanquish.

"Whoa, nice ride Nigel," Ian said admiring the car.

"Get in and buckle up. It's going to be the ride of your life," Cambridge instructed.

"There are two of them and they are driving a very fast car as well," Nigel stated as he buckled in and fired up the big supercar.

The burble of the Aston Martin's exhaust note was heard across the street by the two thugs who turned in an attempt to see where it was coming from. It was the sound they had been waiting to hear since arriving in Woodford knowing that Cambridge drove an Aston Martin. The Vanquish pulled out onto the road. Ian turned and looked behind, noting that the Audi was now pulling onto the road right behind them.

"You'd better step on it Nigel," Ian advised.

As they proceeded north along The Ave, Cambridge noticed the high powered Audi approaching fast in his rear view mirror.

"Hang on," Cambridge warned as the engine roared to life.

Ian marveled at the acceleration that slammed him back in his seat as he watched the digital speedometer reach 70 miles per hour in just a few seconds. Ian turned around and saw the 5.2 liter, 435 horsepower V10 Audi close behind as it matched the Aston Martin's performance.

"This is going to come down to driver skill," Nigel remarked as the two cars began a high speed road race through the English countryside.

The hair raising high performance driving along The Ave hit speeds exceeding 80 miles per hour with every bump launching both vehicles into the air and each dip exerting immense g-forces on the occupants. Less than a mile went by as they approached Church Bottom Road.

"Hold on," Nigel yelled as he slammed on the huge aftermarket brakes and threw the Aston Martin around a 120 degree corner.

The S6 didn't fare so well and almost spun out as it attempted to take the corner way too fast. Recovering, the Audi's wheel spin left a trail of white smoke as it accelerated in pursuit of the Vanquish.

"It's a mile and a half to the A360. Let's see how good these blokes are," Nigel said as he accelerated the Vanquish, deftly clicking on the paddle shifter until they reached 125 miles per hour.

The intersection approached quickly and Nigel once again stood on the big racing brakes rapidly decelerating the 4000 pound supercar. Third, second and then first gear as the RPM gauge showed a motor screaming on the edge of over-speed. Nigel entered the corner at 30 miles per hour and floored the accelerator just as the big car came into the apex, lighting up the rear tires and hanging the tail wildly to the left. Back through the gears the Aston Martin reached 80 miles per hour as Nigel looked in the rear view mirror to see the high powered Audi still in pursuit.

"This lad can really drive," Nigel said as he looked over at white knuckled and speechless Ian MacLeod.

"The next turn isn't so bad," Nigel advised.

Nigel downshifted to second and took the corner onto the A303 at high speed testing the Z rated tires to their limit. Still in pursuit the Audi stayed with the Vanquish as Stonehenge appeared on their left across a big open field.

"OK, we've got to lose these chaps. This is going to get very sketchy," Nigel warned.

A big Lorry approached in the oncoming lane. Just as it was no more than 400 yards away and closing at a combined velocity well in excess of 260 feet per second, Cambridge hit the brakes hard decelerating the big Aston Martin and locking up both shoulder harnesses. The Audi, with far less braking power and now with very hot brakes due to the grueling road race, had no choice but to take evasive action throwing the nimble Audi into the wrong lane, head on into the path of the oncoming Lorry. The Audi's driver had to make a split second survival maneuver and steered his car into the lane just ahead of the Aston Martin to avoid a head on collision with the Lorry. The maneuver exceeded the Audi's performance capabilities causing it to leave the road at high speed into a field near Stonehenge.

The Audi flew off the shoulder and slammed into the ground ripping off the front air dam as it nose-dived into the rain-soaked sod. The Audi's driver, thinking he could make the access road into Stonehenge, gunned it, sending sod and mud flying from the spinning tires, leaving two long tire tracks in the grass and narrowly missing a group of tourists. Losing momentum in the recently rain soaked field the Audi came to a halt, sinking up to its side rails, unable to flee the scene.

The Aston Martin disappeared down the A303.

As the driver, Brian Semple exited the vehicle he heard the sound of approaching sirens. A police vehicle from the Wiltshire Constabulary could be seen some distance away on A303, the main highway leading to Stonehenge. They had been nearby on their way back to the station at Wiltshire when they received a call from the Wiltshire police dispatcher that a car had left the highway at high speed just south of Stonehenge.

"Let's move it," Brian said as he broke into a run across the expansive field towards the highway.

"Yeah, I'm right behind ya mate," his partner said urgently.

The two men, desperate to make the parking lot across the highway from the main monument, attempted to cross the road in front of an approaching car causing the unnerved driver to lock up his brakes and hit the horn. Realizing they didn't have time to reach the parking lot they ran clumsily down the A303 furiously trying to flag down an approaching 'Stones and Bones' tour bus. The bus driver, hearing the sirens and seeing the two seedy looking men, continued driving around them in the other lane. As the wide eyed passengers looked on, Semple gave them the finger as his partner Fred slammed his fist against the side of the slow moving bus.

The police car came to a screeching halt ahead of the two men cutting off their attempted escape. Two officers exited the vehicle with guns drawn and commanded them to stop.

"Down on your bellies," the older male officer yelled. The two men laid face down on the pavement in front of a few onlookers as the officer's partner, a young female, disarmed and handcuffed them.

They were returned back to the scene to ascertain what had happened. As they stood by the grounded Audi the two belligerent men asked why they were being detained.

"Well for starters, you've desecrated the grounds around Stonehenge," the male officer stated.

"Tha's a load of crap. You can't arrest us for tha'," the burly Semple said antagonistically.

"OK, then how about leaving the scene of an accident and possession of illegal firearms?" the senior officer said in a more serious tone.

A witness came forward and approached the officers.

"This car was travelling east down that road over there at tremendous speed when it flew off the highway. It appeared there was a car chase between the Audi and a green Aston Martin," the witness offered.

"Thank you sir," the young female officer said as she jotted down the witness' report in her note book.

"Call in the Aston Martin and let's see if another unit might intercept them up ahead somewhere," the senior officer directed.

The two men were taken into the Wiltshire police station for questioning and identified as known criminals associated with SOCKS. Scotland Yard was notified and detectives drove to Amesbury the next morning to question the two thugs who had been held overnight. The description of the relatively rare racing green Aston Martin Vanquish was put into the system and came back with only a handful of owners in southern England.

"We've narrowed it down to two cars fitting the make, model and color," Detective Gerald Greenspan said as he reported the findings of his investigation to Harry Cosgrove at Scotland Yard headquarters.

"Who are the owners?" Cosgrove asked.

"One is a well-known rock star who lives in the Salisbury district. The other is a lawyer by the name of Nigel Cambridge, our suspect in the MacLeod case and the man wanted by Wiltshire police for dangerous driving," Greenspan replied.

"Well, I hope they survive," Cosgrove said confusing Gerald Greenspan.

"I thought these guys were dangerous felons?" Greenspan asked.

"MI5 has a shoot to kill order on them. We need to find them before secret service agents take them out," Cosgrove said solemnly.

"Why not let MI5 deal with them sir?" Greenspan asked.

"Because I believe they are innocent," Cosgrove said before hanging up.

Detective Chief Inspector Harry Cosgrove called in an APB on Cambridge's car to police across the UK.

Chapter 36

Kyla arrived in Glasgow and purchased copies of every newspaper publication she could get her hands on from local community news to the daily Herald. She then found a Starbucks in the downtown core and set about looking through the want ad section of all the papers. After almost an hour Kyla had compiled a list of 10 possible phone numbers that could be leads to finding Janet McComb. Unfortunately none of them proved fruitful.

'I'm looking in the wrong place,' Kyla thought as she booted up her laptop.

She opened up a Google search.

Bookkeeping and Tax Accounting Glasgow & Edinburgh Scotland

The search came back with so many hits that Kyla was overwhelmed and did not know where to start.

'This is impossible,' Kyla thought feeling completely defeated.

After almost two hours of searching she was about to give up when she came upon an ad that showed promise.

Mature, experienced accountant, available to do bookkeeping right up through full financials and tax advice. Reply only by email jtm@gmail.com

---

"Paydirt?" Kyla asked out loud as the man next to her turned and looked at her.

Kyla typed an email.

Liam Muir

From: Kyla Fraser
To: jtm@gmail.com
Subject: Your Ad
Date: June 22, 2009 2:15 PM

I am a professional woman in need of tax advice for my consulting business. Please advise if you can be of assistance.

Regards

K. Fraser

After an hour Kyla came up with nothing else that seemed likely, so she got in her car and returned to her home on the Isle of Arran. She set up her laptop and after it powered up she once again logged onto her Gmail account. There was a new email from jtm@gmail.com.

From: jtm@gmail.com
To: Kyla Fraser
Subject: Your Ad
Date: June 22, 2009 3:35 PM

Ms. Fraser I can be of assistance. What exactly are you looking for?

Regards

Jtm

Excited, Kyla immediately responded.

From: Kyla Fraser
To: jtm@gmail.com
Subject: Your Ad
Date: June 22, 2009 6:13 PM

I believe you are afraid for your life and I can help. I also have a vested interest in proving Ian MacLeod's innocence. If you are Janet McComb please let me help you.

Regards

K. Fraser

Within minutes there was a return email.

From: jtm@gmail.com
To: Kyla Fraser
Subject: Your Ad
Date: June 22, 2009 6:15 PM

Why should I trust you?

Regards

Jtm

Kyla typed another message.

From: Kyla Fraser
To: jtm@gmail.com
Subject: Your Ad
Date: June 22, 2009 6:17 PM

Because my life is also in danger. These people are relentless and they will find you. Let's work together to put them where they belong – in jail. I know you have information that could help do just that.

Regards

K. Fraser

Yet another email came back from who Kyla now knew was Janet McComb.

From: jtm@gmail.com
To: Kyla Fraser
Subject: Your Ad
Date: June 22, 2009 6:20 PM

I will meet you at a location where I can be sure you have not been followed or have brought them with you. Tomorrow at noon. I will be waiting just inside the entrance of the Strathclyde police headquarters on Pitt Street. If I suspect you are not alone, I'll go right inside and ask for protection.

Regards

jtm

Kyla thought for a moment.

'That's exactly the wrong place to meet.'

Not wanting to frighten her off, Kyla decided not to warn her that McMurphy had insiders at Strathclyde.

From: Kyla Fraser
To: jtm@gmail.com
Subject: Your Ad
Date: June 22, 2009 6:25 PM

OK. Let's meet there tomorrow at noon. Attached is my official Scotland Yard I.D. photo to put your mind at ease. I will wear jeans and a white top. Stand just inside so we can leave quickly and go somewhere nearby and talk. Please do not be afraid, I'm on your side.

Regards

K. Fraser

Kyla did not hear back and had to hope that Janet McComb would show up. Kyla decided not to contact Ian until she had confirmed that this was indeed Janet McComb and that she was willing to cooperate.

The next day Kyla drove into Glasgow, parked her car across from Strathclyde headquarters and watched for Janet McComb. At 11:58 a middle aged woman wearing a scarf and light colored overcoat walked up the street and into the police building. Kyla immediately got out of her car and approached the entrance. She opened the door and smiled as she made eye contact with the woman.

"Are you Janet McComb?" Kyla asked softly.

"Yes."

"Let's go," Kyla said.

Kyla pushed open the door just as Detective Black walked in through the other set of doors. He recognized Kyla Fraser from her visit to Strathclyde a few weeks earlier.

Black took out his mobile phone and dialed Douglas McMurphy's number but hung up after it rang without either an answer or going into voicemail.

The two women got into Kyla's car and drove off towards the entrance to the M8. As they drove they began a conversation.

"I'm so glad I found you Ms. McComb," Kyla said trying to make her feel comfortable.

"Yes, so am I. I've been so anxious waiting for them to track me down," Janet McComb said with a sense of relief in her voice.

"Look, I'm not sure if you know who I am, so let me fill in the blanks. I am a serial murder profiler with Scotland Yard who got involved in a romantic relationship with Ian MacLeod. As you know he was working for RIA and stole money from their client Douglas McMurphy. Based on our investigation, Scotland Yard thinks that he was set up as the patsy in a series of murders perpetrated by the mob. We also now believe that either Ascot or McMurphy pulled strings with the Home Office to get MI5 to issue a shoot to kill order, so we don't have much time to help him," Kyla explained.

"It would have been Ascot. He knows Gordon Kinsey personally," Janet offered.

"Are you willing to help us?" Kyla asked.

"Under the circumstances I don't have much choice do I?" Janet replied.

"I suppose not," Kyla said looking over at her.

Janet McComb looked tired. The lines on her face and the circles around her eyes told of a woman who had been in the throes of acute anxiety and stress.

"I know everything—their business dealings, financial situation, bank accounts, the works. I can testify that Ascot and McMurphy are collaborators in a web of crime and deceit that extends across international boundaries and brings revenue in the billions of dollars."

"Brilliant. I'd like to get you on a private jet under Scotland Yard protection if I can," Kyla offered.

"Alright, but where do I stay in the meantime?" she asked.

"Let's book into a hotel out of town until I can arrange things," Kyla responded.

"Where?" Janet asked.

"There's a hotel in Aberfeldy, the Weem I believe it's called. I think we should go right now," Kyla said glancing over at Janet.

"If that's what you think, then let's go," Janet replied.

The two women drove the 72 mile journey and arrived in Aberfeldy at 2:30. After they checked into their room at the hotel, Kyla was anxious to let Ian know she had found Janet McComb. After dialing Nigel's mobile number and getting no answer Kyla became very worried that MI5 had found them. On the verge of panic she logged into her Gmail on the hotel Wi-Fi.

From: Kyla Fraser
To: Ian MacLeod
Subject: Good News
Date: June 23, 2009 2:45 PM

I found Janet McComb. She's safe with me at a hotel in the country. Let me know when you get this message. I intend on getting her to Scotland Yard via their private jet so we can put an end to this madness.

Luv

Kyla

"I'm not sure when he might get the message so we need to try and relax in the meantime," Kyla said as Janet sat pensively on the couch across from her.

"What are we going to do next?" Janet queried.

"I'm going to arrange things with Detective Chief Inspector Harry Cosgrove to get you out of Scotland and into safe hands," Kyla replied.

Kyla dialed Cosgrove's mobile phone.

"Cosgrove here."

"Sir, I have a witness who can prove that Ascot and McMurphy are the brains behind SOCKS as well as the entire murder conspiracy," Kyla began.

Kyla explained how Janet McComb fit into the complex puzzle of McMurphy's empire and how she was willing to provide evidence that could implicate both Ascot and McMurphy.

"We need to fly her out of Glasgow in the jet sir. She cannot fly a commercial flight or she'll be picked off by their dragnet," Kyla cautioned.

"I'll arrange to fly up myself. That way no one will suspect anything out of the ordinary. I'll let you know when I have the aircraft booked," Cosgrove replied.

"Thank you sir," Kyla replied, relieved at the turn of events.

There was a flash of lightning and then a few seconds later a huge clap of thunder rolled as the entire hotel shook. A sudden downpour whipped by violent winds sent a torrent of rain against the wooden windows of the old three story structure.

"All we can do is sit and wait," Kyla said as she watched the storm from the safety of their room in Aberfeldy.

Chapter 37

"Spybird has a fix on a green Aston Martin sitting near a farmhouse just off the A1 north of the England Scotland border," MI5 technology agent Mathias Dexter said referring to MI5's eye in the sky. He transmitted the GPS coordinates to field operative Kerry Beckinsworth.

"The GPS coordinates are 55.8269375 longitude, -2.0619965 latitude," Beckinsworth noted as he sat in the right hand seat of the idling helicopter, code named for the mission, operation 'Dark Shadow'.

"Let's get this bird in the air," Commanding Officer Bert Hardwick said.

The veteran combat pilot was flying the Griffin HAR2 helicopter on loan to the Secret Service from 84 Squadron at RAF Akrotiri, Cyprus. He calmly keyed in the GPS coordinates to the navigation system and then executed the start checklist.

The rotor blades and tail rotor came to life and the two Pratt & Whitney PT6T-3D turboshafts spooled up lifting the four blade multirole machine into the air from RAF Leuchars, near St Andrews, Scotland at 2200 hours GMT.

Hardwick and the two MI5 operatives were wearing state of the art night vision goggles allowing them to see any movement that occurred on the ground as they flew the low level night mission. Beckinsworth's partner was agent Jarod Smith, a 10 year veteran of the service trained in hand to hand mortal combat techniques. The two operatives were dressed in black from head to toe.

"My plan is to fly in low and slow setting down with enough distance to reduce the opportunity for detection," Commander Hardwick advised.

"10-4," Beckinsworth's acknowledgment crackled over the intercom.

"According to the GPS we're 70 nautical miles inbound to the target, so about 30 minutes," Hardwick noted.

They were flying no more than 100 feet off the ground following the forward looking terrain guidance system as well as being able to see with the night vision equipment. As they approached from about 10 miles out, Hardwick flew off the coastline intending on setting down on a low tide mudflat adjacent to a wooden pier.

"You'll be less than 700 meters from your target once you disembark," Hardwick said as he maintained his heading towards his touchdown point.

"Once we're down, kill the engines and wait. We'll have them dispatched in no more than 20 minutes," Beckinsworth instructed.

Hardwick could see the mudflat ahead of his aircraft as he pitched it up and decreased the collective, slowing the machine to a landing configuration. He gently touched down and killed the engine to reduce noise as the two operatives jumped out onto the marshy ground.

Beckinsworth motioned to his partner to take the lead and they crossed the beach line into a grove of trees.

"The handheld shows the target at 260 degrees and 600 meters. Let's go," Beckinsworth directed.

The two operatives stealthily crossed the farmer's field in the pitch dark of a heavy overcast night. The chill did not bother them as they both wore woolen night assault gear and balaclavas. As they approached the tiny one room farmhouse Jarod Smith went ahead to scout the situation. He crept up behind the Aston Martin and looked inside, seeing no evidence of their targets. After scanning the area with his night vision goggles, Smith looked at his partner and pointed towards a partially opened window on the side of the darkened house.

"They must be asleep," he whispered over his radio headset.

Beckinsworth began to creep towards his partner's location.

"In and out through that window over there."

"10-4," came Smith's barely audible acknowledgement.

Beckinsworth and Smith crossed the 100 feet in less than 10 seconds stopping underneath the partially open window. Smith motioned to Beckinsworth to open the window wider. He reached up and pulled the window out enough for them to make entry.

Smith, the more experienced of the two in hand to hand combat, got up from his crouching position and peered over the windowsill into the room. He could see two sleeping figures on the single beds situated on either side of the room. One at a time the agents launched themselves silently over the sill. Smith stealthily moved to his target while Beckinsworth did the same. In a lightning fast move Smith violently garroted his victim.

"What the fuck?" Smith cried out as he angrily threw a pillow across the room.

The sound of a high powered engine roared to life and without another word, Beckinsworth leapt out the window. Smith followed as Beckinsworth drew his semi-automatic pistol and began firing at the fleeing vehicle now over 300 yards away.

"Goddamit," Beckinsworth yelled as he kicked the dusty ground in frustration.

The two highly trained MI5 operatives stood dumbfounded as the darkened Aston Martin vanished from sight into a thicket of trees. Beckinsworth grabbed his handheld radio.

"Subjects are a code 9, repeat, subjects are a code 9," Beckinsworth informed headquarters over the radio.

The sound of the Aston Martin accelerating and going through the gears could be heard for miles around in the silence of the English Scottish countryside.

"Dark Shadow, start your engines. Mission scrubbed," Beckinsworth barked over his headset.

"10-4," Commander Hardwick responded.

The two MI5 agents scrambled towards the waiting helicopter.

Cambridge and Ian drove north on the A1 as Nigel switched on the powerful halogen headlamps and lit up the road ahead.

"Look over there," Ian said pointing to the shape of the waiting helicopter, its rotor blades spooling up as it sat on the marsh about a quarter of a mile away.

"I think we should head back to Berwick-upon-Tweed," Nigel noted as he turned the big car around in the opposite direction.

"Why?" Ian asked.

"Well, they came by helicopter and no doubt the pilot knows that the mission has been scrubbed. They'll try to tail us. Hopefully he didn't see the headlamps. Open the glove box. There's a pair of night vision goggles I keep for situations just like this," Nigel directed.

Ian did as he was told and handed the goggles to Cambridge who donned them quickly.

"Where are we headed?" Ian asked.

"When they call it in, the whole RAF will be flying reconnaissance across routes in the vicinity. We need to cut across country through Kelso and head back to Carlisle on the less travelled routes. We also need to ditch the Aston Martin for obvious reasons. Once we make Carlisle we can rent a car and see if we can leave the Vanquish in a garage out of sight from detection."

"I'm glad you were standing watch," Ian said referring to their bivouac hidden amongst the trees adjacent to the farmhouse.

"It's tricky business spotting darkened figures at night, especially when they're so highly trained. They didn't have heat signature capability, otherwise we'd be dead by now," Cambridge replied as he concentrated on his driving.

The road was very quiet in the early morning hours and it was disconcerting to be travelling at high speed without any headlamps. Ian looked ahead trying to make out the road sign as they turned right onto a dark country road. The street lamp on the corner illuminated the sign which read: Carlisle, 120 miles.

A few minutes later, Nigel spotted a car parked along the side of the secluded country road.

"You can't see but we're just about to scare off a soon to be lit up decoy," Nigel said as the darkened Aston Martin raced along the deserted route at over 140 miles per hour.

A young couple were making out in the back seat of an older model car when the pressure wave and Doppler Effect of the two-ton Vanquish rocked the parked car violently with a 205 foot per second pressure wave.

"Omigod Jimmy, slow down love," his girlfriend moaned as the back seat moved like a roller coaster.

"What the hell was that?" Jimmy yelled out as his head popped up, wide-eyed.

Putting a hasty end to their lovemaking, the young man leapt into the front seat, started the car and slammed it into gear, pulling a U-turn. The tail lamps of the lovers' car soon disappeared down the deserted country road.

Chapter 38

"McMurphy, it's Black."

"What's up Detective?" McMurphy asked as he switched his mobile phone to speaker.

"I tried to call you several times but you didn't pick up or return the calls," Black said seemingly agitated.

"Yeah, sorry about that. I had no mobile signal on my way up to the Highland bunker. What's going on?" McMurphy asked.

"I saw that nosy Scotland Yard profiler at headquarters with a middle aged woman. Thought you should know. I got a feeling that she was up to something," Black said.

"What'd the other woman look like?" McMurphy asked.

"Didn't get a good look, but she was an older lass, maybe fifty with dirty blond hair from what I could see under her scarf. Not a bad looker," Black advised.

"Jeezus, I'll bet it was Janet McComb. When did you see them?" McMurphy asked urgently.

"The day before yesterday," Black replied.

"Thanks for the tip Black, I gotta go," McMurphy said before ending the call.

McMurphy dialed up Ascot.

"Ascot here."

"My guy at Strathclyde saw both Kyla Fraser and a woman fitting Janet McComb's description leaving the Pitt Street headquarters," McMurphy advised.

"Well for heaven sakes get your bloody men on it McMurphy," Ascot replied curtly.

"Yeah, yeah, I wanted you to know that's all," McMurphy replied.

"Douglas, I told you we were going to tighten the noose around MacLeod's neck and I've done my part. Where the hell have you been in this mess? The noose is getting tight alright, but around the wrong bloody neck. It appears that it is we who are being led to the gallows," Ascot said clearly annoyed with McMurphy's inept handling of the situation.

"Look, don't point your finger at me Alistair. You're the one who brought MacLeod into our midst, not me," McMurphy said heatedly.

"Alright, now let cooler heads prevail Douglas. Divided we fall and all that jazz. I suggest you mobilize your people to look for her and I'll make some calls myself," Ascot said composing himself.

"Will do," McMurphy responded.

"We'll talk later," Ascot said before hanging up.

Ascot stared out the window.

"Oh my," Ascot said as he sat alone in his office.

"Mr. Ascot there's a call for you on Line 3," receptionist Priscilla Hughes advised.

"Thank you," Ascot said as he picked up the phone.

"It's Stoddard here."

"Yes?" Ascot queried.

"Our people have information on an aircraft movement out of Heathrow. Apparently the commanding officer at Scotland Yard has booked a jet to pick up a Janet McComb at Glasgow International. It's in the air as we speak. Agents have been notified," Stoddard advised.

"My, my, this is not good news," Ascot said with audible strain in his voice.

"Also, the RAF reported that two non-military personnel had to scrub a night mission yesterday," Stoddard said.

"What are you saying?" Ascot inquired.

"I'm saying these guys are making it very hard to catch them. Last night we sent in two of our elite commandoes trained in hand to hand combat by military helicopter to a sighting at an old farmhouse. They should have easily taken out MacLeod and Cambridge but it appears that they were very cleverly tricked. They ended up garroting a pillow," Stoddard said his voice sounding stressed.

"Are you saying your most elite people are that stupid?" Ascot asked in a disdainful and accusatory tone.

"Mr. Ascot, I don't appreciate your attitude," Stoddard said becoming angry.

"I'll let the Home Secretary know your sentiments on a mission he himself endorsed Stoddard," Ascot said intimidatingly.

"He'll deny any involvement. This is MI5 business now so I would be very careful what you say or do sir," Stoddard threatened.

"Go to hell," Ascot said slamming the phone down.

Ascot was steaming as he took a deep breath and tried to calm down.

"Bloody great," Ascot said shaking his head.

Ascot paced his office for a few minutes trying to decide what to do next. He spent several minutes scanning his contacts on his computer before picking up his phone and dialing a London number.

"Sir Walter Neville's Scotland Yard office," greeted the receptionist.

"May I speak to Sir Walter please?" Ascot asked politely in his most refined English pronunciation.

"Who shall I say is calling?"

"Alistair Ascot."

"Just a moment please."

"Neville here," an aristocratic voice answered.

"Yes, it's Alistair Ascot calling from RIA in Glasgow. Do you remember me, Sir Walter?" Ascot queried.

"Of course Mr. Ascot. We met at the Prime Minister's inaugural ball," Neville responded.

"Yes that's right," Ascot said relieved that the head of Scotland Yard had remembered him.

"How can I help you?" Neville asked.

"One of our former employees, Janet McComb has been picked up by your commanding officer and is being flown into Heathrow. I'm not sure if you are up to speed, but we want her investigated for tax fraud and misappropriation of trust funds. It is suspected that she was embezzling funds from RIA for years and we would like to have her prosecuted right here in Glasgow. I was hoping you could step in and have her brought back to Strathclyde where a Detective Black is filing charges against her," Ascot said fabricating his lie as he went along.

"Interesting. I'm sorry to hear that she has perpetrated crimes against your own firm Mr. Ascot. Unfortunately MI5 also seems to have an interest in her and as a matter of fact I just got off the line from James Stoddard. She must be a high value target for the Home Secretary's top national security fellow to be involved don't you think?" Sir Neville asked.

"I suppose," Ascot responded.

"I'm afraid there's nothing I can do now that MI5 is involved. My own commanding officer is about to get waylaid and relieved of his custody of Ms. McComb by SIS agents as soon as he touches down at Heathrow," Neville stated.

"Hmm, so sorry to have troubled you Sir Walter," Ascot replied somewhat relieved, knowing he could now access McComb through his contact at MI5.

"No trouble at all," Neville said, ending the call.

Reflecting for a moment, Ascot picked up the phone and dialed another number.

"This is McMurphy."

"Things are unraveling Douglas, but perhaps in our favor if I play things right. I just spoke to Sir Walter Neville at Scotland Yard and he tells me that MI5 is on McComb's trail. Let me see if I might convince Stoddard to release her into your custody so you can have her dispatched before she puts us behind bars," Ascot said coldly.

* * * * *

As the sleek business jet carrying Detective Chief Inspector Harry Cosgrove and Janet McComb reached cruise altitude, Cosgrove prepared to interview her.

"Miss McComb, I know how difficult this has been for you but with your testimony we are going to be able to put these criminals away for a very long time," Cosgrove said.

"I'll have you know that I am terrified because I know how evil McMurphy is," Janet McComb said as she loosened her seat belt.

"Don't worry, as soon as we are on the ground at Heathrow we'll place you in protective custody for as long as it takes to bring them to justice," Cosgrove said in an attempt to calm his witness before asking her to make a statement.

"Before we proceed any further, I have to ask you why you agreed to work under such circumstances. You may have placed yourself in the position of being culpable in the crimes you are about to disclose knowledge of Ms. McComb," Cosgrove cautioned.

"I understand, and I am prepared to face the consequences. Better that than being killed and disposed of," McComb countered.

"Fair enough. I will do my best to absolve you of your participation based on the fact that you are providing important testimony that will incriminate these gangsters. Off the record, you must have been paid very well to be willing to turn a blind eye Ms. McComb," Cosgrove led.

"I was and in hindsight, I regret not coming forward sooner but I was in a Catch 22. I knew full well that they would not think twice about killing me so I continued and kept my mouth shut through coercion," McComb admitted.

During the two hour flight from Glasgow, Cosgrove recorded statements from Janet McComb detailing all of the illegal activities of Douglas McMurphy as well as RIA's involvement in the SOCKS business empire. Cosgrove organized his written notes and made a copy of the digital file of the voice recording. He walked up to the cockpit and asked if he could email the file while in the air and was advised that he could. He walked back to his seat and used his Blackberry to email the files. On the flight deck the pilots prepared for the approach into London.

"Good afternoon, this is Scotland Yard Golf Charlie Alpha Alpha Bravo inbound flight level three zero zero, request decent clearance Heathrow," Captain Alan Harvey said into the microphone on his headset.

"Roger Alpha Alpha Bravo, squawk 4512 for ident please," the controller's voice from Heathrow Center crackled over the cockpit speaker and on his headset.

"Squawking 4512 Alpha Bravo," Captain Harvey responded.

"Alpha Bravo, you are cleared to descend flight level 150 contact Heathrow approach at 119.725," Heathrow Center advised.

"Thank you sir and good day," Harvey said as he throttled back the twin turbofan engines of the BAE-125 belonging to Scotland Yard.

Pushing the nose over Captain Harvey began his descent into Heathrow. A few minutes later the main landing gear touched down on runway 09 left.

The mid-sized business jet taxied to Aviation House where a car was waiting to whisk them off to headquarters as soon as they stepped off the aircraft. The jet came to a halt and immediately the whine of the turbines began to spool down. The first officer exited the cockpit and opened the cabin door where a stairway had already been mobilized for the deplaning passengers.

Cosgrove escorted Janet McComb to the exit where they walked down the stairs to the asphalt ramp that was awash in pouring rain. The two were huddled under Cosgrove's umbrella as they made a dash to the terminal entrance when a man in a black suit pushed open the door in a gesture of etiquette.

"Detective Chief Inspector Harry Cosgrove?" the man asked as they were surrounded by two officious looking men.

Realizing that these were secret service agents and his witness was in dire trouble, Cosgrove grabbed Janet McComb's arm and threw her ahead of him.

"Run," Cosgrove yelled as he turned in an attempt to stop the two men.

He tripped one of them and struggled with the other grabbing him by the arm and flinging him to the ground.

Cosgrove delivered a vicious kick to the man he had tripped but it was futile as the other agent recovered and had him in a headlock before he could inflict any more damage.

"Get his bags and search them," the man with the clean shaven face and shiny head directed.

"You sonsabitches. You can't do this. I'm the commanding officer of Scotland Yard for crissake," Cosgrove said in protest.

"We don't care if you're the President of the United States. We're pulling rank," the man said as he flashed an MI5 badge at Cosgrove.

"Fuck you," Cosgrove said venomously as he was held by the muscular agent who had him immobilized.

"Your witness is now in our custody. We'll release you if you promise not to resist any further, otherwise we'll place you under detention and you'll be held indeterminately sir," the stone faced agent said awaiting Cosgrove's response.

Cosgrove knew well the far reaching powers that MI5 wielded and decided that it was in his best interest to surrender to the situation. He saw that Janet McComb had been intercepted by another agent before she could escape and she looked shaken up by the ordeal.

"Alright," Cosgrove relented.

He addressed Janet McComb.

"Don't worry Ms. McComb, I'll get you released if it's the last thing I do," Harry Cosgrove said with a sneer at the MI5 agents that had roughed him up.

"Where did you send this data?" one of the agents asked holding up the data stick in his hand.

"To my office of course," Cosgrove said as he saw the man pull out his written notes and digital voice recorder placing them in his own briefcase.

The lead MI5 agent instructed his men to release him.

"I'll have you fired for this," Cosgrove threatened as the entourage left with Janet McComb in their custody.

Cosgrove dialed Kyla's mobile phone number.

"Hello?"

"Kyla, SIS has Janet in their custody," Cosgrove advised.

"Oh no. How could they have found out that you had her on the company jet?" Kyla asked.

"Who knows? Maybe my phone was tapped," Cosgrove said exasperated.

"What can we do now?"

"Take matters into our own hands. You need to let me know where MacLeod is so I can help him," Cosgrove said.

"Honestly, I don't know," Kyla replied.

"Are they planning to be in Glasgow?" Cosgrove asked.

"I'm not sure sir."

"OK, let me know if you hear anything," Cosgrove said before ending the call.

Cosgrove headed directly to his home to recover the file containing Janet McComb's statement that he had emailed while enroute from Glasgow.

'I need to get there before MI5 breaks in and hacks my computer,' Cosgrove thought as he drove towards his home in Richmond on the outskirts of London.

After a furious drive to his residence, Cosgrove arrived and parked his BMW in the back lane. Using the rear entrance, he entered the house where he lived alone and proceeded to his study. He sat down, clicked the mouse again and again, but the screen was blank. He tried to reboot the computer without success. He then clicked on his iPhone to open his email and found that his account no longer existed. Cosgrove got up and walked to the front door. It was not locked. Cosgrove slammed his hand against the door.

"Damn!"

Chapter 39

"Ascot, it's Jim Hawkins over at MI5, Stoddard's second. He asked me to call you."

"What is it?" Ascot queried.

"We have Ms. McComb safely in our hands and we'll hold her here pending further instructions," Hawkins advised.

"Excellent. Don't let her talk to anyone," Ascot urged.

"We won't. Stoddard wants you to know that we have her statement to Detective Chief Inspector Harry Cosgrove in our possession," Hawkins replied.

"Good. Send the original files to me right away and destroy the electronic files in your possession please," Ascot instructed.

"They're already on their way via courier. You should have them this afternoon. And Chief Agent Stoddard advised that he would trash the files you are referring to."

"Thank you," Ascot replied.

"Good day sir," Hawkins said as he hung up the phone.

An hour later a special courier package arrived on Ascot's desk and both McMurphy and Ascot were present when he opened it. Ascot pulled out a USB stick and plugged it into the boardroom computer. He then opened the file and put it up on the smart screen in the boardroom.

"Lock the door would you Douglas?" Ascot asked as he scrolled the document for reading. Both men read an excerpt from Janet McComb's statement as it appeared on the screen.

This is the true and full statement of Janet McComb taken by Detective Chief Inspector Harry Cosgrove on this the 25th day of June 2009.

"My name is Janet Teresa McComb. I live at 2749 Dunlevy Crescent, Glasgow Scotland. I was employed as the Chief Financial Officer at RIA Accounting and Consultancy Services Limited at 29 St Vincent Street, Glasgow Scotland. While so employed I became privy to certain illegal activities that occurred between Douglas McMurphy and Alistair Ascot. These activities included establishing business relationships with companies that carried out illegal business operations of which both Ascot and McMurphy were the beneficiaries in varying percentage interests. Although RIA acted in the capacity of auditor and advisor, and I was responsible for all of the financial dealings therein, I was also responsible for the maintenance of bank accounts that were set up under DM Enterprises of which Douglas McMurphy and Alistair Ascot were the sole officers. The bank accounts contained monies in the hundreds of millions of dollars gained from the illegal activities I referred to earlier including but not limited to gambling, prostitution, drug trafficking, sex trade, human trafficking, graft, fraud, bribing of public officials, misappropriation of public trust funds ...

The statement continued on exposing details about the illegal nature of RIA's relationship with Douglas McMurphy.

... In the early spring of 2009 RIA client Mr. Jack Singleton approached RIA Managing Partner, Jordie Dunsmuir seeking assistance in financing his mixed use riverfront project in Manchester, UK. Having been denied financing through conventional channels, Managing Partner Jordie Dunsmuir introduced Singleton to Douglas McMurphy, who offered to provide mezzanine financing. Singleton borrowed £20 million pounds at an interest rate of 25% on the representation that McMurphy would use his influence to secure conventional financing for the project within six months. When Jordie Dunsmuir sent in an independent auditor, Kerry Grant, of Manchester to do a valuation study on Singleton's project Grant suspected that the mezzanine funding was laundered drug money. Grant reported his findings to Dunsmuir thinking he had found a smoking gun and expected to be commended, but instead realized he had opened up a Pandora's Box of criminal involvement in Singleton's project. Grant warned Singleton and threatened to go to the authorities. When Dunsmuir found out about Grant's intentions, he and McMurphy requested that Singleton pay back the loan on demand which, given Singleton's financial troubles, was impossible. Singleton's default allowed McMurphy's company DM Enterprises Ltd. to acquire complete ownership of the project in lieu of repayment of the unsecured loan. McMurphy's son, Joseph, was put in charge of the project and made second in command at Dundee Constructors when they took over the Singleton project from a local Manchester contractor hired by Singleton. Singleton was distraught over McMurphy's actions calling them excessive and punitive, responding by threatening Dunsmuir with the auditor Kerry Grant's findings. In the days following, on or about May 3, 2009, Dunsmuir made a business trip to Manchester after which I found out about Jack Singleton's murder and Grant's disappearance.

A few weeks later, RIA carried out an extensive audit on a business partner suspected of hiding profits that were due to their client, Douglas McMurphy. The client, Lance Mills, was part of a secret partnership in a nationwide street prostitution ring that exploited young eastern European women. Although the RIA audit did not find supporting evidence, it was still suspected that Mills was not honoring his agreement to share profits from the business as had been agreed to with Douglas McMurphy. To that extent it was decided that a secret audit was to take place to expose his fraudulent misreporting and to recover the monies due to McMurphy. In retrospect, it became obvious that they planned to kill Mills even before MacLeod's involvement made him an expedient pawn. Dunsmuir met Ian MacLeod in a chance encounter on the London - Glasgow train on or about May 4, 2009. Upon Dunsmuir's return from London and Manchester, with the knowledge that MacLeod had a personal connection to Mr. Mills as well as further investigation that found there were strained relations between them, he was hired to carry out a so called 'night audit' in an attempt to recover the missing funds Mills was suspected of hiding from McMurphy. The night audit took place on or about June 1, 2009 and successfully uncovered approximately £1,000,000 of hidden profits in an HMQS account. Mills was murdered the next day and I subsequently overheard a conversation between Ascot and Dunsmuir given that my office was next to Dunsmuir's. The gist of that conversation was that MacLeod was to be framed for the murder given his personal connection and known difficult relationship with Lance Mills that resulted in his firing just weeks before the murder. I became increasingly careful what I did and said from that point onward. MacLeod did a second audit at Dundee Constructors, a company that McMurphy was in the process of acquiring from the Dundee family of Edinburgh. After MacLeod audited Dundee, CEO Clive Crawford was subsequently murdered. Two days later, both Dunsmuir and I were called into a meeting with Alistair Ascot and Douglas McMurphy and informed that MacLeod apparently stole four million dollars due from Crawford in a business deal unrelated to the Dundee acquisition. They claimed he had somehow acquired the bank passcodes, passwords and account numbers and transferred the funds from an RIA Swiss bank account into his own personal Swiss account. I was not able to confirm the veracity of their contention as that is where my career with RIA ended and I was subsequently fired.

I went into hiding, fearing for my life and was eventually found by Ian MacLeod's girlfriend Kyla Fraser and brought to the safety of Scotland Yard.

End of Statement.

"Jeezus, how damning," Ascot remarked after reading it.

"No shit," McMurphy remarked.

"However, we can breathe easy now Douglas. I have the original statement so I'll ask Stoddard to release McComb into your people's custody and you can dispose of her," Ascot said indifferently.

"Now what do we do about MacLeod and Fraser?" McMurphy asked.

"We'll take care of them Douglas. But first we need to get our hands on MacLeod and if we can, our money. No more screw ups."

Chapter 40

After driving through the farmlands and mountains that straddle the border of northern England and Scotland, Nigel Cambridge and Ian MacLeod arrived in Carlisle just before dawn. Pulling into a small used car rental company, they parked the Aston Martin behind the metal building that presumably was the mechanic's shop. By 8:00 AM they saw someone opening up the front door.

"Let me do this, you stay in the car," Cambridge said.

He walked over to the entrance.

"Good morning," Cambridge said as he walked up to the sales counter.

"Yes, can I help you?"

"We've got some car trouble and we need to leave the Vanquish over there and rent something to get into Glasgow. We'll be back in a couple of days with the part we need so we can get it roadworthy and be on our way," Cambridge explained.

"Oh, how unfortunate. Very nice car by the way," the freckle faced lad behind the counter noted.

"Thank you. Oh and do you think we could store it inside?" Cambridge asked.

"Don't see why not. I'll open the garage and you can pull it into a corner of the shop."

"That would be brilliant, thanks so much," Cambridge replied.

"What kind of car would you like to rent then?" the counter clerk asked.

"I suppose that little Ford Focus over there would do," Cambridge said pointing at a small white sedan parked nearby.

After completing the transaction and pulling the Vanquish into the shop they were about to leave when Nigel pulled out a £20 note and gave it to the young man.

"Please make sure that the car cover stays on the car. I'm very particular about who touches it," Nigel said.

"No problem sir," the clerk replied looking into the open window of the little white sedan.

They pulled out and were on their way to Glasgow.

"I'd give anything for a proper meal," Ian noted as they passed a MacDonald's.

"You call that proper food?" Nigel asked.

They had been living on fruit and crackers, not daring to stop at a restaurant for fear of being spotted.

"I never thought I'd return to my flat but that's where we'll stay when we get to Glasgow," Ian said as he drove the little car onto the M6 onramp.

"You're sure that no one knows the location of your flat?" Cambridge asked.

"Absolutely, I was very careful not to disclose it to anyone but Kyla," Ian replied.

A few hours later Ian and Nigel arrived at the Dundas Street flat, taking care not to be seen as they walked across the busy street near Queen Street Station and entered the front door to The Ayrshire.

After an exhausting night of driving, Nigel retired to Ian's bedroom for a nap. Ian couldn't sleep so he stood looking out the window while Nigel slept. Nigel's phone rang and Ian answered it.

"Hello."

"Ian, thank God you're OK!" Kyla exclaimed.

"Barely, it's been quite an ordeal, that I can tell you," Ian replied.

"I'm so relieved. Where are you now?" Kyla asked.

"At the flat."

"I need to see you right away. I'm in Glasgow as we speak," Kyla pleaded.

"Not here, it's too risky."

Thoughtful for a moment, Ian continued.

"Let's meet at the Highlander in the triangle just past the bus park. We should be safe there."

"Fine, how about in 20 minutes?"

"Alright, see you then," Ian said before ending the call.

A short time later, Ian walked into the tiny café and noticed Kyla in a corner booth. She got up as soon as she spotted Ian and they embraced. Kyla pulled back and looked up at him.

"Ian, I tried to contact you by phone and email but I never heard back. I thought you were dead."

"I'm sorry. It's been a crazy ride. I've been too busy trying to stay alive to even look at my email."

"Sit down Ian," Kyla said motioning to the booth.

They looked at each other across the table.

"Ian, Janet McComb was captured by MI5."

There was a look of surprise on Ian's face.

"Oh no, I'm sunk then," Ian responded dejectedly.

"Don't say that. The police have all but absolved you."

"Tell that to MI5," Ian countered.

"We've got to stay focussed Ian and do the right things now, including giving up the money you stole," Kyla said looking Ian in the eye.

Ian braced.

"No way, Kyla," Ian replied defensively.

"Ian, the reason they are after you is because of the money and you know it," Kyla countered.

"What? I'm supposed to walk up to McMurphy and apologize, handing over a bag with four million dollars in it?"

"It's theft of laundered money and you must turn it into the authorities," Kyla said raising her voice.

"Kyla, there's no way you'll ever convince me to give up that money after all I've been through."

"Ian, my integrity and sense of right and wrong is deeply offended by your attitude. I expect better than that from someone I am in a relationship with," Kyla said sharply.

Ian glared at Kyla.

"You sit in your safe little sanctuary on Arran while I'm being hunted down as a wanted felon for a crime I didn't commit and you have the nerve to lecture me about integrity?" Ian said loudly.

"Ian, I am going to lose my job over this!" Kyla exclaimed.

Ian steeled his jaw, unresponsive to Kyla's concern.

Kyla glared at Ian for a moment before grabbing her purse, getting up from the table and walking determinedly towards the entrance of the tiny café.

Ian watched in silence as Kyla disappeared through the doors into the rainy Glasgow afternoon. After a few moments, he got up and walked outside. Looking around, Ian pulled up the collar on his windbreaker and walked disconsolately back to The Ayrshire.

Nigel was sitting on the couch reading the newspaper when Ian walked into the flat.

Without saying a word to Nigel, he logged onto the web and surfed mindlessly to ease the pain of what had just happened between him and Kyla. He saw a news story. The headline read 'RIA executive Jordie Dunsmuir found dead in the Clyde.'

"Omigod," MacLeod uttered.

He turned to Cambridge.

"Nigel, we're done for," MacLeod exclaimed.

Cambridge lowered his paper and noticed MacLeod slumped over. He got up and walked to MacLeod's side.

"What's wrong old chap?" Nigel asked.

MacLeod raised his head and slowly turned toward Cambridge.

"What's wrong? You're asking me what's wrong? I've crossed the bloody country, not once but twice, pursued by McMurphy's murderous henchmen and scared half to death by your lunatic driving. We're nearly finished off by MI5. Kyla just walked out on me and now the only hope we have, Janet McComb, is kidnapped. And you ask me what's wrong?"

Cambridge remained calm, raising his eyebrows.

"Are you done?" Cambridge asked.

MacLeod was embarrassed. His face turned red and he looked down at the floor, averting his eyes from Cambridge.

"Look, I'm sorry. I've no right to blame anyone but myself for this mess. I almost had it all. Kyla, a new life, and now it's gone Nigel, gone," Ian stated despondently.

Cambridge placed his hand on MacLeod's shoulder.

"Ian, you're focusing on what hasn't happened yet. I know Kyla. She's a headstrong lass but I know she would never have risked her own career unless she loved you. Look me in the eye, MacLeod," Cambridge said softly.

MacLeod raised his head and made eye contact with Cambridge.

"Now, where there's a will there's a way. It's time you grew some knackers and started acting like a man for God's sake. You took McMurphy on by stealing his money, so what did you expect? A thank you note? Now finish the damn job," Cambridge admonished.

MacLeod was silent for a moment. His face took on a determined look as he gritted his teeth.

"You're right. I'm gonna take McMurphy and Ascot down or die tryin'," MacLeod said determinedly.

Cambridge stood erect and pulled back his chin.

"Well, speaking for myself, I prefer the former option."

MacLeod furiously typed a search into the keyboard.

"I'm gonna break into Ascot's office and get the evidence myself to put them away for good."

"And how do you propose doing that? A security pass and key might help," Cambridge said mockingly.

MacLeod pointed to an image on his computer screen.

"I'll climb the face of 29 St Vincent and go in through the fourth floor window, right there."

Cambridge tried to contain himself, placing his hand over his mouth as he chuckled.

"I'm serious Nigel. What's so funny?" MacLeod asked as he stood up and placed his hands on his hips.

Cambridge put on a straight face.

"I'm so sorry, MacLeod. I had no idea I had befriended Spider-Man himself," Cambridge said with a serious face before breaking into ridiculing laughter.

Humiliated, MacLeod sat down at his computer and studied the image, ignoring Cambridge. Cambridge's facial expression became somber as he glanced at the image again.

"Hmm. You're serious aren't you?"

MacLeod turned and addressed Cambridge.

"Look, when I was younger, one of my hobbies was rock climbing. I've never done a free solo climb, but what other option do I have left?"

As Cambridge looked on, Ian began to survey the building face at 29 St Vincent Street. The images available on Google Earth Street View showed in detail all of the reveals, cornices and articulated forms that Ian would have to negotiate during a free solo climb of the stone monolith.

Cambridge tilted his head and pursed his lips.

"Well young man, you climb that building, I'll crack the bloody safe."

MacLeod smiled.

"It's a deal."

* * * * *

At 10 PM, MacLeod and Cambridge left the flat and walked the short distance to RIA Headquarters at 29 St Vincent Street.

They stood beneath the four story monolith looking at the forbidding stone face that had been weathered with age for over 150 years.

"OK Nigel, wish me luck," Ian said as he looked up at his planned route to the window set back from the large ledge almost 80 feet above him.

"Wait a minute. Let me see if I can make this a little easier, not to mention less threatening to your health. Stay out of sight until I signal you," Nigel stated as he looked over at the lit up lobby.

A lone security guard sat behind a large oak reception desk head down reading a newspaper. Nigel walked over to the entrance and tapped on the glass. The security guard looked up and squinted, trying to make out who was outside at the building entrance. Finally he got up and walked over to the access door next to the revolving turnstile which was locked for the night. He stared out at Nigel holding up his palms in a questioning gesture. Nigel motioned for him to open the door. After a moment of hesitation the guard cracked open the door.

"Yes, I'm Dr. Greenspan. I'm here to meet a chap who is working late on the fourth floor. He asked if you could show me to suite 405."

"There is no suite 40—"

Cutting the guard's words short, Cambridge lashed out violently and struck him in the throat. The guard collapsed and Cambridge entered the lobby. He motioned for MacLeod to join him.

"What did you do?" MacLeod asked.

"Don't worry, he's not dead. Go to the concierge desk and find something to tie him up," Nigel instructed.

Ian ran over to the desk and searched furiously to find some binding material. He came back with a roll of duct tape which Nigel grabbed. They dragged the guard to a rear 'exit only' stairwell and dumped him inside.

"What exactly did you do to him?" Ian asked as he watched Nigel lash his hands and feet together.

"When he answered the door I hit his carotid artery with a knockout shot called dim mak death point stomach 9. Haven't used it for awhile so it was a lucky break when his lights went out," Nigel said, glancing up at Ian as he placed a piece of tape over the guard's mouth.

Next, they walked to the elevator and took it to the fourth floor where they emerged and headed to RIA's entry door.

Cambridge peered inside and sized up the problem of getting into RIA's offices.

"No keypad means it's a silent alarm system, so we have maybe three to five minutes before police arrive."

Cambridge lifted his right foot and kicked at the glass just to the left of the locking device, jumping back as the glass shattered onto the floor. Calmly reaching his hand inside, he opened the door.

They entered and Ian led them to Janet McComb's old office and located the large Chubb safe.

"Now be silent," Nigel said as he listened carefully to the sound of the tumblers while turning the combination dial. Precious minutes passed before Nigel broke the silence.

"OK, I almost have it. 26 … 45 … 83 … and let me listen … ah, there it is … 36."

Nigel pulled the safe door open.

"It's all yours," Nigel said triumphantly.

Ian opened the leather bag Cambridge brought up with him and began stuffing in as many documents as it would hold.

"Damn, the police are here. I'll take the elevator and you take the stairs. If we split up, there's a better chance one of us will get away," Cambridge instructed as he pointed to the oscillating red lights reflecting on the stone outside the windows.

"OK. See you back at the flat," Ian said bidding his partner goodbye.

Nigel rushed out towards the elevators as Ian scurried down the stairwell where he saw a groggy and confused looking security guard at the bottom vestibule. He jumped over him and emerged outside. He looked around before breaking into a run without stopping until he reached the door to The Ayrshire at 666 Dundas Street.

Knowing he had no time to waste, Ian emptied the contents of Cambridge's leather bag onto the counter and was surprised when Nigel's phone spilled out with all the reams of paper. Before long, Ian found what he was looking for. It was the corporate registry document for DM Enterprises showing the share ownership of the company. It confirmed what MacLeod had come to suspect.

"Welcome to the worst day of the rest of your life you pompous ass," Ian said elatedly.

MacLeod went over to the window and waited for Nigel to return.

Chapter 41

"Douglas, there's been a breach," Ascot said sounding uncharacteristically troubled.

"Why, what happened?" McMurphy asked alarmed at Ascot's tone.

"It appears that MacLeod broke into RIA and stole the contents of my personal safe. It exposes the entire criminal dealings of SOCKS. We're in deep trouble if we don't get it back," Ascot said gravely.

"Jeezus, how could you let this happen Ascot?" McMurphy asked angrily.

"This is no time to lose our composure, Douglas," Ascot replied.

"Hang on. I've got a call on the other line," McMurphy advised.

A minute later McMurphy was back on with Ascot.

"Black just called. Cambridge is in custody at Strathclyde," McMurphy said.

"Good," Ascot responded.

"Yeah, but where is MacLeod?" McMurphy asked.

"I presume they didn't get him," Ascot replied.

"Not good," McMurphy said in a somber tone.

"You need to head over to Arran and collect Ms. Fraser. Once we have her, then you're going to get your Detective Black to deliver us Cambridge. We've got McComb contained but we need to convince Mr. MacLeod to give us back our documents in exchange for his cherished companions. Once we have them, then MacLeod and his entourage will mysteriously disappear," Ascot said confidently.

"What are you gonna do?" McMurphy asked.

"Wait as patiently as I can under these most distressing circumstances," Ascot advised.

* * * * *

The next morning McMurphy arrived at Kyla's secluded home on the Isle of Arran. He checked the area and noted that she had no neighbors whose suspicions might be aroused. After knocking on the door and getting no answer, he broke into the cottage and waited for Kyla to return. After almost two hours of watching for her out the window, he heard the sound of her Lotus as it turned into the driveway and parked in the garage.

Wearing a loose fitting blouse that covered her hips, Kyla walked towards the house with an armful of groceries. She placed them on the steps and inserted the key becoming instantly aware that the door was not locked. Alarmed, she gingerly stepped off the veranda and turned, launching into a sprint towards the garage. McMurphy darted from the kitchen door in pursuit. She arrived at the car at the same instant as McMurphy as he grabbed her by the collar and slammed her body onto the hood. Kyla's purse flew through the air before landing on the ground a few feet away. The top buttons of her blouse popped exposing her cleavage and low cut bra as McMurphy grabbed her by the neck and had to control his urge to strangle her. Kyla lifted her right knee hard into McMurphy's crotch with enough force to cause him to release his hold and to fall backwards onto his buttocks. He doubled over in pain. Kyla had a few precious seconds to run into the house and lock the door.

McMurphy got up and grimaced in pain as he ran to the entrance of the cottage.

"Open up the door," the wild eyed McMurphy demanded as he reefed on the door handle.

McMurphy slammed his right foot into the door throwing it open. Kyla was on the landline so McMurphy threw himself at her knocking her away before smashing the phone against the tile floor with his boot.

Kyla stood frozen in fear as McMurphy turned to face her, then came at her again. She sidestepped, deftly grabbing his right arm and flipping him over her hip. McMurphy fell hard onto his back, wide eyed in shock at the petite little redhead's move. She ran for the door, but McMurphy's big hand grasped onto her ankle and she fell to the floor. He rolled onto her pinning her down lifting his fist in the air as she cowered and covered her face.

"Alright," she gasped, struggling for breath.

Kyla was terrified.

McMurphy got to his feet and grabbed her by the arm, pulling her up before throwing her onto the couch.

"Where's yer purse?" McMurphy demanded.

"It's on the ground outside."

McMurphy took a lock of Kyla's hair into his huge crass fingers and looked down at Kyla with a malevolent and lustful expression. In his other hand he held a large black pistol pointing it up at the ceiling and then towards the still open door. He fired off a shot and Kyla jumped, cringing in fear. McMurphy let go of Kyla's hair and walked over to the open door, turning towards Kyla.

"I mean business lassie. Don't fuck with me."

As soon as McMurphy walked outside Kyla pulled out her personal iPhone from her back pocket. After muting it she stuffed it down the front of her jeans.

Outside, McMurphy walked toward where they had struggled and saw Kyla's purse lying on the ground. Picking it up, he hurriedly returned to the open door and back inside. McMurphy dumped the entire contents of Kyla's purse onto the counter. He sorted through them and picked up a blackberry, putting it in his pocket. It was Kyla's Scotland Yard issued mobile phone.

"Who are you?" Kyla asked knowing full well he was Douglas McMurphy.

"Don't play dumb pretty face. I'm the employer of the little prick that's been fucking both of us."

Kyla turned away in disgust just as McMurphy's phone rang. "Hello."

Kyla couldn't hear the voice at the other end but she knew it was Ascot.

"Yeah, she's right here with me."

McMurphy listened for a few moments before talking again.

"Sure, I can do that," McMurphy said ending the call.

"I want you to contact MacLeod," McMurphy said.

"He has no phone," Kyla said.

"You better hope he has," McMurphy said handing Kyla her Blackberry.

"I broke up with MacLeod. He may not take my call," Kyla cautioned.

"He'll take it. Now dial the number," McMurphy said threateningly.

Kyla hoped that Ian was with Nigel as she struggled to remember Nigel's phone number as it was on a speed dial programmed into her iPhone. After fumbling with her blackberry for several seconds, it came to her and she keyed in the number.

The phone rang several times before it was answered.

"Hello."

"Ian, it's Kyla—," she said before McMurphy grabbed the device.

"MacLeod, listen up. This is Douglas McMurphy. Yer bitch is gonna die along with Cambridge unless you return the money and the documents," McMurphy warned.

Ian's mind raced as he struggled to respond intelligently. He realized that Cambridge must have been caught red-handed and Kyla was now in McMurphy's custody.

"Are y' there lover boy?" McMurphy taunted.

"Aye," MacLeod responded.

"Here's how it's gonna go down lad. Yer gonna bring the money and the documents to a location on the banks of the Clyde at Dunglass Roundabout at midnight tonight," McMurphy said threateningly.

"OK," MacLeod replied still dumbfounded.

"Wake up lad. Y' sound like yer sleepin'. Maybe this'll stir you," McMurphy said.

MacLeod heard a gunshot and a bloodcurdling scream.

"Now, that's just for starters. I would take great pleasure in administering unspeakable pain to this gorgeous young lass before I slit her throat," McMurphy said menacingly.

"Don't hurt her!"

"Tonight at Dunglass Roundabout," McMurphy said before ending the call.

Kyla held her forearm where the powder burns from McMurphy's warning shot formed an ugly blackened tattoo. Across the room a slug had buried itself in the plaster wall of Kyla's dining room.

"OK, we're leaving as soon as my driver gets here," McMurphy said walking toward the kitchen door.

"At least let me change my top," Kyla said modestly covering herself up with crossed arms.

"Hurry then," McMurphy replied nodding at her.

Kyla dashed up the stairs to her bedroom, pulling out her iPhone from her jeans. She found Harry Cosgrove's SMS number and furiously typed in a cryptic text message.

Kidnapped by McMurphy. Come to Dunglass Roundabout Tuesday midnight.

2009-06-28 11:09 AM

She pushed the send button before shoving it down her jeans a moment before McMurphy entered her bedroom.

"What 're ya up to lass? I thought you were changin'."

"I used the toilet if you don't mind. Now turn around so I can change," Kyla snapped back.

McMurphy threw up his arms and turned around, standing at the top of the staircase.

Kyla removed her torn blouse and threw it on the bed. She opened her closet and pulled out another loose fitting top that would hide the telltale bulge in her jeans from the iPhone. She pulled the top over her head and straightened it as she walked towards McMurphy.

"Hurry up fer crissake. Let's go," McMurphy said as he turned around, grabbing Kyla by the arm and pushing her towards the stairs.

Kyla heard the Range Rover idling outside.

During the drive back to Glasgow, McMurphy conferred with Ascot on the Range Rover's hands-free phone. As Kyla sat in the backseat she reached down and pulled out her phone from the front of her jeans. Leaning against the window of the Range Rover, Kyla pretended to look out at the passing countryside as she opened her iPhone. Holding it between her body and the door she entered her password. She hoped that McMurphy's speakerphone conversation with Ascot, and the road noise, would mask the telltale clicks as the screen came to life. Next she clicked on the utilities icon and opened up the voice memo function. Kyla touched the red record button activating a new recording. McMurphy glanced back at Kyla as if he had heard something and then turned his attention back to his conversation.

"You'd better bring plenty of armed men with you Douglas. This time we cannot let MacLeod escape. As soon as I have confirmed that we have all the incriminating evidence back, you will have your men finish him off. You can deal with the others yourself," Ascot's voice resonated over the speakerphone.

"I've already arranged everything," McMurphy confirmed.

"Very good," Ascot's voice crackled over the speaker.

"What if he has copied the files?" McMurphy asked.

"He may have … that's a chance we'll have to take as it is out of our control at this point," Ascot said.

"Why don't we just take her to the warehouse and squeeze MacLeod's whereabouts out of her," McMurphy said as he turned and eyed up Kyla.

"No we'll stick to the plan. We need them all together so we can pull at MacLeod's heartstrings," Ascot said coldheartedly.

"What was in the safe exactly?" McMurphy asked.

"Let's just say if the information he has in his hands gets the attention of Scotland Yard, they'd lead us to the scaffold if they still used the noose," Ascot replied.

McMurphy was silent.

"Alright Douglas, I'll meet you at the Dunglass Roundabout at 11:45 this evening. Cheers," Ascot said ending the call.

McMurphy turned to look at Kyla who averted her eyes from his cold black stare. He settled into the supple leather seat and closed his eyes ostensibly nodding off.

Kyla pressed the 'Stop' button that ended the recording. She clicked the 'Share' button and then pressed 'Email'. Kyla then pressed the 'c' on the keyboard, found Cosgrove's email address and entered it as the recipient. As she pressed the send button, the message and file attachment silently transmitted across cyberspace.

The Consultant

From: Kyla Fraser
To: Harry Cosgrove
Subject:
Date: June 28, 2009 12:15 PM

 Memo.m4a
52K Download

Chapter 42

Ian looked at the slip of paper on which he had scrawled the location of the midnight meeting at the Dunglass Roundabout. Not having a clue where it was, Ian searched on Google Earth, locating it on Great Western Way, just west of Glasgow. He studied the surrounding area and noted the secluded space between a grouping of trees and the banks of the Clyde. He also noted a large house nestled in amongst a densely treed area to the east. He glanced at the River Clyde no more than a hundred feet away from the meeting site.

MacLeod slumped in his chair and hung his head in despair for a few moments.

He raised his head and typed a search into Google. His right hand hit the enter key. He clicked on a web page. The screen showed palm trees and white sandy beaches with a large banner that read 'Grand Cayman Islands, A Place to Escape'.

MacLeod sighed. After a few moments he closed the page.

He reached over and grabbed an envelope and began writing down an address: The Glasgow Herald, James Dunlop, Crime Reporter, 200 Renfield St, Glasgow G2 3QB. He placed a stamp on the envelope.

Next, he pulled out a notepad. He wrote a message.

Mr. Dunlop, If you do not hear from me by the time you read this note, use the enclosed key to enter my flat at 103-666 Dundas Street, where you will find evidence that will blow the whistle on the Glaswegian mob. The information is on the USB data transmitter sitting on top of the documents. My user name and password are 'MacLeod' and 'Scotfree.'

MacLeod placed the note and a key to his flat inside the envelope.

He then placed the stack of documents from Ascot's safe on top of the counter.

He plugged the data transmitter into the USB port on his laptop and clicked the enter button on the keyboard. He clicked it again and a photo came up. The photo showed two cashed checks.

The checks read: Pay to the Order of DM Enterprises Ltd, £6,800,000 and the other, Pay to the Order of SXZ Enterprises Ltd, £6,800,000. MacLeod printed it and pulled off the copy. He looked at it for a moment before placing it on top of the stack of documents.

Next, MacLeod inputted some keystrokes into his laptop. A photo stored on the data transmitter came up on the display showing the corporate registry document linking Lance Mills to SXZ Enterprises. He scrolled to the next photo. It showed an image of 'The Backroom' and the young girl Natasha who MacLeod assumed was a victim of McMurphy's illegal activities in the sex trade.

MacLeod pulled out the data transmitter and placed it on top of the stack of documents along with the laptop.

Finally, he opened the briefcase RIA had provided for him and placed a single document into it before closing it.

MacLeod glanced at his watch. It was quarter past eleven. Throwing on his light blue windbreaker, he grabbed the briefcase and quietly locked the door to his flat. He walked down the stairs and out onto Dundas Street.

Spotting the Ford Focus parked on the street, MacLeod walked down the sidewalk towards it. As he passed a post box he stopped, pulled out the addressed envelope and looked at it for a moment. MacLeod looked up to the heavens before bowing his head. He then opened the post box and dropped in the envelope before walking to the little car and getting in.

It was a pitch black moonless night as MacLeod travelled down Great Western Road towards the meeting place on the banks of the Clyde. The headlamps of approaching cars shone in the distance as MacLeod looked through the windshield of the Ford Focus. To his left, were reflections off the river; over his right shoulder, he could see the outline of the darkened rise of the Highlands.

He saw a road sign that read 'Dunglass Roundabout.'

He turned left onto Dumbarton Road, where he noticed a turnoff to his right. MacLeod made the turn and proceeded slowly down a narrow unlit asphalt road lined on the right with large elm trees. In his high beams, he made out the shape of the house that he had seen earlier on Google Maps.

Approaching the banks of the river, Ian rounded a wide corner and spotted a black Range Rover and a silver late model Bentley. Alistair Ascot was standing by the side of the narrow road. Off to the left, standing beside the Range Rover, he spotted Douglas McMurphy. Kyla and Cambridge were blindfolded, kneeling with their hands tied behind their backs. McMurphy held a gun to the back of Kyla's head. MacLeod wondered how badly injured she was from whatever McMurphy had done to her during the phone conversation. The triangular patch of dirt and broken pavement where the party was standing was bounded on one side by the River Clyde and on the other by the thicket of elms, silhouetted against the black of the starlit sky. There were mud puddles from a recent rain inside the asphalt patch.

MacLeod stopped his car, rolled down the driver's side window and turned off the motor. His eyes adjusted to the darkness and he could see Ascot, McMurphy and his friends about 75 feet away.

MacLeod opened the briefcase and looked at the lone document sitting on the bottom.

Through the windshield, MacLeod saw Ascot walking towards him. MacLeod glanced over at the elm thicket.

Ascot approached the driver's window with a somber look on his face.

"Alright MacLeod, your little escapade is over. Give me the documents."

MacLeod looked up at Ascot before picking up the single sheet of paper and handing it over.

As he read it, Ascot's face twisted and grimaced into a look of rage. It was the corporate registry IN01 document that read: DM Enterprises Ltd., Initial shareholdings, Alistair Ascot 51, Douglas McMurphy 49.

His eyes were glaring as he looked down at MacLeod.

"What do you think you're doing, MacLeod?"

MacLeod leaned away and smiled nervously.

"Ascot, no matter what happens to me, the whole world is going to find out that Douglas McMurphy is nothing more than a figurehead. You ... are the real kingpin at SOCKS."

Ascot crumpled the document, tossing it onto the ground.

"Good work MacLeod, but you'll never know how the story ends," Ascot said smugly.

Ascot turned, lifted his arm in the air and pointed toward the elm thicket on the other side of the Ford Focus as he walked toward McMurphy and the hostages.

A dozen armed men emerged from the trees.

Ascot was in the line of fire as he walked back towards McMurphy so the men aimed their weapons waiting until Ascot was out of the kill zone.

"Let her watch him die," Ascot said coldly.

McMurphy reached down and pulled the blindfold off of Kyla's face. Startled, she could see MacLeod sitting in the car. In spite of her fear she looked longingly into his eyes knowing they were both about to die. MacLeod glanced at the armed men before pulling on the latch, pushing open the door and rolling out onto the ground. Gun fire erupted and bullets slammed into the other side of the car as MacLeod curled up into a ball, expecting a fatal shot at any moment.

Suddenly, floodlights illuminated the entire area.

"Drop your weapons. You are surrounded. I repeat, drop your weapons," a voice on a bullhorn blared.

Ascot, McMurphy and his henchmen were all blinded by the intense light. The gunfire continued as McMurphy's goons fired in the direction of the floodlights. The same Griffin HAR2 helicopter that had carried the would-be executioners to the farmhouse just days before, flew in with gunfire blazing, mowing down most of McMurphy's men. A battalion of the British Armed Forces drove up from the Dunglass Roundabout as MacLeod stood up and marveled.

MacLeod bolted as the gunfire continued. Bullets hit the ground in sprays of dirt and sod around him. Douglas McMurphy glanced over at the approaching battalion and saw MacLeod running towards him and his captive, Kyla. He raised his gun taking aim at MacLeod as Ascot stood frozen in shock. Cambridge was oblivious as he remained tied up and blindfolded.

A Special Forces sharpshooter had a bead on McMurphy and fired. The gun flew from McMurphy's hand and fell at Ascot's feet as McMurphy abandoned the group in a feeble escape attempt, running across the road and crossing the dike that bounded the shores of the river. A Hovercraft approached from the west and flashed its floodlight onto McMurphy.

"Code Blue. Suspect on road near river. Do not shoot. Repeat. Do not shoot," MacLeod heard a voice on a radio crackle over the noise of the assault.

He reached the group and tackled Ascot, violently knocking him to the ground. Kyla, still bound with her hands behind her back, stood up and kicked the gun out of reach. MacLeod got to his feet and looked over at Kyla. She nodded her head toward Ascot as he was getting up, facing away from MacLeod.

Ascot noticed the gun and launched towards it in a final futile effort to kill MacLeod in the midst of the melee. MacLeod deftly extended his leg, tripping Ascot and sending him face first into a large puddle. Ascot got up, soaking wet, his face covered in mud. Looking like a raccoon Ascot stared at MacLeod in disbelief.

Rushing over, armed men took Ascot into custody as he did his best to assume his usual distinguished bearing in spite of his disheveled appearance. Cambridge, having been freed, stood off to the side watching with interest.

MacLeod released Kyla from her bonds and they embraced, Kyla throwing back her hair as she looked up at him.

"So, welcome home."

"Aye, and a nice surprise party as well," MacLeod quipped before kissing Kyla.

A soaking wet Douglas McMurphy was dragged back onto the asphalt and over to where a group of official looking men wearing beige trench coats stood in wait. He was taken into custody and surrounded by several armed police.

MacLeod and Kyla stood in a silent embrace oblivious to the background commotion of helicopters, hovercraft, sirens and indistinct men's voices.

Detective Chief Inspector Harry Cosgrove walked over to where Kyla and MacLeod were standing.

"Excuse me," Cosgrove said.

Kyla and MacLeod turned towards him. Kyla broke off from MacLeod's embrace attempting to straighten her clothes as she faced Cosgrove.

"Hello sir. I was afraid you wouldn't come."

Cosgrove smiled and waved his hand at the military presence around them.

"Once the Prime Minister heard about it, he mobilized the whole bloody war machine," Cosgrove said with a smile.

Then Cosgrove turned to MacLeod, his eyebrows raised in a look of feigned dismay.

"This must be the man responsible for all the commotion."

MacLeod looked sheepishly out from the corner of his eye as he responded apologetically.

"Aye, I reckon I am sir."

"Well, as they say, all's well that ends well," Cosgrove said as MI5 head James Stoddard walked up overhearing Cosgrove's words.

"I'm James Stoddard, the head of MI5. My sincere apologies to you and my old compatriot Nigel for what was a terrible miscarriage of justice and abuse of power—"

"Head of MI5? More like a puppet, I'd say—" Cambridge interjected from the sidelines.

"… However, apology accepted, Stoddard."

Stoddard looked at Cambridge, annoyed at his demeaning remark, then continued.

"…None of what you went through should have happened, but thankfully when the Prime Minister was informed of the recordings that Ms. Fraser was able to email, MI5 reversed the trumped up orders against you. The Prime Minister approved a full military assault against the real culprits," Stoddard said as he turned to Alistair Ascot who was listening as he stood detained by police.

"Where's Janet McComb?" Ian asked looking over at Cosgrove.

"Ms. McComb is fine and I have the copy of her statement that I sent as backup to Detective Woods. We've also located missing accountant Kerry Grant who has turned over evidence of money laundering on the Manchester project," Cosgrove replied.

"Oh, and another detail, Ian. Your ex-girlfriend?" Cosgrove led.

MacLeod appeared surprised and noticed that Kyla was taken aback.

"Girlfriend?" Kyla asked startled.

"Ancient history Kyla," Ian said reassuringly, turning towards her for a moment.

MacLeod turned back to Cosgrove.

"Heather Gordon?"

"That's right. She's willing to testify against Douglas McMurphy in the murders of Danny McGinnis and James Ot," Cosgrove stated.

"Apparently she heard everything the killers said as they bludgeoned McGinnis to death. With her testimony, as well as Janet McComb's and Kerry Grant's, your would-be killers are going to spend a long time behind bars," Cosgrove said as he glanced over at McMurphy and Ascot who no doubt had overheard.

Cosgrove walked over to Douglas McMurphy who along with Ascot was surrounded by a throng of police officers and secret service agents.

"Douglas McMurphy, you are charged with kidnapping, murder and racketeering," Cosgrove stated, reading him his rights as Alistair Ascot looked on.

Cosgrove then turned to Alistair Ascot.

"As for you Mr. Ascot, you will be forever known as England's most notorious white collar criminal. You are charged with conspiracy to commit murder, kidnapping, racketeering, human trafficking, money laundering and a host of other charges still pending. You will be turned over to the serious organized crime agency for prosecution under the laws of The Kingdom of Great Britain," Cosgrove said motioning to a waiting detective from Strathclyde to take away the prisoners.

"Detective Black, you and my man Johnson can take them to Strathclyde for booking."

Detectives Black and Johnson escorted both prisoners towards a waiting Strathclyde police cruiser.

Walking away from Kyla and Cosgrove, MacLeod retrieved the crumpled corporate registry document laying on the ground beside his car. He looked over at Ascot and McMurphy as he unwrinkled the paper.

"Excuse me, Mr. Ascot," MacLeod yelled out.

Ascot turned to MacLeod as he was being led away. MacLeod waved the registry document in the air.

"Enjoy your stay at Her Majesty's Wakefield Inn," MacLeod said smugly.

Ascot stopped and turned toward Detective Black, before assuming his normal commanding bearing, returning a sneering look towards MacLeod.

"It's not over MacLeod," Ascot shot back.

The two detectives helped the handcuffed men into the back seat of the police cruiser.

Detective Black glanced over at Ian before getting into the driver's seat and putting the cruiser in gear. The car pulled away down the unlit dirt road.

Ian caught a glimpse of Ascot's face as he looked menacingly out of the rear window. The cruiser's tail lights vanished into the darkened silhouette of the Highlands.

Chapter 43

A few days later, Isle of Arran

Kyla was discharged from her duties and stripped of her badge by Cosgrove the night of their spectacular rescue. Cosgrove apologized but said he had no choice under the circumstances as it was Scotland Yard policy. MacLeod and Kyla went into seclusion, spending the next few days recovering from their ordeal. Although he had made a statement to police that evening and had promised to make himself available for further questioning, Ian knew it was best for him and hopefully Kyla to flee the country and take refuge in warmer climes.

As MacLeod and Kyla sat in the living room of Kyla's home on the Isle of Arran, MacLeod got up and walked over towards the window. He looked out at Holy Island for a moment and then turning to Kyla, he flashed a charming smile.

"I hope all is forgiven lass. I was such a hothead the other night," Ian said sheepishly.

"I'm still serious about the money, Ian."

"I know and we're gonna deal with that, rest assured. But first of all, I need to know if you'll marry me. Not right now, but you know, eventually."

Kyla looked up at him as he stood with his hands in his pockets waiting for her answer. She feigned aloofness, batting her eyelashes and averting her gaze.

"Well first of all, now that I'm out of a job, how are y' gonna support me, Ian MacLeod?"

MacLeod sputtered and furrowed his brow. He cocked his head and pursed his lips, giving Kyla a thoughtful look before responding confidently.

"No worries Kyla, Ascot and McMurphy have taken care of everything."

Walking over to her, MacLeod pulled a ring from his pocket and knelt in front of Kyla. He took her left hand and held the ring in his other.

"I'm askin' again, Kyla."

Her eyes wide in amazement, Kyla took the ring in her fingers and marveled at the sparkling diamond. She squinted suspiciously before responding.

"Now do tell, how did y' pay for this, Ian?" she queried.

MacLeod looked around as if to ensure that no one was listening.

"With the handsome fee I was paid for the Mills job. All above board I'll have y' know," Ian explained.

He pulled two airline tickets out of his back pocket, placing them in Kyla's free hand. She held them up and studied them. The ticket read, departing LHR, Destination MWCR, GCM. Kyla looked over at Ian, confused.

"There's a beachfront house surrounded by palm trees, waitin' for us in the Caymans, Kyla," Ian stated.

Kyla looked at MacLeod seemingly confused.

"Now just hold your tongue and let me say my piece. Obviously you know I took the money, but it remained in an RIA account until yesterday when I transferred two point nine million pounds into a tax free offshore account in the Caymans."

Kyla tilted her head.

"But Ian, how many times do I have to repeat myself? It's the proceeds of crime," Kyla said, her tone ratcheting up.

Still kneeling, MacLeod got up and placed both hands on his hips. With an indignant, wide eyed look on his face, Ian looked straight into Kyla's blue eyes.

"Proceeds of crime fightin', y' mean," Ian said emphatically in a prosodic Glaswegian lilt.

Ian MacLeod cocked his head with a devilish look in his eyes and a smirk on his face. Kyla could not help but laugh before returning to her somber demeanor.

"Well Mr. MacLeod, it's laundered money and you're a criminal as long as you are in possession of it."

"I thought about what y' said and you're right; the money isn't mine to keep. I decided to use it to help drug addicted victims of the sex trade who have been exploited by scum like Ascot and McMurphy," Ian stated passionately.

"Ian, I'm not sure what that means but I'm willing to listen," Kyla said standing up and placing her arms around Ian, looking deeply into his eyes.

Ian leaned back from Kyla and averted his gaze, suddenly lost in thought.

"Kyla, I'll explain later but there is one more thing. I have to get this off my chest. Did you and Nigel ever ... you know."

Kyla raised her eyebrows and stared incredulously at Ian.

"You can't be serious. Never in a million years, Ian."

Ian breathed a sigh of relief. He took Kyla's hand and slipped on the engagement ring.

"Mrs. Ian MacLeod ... I like the sound of it," Ian said looking dreamily up to the ceiling.

Kyla drew her head back slightly to one side, pursed her lips and looked up in a contemplative manner.

"Oh really? I was thinking more like Mr. Ian Fraser," Kyla said mockingly as she looked up at him.

"I'm not that liberated lassie," MacLeod said raising his eyebrows and rolling his eyes.

They both laughed before Ian embraced and kissed Kyla tenderly.

Epilogue

May 2010

The Caribbean sun reflected off the gentle surf as it rolled across the shallow waters on the windward side of Grand Cayman Island just west of its capital of Georgetown. It had been just over nine months since Ian and Kyla had moved into the beachfront home that MacLeod had purchased for them prior to leaving Glasgow.

Kyla, wearing a halter dress, her curls tied back with a brightly coloured scarf, leaned over the rail marveling at the turquoise water and the expanse of white sand that stretched for miles in both directions.

Ian approached from behind, arm in arm with a pretty young platinum blond who was smiling from ear to ear.

"Kyla, it's time to say goodbye to Natasha."

Kyla turned and smiled, taking Natasha's hands in hers and looking intently into the young woman's eyes.

"Ah, lass, we're gonna miss ya," Kyla said tenderly as she and Natasha embraced warmly.

Natasha turned to MacLeod, who gestured for her to go ahead of him. MacLeod walked with Natasha to a set of steps leading down to a pathway surrounded by tropical plants and palm trees. In front of the beachfront house on North Church Street, a taxi waited by an understated wooden sign that read: 'Fallen Angels Recovery Center.'

The Consultant

Liam Muir is a pseudonym for the fictional writings of Lloyd Tosoff. Tosoff spent four decades in the organizational world as a leader and executive, retiring in 2009. He has pursued his passion for writing ever since. Tosoff is a native of British Columbia, Canada. The Consultant is his first novel.

Watch for updates on the sequel in *The Consultant* series at http://liammuirauthor.com/ or on the ORB Press Books website at http://ORBPressBooks.com/

CPSIA information can be obtained at www.ICGtesting.com
Printed in the USA
LVOW05s1946290114

371500LV00033B/1818/P